Vala's
Bed

Joyce Faulkner

Red Engine Press
Pittsburgh, Pennsylvania

Library of Congress Cataloging-in-Publication Data

Names: Faulkner, Joyce, 1948- author.

Title: Vala's bed / Joyce Faulkner.

Description: Pittsburgh, PA : Red Engine Press, [2017] | Summary: In post-World War II America, Emo's investigation into his dimly-remembered childhood in Nazi Germany leads to a shocking discovery that changes everything he knows about his family and himself.

Identifiers: LCCN 2017001415 | ISBN 9781943267231 (trade paperback : alk. paper)

Subjects: | CYAC: Family life--Ohio--Fiction. | Identity--Fiction. | Nazis--Fiction. | Holocaust, Jewish (1939-1945)--Germany--Fiction. | German Americans--Fiction. | Ohio--History--20th century--Fiction. | Germany--History--1945-1955--Fiction.

Classification: LCC PZ7.1.F38 Val 2017 | DDC [Fic]--dc23

LC record available at https://lccn.loc.gov/2017001415

"Vala's Bed" Painting on the cover: Aurora Huston

Editing: Betsy Beard

Printed in the United States

Red Engine Press

What People Are Saying...

EJ Logan is only six when he arrives in a small Ohio town with his mother and brother as refugees from war-torn Nazi Germany. They bring with them keepsakes and secrets and scars from their past. But while little Mick is too young to remember being anything but an American, EJ and his mother are both haunted by fragments of memory, looming shadows, flames, and frightening dreams. As EJ grows up, he gradually learns the truth about his family and about himself, and the reader gains understanding at the same gradual, ominous pace. Perhaps not since *The Diary of Anne Frank* has a story told by a child cast such an unforgiving light on the Holocaust.

Carolyn P. Schriber, award-winning author and historian

* * *

Vala's Bed by award-winning novelist Joyce Faulkner is an exceptional story that will keep you turning the pages to unlock the secrets hidden in the narrative. The shame of the Holocaust haunts this coming-of-age tale about two brothers who have immigrated to America, along with their secretive mother, and the mysteries that surround their German heritage and a massive carved bed. Joyce Faulkner is a master at writing novels peopled with characters that feel as real as your neighbors and friends and plots that are tightly woven with important themes and history. While most of the novel takes place in a quaint town named Cold Creek, Ohio, between 1949 and 1970, chilling scenes abound in a story that could happen again if we aren't careful. My heart raced and the tears flowed the closer I got to the end.

Kathleen M. Rodgers, author of *The Final Salute*, *Johnnie Come Lately*, and *Seven Wings to Glory*

* * *

Vala's Bed reveals the humanity behind the textbook history of World War II and into three decades beyond, from global to community to family to individual perspectives, and immerses the readers in the lives of authentic characters. This novel uncovers the weaknesses and strengths that we all share as children, teens, and young and old adults, and sprinkles us with the occasional, necessary healing of humor.

Joyce Faulkner maintains an alluring, intriguing, suspenseful narrative throughout, surrounding Vala's bed itself. Readers will empathize with these genuine characters who come to realize the darkness of the human ego, yet the light of human sacrifice.

Frank A. Tatone, English Department, Robert Morris University, Pittsburgh, Pennsylvania

* * *

Tightly plotted, emotionally intense, with complex characters and more upending twists than an M.C. Esher drawing, *Vala's Bed* is a gut-punch that gives a horrifying new definition to the term "family values." With *Vala's Bed* author Joyce Faulkner has delivered a emotionally-charged triumph.

Dwight Jon Zimmerman, #1 New York Times bestselling author

* * *

Vala's Bed is a story that takes you on a horrific spiritual journey, filled with the memories and nightmares of Nazi Germany, but woven ever so beautifully with hope and love. Faulkner hits the mark emotionally with her best book to date!

Rev. Bill McDonald, author, founder of American Authors Association and Military Writers Society of America, international motivational speaker, and award-winning poet

* * *

In *Vala's Bed*, Joyce Faulkner confronts one of the most shameful chapters in the history of mankind. As diverse groups of people move on from the tragedy, the lines between perpetrator, accomplice, bystander, and victim become blurred, and it appears that no one is left unscathed. *Vala's Bed* is a powerful tale of man's ability to endure…and survive.

Joe Campolo Jr, award winning author of *The Kansas NCO* and *Back To The World*

* * *

Vala's Bed is an extraordinary historical tale about German survivors of World War II finding a new life in America, but haunted by their past. It's an excellent read.

Joe Epley, author of Revolutionary War novels, *A Passel of Trouble* and *A Passel of Hate*

* * *

There are so many symbols, so many passions, so much pathos and hope in this book that it was an emotional adventure for me. I completed the reading with tears in my eyes, even though the novel ended with a brighter future for those Vala saved.

Michael D. Mullins, award-winning author and poet: *The Drifter, Out of the Mist: Memories of War*, and *Vietnam in Verse: Poetry for Beer Drinkers*

For Micki

List of Characters

German

- Vala Hess Logan: war bride, wife of Sonny Logan, mother of EJ and Mick Logan.
- Emo Johann Hess Logan (American name EJ Logan): narrator, son of Vala Hess Logan, stepson of Sonny Logan.
- Milo Hess Logan (American name Mick Logan): son of Vala Hess Logan, brother of EJ Logan, stepson of Sonny Logan.
- Lana Hess: Vala Hess Logan's older sister.
- Standartenführer Erich Hess: Vala's father, wealthy citizen of Mannheim, member of the Nazi party.
- Frau Anna Hess: Standartenführer Erich Hess's wife, Lana and Vala's mother.
- Gerhardt (American name John Sarris): driver for Standartenführer Erich Hess.
- Oskar Schreiner: past owner of his family's furniture company in Mannheim, Germany, a Jew who escaped to America in the late 1930s to live in North Royalton, Ohio (a suburb of Cleveland).
- Magda Langer: Oskar Schreiner's sweetheart, Emo Hess's babysitter.
- Dolph Jäger (American name Frank Barnes): Nazi guard at Auschwitz, one of Lana Hess's suitors.
- Ulli: an employee at Schreiner's Möbelfabrik in the 1930s.
- Jan: an employee at Schreiner's Möbelfabrik in the 1930s.
- Obergruppenführer Reinhard Heydrich: a high-ranking German Nazi official. He was called "The Blond Beast" by admirers and "The Hangman" by his potential victims. In early 1942, he hosted a conference in Wannsee to facilitate the "final solution."

American

- Sonny Logan: owner of Logan Foods, Army veteran and part of the occupation force in Germany, Vala's husband, stepfather to EJ and Mick.
- Grant Logan: partner with Sonny in the family business Logan Foods, brother of Long John and Sonny, uncle to EJ and Mick.
- Long John Logan: brother of Sonny and Grant Logan, killed during World War II.

- Arial Logan: mother of Long John, Sonny, and Grant Logan, beloved grandmother to EJ and Mick
- Arnold Vilani: school principal and neighbor of Sonny, Vala, EJ, and Mick Logan.
- Teresa Roberts: nurse at the hospital, high school friend of Sonny, Long John, and Grant Logan.
- Skippy: owner of the newsstand, wounded veteran of the Invasion of Normandy, friend of Sonny and Grant Logan.
- Myrtle Jones Kline: owner of the Windshift Inn, wife of Jerry Kline, stepmother of Danny and Pam Kline, friend of Arial Logan, Mags Strickland, Delores Lieberman McDougal, and Shirley Maxwell Reynolds.*
- Jerry Kline: owner of a small airport and the Windshift Inn, father of Danny and Pam Kline, husband to Myrtle Jones Kline.*
- Delores Lieberman McDougal: wounded pilot, married to Tommy McDougal, looking for her Jewish relatives lost during Holocaust, Vala's friend.*
- Shirley Maxwell Reynolds: a wealthy and influential friend of the Logan family, crippled by polio.*
- Jack Reynolds: Shirley Maxwell's husband.
- Mags Strickland: pilot, wealthy adventuress, friend of Myrtle and Jerry Kline, helps Delores Lieberman McDougal search for lost relatives.*
- Danny Kline: wounded veteran of the Battle of Iwo Jima, friend of the Logans, stepson of Myrtle Kline.
- Zona Dixon: Avon lady, Vala Logan's best friend, wife of Deputy Jimmy Dixon.
- Sheriff George Douglas: chief law enforcement officer of Cold Creek, Ohio.
- Deputy Jimmy Dixon: friend of Sonny and Grant Logan, deputy to Sheriff Douglas, husband of Zona Dixon.
- Annie Jones: EJ's classmate and friend.
- Billy Ray Parker: EJ's classmate and friend.
- Rosa: cousin of Delores McDougal and friend of EJ. Rescued from Gurs in Vichy France by the Quakers at the request of Shirley Maxwell Reynolds.*

*Backstory is told in *Windshift*.

Poland

January, 1945

THE CAR STOPPED. Mutti threw open the back door and got out.

"You're a fool," the man in the blue coat said.

"Maybe." Her voice sounded far away and breathless, like she was running.

"What is it?" I climbed over his lap and peered out the window. "A sausage?"

Mutti was squatting over something by the side of the road. She looked up. "Keep Emo busy."

The man pulled me away from the window.

"Mutti!" I screamed and fought him.

"Why does he misbehave this way?" His fingers were tight around my wrists.

Mutti appeared at the window holding a bundle. "He's a child. Can't you see that he's scared?"

Sobbing, I held out my arms. "Don't leave me, Mutti."

"I'm here, Emo. Don't worry. I'll never leave you again." She opened the car door and crawled in.

The man wrinkled his nose. "And what is that?"

"It's what it looks like." She put the bundle on the seat.

"Oh throw it away, Vala."

"No."

"It's a piece of garbage you found in a ditch. Throw it out!"

She shook her head.

"Obey me." He slapped her.

Blood trickled from one of her nostrils.

I squealed and lunged for my mother, trampling him to get to her.

"Bastard." He smacked my buttocks with his gloves.

The driver turned in his seat. "There's a barn up ahead. Looks like people are taking shelter there. Maybe we can get milk from them."

"Yes." Mutti wiped the blood from her upper lip. "He's hungry."

"There's no time for that," the man in the blue coat said. "Drive on, Gerhardt."

"You're not in charge here." Mutti pulled the man's gun out of its holster and pointed it at him.

His eyes widened. "I thought you wanted to go home."

"I don't need you for that."

"It's dangerous out here, Vala. People are desperate."

"Get out of the car!"

"Standartenführer Hess asked me to watch over you and the boy."

"That's not why you came with us."

"We'll go to Mannheim. It's all arranged."

"Not you."

"And why not?"

She put an arm around me. "Look at him."

He leaned forward and stared into my eyes.

I cringed.

"He can't bear you."

The man's teeth glowed in the dim light. "Do you know who I am, Emo?"

I nodded. "A monster."

Part One

Innocence

Cold Creek, Ohio

1949

1

Moving In
July 1, 1949

THE HOUSE WAS big, at least bigger than the apartment over Logan Foods. Mama wouldn't let Sonny bring in any of our furniture until she'd scrubbed every inch of the place. Mick and I ran around the empty rooms, sliding sideways in our stocking feet, giggling and squealing whenever we found something new.

"This is my hiding place." Mick opened a small door under the stairs. "And I'm going to keep all my toys locked up in here."

"Who are you hiding them from, goofy?"

"Nazis."

"This is Ohio. There ain't no Nazis around here. Besides, why would Nazis want your Lincoln Logs?"

"Nobody knows what they might grab next."

I thought about my comics and wondered if I should look for a hiding place, too. "Who told you that?"

"Mr. McKensey."

"Mr. McKensey?"

"The guy who lives at Miss Myrtle's house. He said the Nazis are hunkered down waiting until we forget about them and then they'll come out and rob everyone blind again."

"How does Mr. McKensey know that?"

"He's really, really old."

"Where are they, then?"

"How would I know? I'm only four and a half."

"There's no lock on that door. And the latch is broken."

"I'll buy one."

"You need money for that."

Mick folded his arms over his chest and stuck out his lower lip. "Mama will buy it for me."

"Mama doesn't like to spend money. Ask Sonny. He's easier."

Mick grinned. "I'll ask him when he gets here with our stuff."

* * *

Mama was teetering on a stepladder trying to wipe down the walls when Sonny pulled up in front of our house in the Logan Foods delivery truck. He beeped the horn and Mick and I ran downstairs to greet him.

"Emo! Milo! Slow!" Mama cried as we passed her.

"Who are Emo and Milo?" Mick giggled and nudged me.

"Naughty…Jungen!" She climbed down the ladder.

"You always forget, Mama. I'm EJ. We are Americans now."

"Ja, Sonny put you up to this."

"The kids at school thought Emo was funny. They all have names like Johnny or Bobby or Billy Ray. There are no Emos or Milos at all."

Mick tugged at her skirt. "I'm Mick now, Mama."

"We are Deutsch, not Irish." She climbed down the ladder, rolled up her rag, and squeezed dirty water into the pail at her feet.

Mick pursed his lips and looked at me for help.

"Sonny helped us pick good nicknames," I said.

"Not American." Her voice was stern but her eyes twinkled.

I giggled. "Sounds more American than Milo."

Mick bounced up and down. "Mick, Mick, Mick."

She folded the cloth and laid it on the ladder. "You sound like Sonny more every day, Mausi."

"I'm not a mouse, I'm a Mick." He stuck out his tongue.

"Mickey Mouse!" I bumped him with my elbow. "Get it?"

"Ha ha ha!" He put his hands on his head and wiggled them like mouse ears.

We heard gears grinding, and through the front window I could see the truck backing into our driveway. "There's Sonny now." I pointed.

His eyes sparkling, Mick put his hands on his cheeks. "Oh!"

"You silly boys." Mama pretended to chase us and we all hurried out onto the front porch, letting the screen door slam behind us.

Sonny maneuvered the truck as close to the house as possible.

"Oh, no!" Mama wailed. "You runned over die Rhododendren, Sonny."

Sonny and Uncle Grant started unloading a giant bed out of the truck. "Sorry, Vala."

"He *ran* over them, Mutti," I whispered.

She frowned at me. "Runned or ran, he still messed up that… Blumen bush."

"Flower bush," I said behind my hand.

"Ja, flower bush."

"I'll buy you another." Sonny grunted as he and Uncle Grant struggled to get the wooden bed frame across the yard.

"What is it?" Mick ran up to them.

Uncle Grant, who was facing away from us, nearly stepped back on him. "Mick, you are too little. Get back up on the porch with your momma." Uncle Grant was hard of hearing and little kids made him cranky. Maybe he couldn't make out what we were saying, or maybe he thought we misbehaved. Or maybe he never got used to us being a part of his family.

Mick turned to Mama. "What is it?"

"Das ist mein Bett, Mausi."

"I never saw it before," I said. "Where did it come from?"

"Home." She reached out to touch the enamel mosaic on the headboard, but then drew her hand back as if it burned her. "Mannheim."

Winded from trying to get it to the porch, the men set the bed frame on the lawn.

"No," she cried. "Not on the grass! It isn't gut for it."

Uncle Grant sat down in the rocking chair on the porch, rubbing his hands. "We need to get someone over here to help get it through the door and up those stairs." He sounded funny. Sonny told us that was because he couldn't hear.

"I can help." I held up my hand.

"You are too little to lift it, EJ. We need at least two more big, strong men."

"Is Roger Littleton in town? He's a tough old son of a gun." Uncle Grant straightened his glasses. "I'll call him."

"I heard he's gone up to Cleveland to get a divorce. One more casualty of war, I guess. Seems he and Maxine haven't gotten along since he got home in '46. Last month she caught him with her hairdresser." Sonny sighed.

"You mean that cute little brunette? Used to play the ukulele? Never thought of her as a seductress."

"What's a ukulele?" Mick asked.

Uncle Grant didn't hear him. "How about Jake Jolly? He make it back from war in one piece?"

"He got called back up and he's on his way to Japan as we speak. Everyone with a strong back is either dead, wounded, or back in the Army again."

"Doesn't make any difference," Uncle Grant said. "No matter how many volunteers you get over here, that bed's not going up to the second floor in one piece. The turns are too sharp."

The stairway changed directions every seven steps. Mick and I counted them when we were playing earlier.

Sonny lit a cigarette. "I figure I'll have to widen the door frame to get it into the bedroom anyway.

"No," Mama howled. "No break die Wand."

"We'll rebuild them, sugar."

"This is first place that is mine. Das ist…nice. I want it that way."

"At the very least we'll have to take the front door out to get it into the house," Sonny said.

Mama folded her arms across her bosom. "Nein!"

Sonny took a deep breath. "Okay," he said. "I'll see what other options we have, sugar." He and Uncle Grant wandered around the corner of the house inspecting windows and doors and the big screened-in room in the back. We could hear them tapping on the siding and opening and closing doors. There was a crash. Uncle Grant yelped and Sonny mumbled something.

"Uh oh." I rolled my eyes.

Mama sat down on the top step of the porch, wringing her hands and mumbling in German.

"What's a ukulele?" Mick tried to get Mama's attention.

She shrugged and strained to hear what Sonny and Uncle Grant were saying in back of the house.

Mick turned to me. "What's a ukulele?"

"A plunky little guitar, I think."

"How'd you know that?"

"Heard someone playing it on Arthur Godfrey."

"Oh."

Sonny and Uncle Grant and a stranger came around the opposite corner of the house.

"Arnold, let me introduce you to my wife and family. This is Vala, and that little guy there is Mick. This is our backyard neighbor, Arnold Vilani."

The man beamed at Mama. "Well, aren't you a sweet little thing?"

Mama blushed and tucked her chin. "Nice…er…nice to…" Meeting new people was hard on her.

Mr. Vilani turned to Mick and said, "You the kind of boy that likes to play with a dog?"

Mick's eyes lit up. "A dog?"

"My missus and I live across the back fence from you. My old hound dog Stinker loves to play fetch. Why don't you come see him sometime?"

"I don't want him to cause dog to bark, to…er…bite." Mama put her arms about Mick.

"Oh, Mrs. Logan…Vala…that sweet old beast is fifteen years old. He doesn't have many teeth left. More likely he'll lick the boy to death."

Mama cocked her head and I translated "lick you to death" for her. She looked confused at first but then as the meaning hit her, she giggled. "Okay, okay."

Sonny turned to me. "And this is my man, EJ Logan."

I stuck out my hand. "Nice to meet you, sir."

Mr. Vilani had a shiny bald head, but hair grew out of his nose and ears. "Look at you. Big and strong already." He shook my hand.

"Arnold is going to help us get the bed inside," Sonny said. "Even with the three of us, we have to figure out how to get it through the door." He sat beside Mama and took her hand. "It'll be a struggle, but we'll get it in."

I translated and Mama's face brightened.

I figured things were okay now, but as Mr. Vilani and Uncle Grant examined the huge bed, I realized there really was no way to get it into the house.

"EJ?"

I jumped. "Sir?"

"Get up inside that truck and get the toolbox." Sonny patted Mama's hand. "We'll take the bed apart."

"No!" Mama jerked her hand away and ran to stand in front of the bed. "You will not break it."

Sonny stood up. "It's okay, baby." He reached for her but she wriggled away from him. "I promise I won't break it. We'll take it apart so we can get it up to the bedroom in smaller pieces. It's much bigger than we thought, and Grant and Arnold and I aren't strong enough to wrestle it through that door and up those stairs without scratching it or the walls."

"It's mine. It's all I have left…from home." Tears rolled down her cheeks. "Papi had it made for me special. You can't take it apart. You can't."

Sonny looked at everyone in turn, as if taking stock. Mr. Vilani seemed embarrassed. Uncle Grant stared off toward the warehouse, scowling. Mick and I were both upset because Mama was crying, but neither of us knew why she cared so much about that ugly old piece of furniture.

"We'll put it back together once we get the pieces up into the room," Sonny said. "It'll be good as new."

"Nein!" Mama stamped her foot. "Du drafst nicht. You can't!"

Uncle Grant threw down his cigarette and smothered it with his heel. "You want to leave it in the front yard?"

"Why you care?" Mama cried.

Sonny put one hand on Mama's shoulder and held the other palm out toward Uncle Grant. "Calm down, Vala. It's not that big of a deal. We'll figure it out."

Uncle Grant got into the cab of the truck and slammed the door.

Mr. Vilani caught my eye and raised an eyebrow. I shrugged and shook my head. Mick covered his ears and closed his eyes.

Mama pushed Sonny's hand away. "I should be dead."

"Mutti?" I tried to hug her but she pushed me away, too.

Sonny got red in the face and stomped across the yard toward the Logan Foods warehouse next door. He fumbled with the gate to the fence, cussing up a storm. The latch must have been stuck or something because he started kicking it.

I glanced at Mick. His mouth was open and his eyes wide. Mama stood her ground, determined to protect the bed. Grandma Arial peeked through the picture window of her duplex across the street. A kid riding by on a bicycle stopped to watch the ruckus. Some of the men who worked in the warehouse came out on the loading dock. We could barely see them for the trees, but we could hear them shuffling their feet and asking each other what was going on.

Sonny climbed the fence and we lost sight of him.

Suddenly it was quiet.

A minute passed. We heard noises from inside the warehouse. The back door creaked as it slid on its track. Then we saw Sonny coming back over the fence with an ax in one hand.

Mama screamed and tried to block him.

Afraid that he might hit her with the ax, I jumped between them. And afraid that I might get hurt, Mick did, too. We needn't have bothered. Sonny sidestepped all of us, climbed up on the porch, and swung the ax in a great arc over his head and then into the siding beside the front door.

Terrified of the ax being used in such a manner, Mama tripped and fell backwards onto the bed frame, waving her arms and legs like an upset beetle.

Mr. Vilani ran to help her up. Wide-eyed, she squealed and pulled away from him.

Grunting, Sonny swung again and broke through the wall next to the jamb.

Uncle Grant jumped out of the truck and came running. I didn't know whether he aimed to stop Sonny from bashing in the front of our new house or to rescue Mick and me from the flying wood chips. He lost his balance and fell into the rest of Mama's rhododendrons, breaking his glasses in the process and losing one of his hearing aids.

Sonny swung once more and a large hole opened up beside the door.

Mr. Vilani tried again to help Mama climb out of the bed frame. No longer screaming, she accepted his hand and stood up. Mick and I ran to her and together we stood guard in front of the bed.

"Sonny, what are you doing?" Grandma Arial stormed across the street. "Stop that! Do you hear me? Johnny left this house in such good shape and here you are tearing it apart already! Stop it!"

He ignored her and chopped away at the entrance until it was almost twice as big as it used to be.

Grandma Arial put her hands on her hips. "Now what?"

Sonny handed her the ax. "Now we widen the door to the parlor and put this monstrosity in there."

The ax was almost as tall as my grandmother. She held it out in front of her body until Uncle Grant took it and propped it against the side of the truck.

"Mein Bett, mein Bett." Mama wrung her hands.

"Now Vala, no one is going to hurt that bed. Come on over to my house and let these men get on with their work. They have a lot of fixing up to do before you can move in anyway. I just took some cookies out of the oven, and I'll make some good strong tea." Grandma Arial put her arm around my mother and led her away.

At the curb, Mama looked over her shoulder. "Milo, you come with us."

Mick froze, unsure whether to go with the women or stay with the guys.

Grandma Arial's voice was a soft croon. "Come on, sweetheart. We'll have fun."

Mick ran to our grandmother, and she picked him up.

"Can I have a ukulele, Grandma Arial?" He laid his cheek on her shoulder.

"Of course you can, my darling." She caressed his cheek.

"Milo, you can't ask for things that cost so much."

"It's Mick, Mama."

"Mick." Mama sounded so sad that I wanted to run to her and give her a hug—except I knew she wouldn't like that.

"Let's read a book," Mick said to Grandma Arial.

"Which book do you want to hear this afternoon?"

"Dorothy!" Mick's good humor had returned.

"Okay. After tea, I'll read the next chapter of *The Wizard of Oz* to you and your Mama."

I started to follow them across the street, but Grandma Arial stopped me. "It's a big job, don't you think?"

"What?"

She gestured with her eyes toward our house with the truck in the driveway and the bed in the front yard. "Moving such big furniture and cleaning up that mess Sonny made."

I didn't know what she meant.

"They need another man to help."

I looked at Sonny and Uncle Grant. They both grinned. Mr. Vilani held out a small hammer with one hand and gave me the thumbs-up sign with the other.

"Me?"

"I don't see anyone else around."

I gave grandma a quick hug and ran back to where Mr. Vilani, Sonny, and Uncle Grant were already pulling loose pieces of wood off the door frame and tossing them into a pile in the yard.

"What can I do?"

Uncle Grant sounded funny when he talked, on account of his hearing problems, but I knew exactly what he was saying. "How about you start loading that pile into the garbage can?"

* * *

It took three days to finish converting the front parlor into Mama's bedroom, but when we were done, it looked nice. There was room for her bed, a dresser, and a closet that Sonny built into the back wall. I taped one of Mick's drawings onto the mirror of her dresser and tucked an envelope with a note that said, "I love you. Signed EJ Logan" under her pillow. Sonny put a vase of yellow roses on her nightstand and Grandma Arial made her a lavender sachet that we put in her underwear drawer.

Then we called Mama at Grandma Arial's house and told her that it was ready. We were hiding when she came in the front door and we all jumped out and yelled, "Surprise!"

"Oh!" She walked into the parlor-turned-bedroom and smiled. "Danke."

Then she closed the door in our faces.

"Mama!" Mick wailed.

The lock clicked.

"She's mean," I said and took Mick's hand.

Sonny squatted down in front of us. "Naw, she's not mean." He patted my shoulder. "She's overwhelmed right now. Let's give her some time. Want to go over to Grandma's and make some peach ice cream?"

"Can I turn the crank?" Mick danced from one foot to the other in his excitement.

Sonny picked him up and swung him onto his shoulders. "Sure ya can. And you can put the freezer together if you want."

Mick clapped his hands in the air over his head.

I put my ear against the parlor door.

"Now, EJ. Your Mama needs some privacy right now."

"What's wrong with her?" It sounded like she was crying.

Sonny tried to smile but his eyes weren't in it. "Just woman things, buddy. Stuff we guys can't understand."

"She acts like she hates us."

"You know better than that, EJ. She loves you and Mick with all her heart."

I wiped my nose with the back of my hand. "Doesn't feel like it."

He shooed me out onto the porch. "Let's do ice cream first, and then I'll show you a special place for guys like you and me."

"At least Grandma Arial loves us."

"You can count on Grandma, that's for sure." He laughed and we trudged across the front yard and across the street.

* * *

"Let's go for a walk, EJ." Sonny stood up and put his empty bowl in the sink.

"What about Mick?"

"I think Mick is more interested in figuring out how the ice cream freezer works," Grandma Arial said. "He'll be fine."

I peeked into the back porch where my little brother was playing with the gears. "I'll be back."

"Okay." He didn't look up.

"See. He won't even miss us."

"Where are we going?"

"Not far."

We walked down the back stairs and around the house to the front yard. The Logan Foods warehouse was across the street next to our new house. Sonny unlocked the door and we went inside. After a bit of fumbling, he found the light switch, and I followed him through the rows of foodstuffs.

"Usually there's a lot of people in here, but today is Sunday and they're all home with their families." He pulled a handle down and pushed open a sliding door. It screeched, and the piercing sound hurt my ears. "When you come here the next time, I'll introduce you to everyone."

"Okay." I stepped out onto the loading dock with him.

"You have to be careful when you come here because of the trucks."

I didn't see any trucks, but there was a circular drive leading up to a ramp so I guessed that's where they would be. I still didn't have any idea why Sonny had brought me here. We crossed the driveway and tramped across the grass to a tree at the far end of the property.

A rope dangled from the tree and Sonny gave it a tug. With that, a ladder dropped down.

For the first time, I looked up. "Wow," I said. "Wow!"

"This was my private place. When I was your age, I'd come here to read or think or draw."

"How did you...I mean, where'd it come from?"

"My grandfather built it for my dad, and my dad gave it to me. You want to go up?"

"Yes, sir!" I scrambled up the ladder into the tree house. It was big enough for me to stand up in the middle. I kicked at dead leaves and brushed away a spider web.

"I haven't been up here in a while," Sonny said from the top step of the ladder. "Looks like we'll need to do some housekeeping."

I pulled a tarp off of a trunk. I glanced at Sonny.

"Mostly books and games, if I remember correctly. Go ahead, open it."

I lifted the lid. "Comic books?"

"Old ones."

I reached inside. "Can I have them?"

"Sure you can. Keep them inside the locker when you aren't reading them, though. Things can get damp out here if you don't protect them."

I picked one up and grinned. *Superman.*

As we walked back to Grandma Arial's house, I couldn't help but glance over my shoulder at the tree house. It was my special place, and it had been Sonny's before me and Grandpa John's before that. I felt like I was truly a Logan now. "Thanks, Sonny."

"Just don't let me catch you smoking out here."

"No, sir."

* * *

I sat on the floor banging wooden spoons together.

A woman scooped me up into her arms. "Come meet your mother, Emo," she whispered. "This is the one. I promise."

"No," I wailed. "I'm playing now."

"But your mother, Emo. She's been looking for you for so long."

"Nooooo."

* * *

I was screaming in my sleep. "No!"

Someone was trying to cover me with a blanket. "EJ, darling. It's Grandma."

"No, no, no."

"Wake up, baby." She sat down beside me and rubbed my trembling leg.

I laid my head in her lap. "I don't want them to take you."

"I'm not going anywhere. Do you understand?"

I rubbed my eyes. "I'm sorry."

"You want to tell me about it?"

"They came for you. Mama told them no, but they took you anyway."

"I see. That must have been scary."

We sat quietly in the dark until my breathing slowed and my leg relaxed. "Grandma?"

"I'm here, baby."

"Why do people have bad dreams?"

"Maybe something they ate. Maybe something is worrying them. Maybe it's a story they are making up that gets scary toward the end."

"Why do I have them?"

"Maybe you were overexcited tonight, putting together your mother's room. Surprising her."

"I wanted her to be happy."

"I know, sweetheart."

"Why wasn't she?"

"I think she wanted to be. Maybe she was somewhere deep inside."

2

Who Am I?

August 21, 1949

I PEEKED OUT the back window. Mama was hanging wash on the clothesline. Her laundry basket was almost full. She would be busy for a while. Mick was on the back porch playing with the ukulele that Grandma Arial bought for him. Sonny was at work.

I hurried to the closet under the stairs, slipped open the lock as quietly as I could, and felt around for the flashlight Mick kept inside. Flipping it on, I crawled inside and closed the door behind me. The box was in a dark corner where I had hidden it the day Sonny brought Mama's bed home. I pushed Mick's toys and a stack of books away from my prize and opened it. Mama's belongings from Mannheim were individually wrapped in brown paper. I was about to start second grade but I was a pretty good reader—in English. All these items were labeled in German. I had no idea what "Schulzeugnisse" meant, but a round package with "Hut" printed on top was easy to figure out—and I knew immediately what a book-shaped item labeled "Foto-Album" meant.

I unwrapped it. The cover was dark brown and had "Vogel Fotografie Studio" stamped in gold on the front. The first thing I saw when I opened it was a picture of my mother sitting cross-legged in an open field. She wore a sleeveless white shirt and dark shorts, and her hair hung over her shoulders in long braids. Behind her, other girls dressed like her seemed to be exercising. I wondered where she was and what she was doing. Summer camp, maybe? Under the photograph she had written, "Bund Deutscher Mädel, 1942."

On the next page, there was a picture of a man smoking a pipe. Like Mama, he had light hair and eyes and a short forehead. Below it, Mama had printed "Papi." Was this my grandfather who died before I was old enough to remember him? I squinted at the photo, but it was too dark in the closet to make out much more detail.

I put everything but the photo album back into the box and shoved it into the corner. Pushing open the closet door, I looked both ways. Ukulele music drifted in from the back of the house. I crawled out with the album under my arm. Sliding the bolt home on the closet lock, I stood up.

The kitchen was down the hall and Mama's room was across from it. When she finished hanging up the clothes, she would probably go into the kitchen for a cup of coffee. Turning the other way, I tiptoed up the stairs and into the bathroom that I shared with Mick and Sonny. I sat on the floor and paged through the album. There were pictures of old people posing on a bench in a courtyard. There was a letter, but it was in German so I put it back into its envelope.

The door opened. "Whatcha doing, EJ?"

I pointed to the picture of the older man. "Looking to see if I look like our grandpa in Germany."

Mick crawled up onto the toilet and put his face beside mine. "Do I look like him?"

"Maybe."

"I like him."

"Why?"

"He's not mean."

"How can you tell?"

"He has smiling eyes."

Now that Mick mentioned it, the man's eyes *did* look like they were smiling. I sighed and turned the page. Our grandfather was dead, and we'd never meet him anyway.

"What's that?" A ragged piece of paper fell out of the album and Mick scrambled after it. He picked it up and handed it to me.

I held it to the light. "Newspaper, I think."

"What's it say?"

"Something about a dead doctor." I stuck it in the book again.

"What about him?"

"I don't know. It's too hard for me to read."

"Maybe next year, then."

"Maybe."

* * *

I was little and a tall man held my hand. We walked through an iron gate into a village. Wooden buildings were on either side of the road. We passed a group of people standing in line. There were so many of them—mamas and papas and children.

I saw a little girl holding her mama's hand. We stared at each other and then as we passed, she waved at me.

"Who are they?" I asked the man.

"Ghosts, Emo."

"What are ghosts?"

"Dead people."

3

My Birthday Party

September 6, 1949

SEVERAL CARS WERE parked in the turnaround drive of the big white house. Sonny pulled in behind a large brown one and turned off the engine. Mick and I crawled out of the Logan Foods van and ran toward the porch. A sign over the door said "The Windshift Inn ~ Myrtle and Jerry Kline, Proprietors."

A tiny woman sat in a painted chair. A little white dog lying at her feet yapped as we climbed the steps.

"A doggie!" Mick squealed.

"Hush, Waldo." The woman leaned over and patted the dog. "These are friends."

Waldo wagged his tail.

Mick stopped a few feet away. "Can I touch him?"

"Let him sniff your hand first."

"Okay." He held out his fingers and the little animal trotted right up to him.

It was then that I noticed the metal on the woman's legs and the crutches leaning on the wall behind her chair.

"Well, look who's here." Grandma Arial kissed the woman's cheek. "How beautiful you are, Shirley."

"It's wonderful to see you, Arial. I'm so sorry about John. Cold Creek isn't the same without him."

"I'm not the same either." Grandma Arial sat down on the porch swing. "He would have loved our new family."

"Of course, he would have." Shirley reached out to squeeze Grandma Arial's hand.

Mick scratched Waldo under his ears, and they were new best friends.

Sonny leaned down and pecked Shirley on the forehead. "It's been too long."

"There's been a lot going on in everyone's life since the end of the war."

"I'm grateful for everything you did to get Vala and the boys over here."

"That was Father and Mags and Delores. Health didn't allow me to do as much as I would have liked."

"Nonsense." The swing creaked as Grandma Arial pushed it back and forth with her feet. "Without your help, I don't think we could have managed it."

Shirley turned to Mama. "So is this Vala?"

"Where are my manners? Shirley, this is Vala. Vala, this is Shirley Maxwell. Oh! I guess it's Shirley Reynolds now."

Mama stepped forward, wringing her hands. "Es ist eine Ehre, Dame."

"It's nice to meet you," I whispered behind my hand.

"Nice to meet you, Frau Reynolds." Mama repeated.

Shirley held out a hand.

Mama took it and held it against her cheek. "Das sind meine Jungen." Mama shoved me forward. "This is Emo. Heute ist sein Geburtstag."

I sighed. "She says that we are her sons—Mick and I. And that today is my birthday."

"Happy Birthday, EJ!" Shirley seemed like a nice person, but I had no idea who she was or why Mama and Sonny seemed so excited to see her. Whatever was wrong with her legs scared me.

"Sage etwas, Emo." Mama poked me.

It took me a moment to think of something to say. "Thank you, ma'am."

"Er ist schüchtern." Mama rolled her eyes at me.

I ducked my head. "She says I'm shy."

"Nothing wrong with that. So am I."

I smiled at Shirley and she smiled back. It was like we knew a secret that other people didn't.

Mama grabbed Mick who was playing with Waldo and pushed him toward Shirley. "Und hier ist mein anderer Sohn, Milo."

"She's excited," I said. "She forgets English when she's excited."

Shirley nodded. "So this fellow is Mick."

"He's my little brother."

She turned her attention to Mick. "You and Waldo have been having fun, I see."

Waldo disengaged himself from Mick's grasp and ran to Shirley. With that, Mick finally saw the little woman in the chair instead of the dog. His eyes grew large. "What's wrong with your legs?"

"Mick!" Sonny reached for him.

"No, it's okay," Shirley said. "He's a little boy and he's curious."

"Sorry. Zo sorry!" Mama's English returned—sort of.

"I got sick a few years ago and since then, I can't walk very well," Shirley said to Mick.

A handsome man came out of the house. "Myrtle says dinner is ready."

Mick wasn't deterred. "What are those things on your legs?"

"Braces," Shirley said. "They help me stand up."

"Can I look at them?"

Shirley stiffened, but she said, "Sure."

Mick squatted down beside the chair and examined the leather straps that kept the long strips of metal fastened to her legs. "Does it hurt?"

"Sometimes."

"Who figured out how to make these?"

"That's enough, young man." Sonny lifted Mick onto his shoulders.

As they went into the house, Mick ducked to avoid hitting his head on the door. "Whoever did that was pretty smart," he said to Shirley as they disappeared into the house.

Mama blushed. "Sorry. He is a crazy boy."

"Not so crazy. I don't know who made these things, but they *are* pretty smart. Guess I'll have to find out and thank them."

"Good afternoon, Arial," the young man standing behind Shirley said to my grandmother.

"It's good to see you, Jack." Grandma Arial stood up. "Let's help your pretty girl here get inside. I hear that Myrtle and Jerry have put together quite a feast."

"Is this the birthday boy?"

I grinned and nodded.

"EJ, this is Shirley's husband, Jack Reynolds."

"Hello, Mr. Reynolds. It's nice to meet you."

"You can call me, Jack. Shirley and I don't stand on formality, do we?" He smiled at Shirley and picked up her crutches. "How old are you, EJ?"

"Six."

"Wow, you're big for six. Don't you think, Arial?"

Grandma Arial nodded. "I do indeed. And he's smart, too. So smart that they let him skip the first grade."

"Tell you what, EJ. I need some help getting Shirley into the house. Think you can lend a hand?"

"Sure, what do you want me to do?"

He handed me the funny-looking crutches. "It's easier to carry Miss Priss here into the house—"

"Oh Jack," Shirley laughed.

"—but she won't have any of it, so we need to help her stand up and wait until she gets her balance. Arial, will you take Waldo into the house so he doesn't trip up the works?"

"I've been waiting to get my hands on that baby." Grandma Arial picked up the wiggly dog and opened the screen door.

"Here we go." Jack put his arms around Shirley and lifted her to her feet. She tottered for a moment and he reached for her again.

She pushed him back. "Will you stop? I'm fine."

"See what a pain this girl can be? If I had my way, I'd throw her over my shoulder."

"Ha, ha, ha." Shirley pretended to laugh, but the funny part of it was that she really was laughing. "Give me those sticks, EJ."

"Oh!" I startled. "Sorry, here they are."

"One at a time." She slipped an arm into a circlet of leather and leaned on that crutch while I gave her the other one. "Okay, let's start the parade."

I didn't know what to do at first, but then I ran around them and opened the front door.

"When I get old and gray, I'm afraid Shirley's gonna trade me in for you." Jack kept his eyes on Shirley. I could tell he was worried about her falling but didn't want to let on that he was.

Shirley moved slowly, her braces clanking against the wooden porch flooring. "I may not wait until you are old and gray, Jack," she grunted.

"Hurry up, woman. That birthday cake is gonna mold before we get in there."

* * *

After dinner, everyone sat in Myrtle's parlor.

"Watching little guys grow up gives one a sense of time," Myrtle said as Mick and Waldo romped on the rug. "Otherwise, one day blends into the next until you realize months and years have passed without you even noticing."

Sonny and Mama sat on the couch together. I could tell Mama was trying not to cry and I wondered why, since it had been such a nice evening.

"We used to play piano and sing and dance in here," Shirley said.

"Can I play the piano with you, Miss Myrtle?" Mick tugged at Myrtle's dress.

"Oh no, Mick," Mama shook her head. "The big people, they want to talk."

"Vala, it's fine. I think some music would be great. Come on over here, boy, and I'll show you a tune or two." Myrtle pulled out the piano bench.

Mick trotted over to her and crawled up on the seat.

"What do you want to play?"

"Something fun."

"How about 'Buffalo Gals'? Do you know that one?"

Mick shook his head. "Show me."

Myrtle plinked out a little tune. Mick watched her fingers through the first stanza and the chorus before playing the song himself.

Shirley elbowed Jack. "Look at that little fellow. He picked it up by ear."

Jack turned to me. "How old is he?"

"Four."

Jack leaned forward. "That's amazing."

"Is everyone in your family musical?" Shirley asked.

I shrugged. "Dunno."

She stared at me for a minute. "I bet you and Mick are the great greats of Beethoven or Mozart."

"Maybe."

Shirley laughed—and I laughed because I knew she knew I had no idea who those guys were. As Mick started the melody again, Myrtle started playing the chords, and the music got louder.

Shirley clapped her hands, and then she and Grandma Arial sang,

Buffalo gals won't you come out tonight,
Come out tonight, come out tonight.
Buffalo gals won't you come out tonight
And dance by the light of the moon.

They started again, this time faster.

"Come on, Vala," Grandma Arial called. "Sing with us."

Mama shook her head but by the chorus she was clapping and pretending to sing. She looked pretty in her pink and white checkered dress, her cheeks rosy and her eyes sparkling with fun.

* * *

I went to the bathroom and when I came back downstairs, Mama was chatting with Shirley. The men had gone out on the porch to smoke and talk about guy things. Unsure which group to join, I sat on the bottom step of the hall stairway.

"There's been no word from your family?" Shirley asked Mama.

"They not want me. I am a black lamb."

"Delores said that the house is in good repair now. But she knocked and no one came to the door the last time she was in Germany."

Mama sniffed. "Maybe that's okay."

"Are you happy here? In Cold Creek?"

"Safe, yes. I have the boys, and Sonny is very kind."

"Have you found any friends your own age here?"

Mama shook her head. "Die Frauen are busy with their families. Und they think that I am bad—that all Deutsche Leute are bad."

Shirley sighed. "They only know what they are hearing. They don't know you."

Mama rubbed her eyes. "Soon it will be better, maybe."

"What was it like for you? In Mannheim when EJ was born?"

There was quiet for a long time. I thought about peeking around the door frame to see what was going on.

"Oh, Shirley. It was beautiful there. Emo was born in a nice home where they took care of mothers and babies, especially babies like Emo. He was the right kind, what they wished for future Germans."

"How old were you, Vala?"

"Me?" She seemed surprised by the question. "Er…Fourteen. Almost fifteen."

"You were away from the bombings, then?"

"There were no bombings when Emo was born. The sky was sehr blau, very blue, that day. When the baby came, his daddy sent a nice bag of things for him."

"Did you ever see Emo's daddy after that?"

"He was very important man in Prague, a leader. We heard about him all the time. Then they say he was killed by a bomb on his car."

Shirley's voice was soft, but I think she said, "I'm sorry."

* * *

Mama only made a little fuss when I told them I wanted to spend the night at Grandma Arial's house. She got out of the truck with Mick, who was asleep. "You be good for Grandma."

"He's always good, aren't you, EJ?"

I nodded.

Mama carried Mick into our house.

"Good night, Vala," Grandma Arial called.

"I'll come for you in the morning," Sonny said to me. "Before work."

"Let him stay a bit, Sonny. I get lonely here, now that your dad's gone. I'll make sure he gets to school on time."

"Are you sure you want to be taking care of a kid right now?" Sonny ruffled my hair "Even a smart guy like EJ here?"

"It's my greatest pleasure."

Sonny kissed Grandma Arial on the top of her head. "You want me to walk you to the door?"

She shook her head. "You go take care of that pretty girl of yours and Mick."

As Grandma Arial and I climbed up the stairs to her apartment, I turned around. Sonny was standing on our front porch watching us. I waved and he waved back.

"Do you want a glass of milk before bed?"

I was so full I could hardly breathe, but I wasn't sleepy. "Sure." I sat down on a chair at Grandma Arial's table while she bustled around the kitchen.

"Did you have fun tonight, birthday boy?"

"I did. I like Shirley and Jack. They're nice."

Grandma tied on a fresh apron. "There was a time I thought Shirley was going to marry your Uncle Grant, but it didn't work out."

"Why not?"

"Neither of them told us why. Shirley's father is famous. Maybe it had something to do with that, or maybe it was because of the polio."

"I'm sorry."

"I was, too." She took out a pan and poured milk into it. "Life's like that sometimes, EJ."

"I like Jack, though." I wrinkled my nose. Warm milk wasn't my favorite but Grandma Arial insisted that cold milk before bed gave kids stomach aches.

"Your Grandpa John liked Jack, too," she said as she lit the burner.

"What was Grandpa John like?"

"He was handsome like Grant and Sonny. Your Uncle Johnny looked more like me." She poured the warm milk into my special cup and sprinkled cinnamon and a little sugar into it. She did that to make warm milk taste better to me.

"Your grandpa loved to play chess. He would've played a game of chess with you every Sunday after church if he was still alive."

"I like checkers."

She handed me the cup. "He was looking forward to meeting you when we were trying to get you and Mick and your mom here. I guess it wasn't meant to be. He died one morning at breakfast."

"I wish I had a grandfather. I don't remember my Mannheim Opa at all. Mama thinks he was killed in a car accident when I was a baby, but no one knows for sure. He just didn't come home one day."

"War sometimes makes it hard to know what happened to people," she said. "You'll have time to learn about your family someday. It's complicated right now, though."

"I found a picture of Opa. Mick thinks he was handsome."

"I'm sure he was. Would you like to see a picture of Grandpa John?"

"Yes!"

While she fetched the picture out of her bedroom, I dumped the milk into the sink and rinsed the cup.

"Aren't you a good boy, EJ. Cleaning up like that." She had a photo album under her arm. "Come sit with me on the couch and we'll look at your American family."

I curled up beside her, "Thank you, Grandma."

She opened the book. "You're welcome, sweetheart."

"At least I have you."

"Just try to get rid of me, EJ Logan."

4

Zona Dixon

October 2, 1949

"Yoo hoo! Avon calling."

We were finishing lunch a few weeks after my birthday party.

Mick raced to the front door. "There's a lady with a big bag on the porch." He skipped back into the kitchen, clapping his hands. "Did she bring us something?"

Sonny leaned back in his seat so he could see who was tapping on the front door. "That's Zona, Deputy Jimmy Dixon's wife."

I peered around the door frame. "Who?"

"Her husband works for the sheriff, EJ. You know, police?"

Mama leapt to her feet, knocking over her chair. "Polizei? Why? What did we do?" Her eyes were wide.

"It's okay, sugar. Zona came to see you. She sells Avon. You know, lipstick? That paint women put on their faces?"

"Yoo hoo. You in there, Sonny Logan?"

"Coming, Zona."

"Paint? Wandfarbe?"

"Not the walls. Your face, Vala."

Mama touched her own cheeks. "My face?"

"You'll like Zona. She went to school with me and married my brother Long John's best buddy." Sonny got up and took Mama's hand. "Let's go meet your visitor."

"Nein. Mein Haus." Mama pointed to the lunch dishes still setting on the table. "Ist ba...er..."

"Dirty?" I prompted.

"Not dirty, EJ." Sonny pulled Mama toward the front door, her heels sliding on the wood floor in the hall. "I think she means messy. You know, like not neat."

"Anyone home besides that adorable little boy?" Zona scratched at the screen like a cat.

"Hold your horses, Zona. I had to explain about makeup to the missus. She thought you were going to paint her face with Super Kem-Tone."

Sonny opened the screen door. Mama peeked around him on one side, I peeked around her, and Mick peeked around me.

A round little woman with bright red lips and an equally bright red hat smiled at us.

"These guys aren't used to company yet," Sonny said as he led her into our living room. Mama and Mick and I followed behind. Mama was nervous but excited. Mick and I were curious.

"Sonny, should we have coffee with Frau Dixon?"

"Call me Zona, honey. When folks say Mrs. Dixon, I think of my mother-in-law. Nice lady and all, but she has ten inches and a hundred pounds on me. She casts quite a shadow, if you know what I mean."

"What's that?" Mick loved exploring the insides of purses, boxes, drawers, shelves—anything that held surprises. The Avon lady's black case was as exciting to him as an unopened birthday present.

Sonny pointed to the couch. "Have a seat. I don't know if I'll be any good at translating. The boys are pretty comfortable with English and German, but since you have a specialized female vocabulary with this stuff, I'm going to call Mama Arial to come over and help with this little party."

Mama tugged at his shirtsleeve. "Ask lady if she wants coffee?"

"Folgers, Zona?"

"What's in the case?" Mick's voice got louder.

"Makeup." Zona set it on the floor.

Mick ran his finger up and down the strap and around the clasp. "I like it," he said.

"Aren't you the sweetest thing? Why don't you open it up?"

Mick turned the clasp as soon as Zona gave him permission. "Oh!" He sat back on his heels and stared at the rows of bottles, boxes, and tubes strapped inside the case.

Zona winked at Sonny and turned to Mama. "Thank you, dear. I'd love some coffee with cream and three teaspoons of sugar."

Mama turned to go into the kitchen.

Sonny guided Mama to the chair next to the couch. "The boys and I will serve the coffee. You sit right here."

"EJ, stay. Bleib bei mir." Mama pointed to the space on the couch.

"You can help me talk with your Mama, can't you, EJ?" Zona took a thin book out of the bag and handed it to Mick who thumbed through it looking at the pictures.

"Yes, ma'am." I wasn't used to strangers in our house, but Zona seemed like a nice lady.

"Where did you get those eyes, Vala?"

After I translated, Mama and I looked at each other, unsure how to answer such a question.

"Let me see. You're fair-skinned and light blonde." Zona rummaged through her case. "I'm sure I have the perfect colors for you." She held up a small tube of lipstick. "Ever hear of Loretta Young? She wears Avon all the time. Ever see her in our ad?"

Mama looked at me but I didn't speak Avon yet and shrugged.

"Wow, look at this!" Mick held up the catalog and pointed to the picture of a woman holding something white and fluffy. "Is that a bird?"

"Oh no, sugar. That's a powder puff." Zona reached over Mick and handed Mama the tiny lipstick and a mirror. "Let's see how this looks on you."

Mama stared at it.

"On your mouth. Like this." Zona pantomimed putting on lipstick with her finger and when that didn't clear the confusion from Mama's face, she got out another little tube and colored her own lips with it. Then she gestured toward the makeup in Mama's hand. "Go ahead."

A smile spread across Mama's face as she realized it was okay to try it on. She painted her lips, rubbing a smear off her front tooth.

"Just as I thought. Great shade for you."

Mama puckered up her lips and examined her own reflection in the mirror. "Es ist länger hier."

"It's been a long time," I translated.

"Let me see." Mick took the sample from Mama and sniffed it.

Zona held up several pencils."How about darkening your eyebrows a bit?"

I couldn't remember the German word for eyebrows, so I ran my finger over each of my own.

"Milo, no!" Mama took the sample lipstick away from Mick. "You look like der clown. I am sorry, Zona. Der Junge…"

"The boy, Mama."

"The boy doesn't know Avon."

"Darlin', that's what samples are for." Using the pencils, Zona drew several colors on her wrist from light to dark and held out her arm. Mama examined the colors for a minute before she understood and chose one to try on.

"You want some too, EJ?"

I shook my head.

Mama pointed to a bunch of little bottles strapped to the roof of the cosmetics case. "Parfüm?"

Zona took them out one at a time, opening them, and letting Mama smell first and then Mick and me. I wrinkled my nose and tried not to sneeze.

"Can I try this one?" Mick held up a tiny bottle.

"Nein, Milo. Das ist…not for boys."

"Why not?" He stuck out his lower lip.

"It's okay, Vala. He's curious. He can play with it."

"Ich will das nicht kaufen."

"Mama is worried she will have to buy it and she doesn't want that one," I explained to Zona.

"It's a sample, Vala. The boy can play with it."

"Ja?"

Zona nodded and Mama smiled.

I heard footsteps on the front porch and then I smelled cookies. A moment later, Grandma Arial bustled in with a plate of snicker doodles.

"Sorry I took so long. I'd already put these in the oven when Sonny called."

"Grandma!"

"What's going on here?"

"It's a party for coloring Mama's face."

Grandma Arial and Zona smiled at each other. It felt like they were laughing at me and I frowned.

"In America, we eat at parties to color faces." Grandma Arial patted me on the head and gave me a cookie.

I bit into it and gave Grandma Arial a thumbs up.

She turned to Mrs. Dixon. "Good to see you, Zona."

"Thanks, Arial. I have your last order with me and the new catalog."

"Good. Smells like Sonny's got the coffee percolating. Let me go set these down and then I want to take a look at the rouges. I swear I'm fading away. Pretty soon I'm going to be a ghost and I'll need to put on makeup so folks can see me." Grandma went into the kitchen.

A ghost? Like the little girl-ghost I sometimes dreamed about? I wanted to cry out that I didn't want Grandma Arial to be a ghost, but I knew Mama would scold me for interrupting.

"I go help." Mama got up and hurried into the kitchen, too.

"Why did you bring makeup for Mama to see?" Mick asked Zona when we were alone with her in the living room.

"It's my job, sweetheart. Of course, if I had a million dollars I'd still do Avon, because it lets me dress up and get out of the house and go visit folks."

"But we just moved here. How did you know Mama would like that stuff?"

When Zona smiled, her teeth showed and her cheeks made it hard to see her eyes. "Someone told me that Sonny Logan and his pretty new wife moved into Long John's old house."

"I know who told you," Mick said.

"Who?" I nudged him.

He looked over his shoulder. Mama and Sonny and Grandma Arial were busy pouring coffee and putting cookies on plates. "Grandma Arial?"

"You're a smart little boy." Zona looked at herself in the little mirror Mama had left behind and pushed a strand of hair back into place.

"I'm not smart," Mick said. "But Grandma Arial loves baking cookies, and she's always looking for an excuse to make them."

"Where'd you hear that?" I laughed.

"Mr. McKensey."

"Ah. Your friend Mr. McKensey."

Mick frowned. "He knows things, EJ."

"That he does, young man," Zona said. "And if he doesn't know it for a fact, he has an opinion about it."

"He never said anything interesting to me." In fact, Mr. McKensey never said anything to me but "Get out of the way!" or "Keep it down, pipsqueak."

"When he does say something even half-way nice, we listen," Zona said.

"Why?" I didn't understand why everyone liked Mr. McKensey.

"You will find out for yourself someday, EJ." Sonny set a cup of hot chocolate on the coffee table in front of me.

* * *

I stood on a chair and looked out a window. It was raining. Children jumped in the puddles as people in funny-looking clothes hurried by. I shouted and waved. An old woman with a big bump on her throat looked up at me and frowned. I ducked down below the windowsill.

"Emo, don't bother those people. Come here."

I shook my head.

"Come, baby. Come to Tante Magda."

The floor was scratchy on my feet. I climbed into her lap and laid my head on her shoulder. "That lady had a potato under her chin." I put my thumb into my mouth.

"A what?"

"A potato."

"I see."

A little girl sat down beside Tante Magda. "Mutti, there's bugs in my bed."

"I know, sweet girl."

"I don't like them."

I took my thumb out of my mouth. "I got bugs, too."

The rain on the roof got loud. And lights flashed.

Part Two

Awakening

Cold Creek, Ohio

1953

＃

5

The Newsstand

October 12, 1953

"EJ, YOU BETTER slow down before you fall," Grandma Arial called from her parlor window.

"I will."

"Where are you going?"

"Aw, Grandma, you know it's comics day."

"It is? Then you better hurry. I have plenty of Merthiolate and I'm itching to put it all over you."

I giggled and waved.

Teresa Roberts was coming out of the newsstand with an armload of comic books.

"What'd you get?"

"Mostly Mickey Mouse, and some Tom and Jerry," she said. "Last month's Superman was gone."

"What do you do with all of them?"

"I take them to the kids at the hospital."

"Don't they care that the comics are old and don't have a front cover?"

A dimple appeared beside her mouth when she smiled. "No, they're happy to have something to read."

"Being sick must be pretty boring."

"I imagine it is, especially for smart boys like you."

I watched her until she disappeared around the corner before going into the newsstand.

A man in a plaid shirt was opening packages of comic books and arranging them for sale.

"Hi, Skippy."

"Hey, EJ. How are you today?"

"I'm good."

"I put your books aside. They're over on the table."

"Thanks."

"Too bad you can't get Captain *America* anymore. Your dad used to love the exploits of old Steve Rogers back when we were kids."

"What happened to them all?"

"Don't know. Maybe Mama Arial stored them somewhere when the Army sent Sonny to Germany. He had quite a collection as I recall."

I sorted through my options. I could only afford two today, but Skippy always let me look at the new ones. I picked out one of my least favorites and sat down on the floor with my back against a wooden post. I was absorbed in the exploits of Captain Comet when the bell over the door jingled.

"Danny Kline! Where have you been?"

I looked up to see Skippy embrace a man with a bald spot on the back of his head.

"Been in college up in Cleveland, courtesy of Uncle Sam."

"Who ever thought so many of us would get schooling like that? Your dad must be popping his buttons, especially after you getting all those medals and all. What're you studying?"

"Pre-med. I'm lucky to be alive after Iwo. I spent all that time in the hospital, and I guess I feel comfortable there now."

"You're a better man than I am. I'll be happy never to set foot in one of those places again," Skippy said.

"Where did you get hit?"

"Normandy. I didn't get more than a step or two on the beach. Everything went black and I woke up on a hospital ship. Some nurse was cutting my shirt off. The next time I woke up, I was in England."

"Looks like they did a good job. Your jaw healed up nicer than it was in school. Turned you into a Cary Grant look-alike."

They both laughed. It grew quiet. They stared at each other, the floor, and the ceiling. Finally, Danny picked up a magazine from the shelf below the register and laid it on the counter along with a five-dollar bill. "Can you break that?"

"Sure thing." Skippy pushed some buttons with his stump and the register drawer made a noise as it opened.

Danny accepted the change. "Ever hear anything about Teresa?"

"You just missed her. She made a comic book run for the kids not twenty minutes ago."

"Is she...you know, did they get married?"

Skippy glanced at me but I pretended to be absorbed in Captain Comet.

"I guess it didn't work out and he married someone else."

"Oh no! Is she okay?"

"Anyone else would ask if she's available."

"I know how she felt about him. She must've been devastated."

"If she was, you couldn't tell it now. She's as perky as ever. She's friends with him and his wife."

"That sounds like her."

"So are you going to go see her?"

"I don't know. Last time was before the war. She made it clear she had a new love and that I should move on."

Skippy shrugged. "Well, now she doesn't. What do you have to lose?"

"I'll think about it."

"Cold Creek has a hospital." Skippy grinned. "I hear that the prettiest girl of the class of '41 works there, when she's not at the school."

"You a matchmaker now, Skip?"

"Keeps me occupied, I guess."

"What about you? Picked yourself a woman yet?"

"Several times, but never got one to the altar. Scarred-up jokesters are a dime a dozen these days."

"EJ? EJ!" My grandmother's voice could break glass.

"My God," Danny laughed. "Is that Arial Logan?"

The door to the newsstand burst open and my grandmother bustled in. "There you are, EJ. Aren't you hungry yet? Soup's getting cold."

I put down the comic I was pretending to read and picked up the two I was going to buy. "Coming, Grandma."

"Is that Jerry Kline's baby boy?" Arial squinted and leaned closer.

"It's me, Mama Arial. How have you been?" Danny gave her a long hug.

"I'm fine, fine. Have you met Sonny's eldest?" She pointed at me. "He's like Sonny. Has to have the latest comic as soon as it comes in."

Danny smiled at me. "Well, hello there. What's your name?"

"This is EJ," Grandma Arial said. "Aren't those eyes to die for? His mother's a true beauty. His little brother Mick's going to be a scientist—always taking things apart and putting them together again."

"What are you going to be, EJ?" Danny was just being nice.

Actually, I had no idea. A newspaper reporter like Clark Kent? A circus clown? I glanced around the store looking for options. Skippy leaned forward to see what I was about to say, and I focused on his scars instead of his face. "A doctor," I blurted out.

Grandma Arial beamed.

Skippy chuckled as if I'd told a joke.

"What kind of doctor?" Danny really seemed interested.

"A surgeon." I wasn't sure what a surgeon did but I was suddenly certain that I would indeed be one.

"That makes two of us then, EJ." Danny extended his hand.

"Yes, sir." I grinned and we shook on it.

"I bet you'll be a great doctor," he said, and I knew in that moment that I would be.

Danny patted Grandma Arial on the shoulder like they were old friends. "Looks like Sonny did real well for himself—a beautiful family."

"I'm proud of my boys." She inclined her head toward the register. "Pay Skippy, EJ."

I laid twenty pennies on the counter so Skippy could use his handless left arm to scoop them into his right palm.

"Enjoy your comics." He dropped the pennies into his cash drawer and slipped the books into a paper bag.

"I will."

"Come by for lunch while you're home, Danny," Arial said. "And bring your daddy and Myrtle along. I owe them a meal. I'll make peach strudel."

"I'll do that." Danny held the door for us. "Any day better than another?"

"How about day after tomorrow at noon?"

"I'll check with Myrtle. She's the one who keeps dad's appointment calendar these days."

Grandma Arial leaned back around the door frame under Danny's arm. "You come too, Skippy."

"Thanks, Mama Arial, but I work days, you know."

"Then you come to dinner one night."

I glimpsed Skippy's nod before the door closed behind us.

Grandma Arial herded me across Cold Creek Drive and up the hill. "Your mama will have my hide for letting you stay so long at the newsstand. You must be starving."

"Who was that man?"

"Danny? He was the sweetest boy in Cold Creek. We all knew he'd make something of himself from the time he was a little guy—just like we know it about you."

6

Cold Creek Elementary

October 14, 1953

ANNIE JONES TURNED around in her seat. "You're late again."

I scratched the side of my nose. "The bell just rang."

"We're supposed to be in our seats before the bell." She turned to face the front of the room as Mrs. Wiggins came in.

It was early morning, but tiny strands of hair had already curled out of Annie's braids. I waved my palm close to the back of her head and they moved like iron filings beneath a magnet. It must have tickled because she flinched and patted the back of her head.

"EJ Logan!"

I jumped at Mrs. Wiggins' voice. "Yes ma'am?"

"What are you doing?"

"Nothing."

"You were trying to put something in Annie's hair."

"What?" Annie put both hands on her head. "Gum?" She turned to look at me. "You were putting gum in my hair?"

"No, no. It's nothing like that." My ears burned and I couldn't resist scratching one of them.

"What were you doing then?" Mrs. Wiggins stood by my desk, her hands on her hips.

"I was…you know, thinking about what…uh, funny stuff hair is." I rubbed my nose.

"Are you sure you weren't trying to do something mean to Annie?"

"I'm not allowed to chew gum, and besides, I like Annie. I'd never be mean to her."

Someone giggled and one of the Spencer twins in the back of the class made kissing sounds.

Annie hissed at the guys behind us, "Shush!"

I was sure there was a spider crawling across my left ankle. I scraped it with the heel of my right foot.

Mrs. Wiggins snapped her fingers and everyone quieted down. "Annie, are you sure you're okay?"

"I'm fine. Really, Mrs. Wiggins."

"Then let's start. We've wasted enough time on funny hair."

Annie turned and winked at me.

Any other time, that little bit of attention would have been thrilling, but my head hurt and I needed to lie down.

"Open your books to Chapter Eleven." Mrs. Wiggins sat at her own desk and opened her notebook. "We are going to talk about Lewis and Clark today."

I didn't care about Lewis and Clark. All I could think about was Annie's caramel-colored braids and my sore throat.

"Whoa, what's wrong with you?" Billy Ray Parker in the next row whispered.

"Why?" I coughed into my fist.

"You're all red."

"I need a drink of water." I laid my head on my desk.

"Mr. Logan?"

Mrs. Wiggins sounded far away.

"What?" I grunted.

"EJ!"

Soft hands touched my face. "He's burning up, Mrs. Wiggins."

"Okay, okay. Back away. Give the poor boy some air." Mrs. Wiggins clapped her hands.

I lifted my head and quickly put it back down again. "I don't feel good."

"Come with me." She helped me up and guided me toward the door. "Get out your history books and read Chapter Eleven," she said over her shoulder.

"We already read it," Billy Ray whined.

"Read it again." She pushed me into the hall and closed the door behind us. Immediately voices inside the classroom rose. She rapped on the window with her knuckles. "Read!"

"Where are we going?" I croaked.

"Nurse's office."

"I wanna go home."

"Miss Roberts will decide that." Mrs. Wiggins prodded me along, but I didn't feel like hurrying. In fact, the hall seemed a lot longer than usual.

"I can't make it." I dropped to the floor and curled into a ball clutching my stomach.

"There's no need for this, young man." She tugged at my arm.

"Ow," I grunted before I threw up Grandma Ariel's pancake breakfast all over Mrs. Wiggins's shoelaces.

* * *

"You certainly caused a stir."

I opened my eyes.

"Are you going to throw up again?" Teresa Roberts wiped my mouth with a damp cloth.

"No."

"Good. Let's take your temperature and see what we have here." She rinsed the cloth and wrung it out. "Hold this under your chin. It'll make you feel better."

I doubted a cool rag would do the trick, but I didn't argue with her. My forehead was itchy and my eyes were sore. In fact, the damp coolness of the cloth did feel good.

"Does that help?"

The cloth had warmed up. I refolded it and pressed it to my forehead. "It's okay. Where's Mrs. Wiggins?"

"Cleaning up." She washed her hands in a tiny sink and dried them with a towel. She shook a thermometer and stuck it in my mouth.

"What's wrong with me?"

"Don't know yet."

"Did they call my mom?"

"Someone will be here soon." She put a stethoscope to my chest. "Take a deep breath."

I coughed when I tried.

"Anything hurt?" She put the back of her hand against my cheek.

"My head. And everything itches."

There was a knock on the door. "We have another patient, Miss Roberts." Mrs. Wiggins pushed Billy Ray Parker into the office and retreated.

"Sit over there." Miss Roberts pointed to a wooden chair.

Billy Ray slumped into the assigned seat without a word. There were three large red splotches under his left eye.

She took the thermometer out of my mouth and held it up to the light. "I'll get you some aspirin."

I covered my eyes with the damp cloth. Miss Roberts walked away and I heard a drawer opening somewhere.

"What happened to you?" I muttered.

"Same as you, except I didn't puke on Mrs. Wiggins."

"Guess she's pretty mad, huh?"

"She didn't seem to be mad—more like worried. Two of us getting sick in twenty minutes."

I rubbed one arm and then the other.

"Stop it, EJ. You're making me itch, too."

"I can't help it." I scratched my belly and then my left thigh and then my belly again.

Miss Roberts came back into the room. "Take these."

I lifted the cloth off my face and squinted. "The lights are so bright." I took two white tablets out of her palm and crunched them between my teeth.

"Here." She nudged me.

I took the glass of water out of her hand and gulped it down. "Can I have more?"

"I'm thirsty too, Miss Roberts." Billy Ray's voice cracked.

She touched his forehead and frowned. "Let's check you too, young man." She put another thermometer in his mouth and went back into the storeroom.

"My head hurts." Billy Ray's rash covered his cheek and neck now.

Miss Roberts came back with a cloth for Billy Ray and read his temperature. Sighing, she hurried away to fetch more aspirin and water.

We were finishing off our glasses when the fifth-grade teacher arrived with a spotty girl who was crying and scratching. Miss Roberts herded her into our itchy little club and started her usual ministrations.

I squirmed, trying to find a comfortable position in the armless office chair. "I have to go to the bathroom," I said at last.

Miss Roberts was tending to the little girl. "That door." She pointed.

After using the toilet, I washed my hands. The cool water soothed the stinging. I started to splash it on my face when I caught sight of myself in the mirror. The rash covered my forehead and both eyelids.

"Great." I looked around. The fixtures in the tiny bathroom were very clean and very white. So was the floor. I switched off the lights, pressed my back against the wall, and slid down until my legs stretched out in front of me. I sat there a minute before curling up on my side and resting my cheek on the cool tile.

I was almost asleep when Sonny opened the door and picked me up. "Come on, buddy. I'm taking you over to see Doc Riley."

I covered my eyes and whimpered as he carried me out into the nurse's office.

"Where's his jacket?" Sonny sounded scared.

Miss Roberts threw a blanket over my shoulders. "In his locker I guess. But you need to get him to the doctor. I'll bring his stuff after I take care of these two."

Sonny tucked the blanket around my legs while Miss Roberts put a colorful knitted hat on my head, pulling it down over my ears.

I fought her. "It's a girl's hat."

"No, it's not."

"Yes, it is."

"No. I knitted it for Superman."

I sighed and relaxed against Sonny's shoulder. Miss Roberts was lying and I knew it, but I was too sick to care.

She opened the office door.

I opened one eye. Billy Ray Parker was still sitting there, shivering and wrapped in a woman's shawl.

I buried my face in Sonny's chest as he carried me out of the school.

* * *

"Measles?" Mama frowned. "Where did he get measles?"

"School, church, playground, newsstand. Take your pick." Sonny squeezed past her and laid me on the couch in the living room.

"Not a good place." She gestured with her head. "I have company."

"He can't stay in his room with Mick unless Mick gets it, too."

"Nein. No good." Mama twisted her hands. "Emo cannot be sick now."

"The boy has measles, Vala. He can't help that."

"Maybe your mama will keep Mick?"

"I'm sure she'd love it. I'll call her when we get EJ settled in."

I closed my eyes and willed their voices to go away.

"It's okay, Vala." A woman came out of the kitchen. "I can go to the inn and come back when things are calmer."

"Things are calm. Emo is sick and we don't know where to put him."

Sonny tucked the crocheted sofa throw around my legs. "Now, Vala, you don't want Delores to get sick too."

"I had the measles when I was in the first grade. Twice." The woman held up two fingers. They were shiny white and looked weird—like fishhooks. "Unless they come up with a different strain, I'll be fine. Don't worry about me." She saw me looking at her hands and put them in the pockets of her cardigan.

Mama frowned. "Poor Emo. You look all...what's that called? A dress with spots?"

"Polka dots?" The visitor's voice came closer.

"Ja. He has polka dots."

"Why not put him in there?" Delores pointed at Mama's bedroom across the hall. "He'd be downstairs, away from the little guy, and where you can take care of him."

"And where would I sleep?" Mama's eyes were wide.

Delores glanced at Sonny, who shrugged and shook his head. "You could sleep in EJ's bed in the boys' room," he said. "At least until EJ starts feeling better."

"No, no. The couch is better. You like the couch, don't you, Emo?"

I groaned and rolled away from them.

"He needs more aspirin to keep the fever down. I'll get you some water, EJ." Sonny went into the kitchen.

Delores sat on the sofa and put her funny-looking hand on my ankle. "He's gotten so big, Vala—and handsome."

"Ja, he's big."

"Here you go." Sonny hustled into the room and I heard him set something on Mama's end table. He tapped me on the shoulder. "Sit up for a minute."

"Sonny, my table! Use an…er…Untersetzer." Mama picked up the glass and rubbed at the table with her apron.

I coughed into my fist, and that started another round of itching. Before I knew it I was crying. I wanted them all to go away and let me sleep.

Sonny sat down beside me and put his arm around my shoulders. "Try to relax, okay? The measles aren't that bad. You get to stay home from school and take naps and let Grandma Arial spoil you." He handed me aspirin and took the glass of water from Mama.

I swallowed the pills so I could have the water. "Thanks, Sonny."

He eased me back on the couch again. "There you go. We'll be in the kitchen if you need anything."

I pretended to sleep, and soon I wasn't pretending anymore.

* * *

It was dark and the room rocked from side to side. There were people with us. I could hear them breathing, coughing, sniffling.

"Where are we going?"

My voice was small and no one heard me.

The room rattled and in the distance, I heard a whistle.

"Where are we going?" I stamped my foot.

"Air. I need air." A man pushed me against the wall and stuck his nose against a small slit over my head. "Air."

I hit his leg with my fist. "Where are we going?"

* * *

My heart pounded. I sat up and scratched. Somewhere in the gloom, I heard my mother's voice. In my stocking feet, I followed the sound.

The moonlight came in through the window over the kitchen sink and shone on her hair. She sat with her face and both arms on the table, sobbing. I watched from the doorway for a few seconds before returning to my couch.

7

Guests and Threats

"I DON'T THINK it was Skippy, Vala."

I tried to open my eyes, but the sun coming in the living room window made me squeeze them shut again.

"I think he followed me to Cleveland last year."

"Skippy is like Tommy. The war is over. All he wants is to be happy now, focus on building things."

I recognized the voice. The lady with the funny-looking hands was visiting Mama again. I tried to remember her name. Oh yes, Delores.

"Then who would call and say such things?" My mother blew her nose.

I lay still, eyes wide—listening.

"Who knows?" The woman sitting in the kitchen with Mama kept her voice low. "Bitterness makes ordinary people do ugly things."

"I feel their eyes on me sometimes. They make…eh…machen meine Haut kriechen…my skin itch."

"Who?"

"Monsters!" Mama cried. "I feel them out there at night, circling the house, waiting for me and the boys."

I shuddered. Not the monsters again.

"Well, that might be, but Skippy isn't one of them. Ask Sonny. They went to school together. The Klines know him."

"The burned ones are so angry with me—like you."

"I'm not mad at you, Vala. You know that."

I pushed back the blankets and sat up.

"You all think I did those things."

"We are angry those things happened, but you were a young girl. You were a victim, too."

"Those women in Mannheim…their faces…they wanted to kill me."

Who would want to kill Mama? She was fragile and a little crazy, but she was…you know… my mama.

"They thought they recognized you, but that's no excuse for what they did to you."

"I would be dead except for you and Mags and Sonny."

I got up and peeked around the corner into the kitchen. Delores was leaning across the table, her ugly white claw resting on my mother's hand. "Mama?"

They both looked up at me. Tears were running down Mama's face.

"Emo, go back and lie down!"

"Are you okay?"

"Your mama's fine, EJ."

"Somebody hurt you?"

Mama opened her arms and I ran to hug her. "I'm okay, Emo. Someone called and said mean things. That's all."

"Where's Sonny?"

"He went to get Mick," Delores said. "They'll be back soon. Are you feeling better?"

"I itch, mostly, but my head doesn't hurt so much."

"You want some orange juice?"

I nodded.

"Go lie on the couch, Emo," Mama said. "I will bring it to you."

She sounded more like herself and I relaxed. "Okay." I looked over at Delores and smiled. "Thank you."

She cocked her head to one side. "For what, EJ?"

"For being Mama's friend."

She nodded and smiled back at me. "Get some rest."

As I lay back down on the couch I heard her say, "He's a great kid, Vala."

* * *

There were voices all around me. Some were harsh and scary. Some cries were loud at first and then softened and other wails replaced them. Babies' screams rose above the babble—and there were beasts with sharp teeth and red eyes.

No, it wasn't voices. It was metal screeching against metal. My ears hurt...

No, it wasn't metal. It was fire! I was burning up...

* * *

The light was on in the kitchen.

"He was so handsome, Delores, and famous."

"He took advantage of you?"

They made no effort to lower their voices and I tensed, listening.

"Nein. I had a... clash on him?"

Delores laughed. "A crush."

"Ja! A crush. I tried to make him see me, but he ignored me. I was too young, you understand. Everyone thought he would make beautiful babies. They told us that is what we should do for our country, and I wanted to be a part of it, like any German girl. Of course, I was sad when he chose…"

I wanted to jump up and ask Mama who they were talking about, but then I thought maybe I would learn more by pretending to be asleep. Besides, it was so comfortable on the couch and I wasn't sure if I was awake or if this was another dream.

A sigh broke the silence in the kitchen. "Meiner mutter thought that they were Zukunft von Deutschland…the tomorrow of Germany."

"And your father?"

"Fathers want their daughters to…haben ein besseres Leben… be happy. He thought men like Reinhard could do that. It was Politik. I didn't want to know."

There was another long pause.

"When did you find them?"

"I didn't, it was Papi. Irgendwann im Jahr 1942. Before they left Gurs camp, but they were so far away and no one was sure it was them."

"How long were they in France?"

"Two years, I think. Almost."

"Why didn't your father go get them there? He was a Standartenführer by then, right? A very important man?"

Mama's breathing got faster. "Ich weiß es nicht."

"It would have been easier to get them from France, wouldn't it? Lots of people escaped from Gurs. The Quakers found Rosa there."

"I was young. They didn't tell me that."

"How old?"

"Thirteen in 1942. Mutti was sick after it happened. Papi gave her medicine from the pharmacy that make…um, made her sleep all the time."

"He didn't even try?"

"He sent his driver Gerhardt to look for them but they were riding a train then. Sometime in the summer."

"It's a miracle, Vala."

"Ja, a pin in a field."

"A what?"

"You know how pins are little. Hard to find."

Delores snorted and I realized she was laughing. "How did Herr Hess do it?" she finally asked.

"Ich weiß es nicht. They took so many Mannheimers, you know. I think he paid someone to watch for them at the camp. And of course, Reinhard was so berühmt. So…famous. Papi paid a nasty man to rescue them when the train got to camp. Was dangerous. We thought he put them all in Krakow with Polish people, but we find out later, it was just die…um…the important one."

"But why did Herr Hess send you, Vala? You were a baby yourself."

"It was late 1944 by then. The war was close. Die jungen Männer were at the front. There was no one but Papi's driver, Gerhardt, und me who could fetch them…you know…before russische Soldaten…get there. Papi made a plan with die…papers und contacts. Places to stay."

"You could have been killed."

"The Führung protect me. They knew that Papi und the Reich would punish this mistake."

"Did you know what the Nazis were doing in the camp?"

"Not at first. Then they sent Sturmbannführer Jäger…and I knew…"

I held my breath.

"One day while I was waiting for them to…er…fix it, I wanted to go to the salt mines. You know, where there are big statues of Joseph and Mary? They were making airplanes there, I think, but the Sturmbannführer didn't want to be my baby… er…babysitter. Then I say I wanted to go for a walk, but he said he was walking all day, working eine große Sendung…um…delivery?"

There was a soft inhalation. I couldn't tell if it was from Mama or Delores.

"Vergib mir. I didn't know what that mean then."

"No one wanted to believe it." Delores's voice had changed.

"I only understand it now as I tell you this story. He was tired from killing people."

I got up and stretched. "I'm hungry," I announced as I reached the door to the kitchen.

They startled.

"What's wrong?"

"It's nothing, Emo." Mama put her arms around me. "Would you like eggs?"

"You were crying again."

"Your mama and I were talking about old times." Delores's eyes were sad—so sad that I needed to look away from them.

"Why talk about things that make you cry?"

"Why, indeed?" Delores patted me on the shoulder.

Mama took her heavy iron frying pan out of the oven and put it on the cook top. "You want omelet? I have cheese and onions."

"Okay." I sat down across from Delores. She smiled at me and I smiled back.

"Do you remember me, EJ? From Mannheim?"

I shook my head.

"Just as well. Let's start our friendship today, okay?"

She was nice, so I nodded.

"You want some eggs too?" Mama held up the carton.

"It's getting late. I'm sure Myrtle is planning on feeding me. And Tommy will be calling at nine, after the children are in bed. I should go."

My mother's eyes were wet. "I'm sorry about before."

Delores stood up. Mama put her arms around her and laid her face on Delores's shoulder.

"It's a strange world we live in, Vala." Delores patted Mama's back. "None of this stuff is our fault."

"That doesn't make it go away."

Delores disengaged herself from Mama's grasp. "No, it doesn't." She took her jacket off the back of her chair and put it on. "Someday, we'll figure it all out."

* * *

After Delores left, I ate my eggs.

Mama felt my forehead. "You should wash your face and brush your teeth, Emo. That will make you feel better," she said in German.

"Did we know Delores in Germany?"

Mama nodded. "Her great aunt's family lived in Mannheim before the war. We met after the war, when she came there looking for them."

"I don't remember."

"You were little."

I drank my orange juice. "Was Delores's family nice?"

"I don't know. Everyone stayed away from them. They were Jews, you know."

"What's that mean?"

Mama sat down at the table with her coffee. "People thought they were a threat to Germany."

"Did you?"

"Ja. I did." She stared out the window as she stirred her coffee.

"Where's Delores's family now?"

"Who knows? People got lost in those days. Except for one little girl, they haven't found anyone who used to live in Mannheim."

"Were we lost?"

"Some people think we still are." She reached for my plate. "Get cleaned up now."

I frowned. When Mama didn't want to answer my questions, she either answered with a riddle or changed the subject.

In the bathroom, I splashed cool water on my raw face and put on fresh pajamas. I looked awful, but I didn't feel quite as bad as I had earlier in the day. I was brushing my teeth when I heard a crash, and my mother cried out.

I rushed into the kitchen to see a stranger standing inside the back door. He wore a dark hat and glasses.

"You have grown, Emo," he said in German.

Mama grabbed me and pulled me behind her. "What you want?"

"I see that you have left German behind, Vala." His voice was scratchy, like he needed to cough. "Gut. It is safer, but I do miss it sometimes. English is so limiting, don't you think?"

Mama trembled. "You should not be here."

"You should have answered the phone."

"It was you? Saying such things?"

The stranger sighed and lapsed back into German. "How could I say anything when you won't answer. I came to tell you that he found me."

"How?" Mama gasped.

"A coincidence. I got a job at the auto factory in Cleveland. The first day, I met a man who told me that someone was looking for a war bride living in Ohio. A pretty girl from Mannheim with one blue eye and one gray."

She gasped. "And you told him about me?"

The stranger lowered his eyes. "No, of course not, but I think this man guessed some connection. Perhaps some research. Perhaps a description."

"Why do you think that?"

"Because a week later, I saw another man in the parking lot. I don't think he saw me because I ducked back inside, but I think it was the Obergruppenführer. And the only reason in the world he would be looking for me would be to…" The man glanced at me and then back at Mama.

"Oh, Gerhardt, are you sure?"

"I think so."

Mama squeezed my shoulder. "It's okay, Emo. Go upstairs now."

"No."

"Emo, do what I say."

I stuck out my lower lip and scowled.

"Obey your mother, Emo." Gerhardt frowned behind his dark glasses.

I folded my arms over my chest.

He chuckled. "Still stubborn, I see."

"The boy knows his own mind."

"What else does he know?"

Mama tensed.

I looked up at her.

"Nothing." She avoided my eyes. "You should go now."

"I think he follows me sometimes, Vala."

"And you led him here?" Her voice rose.

"You should have answered your phone. But don't worry. I took precautions."

"Don't come back to Cold Creek. Ever. It's too risky."

"I didn't know how else to tell you. I promised your father…"

"He won't find me."

"How can you be so sure?"

"There are many brides in Ohio."

"With two young boys?"

"He can't know that."

"He must."

I touched her arm. "Mama?" She was trembling.

Gerhardt's eyes found mine. "What's wrong with you, Emo? You are sick?"

I nodded.

"Maybe you should go lie down now."

I shook my head.

"Go." Mama pinched my arm.

"Ow!"

The floor creaked behind us. "Who are you?"

I spun around to see Sonny standing in the hallway. I had been so absorbed in our unexpected visitor that I didn't hear the truck pull into the drive. Mick peered out from behind Sonny.

"Sonny!" Mama sounded happy that he was home.

I certainly was.

Sonny tapped Mick's shoulder. "Go upstairs, son."

"I don't want to."

"Go."

Mick ran up the stairs and slammed our bedroom door.

"You too, EJ."

I shook my head.

"Go!"

I grabbed my mother's hand. "No, sir."

"You must be the man of the house." Gerhardt switched to English.

Sonny looked at Mama and gestured toward the man. "Did you invite him?"

"No." Mama sounded angry now that we weren't alone with this fellow.

Sonny clenched his fists and narrowed his eyes. "Who are you?"

"In America, I am John Sarris. But I knew Vala in Germany, under another name, of course."

"Is that true?"

Mama nodded.

"Do you want him here?"

Her head popped up. "No!"

"Then you are leaving now, John Sarris."

"Yes. Thank you." John Sarris touched the brim of his hat and backed away.

"I don't want to see you in my house or around this town again. Is that understood?"

"Ah, yes."

The kitchen door slammed shut behind him. I ran to the window and watched him hurry down Cold Creek Drive with his body bent against the wind.

"Where is he going, EJ?"

"Looks like he's headed toward Main. Maybe the train station?"

"Keep an eye on him."

"Yes, sir."

"Was he at Auschwitz?"

Mama's voice quivered. "Ja."

I turned to look at them.

Sonny had both arms around Mama. "It's okay, sugar."

"No. It's never okay." She sobbed onto his shoulder.

"I'll take care of you. I promise."

She pulled away and dug a tissue out of her apron pocket. "I have no one but you, Sonny." She blew her nose.

"And me, Mama."

"Ja, und Emo und Milo."

8

Another Visitor

October 15, 1953

I HEARD THE music before I opened the bedroom door.

"You look funny." Mick sat on his bed strumming his guitar.

"I'm not supposed to get close to you."

"Why?"

"Cuz it's catchy." I watched his fingers moving on the strings. He was only eight and he could already play the ukulele and the accordion. And Myrtle let him practice on her piano at The Windshift Inn every time we visited. "You're just a little kid. How come you're so good at this stuff?"

"I don't know."

"How come I can't play?"

"You never try."

I shrugged. "Sonny says to come down for a family meeting."

"Is it about that guy?"

"I think so."

"Mama was scared."

"Yeah. Me too."

Mick laid his guitar down and stood up. "Maybe he's not gone yet."

"What do you mean?"

"There's someone in Grandma Arial's yard." He pointed out the window.

A tall man stood at the foot of the side stairs to our grandmother's house.

I squinted. "Who is that?"

"I don't like him," Mick whispered.

"Why?"

"He's stiff like a stick."

The man looked around and when he didn't see anyone, he started up the steps.

Terror raced through me. I ran down the steps croaking, "Sonny! There's another guy! A different one."

Sonny met me at the bottom of the staircase, frowning. "What? Where?"

"At Grandma's."

"Oh my God." He ran out the front door. "Call the sheriff, EJ," he yelled over his shoulder.

When I hurried to the kitchen to telephone, Mama was backed into a corner, eyes wide and arms folded over her chest.

"Sonny said to call Sheriff Douglas!"

She didn't move.

Mick wasn't far behind me. "Mama?" He went to her and she put her arms around him. "Who was that guy in our house?"

"Shush, Milo. You don't need to know," she said.

I called Sheriff Douglas and went out onto the front porch to find Sonny.

"No, Emo!" The slamming door muffled Mama's scream.

As I crossed the yard, I could see Grandma standing at her picture window. She looked scared, and I wondered if the intruder had found his way inside her house like John Sarris had ours.

I stopped at the edge of the street. I couldn't see the man anymore, but there were voices coming from Grandma Arial's back yard.

Grandma Arial knocked on her window with her knuckles and gestured that I should go back inside.

"Don't let that guy in," I shouted.

Grandma Arial pantomimed locking a door and then held up her thumb.

I felt like I was going to throw up and might have, if Mama had not grabbed me from behind. "Come, Emo. Sonny is taking care of Arial."

"Who are these people, Mama?"

She dragged me across the yard by one arm and pushed me up onto the porch where Mick was waiting. "Go inside, both of you."

In the distance, a siren told me that Sheriff Douglas was on his way.

"Mama!"

"Now, Emo."

I went inside with my brother and closed the front door. As soon as the warmth hit me, I started coughing. "Stay away from me, Mick." I covered my mouth with one hand and pointed to the hallway with the other. "Go upstairs."

"Fine." He stomped up the steps and slammed the bedroom door. As I peeked through the front-room blinds, the light fixture on the ceiling rattled and I figured Mick was watching the scene from our window directly above.

Sonny and the new stranger came around the side of Grandma Arial's house just as Sheriff Douglas arrived, lights flashing and siren screaming. Mick was right. The man walked like he was marching. He held his head high so that it seemed like he had a very long neck and very broad shoulders. He acted like he was better than Sonny, even though Sonny had hold of the man's upper arm and was clearly in charge.

A skinny fellow with a big shotgun came running from town. He said something to Sonny, and I realized it was Skippy. He pointed the gun at the man while the sheriff handcuffed him.

Mama stood at the curb on our side of the street, her arms folded across her chest. I was focused on the sheriff, Skippy, and Sonny when Mama's hands went up to her face. Sonny's prisoner glanced at her and then again. Then he turned to stare.

Mama backed away from the curb. When she was in front of the Spencer's house next door, she wheeled and ran down the street. I wondered where she was going. Downtown Cold Creek was the opposite direction.

Sheriff Douglas opened the car door and the motion drew my attention back to the men in Grandma Arial's yard. I could only see the stranger's high forehead and prominent nose. I loathed him for coming into our neighborhood and scaring us, for staring at my mother, and for some instinctive feeling of danger that churned in the pit of my stomach.

Sheriff Douglas took the man's arm and walked him to the black and white car. The prisoner was still looking over his shoulder in the direction Mama had gone. As Sheriff Douglas drove away, Sonny stood in the middle of the street with his hands on his hips. A moment later, Skippy joined him with the shotgun cradled in the crook of his bad arm. They were watching the sheriff's car turn the corner a block away, when the Logan Foods van pulled up in front of Grandma Arial's house. Uncle Grant jumped out and after a short conversation with Sonny and Skippy, went to see about Grandma Arial.

Sonny clapped Skippy on the back and waved at me.

I looked down the street but couldn't see Mama. There was nowhere for her to go that way, except to the Kline's airport or the Windshift Inn.

It was getting late in the day and the excitement had exhausted me. My head hurt and my neck was stiff. I lay down on the couch. The pillow felt wonderful, but the blankets weren't warm enough. I coughed and shivered and worried about Mama.

Then Grandma Arial was fussing over me, bringing me aspirin and water and extra blankets and replacing my sweaty pillowcase with a fresh one.

"You poor baby," she whispered as she wiped my face with a cool washcloth. "Your grandma is here."

I wondered about Mama but couldn't stay awake long enough to ask.

* * *

My toes hurt. Crying, I tried to sit down.

"Keep that child quiet," a passing figure growled.

Tante Magda picked me up. "Shush, baby." We have to keep walking.

"I don't want them." I pointed to my shoes.

"You have to wear them, baby. It's cold. You will get sick."

The little girl said, "He can wear mine, Mutti."

"Your shoes won't fit Emo, Liebchen. Besides, you need them yourself."

I tugged at my shoes, sobbing. "Off, off."

"What's wrong with that kid?" It was a man's angry voice.

"His shoes are too small."

"Just take them off."

"His little feet will freeze."

"He's going to get the rest of us killed," an old woman said. "Do something."

"I'm trying, Frau Weiss. He's a baby, he doesn't know anything but that his feet hurt."

"Keep walking, Frau Weiss. I will think of something." The man pointed down the road.

"That little thing won't live until morning anyway," Frau Weiss grumbled.

* * *

A knock at the front door woke me—then my grandmother's clicking footsteps in the hall.

"Wait! Let me check who it is first." I recognized the voice but it confused me. Why was Skippy in our house? I sat up. Uncle Grant stood in the doorway between the living room where I'd been sleeping and the front hall. I started to ask what was going on, but he put his finger to his lips. I nodded.

"It's me, Arial." It was a woman's voice. "Teresa Roberts. I've brought EJ's jacket."

"Teresa!" My grandmother sounded surprised. "Come in."

"Skippy, what's wrong? Is Sonny okay?"

Uncle Grant winked at me and I relaxed.

Sonny called from the kitchen. "In here. I'm fine. We just had a situation."

I mouthed, "Where's Mama?"

Uncle Grant shook his head and shrugged.

Grandma Arial scurried through the living room, pausing only to put her cold hands on my cheeks. "This child is still feverish."

"Aw Grandma, I'm not dying. Just itchy." I tried to look healthy.

Teresa came over to the couch and smiled down at me. "You certainly started something at school, young man. Six in your class are sick, three in the fifth grade, and half of the fourth grade."

"How did I get it?"

"Who knows? The good news is that once you get well, you won't get this kind of measles again." She held up my jacket. "You're going to need this."

"Thank you, Miss Roberts."

She handed me a brown bag from the newsstand. "And maybe tomorrow, you'll feel like looking at these."

I peeked into the bag. I already had those two comics. I looked up. I could see myself in her eyes. "I've been looking forward to these. Thanks."

Over Miss Roberts's shoulder, Skippy winked at me. Great. The only person in the world who knew I was lying was standing in our living room. For a moment, I thought he was going to tell on me. When I realized he was going to keep my secret, I relaxed and grinned at him.

Grandma Arial stuck her head into the room. "Coffee, everyone. Come get some coffee."

Skippy lowered his voice. "Does she still slip cinnamon into the coffee?"

I nodded. "And cream."

He stuck out his tongue and crossed his eyes.

I laughed.

"Skippy doesn't like cinnamon," Teresa said. "Says it burns his tongue."

"Why don't you tell her that, and she won't put it in yours," I suggested.

"She's been serving us strudel and coffee since I can remember. Why mess with a good thing now?"

"You're a nice man, Skippy." Teresa stood on tiptoe and kissed him on the cheek.

He looked at me over her shoulder. "Keep that under your hat."

I grinned.

"On second thought, tell Vala so she'll stop worrying that I'm the devil."

"Skippy, get in here," Grandma called.

"Coming, Mama Arial!"

After they went into the kitchen, I lay back on the couch and straightened my blanket. It was embarrassing that Skippy had already heard that Mama thought he was one of her monsters. I could hear the adults in the other room, but their conversations overlapped and I couldn't understand what anyone was saying. Mick must have been upstairs. Soft notes drifted down from the ceiling. They lulled me and I relaxed. Nothing bad would happen now. I could finish being sick.

* * *

The phone rang and Sonny answered it.

"Hello. Is she okay? Yes, I imagine so. Sure, that would be fine. Tell her the boys are safe. Mama and I will watch over them. Thanks, Delores. And tell Myrtle that I owe her big time."

I opened my eyes. "She's at the inn, isn't she?"

The light in the kitchen made Sonny look like a shadow. "The Klines will take care of her. She's too scared to come home right now."

"Where's everyone else?"

"Teresa and Skippy went home a half hour ago, and your Uncle Grant is going to stay here with us tonight."

"Grandma?"

"I'm here, sweet boy." Grandma Arial started to turn on the lamp.

"No light, please. It makes my eyes hurt."

"Just a little bit, sugar." She put her dishtowel over the shade. "How's that?"

"Okay."

She sat down on the far end of the couch.

"Who were those guys?"

She took off my socks and rubbed my feet. "It's hard to know, EJ. Your mama led another life before Cold Creek. Until Sonny can talk to her, we can only guess. One thing's for sure, you and Mick are my little heroes."

"What if I hadn't got the measles?"

"What do you mean?"

"What if I hadn't been here when John Sarris broke in?"

Grandma held up my foot. "Look at this, Sonny. He's got spots between his toes. Just like you did."

"Hmm." I wasn't sure if Sonny's grunt was in response to my spotty toes or to my question.

"You boys need to know what to do if there's ever another unwanted visitor." Uncle Grant's voice startled me. He seldom had much to say.

"Mick's too young to deal with this nonsense," Sonny said. "That means you'll need to keep an eye on him when an adult isn't around, EJ."

"Okay."

"Even if your mother is here," Uncle Grant added.

"But Mama takes good care of Mick…"

"He didn't mean it that way, boy," Sonny said. "Your mama knows how to survive. She's been doing it for half her life. But if someone hurt you or Mick…well, she would give herself to the bad guys before she'd let anything happen to you."

I shuddered at the thought of anyone hurting Mama or Mick.

Grandma Arial squeezed my foot. "If something like this happens again, you grab your brother and come to my house."

Uncle Grant leaned forward in his chair. "And if your grandmother isn't home, do you know how to get into the warehouse?"

I nodded.

"There's a phone in the office. You call Sheriff Douglas."

It was the first time I realized that Uncle Grant was on my side. I wanted to hug him, but I didn't feel like getting up. And Uncle Grant wasn't much of a hugger anyway.

9

Coach Littleton vs. Mr. McKensey

October 16, 1953

BY THE NEXT morning, my fever had subsided, and while I was still itchy, I felt better except for a sore throat. I got up and pressed my face against the front window. It was raining. Coach Littleton hurried by under a big black umbrella. Mr. McKensey drove past in his dented old Ford. When he got even with Mr. Littleton, he beeped his horn and shouted out the window.

Mr. Littleton startled and jumped back, but muddy water splattered his pants anyway. Furious, he shouted and waved his arms and tried to pound on the trunk of Mr. McKensey's car with his umbrella—which broke with the first blow. Mr. McKensey stuck up his middle finger and zoomed away. The resulting wave drenched Mr. Littleton, who screamed and shook his fist.

I laughed to myself. Round one went to Mr. McKensey.

"What's happening in the rain, Emo?" Mama called from the kitchen where she was making my breakfast.

"Mr. McKensey was being Mr. McKensey, and Mr. Littleton didn't like it."

"Why?"

"I don't know why, Mama. Shirley and Myrtle said that Mr. McKensey's always been cranky. Everyone knows to keep out of his way when he's driving."

"Cranky? What's cranky?"

"Empfindlich."

"Empfindlich?"

"Or maybe griesgrämig is better."

"Ach. English is so hard, Emo."

"German has a lot of words that mean close to the same thing. English doesn't have so many."

The coach tried to close his broken umbrella but it was stuck. He threw it down in the middle of the street and stamped on it.

"He has ein Temperament," Mama said over my shoulder.

"A temper, Mama. He has a temper."

"Ja. A temper."

"Look at all the windows." I pointed. "Grandma Arial's watching, and there's Skippy over there in the newsstand. And I bet the guys at Logan Foods are all watching out the front door."

The figure outside finally dropped to the curb, soaking wet and exhausted by his tantrum. Mick or I would have been punished for such bad behavior in public.

"That man is crazy," Mama declared. "We should call Sonny to come for him." She went into the other room, and I heard her dialing the phone.

Mr. Littleton was facing away from us, his face in his hands and his shoulders shaking.

Why was he so upset, I wondered. Mr. McKensey had been tooling around Cold Creek in that wreck of his for years. If the coach grew up here, why didn't he know that? I never expected a teacher to act that way—or any adult for that matter. He seemed like a scared, angry kid.

Then people started coming. First it was Skippy with a big towel to wrap around Mr. Littleton. Then Uncle Grant and Sonny pulled up and parked the van in Grandma Arial's driveway.

"They're here, Mama," I called over my shoulder.

"Emo, save your voice."

"Sorry." I turned back to the window.

Together, the three men helped Roger Littleton to his feet and headed across the street to Grandma's house. They were halfway up the steps when Skippy turned around and came back to pick up the broken umbrella.

I waved at him.

Sad faced, he waved back before hurrying to help the others get their old friend out of the rain. I knew Grandma Arial was already making hot tea and searching her closets for something warm for Mr. Littleton to wear while his suit dried.

I was tired and I hadn't even been up an hour. I tried to eat the breakfast Mama made me, but every bite hurt my throat. Finally I lay down on the couch and covered up. The room was hot so I kicked the blanket onto the floor and sat up. Scratching my thigh, I grabbed the bag of comics that Teresa had brought me and thumbed through them. Repeats. I tossed them on the coffee table. I wished I had the comics I'd picked out at the newsstand the day before I got sick, but they were across the street in Grandma Arial's living room. I stretched and closed my eyes.

Mama bustled around in her room. She must have been changing the sheets because I could hear her bumping into things and moving furniture around. After a few minutes, she came out with a basket full of linens.

"Are you okay, Emo?"

"Bored."

"Would you like the radio?"

"There's nothing on." I squirmed and scratched.

"What about Vater Knows Right?"

"Father Knows Best, Mama. And that's tonight, hours away."

"Want something to drink?"

I shook my head. Yesterday I'd been so thirsty that I'd have traded chocolate ice cream for a glass of water. Not so today.

"What's wrong, then?"

"Just bored." I folded my arms over my chest.

She set the laundry basket down in the hallway and came into the living room. "You want a toy?"

What toy did she have in mind? I folded my arms across my chest. "No."

She tucked the blankets around my feet and felt my forehead. "How about a book?"

"I already read the ones that Teresa brought me, and the new ones are at Grandma's."

She went back to pick up the laundry again. "I can fetch your comics after I wash these."

"When would that be?" I could be dead by the time she was done cleaning.

"Ah," she said. "You are...launenhaft today."

"You mean cranky, Mama." I rolled over to face the back of the sofa.

"Ja, griesgrämig!"

She went into the kitchen, mumbling to herself in German.

I fumed. It didn't feel right being home in the middle of the day. Everyone else was busy doing something—working, going to school, and talking to each other. I was stuck in the house.

The washing machine in the back room started, and the whole house vibrated. I curled into a ball and pulled the pillow over my face. A few minutes later, Mama went out the back door and around the house. As she walked past the front window, she was still muttering to herself. I sat up and watched as she crossed the street and climbed the steps to Grandma Arial's house.

I got up and went to the bathroom. On the way back down the stairs, I noticed that the door to Mama's room was ajar. She usually kept it locked when she wasn't home. Even though I knew I was alone in the house, I looked around before ducking inside. The room was decorated in light blues and grays. It felt cooler than it really was.

We were forbidden to climb on Mama's bed for any reason. I ran my fingers over the fresh linen and enjoyed its starched crispness. An elaborate carving and ceramic mosaic on the headboard looked like a bunch of wolves howling at the moon. I belly-flopped onto the bed and ran my fingers over it, imagining a story to go along with the image. Then I rolled over and stared at the pattern the window light shining through the canopy made on my arms and legs. A piece of lace dangled from the arch of the top frame. I stood up and touched it. On impulse, I sniffed. It smelled like purple flowers.

I knew I would be in trouble if she found me there. I looked around the room. The door to her closet was opened slightly, and I could see her nightgown hanging on a hook. I jumped down off the bed and went to explore.

There was a light inside the closet. Her clothes hanging on their wooden hangers all faced the same way. Her shoes were all in a row too. A brown suitcase was wedged into the corner. I'd never seen that one before. Maybe there was something of hers that I hadn't seen yet, but I didn't have the strength today. I already felt sweaty.

I was back in the living room when I saw Mama come out of Grandma's house with a bag under her arm. I peered through the curtains. She had the new bag of comics—the ones that I wanted. Even though she was busy and I was sick and cranky, she'd gone over to get them for me in the pouring rain. I felt like a jerk and a spy. She deserved a better son than me.

I hurried back to her bedroom to make sure that the closet door was at the proper angle and that the light was off. I was in the hall when I remembered the bedspread. I went back a second time and smoothed the coverlet so that there were no wrinkles or indentations from my feet.

As I crawled onto the couch and covered myself with the blanket, Mama's footsteps thumped on the front porch. I closed my eyes and tried to slow my breathing. The door opened and she came in. Her teeth were chattering because she'd forgotten to wear her coat. She would have scolded me for that. She tiptoed across the living room to where I was playing possum, kissed my forehead, and gently laid the bag with my comic books on my chest. She had to be the most wonderful mother in the world.

10

American View Magazine

October 17, 1953

"YOU MUST LET me wash you, Emo." Mama stood over me with a washcloth. "You are like…running horses."

"What?"

"Like hot water…"

"You mean sweaty, Mama."

"Ja."

"I can do it myself." I stood up and headed toward the stairs.

"No shower." She held up a small square of terry cloth. "Waschlappen!"

"Okay."

"Change to saubere Kleidung—on your Bett."

"I will."

"Don't forget socks."

"Mama!" I went into my room and collected my fresh clothes. In the bathroom, I stripped down and used a soapy washcloth to clean myself. The long scar on my thigh was shiny white against the measles-red dots. I ran my finger over it. Mama said I got it when I was a baby but like everything else, she avoided telling me how I got it. Doc Wiley told us it would fade as I got older and not to worry about it, which wasn't the point.

I was chilly so I pulled on long underwear and put my red flannel robe on top of them. I brushed my teeth, examined them in the mirror, and then brushed them again. My mouth still tasted bad.

I wasn't well, but washing up did make me feel better. I started downstairs.

"Socks, Emo!"

How did she know? "I have them in my pocket, Mama!"

"The wooden floor in the hall is cold. Put them on up there where there is carpet."

I sighed and sat down on the top step to put on my socks.

The phone rang.

"Hallo?"

I shouted, "Who is it?"

She slammed the receiver down. "No one. Wrong dial."

I came into the living room. "We get a lot of them."

"Ja."

I crawled onto the sofa and wrapped myself in the fresh blanket she had put out for me. "You aren't getting sick are you, Mama?" Her cheeks were as red as mine.

"I must buy baking powder for your dots," she said.

"You mean talcum powder?"

"Ja, talcum powder so you don't screetch."

"You mean scratch, Mama."

"Ja, ja. Scratch, screetch. Who cares?"

"Depends on if you are baking a cake or doctoring a rash."

She shrugged and disappeared into her room.

When she came out she slipped on her coat. "Will you be okay?"

"Fine."

She picked up her purse. "I won't be too long. Call Grandma Arial if you need bananas or something."

Sure that I wouldn't have a sudden need for bananas while Mama was gone, I glared at her. Mama never went shopping. Sonny brought home what we needed from Logan Foods. I didn't want her to leave me, because I was worried about her and because I didn't want to be alone. We'd had two different strangers nosing around the neighborhood. I could tell she was afraid of something, and that was scary for me.

"Don't look at me like a mean cat, Emo. I must to go."

I wrapped myself in the blanket and turned my back, trying not to laugh at her English or cry because she was leaving me alone.

* * *

When the door slammed, I counted to ten before reaching for my comics. "I can't believe it," I groaned. There was only a glossy *American View Magazine* in the bag. "Why is it so hard to get a couple of Superman comic books?" Mama must not have looked inside the bag she picked up at Grandma's. I threw the magazine on the coffee table and fidgeted.

A soft rattle made the hair on my arms stand up. When I couldn't ignore it any longer, I got up and crept into the kitchen. Sonny had already fixed the back door where John Sarris had broken the lock. I felt a little better, until I realized that if John Sarris got himself inside our house once, he could do it again. I peeked through Mama's frilly kitchen curtains—just the picnic table and an old box of Mick's trains on the porch. The wind made the screens shiver in their frames. Relieved, I retreated to the living room couch.

Too nervous to relax, I picked up the *American View Magazine*. The cover was black, and in bold white letters it said, "Germany's Shame!" Dreading what I might see, but too curious to resist, I opened it.

A headline on page five said "Hitler's Victims" and there were pictures of skinny people. American soldiers were giving them bread, and they were shoving big pieces into their mouths.

Naked dead people were on the next two pages. Did they just die like that? What happened to their clothes? Weren't they cold? Where did they come from? Who were they? One man's skin was so thin that I could see his bones through it. His ears and knees were huge. In some pictures, people lay on the on the ground with their mouths open. In others, they were in train cars and truck beds and wooden buildings and big ditches. They were being carried over the shoulders of soldiers whose faces were screwed up like they smelled something bad.

I thumbed through several pages of advertisements before I got to the second half of the article. I was too caught up in the pictures to read. The last photo showed a bunch of kids, about the same age as Mick. They held their arms up to the camera like they were trying to show me something. I held the magazine close to my face, but I couldn't make out what was on their arms.

A dark-haired girl in the middle of the photograph looked familiar, like someone I'd seen before. Was she German? Did she come from Mannheim, too? I scratched my face. We were American now. It didn't matter if she was a Mannheimer or not. I didn't remember ever being there anyway.

The magazine confused me. I knew that Americans were the good guys. They rescued the people who were still alive when the war was over. But what about the bad guys? Were Germans and Nazis the same thing? Did Nazis capture and kill all of these people? I thought about Mr. McKensey's theory that Nazis would come back and steal us blind. I wondered if they tried to kill us when we were in Germany. Did we become Americans to escape from them? Or were *we* the bad guys?

I dragged Mama's box of papers out of Mick's under-the-stairs closet. Surely there was something that would help me understand. I set aside the picture album. A thick manila envelope was under it. I peered inside. Mama and Sonny's marriage certificate. I thumbed through the other documents, all English. Most were stamped "U.S. Army," although a few were from the courthouse in Cleveland. Two were from St. Mike's, stating the date when Mick and I were baptized. I stuffed them back inside the envelope. Anything about our lives in America didn't interest me.

I started to feel sick again so I repacked everything and dragged the carton back to the closet. Then I hurried around the house to peek out all of the windows. After rechecking the back door, I headed back to the couch. Dizzy, I laid my head on the pillow and curled into a ball.

* * *

"What have you done?"
"Stay back!"
"Sweet baby."
Dark.
A hand against the back of my head.
My cheek against cloth.
Stairs.
A slamming door.
More stairs. More.
Dust. I waved my arms and coughed.
"Hush. Hush."
Dark.
Gasping. Choking.
My leg quivered.
Let me go. Let me go.
Far away behind us—
    Screams
        Screams
           Screams.

* * *

The smoke from Sonny's cigarette burned my nose. I opened my eyes. He sat in the easy chair by the window. Upstairs, Mick was practicing his accordion.

"Where is she?"

"Go back to sleep."

I sat up. "I'm thirsty. You want a drink?"

He lifted his coffee cup. "Thanks, son. I'm good."

I shuffled into the other room and drank a glass of water. I peeked out the back window. The sun was going down, and the shadows on the back porch were deepening. I was worried. We weren't used to being home when Mama wasn't there.

"I had a bad dream," I said from the arch between the kitchen and the living room.

Sonny looked up. "Maybe it's the measles."

"Measles cause bad dreams?"

He shrugged. "Maybe being sick or the commotion of the last couple of days upset you. I imagine being anxious would cause nightmares."

"How's Mr. Littleton?"

"Troubled."

"He's crazy."

"Don't say crazy."

"What's wrong with him then?"

"Roger's always been fragile. The war didn't help."

"Skippy and Danny said he was a POW."

Sonny blew smoke out through his nose. "Yep."

"What's that?"

"A prisoner of war."

"Yeah, but what exactly does that mean?"

"He was captured by the Ger—by the enemy and put into a camp."

"Concentration camps?"

"You know about them?"

I pointed to coffee table. "There's a magazine. Pictures."

He picked it up. "Oh, I see."

"Germans were killing people in camps?"

"It appears that they were."

"Why?"

"They—well, I don't really know. They claimed they had good reason. Fact is, some folks here agreed with them about Jews and Gypsies."

"Did you?"

"I didn't know any Jews."

"Is that why you joined the army? To rescue them?"

He lowered his eyes. "No."

I felt like I might throw up. "People here in Cold Creek hated Jews?"

"Kind of like they are with the coloreds."

"Did you hate Jews?"

Sonny lit a new cigarette with the butt of the old on. "Seems to me one group is no worse or better than another. Besides, Grandma Arial would have worn me out if she ever heard me say an ill word about anyone."

"The Nazis killed little kids like me and Mick."

He exhaled. "Yes."

"Did my Opa do that?"

"I don't think so. I hope not."

"What about my real father?"

He sat quietly, but I could tell my question bothered him.

"Did he?"

"Maybe."

"Auschwitz?"

"You know about that, too?"

"I heard you ask Mama. And it's in the magazine."

He sighed.

"Was Mama there?"

"Not in any official capacity."

"What's that mean?"

"I don't know exactly. She went to Poland to get something. She's never told me what."

The house got darker as the sun went down. My leg twitched and I rubbed it until the muscles relaxed.

"Will that happen here?"

"I hope we won't ever let that happen again—anywhere." Smoke came out of his mouth as he answered.

I thought about soldiers killing kids. It was embarrassing to think that I might be related to a murderer—and scary. "What happened to the people who did that?"

"The ones that they caught, they hanged."

I swallowed. "My real dad?"

Sonny shrugged. "Since we don't know who he is, you and Mick and I will never know his fate."

The real question floated between us. I started to ask several times but the words wouldn't come.

"Use your handkerchief, boy."

"Yes, sir."

I wiped my eyes and blew my nose. "Was she...was Mama a Nazi, too?"

"You know her, EJ. What do you think?"

"I'm scared. The other guys are proud of their fathers. They know they were right. They know they were heroes. The only thing I know about my father is that he might have killed people. And Mama won't say one way or another."

"You have me. And I promise you, I never killed anyone."

I avoided his eyes. "I know. You took us in and made us your family. Helped us become American. I appreciate it. I do. I just didn't realize...I didn't know..."

"And you have your mother."

"Do I?" It was a question I couldn't stop asking.

"You and Mick are the most important people in the world to her. She would do anything for you—has done more than anyone can imagine to make sure that you were safe and happy."

I ducked my chin. "I love her so much."

"Sure ya do, boy. She's your mom. And she's worth every ounce of affection you can give her."

A shadow passed the window behind Sonny, and we heard Mama's footsteps on the front porch. He tossed the magazine to me and gestured that I should put it back into the bag.

I was no more interested in upsetting Mama with Auschwitz pictures than Sonny was, so I put it under the cushion where I was sitting. Mama cleaned the living room every Tuesday and Friday, and she would surely find it when she vacuumed the couch. I'd have to move it as soon as she left me alone for a minute. The only place I had any privacy was the tree house. Maybe I'd put it out there when I felt better. Or maybe I'd get Sonny to hide it up there. I didn't want Mick to see it. He was a little guy and I didn't want him to feel sad.

Mama unlocked the door and came into the hallway. "Oh, you two. I didn't expect you...sitting without lights." She turned on the lamp beside the archway. "Hungry?"

"I could eat a bear." Sonny winked at me.

There were no groceries in her hands. "Where did you go, Mama?"

A little V formed between her eyes. "Don't bother me now, Emo. I have to clean and cook."

"Want me to help?" Sonny intervened.

She took off her coat and hung it in the closet. "I will do it."

He followed her into the kitchen anyway. "Maybe I can set the table."

"Oh Sonny, don't you have something to do?"

He put his arm around her shoulders and kissed her cheek. "I have nothing to do but help you, Mrs. Logan."

She smiled up at him. "You make cranzies feel better."

"I do what?"

I leaned forward. "Cranky people, Mama. He makes cranky people feel better."

"Ja. Cranky. Why is it so easy for Emo to remember the words and so hard for me?"

He looked over his shoulder and raised one eyebrow.

I knew that look. It meant shut up. Mama had successfully changed the subject, mostly because Sonny let her off the hook. After all we had just gone through, after our private conversation and knowing that I was upset, Sonny went right back to their version of normal. I punched my pillow and lay down again, thinking about the *American View* hidden in the cushions below me.

* * *

A truck full of soldiers drove past us.

"Magda, wait."

I lifted my head from Tante Magda's shoulder. A young man hurried toward us.

Tante Magda stopped and looked behind us. "What is it?"

"You don't have to carry the boy."

"Emo is a baby. He can barely walk anyway. The rags you tied around his feet are keeping frostbite away, but he can't walk without shoes."

"I found shoes, Magda."

"Baby shoes? Where?"

"On the road, right back there." Ulli pointed.

"You didn't find them, you stole them."

Ulli took me from Tante Magda's arms. "What does it matter where I got them. It only matters that they fit the boy."

"No," I cried when he tried to put the shoes on me.

"It'll be okay, Emo," the little girl said. "Try them on."

"Hold still," Ulli said. "Let me tie them."

"Look there, Emo. New shoes," Tante Magda said.

Ulli helped me stand up.

"There now. Want to walk a little?" Tante Magda held out her arms.

I took a few steps toward her.

"There you go." She took my hand. "Thank you, Ulli.

11

Vala's Explanation

I FELT BETTER but the rash still covered my face and torso. There was no school for me just yet, and Mama wouldn't let me help her do housework. I couldn't go back to the room I shared with Mick, either. Mama wanted to be sure I wasn't contagious, no matter what the doctor said. I felt like I was growing out of the couch, like a weed out of manure.

Mama stood on a stool, washing the picture window with a wadded-up newspaper dipped in vinegar and water.

I wrinkled my nose. "That makes my eyes water."

"It's not that bad, Emo." She puffed as she scrubbed.

"But the windows aren't dirty yet. You did them last week."

"I like a clean house."

We had a rigid schedule. We changed the bed linens on Monday and washed and hung them on the line in the back yard on nice days, and in the basement on rainy ones. Mama did all the windows and light fixtures on Monday, too. On Tuesdays, we dusted and vacuumed the living room. On odd Tuesdays, we also cleaned out the refrigerator and wiped it down, inside and out, and put in a fresh half-cup of Arm and Hammer. We also defrosted the two freezers and scrubbed the inside of the oven with a wire brush. Once a month, we took everything out of the cabinets, washed the dishes and wiped down cans and jars, and put down new shelf paper. Wednesday was grocery day. Sonny brought in sacks from Logan Foods and Mama examined each item, labeled it, and handed it to Mick or me to put away. We'd move the older stuff forward and put the newer canned goods on the back of the shelf. Thursday was garbage day. We went through closets, boxes, and trash pails, separating the stuff we would give away from the stuff we would put out on the street for pickup. On Friday, Mama cooked and canned. Saturday, she baked.

After all of that, you'd think that Sunday would be restful, but we always had a dinner at Grandma Arial's on Sunday, and we brought wiener schnitzel. It was the only time Mama wanted to be around anyone. I guess if Grandma Arial invited someone to dinner, Mama figured they were okay. But she would never invite anyone to our house herself, regardless of how much she liked them. People came to see us because of Sonny. Mama was gracious, but nervous. The only exception was Zona Dixon. Mama looked forward to trying on makeup and drinking tea and chatting with her.

"Emo, there's a girl for you."

I looked around Mama. Annie Jones was on the sidewalk in front of our house, holding her books to her chest. When she saw me, she giggled and waved before heading off to school with her best friend Margie Jenkins.

"She's your friend?"

"I know her from school."

"She's your friend." Mama laughed.

I sat back on the couch and folded my arms over my chest.

Mama got down off the stool. "Is okay to be friends, Emo."

"Then why did you laugh?"

"Maybe I forget what it's like when young?"

"Why did you forget?"

She sighed and lapsed into German. "Because things are different and I am lost."

She *did* seem lost sometimes. "What was it like in Mannheim when you were a kid?" I asked in English.

She took the hint. "Oh…nice. I lived in a nice house in a nice city. I had a Mutti and a Papi and a sister and a dog named Sonnenschein. I went to school, and when I was your age, I joined the Jungmädelbund. My sister Lana was seven years older than me and already in the Bund Deutscher Mädel."

"What was the Young Girls' League?"

"It was the girls' version of the Hitler Jungen, part of the Führer's plan to make Germany with strong, healthy people. An Aryan girl must join the Jungmädelbund when she is ten." She slid back into German. "We wore uniforms and exercised and went camping, and learned how to keep a proper home. I was excited when I got my certificate. It was April 20, 1940. I know the date because that was the Führer's birthday. My father was proud. And I would have gone on to the BDM like Lana when I turned fourteen, but that was when you came to me."

"You mean you had me before you were old enough to be in the Bund Deutscher Mädel?" I was born in 1943. "Does that mean you were only three years older than I am now when I was born?"

"It was a big day." She came back to English because I refused to respond in German. "German girls thought it was an honor to be mothers. We thought it was patriotic. Besides, I loved you the minute I saw you." She kissed the top of my head.

I thought about the *American View Magazine* hidden under the cushions. Along with the pictures of Auschwitz and the other camps, I had read all the articles during my long weeks at home. "I thought the Hitler Youth was where they taught you to hate people."

She was quiet for a long time, and I thought maybe I'd messed up.

"I didn't think that at the time, Emo. It was how things were. We thought we were better than other people. We thought we were like your comics. What is it when people are bigger and better?"

"Supermen?"

"Ja, we thought that the others were not so good. They were dirty, you know, and dangerous to our race. They cheated proper German families."

"How did they do that?"

She thought for a moment. "I don't know, but everyone said that it was true."

"Who thought that?"

"Everyone. Our neighbors, teachers, my parents, my sister. Newspapers. Signs in shop windows. Church."

"Did you believe it?"

Her eyes glistened with tears. "Ja. Why wouldn't I?"

At first I was stunned. Then I began thinking about it. How did anyone know anything was true? Just because Reverend Miller said Jesus was God, didn't make it so, did it? Just because he pointed out a passage in the Bible didn't make it so, either. You believed what people told you because you had no reason not to believe. Why wouldn't you believe your parents?

"Did you think Nazis should kill Jewish families? Mamas and papas and babies?"

She put her arm around me and rested her temple against mine. "They never asked me what I thought. They just did it."

"When you found out, how did you feel?"

"Oh, Emo! Such a question."

"I want to know." I pulled away from her embrace.

"It was war. The Americans and English were bomb—"

"That's different!" My voice cracked and I realized I was yelling at her. "What did you think when you found out that the people you loved were killing little girls and burning them up?"

She stood up, her arms straight at her sides, her hands clenched. "I was furious."

"You were mad about the babies?"

She lapsed into German again. "They took away everything that made me feel proud. I no longer had anything to hang on to or look forward to. The people I adored let me down. Everything that I thought was right...wasn't. Everything I thought was wrong got turned upside down. I am embarrassed and ashamed and confused. Am I to blame for what Nazis did?" Tears filled her eyes. "I don't know anymore."

I reached for her hand. "You didn't kill anyone, Mama."

She pulled her handkerchief out of her apron pocket and wiped her face.

"I just want to know," I murmured.

She was trembling. "You don't. It's better not to know some things."

I searched for a different topic, one that wouldn't upset her so much. "What are the good memories?"

She picked up the newspaper and went to clean the window beside the front door. "It doesn't seem so long ago—a little more than ten years." Her English returned with her good humor. "I had so much fun going places with my Papi, playing with the children in my neighborhood, teasing my sister Lana who had a clash on a handsome young man in the Hitler Youth."

"Crush, Mama."

"Ja, a crush. I always get that one wrong."

"What was my Aunt Lana like?"

"Oh, she was beautiful, Emo. You look like her."

"Did she like the Bund Deutscher Mädel?"

"She did at first. Then, something went wrong at one of the camps she went to, and she came home early."

"When did she die?"

She pulled away from me and applied herself to the window so that I could barely hear her. "1940."

12

Sorrow

October 25, 1953

ZONA KNOCKED ON our door mid-morning.

"What are you doing home, sugar?"

"Getting over the measles." She wasn't dressed in her Avon out-fit—in fact, she didn't have on any makeup at all. I unhooked the screen. "Is something wrong?"

"I was lonesome and couldn't stand the quiet in that big old house. Is your mama home?"

"She's out on the back porch." I led Zona through the house. "She'll be glad to see you."

"You're a sweet boy, EJ." Zona dabbed at her nose with a balled-up handkerchief.

I pushed open the back door and led her onto the porch. "Mama, you have company."

"Oh?" She was staring out into the backyard, holding a cup of coffee in both hands. "Who is it?"

"It's me, Vala."

"Oh, Zona! Is Avon calling again?" Mama stood up.

"No, it's nothing like that. Jimmy's off chasing criminals and… I'm sorry, Vala. I just…I'm lonely."

"Sit. We will drink coffee."

"I'd love coffee." Zona sat down across the table from Mama. "The hairdo looks great." The week before I got sick, they'd gone to the hairdressers together to get the latest style. It was the first time Mama went out with a friend. In fact, Zona was the only friend I could remember Mama having.

Mama touched her hair. "The Italian's not so nice for me."

"No, no," Zona protested. "You look wonderful. We are like Rosalind and Marilyn."

"Ja. Those crazy movie stars."

Neither one of them seemed happy this morning. Zona's hair was growing out and had turned frizzy. Mama's short silky version of the Italian clung to her scalp and refused to curl at all.

"I'll make fresh coffee." I went back into the kitchen.

"Don't go far," Mama said as I came back with a half box of donuts Sonny had brought from Spencer's Bakery earlier that morning. I nodded. She wanted me close enough to translate.

Back in the kitchen, I could hear them talking, but I couldn't quite make out what they were saying. When the percolator light went on, I unplugged it, took out the coffee-grounds basket, and emptied it into a tomato juice can for Mama's rhododendrons.

"I don't have anyone else to tell…" Zona's voice trailed off into silence when I went out onto the porch with their coffee.

"I'll be in the kitchen if you need me."

Mama smiled at me. "Danke, EJ."

Zona grabbed my hand. "You and Mick are nice boys."

"Thanks."

"You're lucky to have them, Vala."

"Ja. So lucky."

I went back inside and sat down by the window. I couldn't quite hear their conversation, but I was close enough to translate if Mama needed me. Happy to have time to myself, I examined the cover of my new comic. Superman floated above a city street at the level of a telephone pole. A crook below was hitting him with a beam of light that seemed to come from a ring. The headline read, "Has the underworld found a new flaw in the Man of Steel's armor?"

I wasn't worried. No matter what the bad guys threw at him, Superman was bigger, stronger, and smarter than anyone else. He always came out ahead. Everyone knew that. He was super good, and super good guys made everyone feel safe. You could count on that just like you could count on black being black and white being white.

"I thought this time would be different. I was almost six weeks." Zona's hoarse whisper intruded on Superman. "Jimmy had already told his mother, and now I've disappointed everyone again."

I opened the comic, trying to ignore her.

"Oh, Zona, I am so sorry." Mama's voice rose and then softened so that I couldn't hear her anymore. Good.

A few seconds later, there was a gurgle and then a sob.

I closed my book and peeked out the window. Mama had her arms around Zona. "Shush, Zona, meine Freundin. It's okay. Ich weiß wie du dich fühlst. I know, I know."

"Jimmy wanted a big family," Zona sobbed. "This is not what I thought would happen to us."

"I know," Mama repeated, tears sliding down her cheeks, too.

"Even when we think *maybe*, we're scared. This is the fifth time. I don't think I can do it again."

"What can you do but try? At least there is maybe."

"There were a lot of women in this town interested in Jimmy. His mother had her eye on Eileen Spencer, but Jimmy insisted on marrying me before he left for the war. Who knows why? I thought my dreams had come true, but now it's been so many years. Eileen has three girls and Jimmy and I have nothing."

Mama stroked Zona's hair. "Shush."

"Even if I can't live up to my part of the bargain, it's not too late for Jimmy. Why should he stay with me? But I can't bear to think about living without him."

"Jimmy loves you."

"He is an only son. If he stays with me, it changes his family forever. How can I ask it of him?"

Over Zona's shoulder, Mama saw me spying on them. "I don't know why they love us."

I wasn't sure if she was talking to Zona or me...or if she had simply confused her tenses again. I closed the curtain and backed away from the window.

"Oh, Vala," Zona wailed.

I went upstairs where I couldn't hear them anymore.

Part Three

Questioning

Cold Creek, Ohio

1956

13

High School
August 30, 1956

THE MAN LET go of my hand.

Red clouds rose into the dark sky. Hundreds of legs moved around me. Everyone carried suitcases and bundles. I moved forward with them. I couldn't help it. I looked around but they were bigger than me.

"Help!"

No one heard me.

Soldiers lined the road, watching us.

I yawned and rubbed my eyes. Everyone was going the same direction, but I didn't want to go that way. I stopped and everyone continued on around me. When they were gone, I sat down by a building.

More people passed.

I curled up on the grass and fell asleep.

Big hands grabbed me. I screamed and kicked.

"I found him. He's here." A soldier lifted me up.

"Are you sure it's him?"

"Yes, Herr Obergruppenführer. It's right here on his coat."

A man in a fancy outfit took me from the soldier. He held me up and looked at me. "Yes. There is no doubt."

"Yes, Herr Obergruppenführer."

"Don't call me that, Dolph."

"I'm sorry, sir."

"Take him to my car."

"Yes, Herr Obergrupp..."

"Protect him."

"Jawohl."

"You lose him again and I won't just kill you. I'll find your family. Do you understand?"

The soldier bowed his head.

* * *

"My God, EJ! What happened to you?" Annie Jones's locker was right next to mine.

"What do you mean?"

"All the other boys look like Mickey Rooney and you show up looking like Burt Lancaster?"

"Who?" I focused on spinning my combination lock rather than look at her.

"Learn to take a compliment." She hugged her books and headed down the hall, her ponytail bouncing on her collar. Just before she went into the classroom, she peeked over her shoulder and caught me watching her.

I coughed and straightened my glasses.

"She's pretty and she knows it," Billy Ray Parker said as he put his jacket into his locker. "Every guy in the class wants her."

"She's pretty all right." I took out my American History book.

"So what did you do this summer? Lift weights?"

I shrugged. "Went to camp and did some rowing on the lake."

"Must have been a big lake or a big canoe."

"No, nothing like that. What did you do this summer?"

"My family doesn't have the dough for fancy summer camps. I worked at the farm like usual."

"That sounds like fun, too."

He rolled his eyes. "Hardly."

"I'm sorry…"

He pushed around me and headed toward the gym.

So far, high school felt weird. I slammed the locker and walked three paces before I realized I didn't know where to go. I fished my schedule out of my back pocket. American History, B22."

"Are you lost?"

I spun around. Coach Littleton stood in the middle of the hall, his hands on his hips.

"No, sir. I'm checking to see what room my class is in."

"Is that you, EJ Logan?" He took off his ball cap and wiped his forehead with his sleeve.

"Yes, sir."

"I would never have recognized you."

I looked around, hoping to find the right hallway.

"Should have noticed that fidget, though. All nervous energy, aren't ya, boy?"

"Yes, sir."

"You like running?"

"I guess so." My hall was just past the coach and to the right.

"How about tackle? You afraid to tackle another kid your size?"

I was uninterested in tackling anyone, but I wasn't afraid of it. "No, sir."

"Got that good Kraut blood in you, don't you, boy?" He punched my arm.

I tried not to flinch.

"We need big strong kids like you for the football team. You trying out this afternoon?"

"How do I do that?"

"Just show up at the field at 3:15."

"Today?"

"You got a date?"

"My grandmother is coming for me."

"You a sissy? Still need your grandmother?" His eyes glittered.

"It's polite to be where you say you will be."

"Tomorrow, then. On the track."

I didn't want to play football, but I didn't want to get in trouble either. "Okay."

"Shouldn't you be finding your classroom?"

"Yes, sir." I went around him and found B22. As I opened the door, I looked back and saw him standing at the head of the hall, his arms crossed over his chest.

* * *

Grandma Arial sat on a bench across from the front entrance of Cold Creek High. Mick bounced a ball against an oak behind her.

"You look so grown up and handsome, EJ."

I leaned down and kissed her cheek. "Thanks, Grandma."

"Are you hungry?"

"I'm always hungry." I caught Mick's toss with one hand. "How was your first day, squirt?"

"I'm going to learn how to play the clarinet."

"Wow!"

"The teacher didn't believe that I could play the ukulele, accordion, guitar, and piano already, so she made me play them all to prove it."

Grandma nudged Mick. "Tell EJ what tune you played for her."

"'Buffalo Gals'!"

I laughed. "Was she impressed?"

"Yeah, but she still wouldn't let me study any of those instruments. She said I was already pro...prof..."

"Proficient?"

"Yeah, and I should learn something entirely different. I asked for drums, but she said a clarinet is better."

"I like clarinets," Grandma Arial said. "Nothing like Benny Goodman playing 'Moonlight Serenade.'"

"And I bet if you had drums, you could figure them out."

"If I had them." Mick grinned and glanced at Grandma.

We all knew that if Mick wanted drums, he would get drums. Either Grandma or Sonny would see to it.

"They give you a clarinet to learn on, don't they?"

He held up a case. "I already figured out a couple of little things on it. It's fun."

"Hope it's not another version of 'Buffalo Gals.'" I winked at Grandma Arial.

"That little ditty is Mick's go-to song for all occasions." She stood up and shouldered her purse. "Let's get going. Your mama will be worried."

We walked to the corner and crossed Spencer Avenue. A couple of young men with their cigarettes rolled up in the sleeves of their T-shirts drove past us in a low-rider Mercury. The car stopped a few yards away, and the driver gunned the engine.

"What in the world is going on with Butch Murphy?"

"Nothing, Grandma. He's just showing off."

The driver backed up until he was in front of us, blocking our way across Logan's Ferry Road. "I hear you told Coach you didn't want to play football?"

I looked around before I realized Butch was talking to me.

"EJ is not fourteen yet. He's too young for such a rough game. Mind your own business, Butch, or I'll call your daddy."

"He's big as an ox." Butch turned to me. "Coach Littleton thinks you're weaseling out of your responsibility to the school."

"I just started high school today. I don't—"

"Doesn't matter what the coach thinks," Grandma Arial said. "If I catch you bullying EJ—or anyone else for that matter—you are going to have to deal with me." She put her hands on her hips and glared until Butch ducked his head.

"Yes, ma'am."

"Now you take that noisy contraption home and tell your daddy I said he should have his head examined for letting you out on the streets of Cold Creek. You're a menace."

"Yes, ma'am."

Butch took off, nearly hitting a couple of girls who were crossing the street.

"Oh, for heaven's sake." Grandma Arial rolled her eyes and we continued walking down Spencer.

"Thanks, Grandma."

"No problem. Besides, I seriously doubt Doc Wiley would sign off on football for you."

"Why?"

"What if you had a seizure on the field? What if it caused you to get hurt?"

"I haven't had one in a long time. Maybe I've grown out of it."

"I don't think you can grow out of epilepsy, sugar."

I hated the idea of football, but I also hated the idea that I couldn't play it if I wanted to.

Two blocks from Logan Foods, we saw Mrs. Jolly sipping iced tea on her front porch. When she saw us, she stood up. "Is it true?"

"Is what true, Etta?" Grandma shaded her eyes with her arm so she could see Mrs. Jolly.

"I heard that Sonny's kids are Nazis."

"Who told you such a thing?"

"Gladys Miller called me this afternoon. She said Meryl Jean Conrad told her that someone told her that these boys were Nazis."

"Etta, they've been here since 1948. They were babies. They don't remember Germany."

"Meryl Jean said they don't even go to church."

"What church does Meryl Jean go to, exactly?"

I felt sick at my stomach. What was going on here? These were our neighbors. I'd gone to school with Ronnie Jolly and Amanda Conrad since first grade. In fact, Ronnie was in the sixth-grade play with me.

"Meryl Jean might not go to church regular, but she's a good Christian woman all the same."

"What do you think we are? Heathens?"

"I'm not talking about you, Arial Logan. I'm talking about those boys and that woman Sonny brought over here. Not everyone feels comfortable with them. Our husbands and sons fought against those people. Some never came home."

Grandma stood up taller. "You mean like my son Johnny? The one who is buried in France?"

Mrs. Jolly sat back down in her rocker, her mouth agape as if someone had punched her in the stomach.

"How dare you imply that my family didn't do its part during the war. And how dare you badmouth my grandchildren." Grandma Arial actually stamped her foot. "You benefited from my husband's kindness throughout the depression and the war, and my Grant saw to it that you had everything you needed when you were down with shingles, not six months ago. Sonny's been over here repairing your doors and windows and never once did he ask for money. Moreover, our little Vala, that darling girl, made the stew he brought you. Did you know that? And the strudel!"

Grandma was shaking. I put my arm around her, and Mick closed in on her other side.

"We gave those things because we are neighbors, and you took them because we are neighbors. Well, these boys," Grandma shoved us forward so that Mrs. Jolly got a good look at us, "these boys are American. Just like me and just like you, Etta Jolly. And you will treat them with the respect they deserve. Or you will have to deal with me."

"I wasn't saying—"

"You were saying exactly that."

"Calm down, Arial. I was just—"

"You were listening to gossip. Evil, mean-spirited gossip about children."

"They said that they murdered all those Jews."

"Look at them. Do they look like murderers?"

Mrs. Jolly's eyes darted from Mick to me and back to Mick. "They are the seed of murderers."

My eyes filled with tears. How could this ugly old woman think such things about us? Where did that come from after all this time? Did she know something that we didn't? Like Grandma said, we were babies then. And Mama wasn't much older than me when that all happened. It wasn't true. It wasn't.

"Etta, you are no longer welcome in my home or in any of the Logan enterprises. And I expect you to pay up your past due accounts by the end of the month." Grandma grabbed Mick's hand and herded us away from Mrs. Jolly's house.

"Grandma—"

"Shush, Mick. Don't look back." We turned the corner onto Cold Creek Drive.

"Why was she so mean?"

"She's scared."

"What's she scared of?"

We stopped in front of our house. "Right now, the Russians. But we have been scared so long that it's habit now, and it doesn't take but one evil person to get everyone upset. If there isn't a clear enemy around, we'll make one up."

I wasn't ready to go in and face Mama. "Does she really think we killed Jews?"

Grandma put her hand on my cheek. "No, I think she's hooked in with the gossip. And for some reason, we were the object of it this time."

"Will she change her mind?"

"People who are wrong don't usually do that, sweetheart. They search for reasons to prove they're right."

Mick tugged at Grandma's arm. "You really won't ever let her come visit again?"

"Not as long as she talks like she talked today."

"But you've been friends since you were little girls."

"You boys are more important than that."

Mick hugged her for a long time before she shooed him into the house.

I sat down on the front porch step and laid my books beside me. "What do we tell Mama?"

"That's up to you, EJ. What do you want to tell her?"

"I don't want to hurt her. She's been hurt enough."

"That's a mature thing to say."

"Is it?"

"I expect you wanted to go in there and cry on her shoulder and have her take care of things, but you're putting all that aside so that she doesn't have a bad day too. Little kids don't think that far ahead."

"Thanks, Grandma."

"So you are feeling sad?"

"Yeah." I rubbed my eyes. "Real sad."

"Me too."

14

The Tree House
September 1, 1956

I TOOK MY copy of *Tarzan of the Apes* and slipped away to the tree house. I lay back on Grandma's old quilt, propped my head up on an old chair cushion, and settled in for the afternoon.

The door from the warehouse to the loading dock squealed and rumbled on its track. Then there were footsteps.

"I'm not an expert, Sonny." A familiar woman's voice tugged at my heart.

"I don't know what to do for her. She cries in her sleep. Something about an old woman on Georgenstraße. She says, 'Es ist meine Schuld' over and over or 'ich war dumm.' When I can't bear it anymore and knock on her door, she says it was just a dream about a wolf chasing her."

"A wolf?"

I folded down the corner of a page and closed my book.

"I ask her what I can do and she says, this is her bed and she must lie in it. Then she turns her back on me and pretends to be asleep."

"Has Vala ever told you why those women were chasing her in Mannheim that day?"

"They wanted her food."

"Do you believe that?"

"No."

I rolled over and peeked through the slats. Sonny and Teresa sat on the loading dock with their legs dangling over the edge. I squinted. They were holding hands!

"I know she's miserable, but I don't know how to make it better," Sonny said. "Seems like I messed up everyone's life. Yours, mine, hers, the boys."

"You saved her and the boys by bringing them here. Think how awful it was in Germany when you found her."

Sonny slid off the dock and turned to lift Teresa down. "Vala was as beaten down as a person could be," he said. "Not defensive and angry like she is now, but lost and desperate. I remember that after we rescued her that day, we took her to a cafe and bought her a meal. She was hungry but she couldn't eat. She just sat there—her eyes darting every which way—like she was still being chased."

Teresa sighed and took his arm. "Maybe she still is."

They walked around the field, stopping now and again to pick a wild flower or pick up a stick and pitch it over the fence. This must have been be their special place, I realized. They'd probably been coming here since they were my age.

"I thought I could help her. That there was a reason I happened to be in that plaza in Mannheim at that moment."

"That God put you there?"

They were close enough that I could see his face flush. "Maybe."

Teresa tucked her hair behind her ear. It was soft and glossy and made me want to reach out and touch it. They walked under the branches and I moved to another crack in the tree house walls to keep them in sight.

She squeezed his arm. "You always took in abandoned puppies."

"I don't know if that's a strength or weakness."

So Mick and I were just another litter of puppies that Sonny found on the side of the road? Another example of a bad habit? Outrage replaced my fascination with Teresa's hair, and then guilt. After all, we were American because of Sonny, and I couldn't imagine any other life.

They paused under my tree, and Sonny put his arms around Teresa. I could hear him breathing. Watching them made me feel funny, but I couldn't look away. At first Teresa accepted his embrace but then she moaned and squirmed away.

"I'm sorry, Teresa."

She came toward the ladder and at first I thought she was going to climb up and catch me spying on them. Just as I was about to panic she stopped and laid her head against the trunk.

"I know I'm a jerk. I broke my promise again." Sonny pressed himself against her back, caressing her shoulders.

"No, it's me too." Her voice was hoarse and I realized that she was crying. "I was young and stupid back then. I thought I was doing the right thing—that you were. Now I see that I was caught up in the emotion of the moment. Marrying to rescue a family from a bad situation seemed romantic. I agreed because I wanted to be a good girl and because I had no concept of how long forever would be."

Sonny kissed the back of her neck.

She turned and kissed his lips. I held my breath and twisted my head so could see them better.

"No." She pushed him away and they stared at each other.

I couldn't tell if they were mad or if they were hurting. Something changed in her face and she stepped back into his embrace and buried her face in his shoulder, slowly hitting his biceps with her fist.

"We must not meet alone again, Sonny."

"Yes." He stared over her head into the bushes that separated this lot from our yard.

"We are too weak."

"Weak," he mumbled.

She sighed. "I can do it now."

"Do what?"

"Stop."

"Okay." He didn't let go, and she didn't push him away.

"I wanted to help Vala, but now it's hard to even like her. You and I gave up our future together, but we didn't let go like we planned—like we should have—and now I feel cheated and wicked."

"No, no!" He looked down into her face. "You were good. Good then and good now. I should have made a choice and stuck with it instead of torturing us this way."

"You need to find a life with Vala. You need to focus on making her happy and letting her make you happy. Have more children."

"There's no getting that close to her," he said.

Teresa pulled away.

"Don't be like that." Sonny's shoulders slumped. "I told you back when I married her that it wasn't love like you and I had."

I swallowed—and swallowed again.

"Maybe that kind of love can't be maintained anyway."

"Don't say that, Teresa."

I had to strain to hear his voice.

"What good does it do us? You have a wife and family. I have the hospital and a gentleman friend. It may not be what we expected, but it's what we have."

Sonny wiped his eyes with the back of his arm. "I'm not trying to go back on our agreement or betray my family, but sometimes I feel lost and useless."

"You make sure they have a place to live and something to eat every day, don't you?"

Sonny nodded.

"And you make sure the boys are getting an education and lots of exercise?"

"I do my best."

"And you would move heaven and earth if Vala asked for help?"

"Of course I would. We may not be lovers, but I do care about her. And I adore those kids."

"And that's the way Vala wants it?"

Sonny took a deep breath. "I don't know what Vala wants."

Teresa took a deep breath. "I came to tell you that I'm getting married."

He seemed as surprised as I was. "I'm happy for you. And a little jealous."

She kissed his forehead and turned to go. "So am I."

* * *

"Sonny, we are invited to Teresa and Danny's wedding!" Mama laid a thick white envelope on the kitchen table. "We need to go shopping."

"Shopping?" Sonny peeked over his newspaper. "You never want to leave the house."

"I need a dress."

"Okay, let's go get a dress. Want to go to Cleveland?"

"Oh no, not Cleveland." Her smile faded.

"There are some nice stores in the city. Mama Ariel likes to go up there from time to time. I bet she'd come with us."

Mama lowered her eyes and twisted the edge of her apron. "Maybe I can find something at Sherry's Dress Shoppe here in Cold Creek."

Sonny sighed. "Okay. I'll drive you over there if you want."

Saved from the prospect of a trip to the big city, the twinkle in Mama's eyes returned. "What kind of dress should I buy?"

"You'd look beautiful in a flour sack, sugar."

"Oh no, I want lace."

"Then lace it will be."

"Pink."

The corners of Sonny's mouth twitched. "Okay."

"You don't mind?"

"We've been married over ten years now, and in all that time, you've never asked for anything for yourself. I'd love to treat you to something pretty."

Mama danced in a circle.

Mick and I laughed. We didn't see our mother dance very often. I took my last bite of oatmeal and laid down my spoon. "Will Mick and I go to the wedding?"

"I don't know," Mama said. "Can they go, Sonny?"

"The guys aren't babies anymore—and besides I think Teresa has a crush on old Mick there. I'm sure the invitation includes them."

"I never saw a wedding in United States America."

"I can't imagine it's much different from weddings in Mannheim—a white dress and veil, a nervous groom in a dark suit." Sonny hid behind the *Plain Dealer*.

"Suits!" Mama put her hands on her cheeks. "The boys need suits."

"We can do that, too."

Mick fingered the invitation. "Will there be music?"

Sonny laughed and put down the paper. "At a minimum, there will be 'Here Comes the Bride.'"

"That's an American song?"

"It probably has another name. When we were kids, Danny and my brother Long John and Skippy and I would sing, 'Here comes the bride, big, fat, and wide.'"

I spewed milk out of my nose and Mick giggled.

"Oh no, not nice, Sonny. That poor bride, she's not fat at all. She's beautiful."

"We weren't singing about Teresa at the time." He wiggled his eyebrows and Mick and I laughed.

"Any bride would not like that song." Mama refilled Sonny's coffee cup.

"So what was your wedding like, Mama?"

Mama glanced at Sonny. "Oh, Milo. Not so nice, I think."

"The Army chaplain married us on the fly so we could get the papers to bring you guys over here," Sonny said. "The ceremony didn't take five minutes."

We were all quiet for a moment.

"What did you wear?" Mick asked.

Mama frowned. "Not lace."

15

A Wedding

October 1, 1956

It was cold and wet the day Teresa married Danny Kline. The ceremony took place at St. Mike's at noon. The red flowers that decorated the pews and the altar awed us.

"Look at the carvings on the walls." Mick pointed.

"Those are the stations of the cross," Sonny explained as we took our seats. "They represent the suffering Jesus endured before he was killed."

"They are sad."

"Yes," Sonny said, "they are."

"There are beautiful churches in Germany," Mama said. "In Heidelberg, the churches are more...how do you say...die Kirchen sind reich verziert ?"

"Ornate, Mama. The Heidelberg churches are more ornate."

"Okay." She squeezed my hand and shivered in her new dress, which was meant for summer, not late fall.

"There's Miss Myrtle and Jerry Kline," I nudged Sonny. "And there's Skippy from the newsstand. Why is he with them?"

"Skippy and your Uncle Grant are good friends with Danny and Teresa. They're escorting the guests to their seats."

"Why didn't they escort us?"

Mama lifted her chin. "We will always be strangers, EJ."

Sonny put his hand on hers. "That's not it."

"No?"

"First off, we were early and came in to look at the church, and since we were already in here, we found our own seats. But you know Jerry Kline is Danny and Pam's dad. After their mom died, he married Myrtle so that makes her Danny's stepmother. Skippy is showing them to a special seat reserved for the groom's parents."

"Oh." Mama was unconvinced.

"Uncle Grant knows us."

"Yes, he does." Sonny winked at Mick.

"He's nice to us."

"Of course he is."

I thought that was stretching things a bit, but Uncle Grant was family and could be expected to take our side.

"Oh," Mama sighed. "Look at Delores. Sie ist sehr schön."

Wearing a deep, blue, velvet dress that looked a lot warmer than Mama's pink lace, Delores came down the center aisle with Uncle Grant. A red-faced, red-haired man and a teenage girl followed them. As they passed us, Delores nodded at Sonny and smiled at Mama.

Mick tugged at Mama's hand. "Who is that with her?"

"That's her husband, Mausi. That's Tommy McDougal."

"What happened to his face?"

"Shush." Mama turned around to watch the other guests as they came in.

Mama was like that sometimes, changing the subject just when the conversation got interesting.

Sonny leaned toward us. "Both Delores and Tommy were pilots during the war. Tommy was flying a big bomber when he got shot. He was hurt bad, but he landed that plane and saved almost everyone on board."

"Oh, then he's a hero," Mick stared at the man sitting beside Delores.

"Around these parts, he sure is."

That was enough for Mick and he turned around to watch the other guests as they came in.

I imagined what it must have been like for Tommy to be shot like that. "Where was he flying that bomber?"

"Germany." Sonny's voice was low enough that the people around us couldn't hear.

"Was he ... you know ... bombing? "

He squeezed my shoulder and nodded.

"Shhh!" Mama hissed. "Enough talking. This is wedding."

I sat down in the pew. Mama's strange attachment to Delores and her family confused me. My nonexistent memories of Germany didn't help. I'd just started learning about World War I in school. All I knew about World War II was that my American and German relations had fought bitterly, and America won. And of course, there were those ugly pictures in *American View Magazine*.

Uncle Grant escorted Zona and her husband Jimmy to the pew in front of us. Mick and I waved at Uncle Grant who winked and went back up the aisle to greet the next group.

Zona turned around and whispered, "Look at you, Vala."

"You like? Sonny bought it for me."

"I should have hit Jimmy up for a new dress." Zona elbowed her husband who rolled his eyes. "Shoes, too."

"And pearls." Mama caressed her necklace. "Sonny surprised me."

"You're getting me in trouble, man." Deputy Jim shook Sonny's hand. "You know these two are thick as thieves."

"The two most beautiful women in Cold Creek," Sonny said.

I groaned inside. Pretend-nice was creepy.

Skippy led Grandma Arial toward us but she stopped and spoke to Delores and Tommy.

The young girl sitting with the McDougals called out, "Mrs. Logan!"

"Oh my goodness, is that Rosa?" Grandma Arial put both gloved hands to her cheeks. "I didn't recognize you."

"I've grown up." The space between the seat of one bench and the back of the next was narrow, and Rosa was awkward, but she stood up and spun around smiling. She wore glasses and had braces on her teeth.

"You have, at that," Grandma Arial said. Rosa giggled behind her gloved fist.

"It's almost time." Skippy held out his arm for Grandma Arial.

"Yes, yes. They won't start until I'm ready, will they?" Grandma Arial laughed. "I'll talk to you later, Rosa."

The girl nodded and sat back down.

"Okay, Skippy." Grandma Arial took Skippy's arm. "Where do you want to put me?"

"Danny and Teresa want you up front, ma'am."

I turned to ask Sonny why Grandma had a seat up front, but he was holding Mama's hand and staring at Skippy and his mother. It didn't seem like the best time to say anything.

Once everyone was settled in the pews, nothing much happened for a while except soft music. Mick and I looked forward to singing "Here Comes the Bride" but I guess Catholics didn't like that song, because the organist never played it.

Finally, two men in dark suits came in through a side door and made their way to the front of the church.

"There's Danny." Mick pointed. "And Coach Littleton."

The music changed.

Every one stood up and turned to look at the back of the church. Not knowing what was going on, Mick and I stood up, too.

"I can't see anything." Mick stood on his toes and tried to peer around the people behind us.

"Shush, Milo. You will in a minute." Mama's voice was soft and happy.

"Here, buddy." Sonny stepped aside so Mick could get a better view.

A young woman in a green dress was coming up the aisle holding some flowers. I squinted and realized it was Pam Kline, Danny's sister. She looked nicer than usual. I had never seen her wear anything but jeans and a red plaid shirt. I saw her sometimes at the newsstand, and I thought she might be sweet on Skippy. She passed us and went up to stand in front of the altar.

The music grew louder and grander.

I nudged Mick. "Bet you can't play that."

"I could if I had an organ." He pushed me back.

"Here she comes," Mama said.

Sure enough, Teresa Roberts was walking down the aisle wearing a shiny white dress and a funny-looking white hat.

"Where's her Papi?" Mama turned to Sonny.

"He died in the war."

"Oh," she sounded sad. "Like mein Vater."

"Not exactly."

"She's like me, though," Mama went on, "without family on her wedding day."

Sonny stiffened. "Yes."

"Oh, look, Vala," Zona whispered. "I sold her that lipstick."

"So pretty," Mama said. "Can you order me the same shade?"

"Tomorrow."

"Look at Miss Roberts," Mick yanked at Sonny's jacket. "Isn't she beautiful?"

* * *

"I'm hungry." Mick tugged at his bow tie.

"It won't be long. Your Grandma Arial made peach strudel for the reception," Sonny said. Whenever Mick or I got cranky, Sonny used Grandma's peach strudel as bait.

Mama and Zona had gone off looking for a bathroom while Jimmy, Sonny, Mick, and I waited in line to shake hands with the bride and groom. A woman with a tall flowered hat chatted with Danny and Teresa. She must have said something funny, because Teresa laughed and spun around to show off the back of her dress.

"Why do brides always wear white?" Mick asked.

"So you know she is the bride." I thumped Mick's head with my knuckles.

"We got an invitation saying Teresa was the bride."

Mick's reasonableness was annoying. Especially since I had no idea why brides wore white. I looked to Sonny who didn't seem to have heard our bridal wardrobe conversation. "Is something wrong?"

He was watching a bearded man in a checked suit step forward to introduce himself to Teresa.

"Sonny?" I touched his arm.

"What?" He jumped. "Is something wrong?"

Mick and I laughed. "I just asked you that."

"I'm sorry, boys. I was wondering who that fellow is."

Teresa introduced the stranger to Danny, who shook his hand.

Mick peered around the family in front of us. "Why would someone who doesn't know either Teresa or Danny come to their wedding?"

"I was wondering the same thing," Sonny said.

There were only three people in front of us when Mama came back from the bathroom. She'd freshened her lipstick and straightened her hat.

"There's lavender soap wrapped in netting in the ladies' room, Sonny."

His eyes lingered on Teresa and Danny for a moment longer than necessary before he turned to Mama and said, "Oh?"

She held out her wrist so he could smell it. "It reminds me of home when I was a girl. I kept little packets of dried lavender in my handkerchief drawer."

"It's lovely, Vala—like you." He put his arm around her.

I wanted to go sulk in the tree house, but I knew Sonny and Mama weren't ready to walk out of this silly party yet. And besides, sulking wouldn't change anything anyway.

Once we'd greeted Danny and Teresa, we went through a door into a large hall.

"Wow," Mick said. "There's a band." He took off across the room to torment the musicians who were unpacking their instruments.

"Don't annoy the playing people," Mama called after him.

"I won't." He never looked back.

Sonny squeezed Mama's arm. "Let him enjoy the day. You know how he loves to play."

"Ja, he loves the music."

Grandma Arial was on the other side of the room, talking to the bearded man in the ugly checked suit. "Sonny, Vala!" She waved us over. "Sonny, do you remember your father's cousin Magda? This is Oskar Schreiner. He lived next door to her in Germany, when they were children."

"Nice to meet you, Mr. Schreiner." Sonny stuck out his hand.

"Herr Logan, it's lovely to meet Magda's family after all of these years."

"So you are from Germany?"

"Cleveland, now. I moved in 1939 after things got bad over there. Was lucky to get away when I did. I work at the gas company."

"Let me introduce my wife, Vala. She grew up in Mannheim."

The man bent to kiss Mama's hand. "Frau Logan, I believe we've met before. A long time ago."

She winced and pulled her hand out of his grasp. Sonny rescued her. "This is my son, EJ."

"EJ."

"Nice to meet you, Mr. Schreiner." The overwhelming smell of mothballs burned my nose. I wiped my sweaty palm on the seat of my new pants. Now I reeked of mothballs too. "How did you know about this wedding?"

Schreiner wasn't interested in me. "Your grandmother would like some punch, I think."

I looked at her. "Would you?"

"That would be lovely, EJ."

Schreiner turned his attention to Mama, blathering on about Ludwigshafen, which I gathered was near Mannheim.

I touched her sleeve. "You want some too, Mama?"

"Please." Mama seemed upset. She sat down at a long folding table covered with starched tablecloths. Schreiner grabbed the chair across from her. He pulled a wooden cigarette case out of his pocket. Popping it open, he leaned forward. "Would you like a Chesterfield, Frau Logan?"

Mama pretended not to hear him, but Grandma Arial took one.

"Thank you, Oskar." She held it under her nose. "I'm not much of a smoker, but my husband John loved these. They remind me of him."

"And you, Vala?"

Schreiner's abrupt switch from the more formal Frau Logan to Vala irritated me.

"Nein, danke." Mama avoided looking at him.

He leaned forward. "You grew up to be a beautiful woman."

Sonny and I exchanged glances.

Mama stared at her hands, and neither Sonny nor I could get her attention.

Was this smelly old guy flirting with my mother?

I scowled at him, but of course, I was a kid and my opinion mattered little to him.

It did matter to Grandma Arial, though. She gave me the evil eye. Being rude was a major sin to her, and I knew better than to further express my suspicions.

I turned to Sonny. "You want something, too?"

As he shook his head, his eyes never left Schreiner—or Mama.

* * *

My sixth grade teacher, Mrs. Wiggins, was serving the punch. "How are you, EJ?"

"I'm fine, ma'am."

"Still making good grades?"

"Yes, ma'am."

She ladled red punch into a fancy glass cup.

"I'll need two," I told her. "One for Grandma Arial and one for Mama."

"Who is that with your Mama?"

"Who knows?"

"A family friend of the Logans, they said."

"That's what they said." I took the two cups of punch and headed back toward the table where Mama sat quietly and Grandma Arial chatted with the mysterious Oskar Schreiner.

"Thank you, sweetheart." Grandma Arial set the punch on the table and gave me a quick kiss on the cheek. "Oh!" She frowned and rubbed my face with her fancy handkerchief. "Lipstick. Might cause a few comments."

I struggled to keep from spilling red punch on myself. "Yes, ma'am." I edged away until I was out of reach before saying, "Thanks, Grandma."

Mama seemed lost in thought and didn't notice me standing beside her. I sighed and set the cup down in front of her. I didn't see Sonny at first and glanced around the room. Teresa was in the far corner, surrounded by a group of giggling women. I relaxed and when I turned around, I realized that Sonny was sitting on the other side of Mama—in guard mode.

I started to join them but Grandma Arial jerked her eyes toward the girl sitting with Delores and Tommy McDougal at the next table.

My mouth went dry and I shook my head, but Grandma Arial's disapproval was more than anyone could bear for very long. Arguing with her over being nice to someone was a losing battle.

The music started and Grandma Arial and Oskar Schreiner raised their voices to compensate.

Sonny caught my eye. "Go on," he mouthed.

I stood there a moment longer—first, silently pleading with Grandma Arial to free me from teenage-girl duty and then making sure Sonny knew I'd help get rid of Schreiner if necessary.

Mama's earlier glow had been replaced with a ruddy flush. "Go, EJ," she hissed.

I clenched my fists.

"Go!"

Whatever was wrong, Mama didn't want me to be a part of it either. I felt Schreiner's chuckle more than heard it. I wanted to smash him in the nose but I couldn't fight everyone—certainly not Sonny and Grandma anyway.

Delores and Tommy were dancing now, and their young charge sat by herself.

Somehow I found a bit of courage and walked over to her. "Would you like some punch?"

The girl peered at me over thick cat-eye glasses. "I don't like sweet drinks. How about water instead?"

"Okay." I didn't quite know what to do. Should I grab a cup and find a sink? I wandered over to the table where Mrs. Wiggins was minding the punch bowl.

"What do you think of that brother of yours?"

"What?"

Mrs. Wiggins pointed.

Mick was playing guitar with the band.

I laughed. "That boy has yet to find an instrument he couldn't play."

"Does anyone else in your family have musical talent?"

I shrugged. "Not that I know of."

"You need another cup of punch?"

I had forgotten my mission. "Actually, where can I get water?"

"Something wrong with the punch?"

"I'm getting a drink for that girl over there, and she didn't want punch." I pointed at the figure sitting alone.

"I didn't know you knew Rosa."

"I don't."

"She's a nice girl. You'll like her."

"Only if I can find water." I held up the cup.

"There's a pitcher of ice water in the kitchen. Just tell Mabel to give you some."

Mrs. Wiggins was a lot nicer now that I wasn't in her class.

* * *

"Thank you," Rosa said when I handed her the cup.

"I'm EJ Logan."

"I know who you are."

"You do?"

"Sure. Your mother is a friend of my cousin Delores."

"Where do you live?" I sat down beside her so I could see the dancers.

"In Pittsburgh, now. I'm going to high school there, but I lived in Cold Creek for a while. Even went to elementary school here."

"How old are you?"

"You are a nosey kid, aren't you?"

"It's because I'm the last person to know anything." I checked to see if Mama and Sonny were okay. He rested his arm on the back of Mama's chair while Schreiner entertained Grandma.

"The curse of our generation, I'm afraid." Rosa smiled and I realized that under those ugly glasses and all that curly hair, she was pretty.

"I'm thirteen," I said. "I'm from Germany, but I don't remember anything about it."

"Me, too. From Germany, I mean, and I'm sixteen."

"What part of Germany?"

"Mannheim."

"Me, too. When did your parents come here?"

"They didn't. They died during the war."

I watched Teresa and Danny dance together, my mind whirling. "Were they soldiers?"

"No, just ordinary people."

"What happened to them?"

"The Gestapo put us in a camp in France. Gurs. The Quakers rescued me and brought me here as a baby. After that, the Nazis murdered my parents, both grandmothers, and most of my cousins in Auschwitz."

I was shocked into silence. Mick and the band played "True Love," and one of the young men sang it. I fidgeted, thinking about the pictures of the dead bodies in the old *American View Magazine*. Could they be pictures of Rosa's family?

"That's a pretty song," Rosa said. "Perfect for a wedding."

"I guess so." Why would Nazis murder Mannheimers in Poland? If they were going to kill them, why run them around all over Europe? I'd read everything I could find, but none of it ever made sense.

"Who is that little guy playing guitar?"

"That's my brother Mick."

"He's cute."

We watched Mick play while I searched for something else to say. "How come everyone I ever met who was German came from Mannheim?"

She seemed relieved and turned her attention back to me. "I asked my Aunt Delores about that once. She said that the people who got out and came here, all got out the same way. The United States required new immigrants to have assets. Money, usually. And family here. The Nazis had already robbed most folks blind. So someone here—a Jew from Mannheim I guess—raised $5,000 and put it in a bank account under his sister's name. That got her family out and they came to Pittsburgh, where he lived. Then they opened an account with the same $5,000 in another bank under the name of another family, and so on and so on. So a lot of the Mannheim Jews who made it out know each other."

"What happened to that money when the last family got here?"

She looked at me and giggled. "I don't know. An extra special bas mitzvah?"

I laughed with her, even though I had no idea what a bas mitzvah was, and once again retreated into uncomfortable silence.

Rosa watched the band for a long time, tapping the table with her fingertips. "Isn't music interesting?" She half-closed her eyes and rocked her head from side to side. "How it can lift your mood?"

"Maybe you only listen to music when you're in a good mood."

She took a sip of the water I'd brought her. "Maybe. Sometimes the people around me are sad and I feel like I should be sad with them, but I'm a kid and I don't remember the bad things. I've always lived with people who love me, and I have plenty to eat and nice things to wear, and friends. I can't help being happy."

I didn't know what to do with all of that, so I said nothing.

"Are you happy, EJ?"

"I don't have any complaints."

The band began "To Know You Is to Love You," and Sonny led Mama out onto the dance floor.

I twisted in my seat to watch. I couldn't figure them out. Sonny seemed dedicated to Mama, and yet I couldn't forget the sight of him kissing Teresa only a few months ago.

"Vala is beautiful." Rosa craned her neck. "Don't you think?"

"We all think our mothers are beautiful."

"If you have one."

"I'm sorry." I was afraid to look at her. "That was stupid of me."
She didn't answer.

"Look, I didn't mean to upset you. I'm not very good at talking
to girls."

"You'll be a lonely old goat if you don't figure it out soon."

Schreiner was trying to get Mama to dance with him. She shook
her head and Sonny guided her back to the table. Schreiner stood in
the middle of the crowded dance floor for a moment before following them.

"Like that one?"

"You mean Oskar?"

"The one bearing down on my mother."

Rosa giggled behind her knuckles. "Well, he's definitely a lonely
old goat."

"If that's my fate, I better learn to entertain pretty girls."

Schreiner loomed over Mama, but she turned away from him
and said something to Grandma Arial.

"Look at him," she said. "He doesn't know how repulsive he is."

"Doesn't he know that Mama is married to Sonny?"

"Do fools know they are fools?"

"Who is he?"

"His family owned a furniture business in Mannheim. They
lived across the river in Ludwigshafen."

"Why do you think he's so interested in Mama?"

"Maybe they knew each other?"

I squinted. "He looks older."

"Maybe her family bought furniture at Schreiner's."

"How come you know so much about Mannheim?"

"Delores is over there all the time, looking for relatives."

"Whenever I try to think about Germany, it's all mixed up in my
head. I don't know what I remember and what people have told me."

Rosa nodded. "Me, too."

"And they lie to me."

"Why do you think that, EJ?"

"Because it's always different."

She was silent for a while. "Different?"

I was stuck now. I took a breath. "Mama says that I was born in
a beautiful birthing home on a beautiful day and everyone gave us
beautiful things."

"That sounds nice."

"But my birthday is September 6, 1943. I read a letter in one of her folders that said that date was a terrible day for Mannheim. It was bombed that night. Lots of people were killed. Even more were hurt. I don't think it was as glorious a day as she says."

"You're being hard on your mother. Maybe she got the date wrong or maybe she wasn't in Mannheim at all."

"It's hard to figure out."

"It must be." She took her glasses off and rubbed her nose.

"At least you know what happened."

She avoided my eyes.

"I wasn't trying to be mean. It's just that you know who you are…who your parents and grandparents were…and that they were innocent."

"You don't think yours were?"

"All I know is that they lie about Germany."

"That's scary," she conceded.

"Yeah."

"How does your brother feel about it?"

"He's too busy being Mick Logan to worry about how he came to be Mick Logan. Everyone adores him and he's fun to be around. I'm quiet and shy, always wondering about things that make people uncomfortable. Grandma Arial says it has to do with our relative ages when we came here. Maybe it does, but I think it's more than that. Mick is absorbed with building things and with music and math. He thinks numbers and musical notes instead of thoughts. And he's never, ever bored."

"That in itself is a blessing."

We watched Schreiner still trying to get Mama's attention. Finally, she got up and went to the bathroom. Schreiner watched until she disappeared down the hallway. Then he went to fill his plate at the buffet table.

Rosa shook her head. "Where did Oskar get that suit?"

"I can't even guess," I said. "I never saw anything like it in my life. I figure it's the only one he has, and he got it out of storage just for the occasion."

"What makes you think that?"

"It burns my nose. Mothballs."

"Ah, so that's why you came over to talk to me!"

"I confess. You smell a lot better than Oskar Schreiner."

"Well, that suit hurts my eyes." Rosa rummaged in her purse and replaced her fancy jeweled glasses with plain ones with dark lenses. Mrs. Wiggins was right. Rosa was a nice girl and I liked her.

16

Oskar Schreiner

October 8, 1956

A WEEK AFTER Danny and Teresa left on their honeymoon, I climbed up Grandma Arial's back porch stairs. "I'm here, Grandma!" I tossed my books on the kitchen table and opened the refrigerator door.

"Don't drink out of the milk bottle, EJ Logan!"

Grandma Arial's screech made me feel at home. I set the bottle on the counter and got out a glass. "Okay."

"There are cookies in the jar."

"Thanks, Grandma." I filled the glass with milk and loaded a napkin with cookies. "Mick will be late today. He's going to play with The Cold Creek Crooners again this Saturday. They want to teach him some of their Rock and Roll tune—" I stopped dead still in the arch leading to the living room.

"Good afternoon, EJ." Oskar Schreiner sat on my grandmother's plastic-covered sofa, sipping tea and eating snickerdoodles.

"You remember Oskar, don't you?"

I cocked my head. In regular clothes, he seemed…more regular. "Sure."

"Come sit down and chat with our guest."

"Okay."

"I came back to talk with your mother, but she won't see me." Schreiner slurped his tea and set the cup on its saucer. "So I decided to visit your grandmother here. Imagine my surprise when she told me you came here every day after school."

"Uh huh."

"I thought you might be willing to help me find where some of my family's property ended up after the war."

"Me? You think I know anything about all that?"

"I think you know people who might know."

I took a quick bite of my brownie. "I doubt it. No one tells me anything."

"Well, your mother and I are from the same city in Germany. We weren't friends or anything, but our families did business."

It struck me that maybe I'd been too quick to snub Oskar Schreiner. "So you knew my grandfather?"

"The Hesses used to buy furniture from us. When I was a young man, I worked in the showroom of Schreiner Möbelfabrik. People came to us for custom furniture—high quality woods and veneers, carved chests, tables, chairs, beds. My great-grandfather started the company in the 1800s. The business would have been mine eventually, except..." He lowered his head and took a deep breath.

"I'm sorry, Oskar," Grandma Arial said.

His cheeks were shiny with sweat. Despite his wheeze, he didn't seem as obnoxious as he had at the wedding reception. But he made me uncomfortable anyway.

"Except for what?"

"Shush, EJ." Grandma Arial put her finger over pursed lips.

"What?" I rolled my eyes and sighed loudly.

Schreiner pulled a mended handkerchief out of his coat pocket and wiped his face. "No, Arial. How will they know if we don't tell them?"

"We've tried to protect them. Wouldn't you rather have had your youth uninterrupted?"

"I would give *anything* for that," he said.

Grandma put her hand on Schreiner's sleeve.

He stared at her tiny fingers. "I hate them for what they did to my Germany."

Grandma Arial sighed. "Me too, Oskar."

I was shocked. I couldn't fathom a world where my grandmother hated anyone. "What happened?"

"We were patriotic," Schreiner said. "Germany was our home. My family had lived there for hundreds of years. My father was a veteran of the first World War. I didn't even know we were Jewish until 1935 when the labeling began in earnest. Seems we had lots of Jewish blood as defined by the new laws. I was a sturdy young man of fifteen, and I was learning my father's business. I had my eye on a pretty girl. I thought that would be my life. I didn't yet know that our neighbors despised us."

"What happened?" I chased the last bit of brownie with a swallow of milk and set the plate on Grandma's ottoman.

"They say it was the Nazis, but it was more complicated than that. People hated Jews for many reasons, but my family wasn't religious or political or rich. I think..." He wiped his upper lip with his handkerchief. "I think that the Nazis gave people a target and permission."

Grandma sat with her arms folded over her chest, rocking back and forth in her seat.

My leg twitched. "Why do you think Mama knows anything about this?"

"After the Nuremberg Laws changed everything, our business dropped off. By 1937, we were struggling. One day, your grandfather visited us with his two daughters, your aunt and your mother. We were excited. He loved unique pieces and in the past had paid us well to create the unusual furniture that graced his home in Mannheim."

"What was my grandfather like?" I was surprised by my own voice. I hadn't meant to say it out loud.

"He was slim and very fair, like Vala and you."

"So what did he want?"

"He said they were planning on redecorating the older girl's room, since she was almost a woman and her taste in furnishings did not coincide with her mother's. I can't remember her name right now."

"Lana," I said. "Her name was Lana. I once saw a picture of her in Mama's photo album."

"You never met her?" Schreiner seemed surprised.

"No. She died before I was born."

"I'm sorry," he said. "I didn't know."

I shrugged. Other than that picture, I knew nothing about her. "So did they order something?"

Now it was Schreiner's turn to shrug. "Lana wasn't interested in our products. She stood by herself staring out the window. Vala was a different story. She skipped around asking questions, opening cabinet doors, and climbing on sofas. Secret compartments were popular at the time and Vala loved running her little hands over the carved surfaces until she found the hidden latches. I remember her laughing about everything. However, they didn't buy anything that day."

"Why do you remember that one visit all these years later?"

He turned to my grandmother. "Because Herr Hess came back the next week and wanted to buy our company. Jews were no longer allowed to own anything, but he said he hated to see our special artistry die out. Since he would be the owner of record, we would work for him. My father said no, of course. We didn't yet realize the situation."

I couldn't make out where my family stood in all of this. "Why did my grandfather want to buy a furniture manufacturing company? He owned a farm, I thought."

"I never knew anything about a farm." Schreiner dug into his pocket and pulled out a beautiful wooden pipe. "He was a pharmacist until he joined the party. Like other businessmen, he saw opportunity in the world Hitler was instituting."

Grandma Arial and I looked at each other. Mama had told us stories about a farm, about a black pig named Brunhilda and a pushy rooster named Emmet. Was it all a lie?

A soft tapping sound filled the room.

"Are you okay, young man?" Schreiner's eyes were as round as his cheeks.

"EJ?" Grandma Arial whispered.

"What?"

She cocked her eyes toward my left leg.

I looked down. It was shaking, and the heel of my shoe clicked against the hardwood floor. I put both hands on my knee. "Sorry." I closed my eyes for a moment and took in deep breaths.

"Is there something wrong with you?"

"No, I'm fine." I frowned at Schreiner.

"EJ has muscle spasms sometimes, that's all." Grandma Arial came to my defense.

Schreiner didn't know everything. My grandparents lived in a big house in Mannheim. They probably owned a farm, too. I knew Mama, and I didn't know Oskar Schreiner at all. I decided to believe my mother and forced myself to calm down. "Go on," I said to him. "Why did Opa want your company?"

"Schreiner's was a family business," he continued. "Our workers were highly skilled, creative. They'd been learning the trade all their lives. We made unique, beautiful things." He held up the elaborately carved pipe. "One of our young artisans made this." He handed it to me. "We did this kind of ornamentation on larger pieces too."

The pipe was dark and shiny. A carved snake curled around the bowl and wound itself up the stem. It wasn't like anything I remembered seeing before, but it was familiar. I just couldn't place why. "Wow!" I handed it to Grandma Arial.

"Oh, Oskar. It's exquisite."

He preened like a peacock. "We sold hundreds of them over the years. No two alike."

"Your employee was a talented man."

"Thank you. You should have seen the larger pieces in our showroom."

She handed the pipe back to him.

I couldn't contain my curiosity any longer. "So what happened next?"

"My father turned Herr Hess down the first time and the next as well," Schreiner said. "After a while, other Mannheimers with money and no inconvenient Jewish blood started coming by with offers, too. Our neighbors became more vocal with their contempt for us. It was confusing, because we never had trouble with them before. Then someone broke the showroom windows one afternoon. One of our employees ran to the front of the store when he heard the crash, and the culprit pelted him with rocks. Broke poor Ulli's front tooth and bloodied his nose."

I was getting restless and Schreiner still hadn't got to the point. "So did your father sell the business to my grandfather?"

"EJ!" Grandma Arial wagged her finger. "Your manners, young man."

"Okay."

Schreiner looked at Grandma, "Where was I?"

"The windows. Someone broke the windows."

"Yes. That was 1938. Sometime in late October I think. We still made furniture, but we couldn't always sell it. Fewer people risked doing business with us. We couldn't pay our employees, and one by one, they left. Finally, in November, my father and I visited Herr Hess to see if he was still interested in buying Schreiner's."

This was it. I leaned forward. "What did he say?"

"There was a party at the Hess home. You could hear people's voices a half block away. It was in the courtyard, which was lit with strings of colored lights. Women in bright dresses and furs were chatting with men in black uniforms. They even had someone playing a Schrammelharmonika. It was quite festive, and we realized at once that it would be bad for Herr Hess if his guests saw us knocking on his door. So we kept on walking."

I tried to imagine all those elegant people visiting Mama's family. Perhaps my grandfather was important after all?

"As we crossed the street, we saw Frau Hess and the two girls. Lana caught my eye and shook her head, but it was too late. Vala raced up to us calling, 'Herr Schreiner, how are you? Did you bring us some furniture?' "

"What was my Oma like?"

"Don't you remember her, EJ?" There were wrinkles in Grandma Arial's forehead.

"I'm not sure. What was her name?"

"Anna."

I closed my eyes. "No," I said after a moment. "I don't think I do. Mama has a picture of Opa, but I've never seen one of Oma." I leaned back in my chair and the plastic crackled. I was lying, sort of. I couldn't bring a face to mind, but I remembered a feeling—no, a smell. I wrinkled my nose, trying to capture the elusive scent. Leaves maybe?

We both looked at Schreiner.

"She was a rich lady. Not particularly rude nor particularly welcoming," he said.

"Was she beautiful?"

He frowned. "Not as beautiful as Herr Hess."

We were quiet for a few moments as Grandma Arial and I each pondered what he meant.

Grandma broke the silence first. "So what happened that day, Oskar?"

"Frau Hess said, 'Go around back. I'll send Erich to talk to you.' She herded her girls past us to the front door of her home. Lana and Vala went inside. Frau Hess turned to look at us before joining the party in the courtyard. We had not said a word to each other, but I could tell she disliked me."

"Surely you are mistaken."

Schreiner's laugh was a bitter cough. "No mistake, Arial. She didn't want me walking on her street."

I remembered my reaction to Schreiner when I first met him at the wedding. That smelly suit was part of it. But he was vulnerable and it showed. It made people uneasy. It made me uneasy. Maybe it was like that with Oma. Maybe she was just protecting her children from a stranger. Yes. That explained it.

I felt rather than saw Grandma Arial cringe when Schreiner stirred his tea with his finger rather than use her shiny silver teaspoon. She was appalled at his manners, but she was kind to him no matter how many rules he broke. My American grandma would never make anyone feel like they had no right to walk past her house.

Schreiner was oblivious to his social missteps. "I know that it is shocking to you, but that's how things were."

I couldn't meet his eyes, but I nodded. "So did you talk to my grandfather that day?"

"Herr Hess met us at the back door. It was the first time I'd seen him in his uniform, and he was impressive. His jacket sparkled with buttons and medals and decorations. We stood on his porch with our hats in our hands. 'Herr Schreiner. Oskar,' he said in welcome. 'What can I do for you?' My father said, 'It's about my business, Herr Hess.'

"Erich Hess squared his shoulders. 'It's Standartenführer now, Herr Schreiner.' And my father bowed his head and said, 'Standartenführer.' Hess looked like he'd eaten a lime and said, 'And It is no longer *your* business, Herr Schreiner. It officially became mine yesterday.'

"The news overwhelmed my father. He staggered backwards as if the Standartenführer had punched him in the stomach. 'Why? Why didn't we know?'

"He said, 'They are coming for you soon. I didn't want it to fall into the wrong hands or to be abandoned. I had to move fast. It's to your advantage to make sure the authorities know I own Schreiner's now.'

Oskar shrugged. "One day, I was the heir to Schreiner's, and the next, my family company belonged to Erich Hess. I will say that act kept me alive long enough to escape. However, I was furious at the time."

I wanted Opa to be a hero. I wanted him to be wise and kind—someone who would buy a struggling company to keep it from going under. Still, the way it happened seemed so awful. Did he really steal it to keep someone else from stealing it?

Oskar's eyes rested on me. In that moment, I realized that he appreciated how shocking I found his story.

"There was nothing we could do about it," he said. "My father and I walked back to the showroom. Jan and Ulli, our young woodworkers, were the only employees left. My father told them the bad news.

"Ulli was a distant relative. He left without saying a word, but Jan was in tears. He'd just gotten married. Without a job, he was afraid he couldn't afford rent or food. My father put his arm around him and said, 'Take your tools. I will destroy the paperwork and no one will notice they are missing. You don't look Jewish. Perhaps you can get a commission here and there.'

"Jan collected his kit and disappeared. I heard he worked out of his father-in-law's jewelry store for a few days, until local hooligans attacked Jewish homes and businesses on November 9. Kristallnacht. Jan and the other men in his family were beaten and marched off to Dachau. The rioters destroyed their store too—the same night they burned the synagogue."

"Were they just targeting Jews?" I didn't understand. If religion was the problem, the Schreiners didn't practice that one.

"Not necessarily. The Nazis were concerned with building a generation of perfect people. The dream was so important to Hitler and his gang that they were willing to do anything to get rid of anyone who didn't fit the picture. If you were sick or deformed in some way, you were a target. They killed or neutered people who were mentally deficient."

My heart beat faster. "What did they mean by perfect?"

Schreiner's eyes were chilly. "People like you. They wanted lots of people like you."

I opened and closed my mouth like a fish on the beach. There were no words for the horror I felt or the relief that they wouldn't have come after me or my family—and the guilt that relief brought.

"Oskar!" Grandma Arial's shrill voice got louder. "I know that you endured much. But EJ is a boy. He grew up in Cold Creek. He may have German blood, but that doesn't make him a Nazi any more than your Jewish ancestry made you a Jew."

My grandmother's words were reassuring, but clearly my German family had been at odds with the Schreiners. Mama was probably tired of hearing this angry man blame her for what happened to his father's business. No wonder she wouldn't see him. The people who hurt the Schreiners were dead now. All of them.

"What happened to Schreiner's?"

Oskar sniffed and dabbed at his nose with his handkerchief. "If you mean the business, it was unscathed. It belonged to a German, after all."

Yes, I thought. Opa was a powerful man. One who could make things happen.

"If you mean my family," Schreiner continued, "my father and Uncle Aldo were dragged out into the street, humiliated, and shipped off to Dachau. My aunt and grandmother hid on the third floor. When the thugs were through with the men, they tromped up the steps after the women. My Oma fought them. A young storm trooper pistol-whipped her. Can you imagine that? A twenty-year-old boy with a gun thought it was okay to beat a seventy-year-old woman into submission."

"Oh!" Grandma Arial covered her mouth with both hands.

"My beautiful grandmother lay on the floor for hours until the violence was over. By then, she was dead, of course. I heard this from my aunt when she bought my father's release from Dachau with the little bit of jewelry and cash we'd hidden. Uncle Aldo had already died by that point."

"I'm sorry."

"Me too, EJ." He rubbed his eye with his knuckle.

"Where were you when it happened?"

He picked up the carved pipe again. "I had stepped out with my sweetheart—your relative, Magda Langer. I'd known her most of my life. We were eighteen then."

"My husband had many letters from his cousin, Magda's mother," Grandma Arial said. "She wrote that Magda was in love and wanted to get married."

Oskar nodded and caressed the polished pipe. "That night, we saw a group of men coming toward us, but we didn't yet appreciate the danger. Then one of them threw a brick through the window of Weiss Juweliergeschäft and the lot of them set about destroying the place. I started to go after them—I was a big strong kid at the time—but Magda grabbed my hand and pulled me into an alley behind the building. She led me to a door hidden by a dustbin. I had to crouch down to avoid hitting my head. She closed the door behind us. I remember that I was out of breath and she patted my back and whispered that I must be quiet. Then we heard the rioters in the front part of the building, smashing things. I realized that we must be in a closet or storage room behind a false wall. It was so dark in the little space we couldn't see each other. Then as our eyes got used to the gloom, I made out stacks of small boxes on shelves on one side of the room and a large safe in the corner. The Weiss family had prepared for problems and stashed their diamond inventory where thieves weren't likely to find it."

"How did Magda know about the hiding place?" I jumped in while Schreiner took a quick sip of tea.

"She worked for the Weisses until Hitler made it against the law for Aryans to work for Jews." He chuckled to himself. "Once they decided that we were Jewish, it was also against the law for Magda and me to see each other, but she was convinced that love would find a way, so we ignored—"

The back door flew open. "What is going on here?" Sonny stormed into the room, scowling. I'd never seen him that upset before, and his anger scared me. I focused on keeping my leg from shaking.

"Would you like some tea?" Grandma stood up.

"I want to know why Mr. Schreiner is here."

"Just a little tea party, Sonny. Some brownies and tart. Some conversation. Join us," she said.

"Conversation? About what?"

The corners of Schreiner's mouth turned up. I couldn't tell if it was a smile or a grimace. "We were having a pleasant afternoon talking about old times," he said.

"They are innocent. Why would you want to impose the past on them?"

Grandma Arial took Sonny's hand, "Please calm down. Let me get you something. Then we can hash this out calmly."

"He's been bothering Vala since the wedding, calling her every day, showing up on our doorstep, implying things."

Schreiner struggled to get up from Grandma's soft, crackling sofa. "So Vala doesn't want to go back to Mannheim. She doesn't want to take responsibility for anything. Okay. I accept that. But EJ and Arial? Why shouldn't they know how it was? Maybe they know something they don't realize they know. Maybe you do, too. Surely Vala has opened up over the years." He tucked in his shirt where it had pulled out of his pants.

"Vala has enough grief of her own. She really can't help you with yours."

Schreiner bowed his head. "I'm sorry to have disturbed your peace, but I can't let it go."

Sonny's posture relaxed. "I know. That's your curse, but I have two boys to raise. I want them to feel safe and loved. I want Vala to taste a little security someday as well. I won't let you destroy what I'm building."

Schreiner took a deep breath. "Then I will go."

"I'm sorry, Oskar," my grandmother said.

"Thank you for your hospitality, Arial." Schreiner turned to me. "Just forget about Mannheim, EJ. It was nothing really. Didn't matter at all."

"Enough of that. Leave the kid alone. I mean it." Sonny clapped Schreiner on the back and guided him to the door.

"If you change your mind or if Vala ever wants to talk, I live in North Royalton. You can find me there."

"I won't change my mind." Sonny pushed him gently out the door and closed it behind him.

"Sonny! I can't believe you were so rude to him. He seems harmless enough."

"He has a flock of demons on his back, Mama. It's not his fault, but even after all these years, there are forces in play that could be dangerous. Besides, Vala and I have worked hard to give EJ and the Mickster a good life. Escapes should have happy endings."

Grandma Arial smiled at me. "True enough. The boys are my happy ending. What would I have done without them, after Johnny was killed and your father died."

Sonny put his hand on my shoulder. "They're my happy ending as well."

"Now that you got rid of Oskar, do you want some brownies?"

"You bet. How about some cocoa, too?"

"I know you're giving me something to do so you can talk to EJ alone," she said over her shoulder.

Sonny winked at me. "Who? Me? Shamelessly manipulating my own mother?"

I laughed with them and for a moment, it did seem like everything was normal and that we hadn't spent the afternoon talking about That Which Shouldn't Be Discussed.

The sofa crunched as Sonny sat down. "So. Oskar told you some stories?"

"Yeah."

"Anything you want to ask me?"

"Did you ever meet Opa or Oma?"

"They say Herr Hess was killed in a car accident in 1945, but no one knows for sure. Vala was in Poland and telegraphed him that she needed help. He sent Gerhardt in his car, and then hired a car and drove off in the night to rescue the three of you. About that time, the Soviet army pushed back the Germans, and Vala found her own way home. Herr Hess never returned to Mannheim. Years later they found his car overturned in a ravine."

It was the same old story. "That's it?"

"That's all I know."

"Was Opa a Nazi?"

Sonny stared at his hands. "I think he was. Yes."

"So Schreiner's story about Opa stealing his family's business was true?"

"I don't know. It's possible. Lots of awful things happened over there—before, during, and after the war."

"And Oma?"

"She was a strange, sad woman. Her world—as she knew and liked it—was gone. She struggled to adapt, I imagine."

"Did you like her?"

He sighed. "I only met her once."

"And?"

"She didn't like me."

"Why not?"

"Probably because I was an American soldier."

"What did she look like?"

"Hard to say. She had been sick for a while."

"Cancer?"

"That's what they said. She turned your mother away. I thought it was because of me but Vala says no."

"Why, then?"

"There's a whole lot of your mother's story that I don't know."

"You'd tell me if you knew, though?"

"Depends on whether Vala agreed."

"If you wait for her permission, I'll never know."

"It's her story. Her life."

"It's mine, too, and Mick's. Don't we have a right to our own family history?"

"Here in Cold Creek, we have no secrets, EJ—well, not exactly." He laughed. "It's just that our secrets aren't as ugly right now. Ask me anything about the Logans and I'll tell you."

"I can handle it, you know."

"Eventually, I suppose you will handle whatever it is."

"If anyone ever sees fit to tell me."

"She will tell us what she can bear to tell us, buddy. In the meantime, we try to be a loving supportive family."

He had me. "Okay."

His eyes fell on the elaborate pipe Schreiner had left between the cushions of the couch. "What's this?"

"It's Schreiner's. I guess he forgot it."

Sonny examined it. "Maybe he forgot it on purpose."

"Why?"

He pocketed it. "So he can convince us to let him come back for it."

"Can I come back in?" Grandma Arial peered around the door frame. "I have your cocoa."

"Your grandma thinks food and drink solves everything."

"It's a good distraction," she yelled from the kitchen.

Sonny and I laughed.

* * *

"Come with me, Emo." My arm around his neck was sweaty.

"Where are we going?"

"For a ride. See the car? Just down there."

I thought about the little girl-ghost. "Will I see children?"

"Yes," he said. "There will be children and my colleagues. Your mommy will be there, too."

Satisfied, I stuck my thumb in my mouth.

"Emo," he pulled my hand away from my face. "You are too old for that."

I tried to pull my hand away from him.

"Emo!"

I twisted in his arms, sobbing."

The slap shocked me into silence.

"This is not a place for tantrums." He pulled my handkerchief out of my pocket. "Blow your nose and keep your fingers out of your mouth." He set me on my feet. "Stand up straight. Good. Hold my hand at all times."

"There's Gerhardt," I said as we went outside.

"Yes and he's going to drive us to pick up your mommy."

Gerhardt opened the car door and we got into the back seat. "Hi, Gerhardt!"

Gerhardt wore a thick black coat and gloves. "Good morning, Emo. Are you ready to go?"

I shook my head and looked up at the man beside me. "My shoe is untied!"

"I'll tie it while Gerhardt drives."

The man picked up my foot and pulled one of the strings out of my sock.

Gerhardt climbed into the front seat and started the engine. As we drove away from our house, the people on our street turned to watch. I saw Frau Koblenz in her window, but she ducked behind the curtains and pretended she didn't see me. I felt sad—like I might not see her again.

A truck with flashing lights and a siren sped past us as we drove out of town. I waved at the men with guns who were riding in it, but they didn't wave back.

"Where are they going?"

"To visit Frau Koblenz."

"Why?"

"Because you are with me now."

"Oh."

We drove down a long gravel road beside the railroad tracks. We came to a funny building that arched over our heads as we went under it. I turned around as we drove away and only then realized it was a room over a gate. A soldier in a window waved at me.

We bumped along for a while. There were lots of people like he said there would be. Some were in their pajamas and wore wooden shoes. They looked like they needed a bath. They didn't wave or smile.

The soldiers were friendlier. They clicked their heels and stuck out their arms. We passed lots of buildings before we turned and stopped. Gerhardt got out and opened the back door for us.

"We won't be long," the man said to Gerhardt as we got out. "For God's sake, don't let any of those wretched souls get near the car. Shoot them if you have to."

"Don't worry."

Gerhardt helped me jump over a puddle of smelly water. "Where are we?"

"Leave Gerhardt alone." The man took my hand. "He has work to do."

"Where's Mama?"

"She's looking at furniture."

"What kind of furniture?"

"Emo, can you be quiet for once in your life?"

I puckered up, but before the tears started, I saw Mama. She was talking to one of the pajama men. I ran to her and clung to her dress.

"Hello, my darling." She picked me up and kissed my forehead. "We are almost done here."

I wrapped my arms around her neck and my legs around her waist. "Where were you?"

"Preparing for our trip, Mausi."

"Where are we going?"

"Home. Mannheim."

"I missed you." I laid my head on her shoulder.

"I missed you, too." She stroked my hair.

"Yes, yes. You haven't been apart two hours. Let's get this business done before they change their minds." The man in the blue coat walked around us. "It's time to go."

"Make sure it goes to Schreiner's," Mama said to the pajama man. "The warehouse has plenty of space."

"I will make the arrangements." The pajama man turned away from us.

"You are too thin, Ulli," Mama said.

He stopped and looked back at us. "I do better than most."

"Any word on the Schreiners?"

"I haven't seen them since 1938."

"Stefan or Jan?"

The pajama man shook his head.

The man in the blue coat took Mama's arm. "Come, Vala. We must get started. The war is coming our way."

"Good luck, Ulli," Mama said over her shoulder as the man pulled us away.

As we reached the door, I heard a snort and watched Ulli spit on the floor.

* * *

"What's wrong, EJ?" Mick stood by my bed, his face crumpled with concern.

I rose up on one elbow and rubbed my eyes with the other fist. "Nothing." I yawned. "Why?"

"You were sleeping so hard and so loud."

"What?"

"I could feel you clear over here. You were unhappy."

I sat up. "It was a dream or maybe a memory. It's crazy and confusing."

"How so?"

"I sometimes dream about Mama and me before you were born. We are in a car with someone, and I can't figure out who he is. Is he our father? Our grandfather? Someone else? It makes me crazy sometimes."

"I don't remember either of them." Mick crawled back into his own bed and pulled the quilt up to his chin. "I don't feel like they are mine. Sonny is the only dad I know."

I stretched. "I should remember something, but I don't really. Just these dreams, and maybe this one is just stuff I made up from what Oskar Schreiner told Grandma Arial and me the other day. He mentioned someone named Ulli and I might remember someone named Ulli but maybe not."

"I dream about music."

"You mean you hear it in your dream?"

"No, I see the notes flying past me on the staff. I know the sounds they make, but I don't hear them exactly."

"Do you remember them when you wake up?"

"Sometimes, but usually not."

"Do they come back?"

"I'm not sure. Sometimes when I play my guitar or the piano, I play things I know I've never heard before, but they seem familiar."

I stared at my toes. "You are a weird kid, Mick. Everyone knows it. I know it. But lately, I realize that weird is the wrong word."

"What's the right one?"

"Special."

He was quiet for a long time. "Thank you, EJ," he said. "That sounds better than weird."

"Yeah it does, but that's because I also just realized that I'm the weird one."

"You worry a lot," he said. "And you feel bad inside when you have those dreams."

"I wish I could stop having them."

"Why can't you?"

"It's like Mama's wolf dream. You know the one where she's going somewhere and when she comes out onto the porch, she feels a wolf on the hill outside. She knows he's coming and she rushes to get us all into the car before the beast arrives to devour us. We close the doors just as he reaches our yard and we hurry to press the locks."

"That makes no sense, EJ. Wolves can't open car doors."

"The part that scares her the most is when he puts his paws on the window and growls at us through the glass."

"She's had that dream ever since I can remember," Mick said. "Sometimes when I come down for breakfast, I can tell she's had it. Her eyes are all red and her hands are shaking."

He hadn't yet realized that Mama's shakes came from the Bordeaux she kept in the cupboard above the sink. Of course, maybe that was why she saw the wolf in the first place. Or maybe, the wolf dream scared her to drink.

"I can't help but think my dreams connect to hers some how. Maybe there's a real wolf heading our way and Mama knows him."

Mick scowled. "Now you're scaring me."

"I'm sorry."

"Go to sleep, EJ, and dream about that pretty girl you met at Teresa and Danny's wedding."

I startled. "What made you think about Rosa?"

"Because she's a lot nicer than Mama's wolf."

17

Mr. McKensey
November 12, 1956

I PUSHED OPEN the door to the newsstand. "Hi, Skippy!"

"EJ! The new *Hot Rod* came in. You want to take one for Sonny? I'll put it on his charge."

"Sure." I felt like I'd known Skippy forever now. His scars had either faded or I was so used to them I didn't even notice anymore. "What about *Mad Magazine* for Mick? And Mama's *Life*? And *American View* for all of us?"

"Already got them in a bag for you."

"And *Superman*?"

Just came in. I'll unpack them and get one for you."

"Sonny said you've been spending time with Elizabeth Jenkins."

He grinned. "You know, EJ, I don't know what was wrong with me. Growing up, I knew Elizabeth was sweet on me, but I had my eye on a little cutie who never gave me the time of day. Every time I got turned down, I'd hang out at Balboa's where Elizabeth was a waitress. I'd drown my sorrows in malteds and tell bad jokes. Elizabeth came right back at me, and we'd laugh and fool around when it wasn't busy. That girl is a lot of fun, and Balboa's was the perfect place to go to raise a reject's spirits."

"So why didn't you ask her out sooner?"

Skippy sighed. "I was a blamed fool. She had these really thick black eyebrows and was a bit chunky for my tastes. It was stupid, really. Wasn't that I didn't like her, but I was worried what the other guys would say if I started dating her."

"You *are* a blamed fool, Skippy Foster."

I jumped and looked around. A very old man was rummaging through the old newspaper bin.

"I know that now, Mr. McKensey."

"Humph." Mr. McKensey's face was set in a perpetual scowl. I didn't know if it was because he was in a bad mood all the time or because he wanted you to think he was. To hear Mick tell it, the old codger was a sweetheart. I wouldn't go that far myself, but I figured the grouch thing was an act.

"So what can I get you? Need a bag for all that stuff?"

"I can carry it. Car's parked right out front."

"I'll help, Mr. McKensey," I said. "That way we can get everything out in one trip."

"Humph." Mr. McKensey filled my arms with out-of-date magazines and newspapers.

"What are you doing with this stuff?" I bent my knees to absorb the next pile of papers. "Do you read it all?"

He scowled at me over his glasses. "None of your business."

I blushed. "I meant no harm, sir." Grandma Arial would have my hide for insulting Mr. McKensey. They went way back.

"Helping doesn't give you the right to pry."

"I'm sorry."

I wanted to drop the load of papers on the floor and storm out but he was on the edge of infirm. I swallowed my irritation. He might not like me, but he'd taken a shine to Mick and vice versa. There must be something inside that old bag of bones besides rancor and bad breath.

"Don't give me that face, EJ Logan, or I'll tell Arial."

"Yes, sir." I lowered my lids.

Skippy opened the door and Mr. McKensey limped through it with me on his heels, my arms stacked with reams of paper right up to my chin.

"A few more yards," the old man grumbled as we crossed Cold Creek Drive and headed up the hill.

I was freezing by the time we reached his car in the McKensey Park parking lot seven blocks away.

"Stand right there," he rummaged in his pocket.

At first, I thought he was looking for a key, but his dilapidated wreck wasn't locked. In fact, it didn't have any locks. He pushed a button and lifted the rusty trunk lid. "Drop them in here."

"Yes, sir." It felt great to flex my hands and stretch my arms.

"You a sissy, boy?"

I gritted my teeth. "No, sir."

"I heard you didn't want to play football?"

"I don't." I zipped my jacket up under my chin. "That doesn't make me a sissy, does it?"

"You scared to play?"

Why exactly I couldn't play was none of his business. "No. I have better things to do in the afternoons."

"Like what?"

"Study."

"Why?"

"I want to be a surgeon like Danny Kline and I don't want to bust up my hands playing some stupid game."

"Do they tease you?"

"A little, but I don't care."

"Good, good." He got into his car and rolled down his window. "At least you aren't a juvenile delinquent like Butch Murphy."

"I got too much to do for that stuff, Mr. McKensey."

He rolled his window half way up, and then changed his mind and rolled it down again. "You don't have to try so hard, EJ."

It was the first kind thing the man ever said to me. "Yes, sir."

With that, Mr. McKensey roared out of the parking lot and into traffic. Cars blew their horns and swerved to avoid him.

I shook my head and chuckled.

* * *

I walked back to the newsstand thinking about Mr. McKensey and rubbing my reddened hands. Why did he love annoying people so much?

"I saw Mr. McKensey zoom past a minute ago," Skippy said as I opened the door. "He give you the business?"

"Let's say that I enjoyed his charming personality."

"It was nice of you to help him, EJ."

"He was such a pain I almost walked off and left him to load all of that stuff by himself. Then out of the blue, he's sweet as pie."

"When he isn't being a pain, he can be pretty observant."

"My brother loves the old guy. I trust Mick's judgment, but in this case—" I put my hand to my ear. A long loud horn sounded in the distance. "What gives?"

Skippy listened for a moment and then shrugged. "Traffic?" He put all of my magazines into a bag. "The crazy thing about Mr. McKensey is that if you're around him much, you like him."

"I can see that. My brother Mick thinks he's gr—"

The door banged open. "Hey Billy Ray," Skippy waved with his good arm. "You here for your dad's *Plain Dealer*?"

"To call an ambulance." Billy Ray panted. "Mr. McKensey bounced off the curb on Main Street and ran into Coach Littleton's new Chevy that was parked outside St. Mike's."

"How bad is he hurt?" Skippy held the receiver under his chin and dialed.

"Hard to say. His nose is bloody and there's a bump over his left eye. Broke his glasses and he's jabbering on about how expensive it is to get them fixed."

"I'm calling now." Skippy picked up the phone. "Anyone else hurt?"

"No, but the coach is pretty upset over his car."

I dropped my bag of magazines and ran out into the street. People were hurrying toward the corner three blocks away. The horn stopped, and the sudden silence was unnerving. I turned to see if Grandma Arial had come out of her house yet. I didn't know whether to go get her or go check on Mr. McKensey first. Then Mick appeared and Grandma followed. I waved to them and headed toward the crowd gathering on the corner.

In the distance, I heard a siren. I walked faster. Billy Ray Parker ran past me and then Skippy. As the ambulance got closer, something told me I needed to run, too. I pumped my arms and stretched my legs. Ahead of me, a woman screamed.

Faster. Faster. Faster.

I approached a mother and her little girl standing on the sidewalk, straining their necks to see what was happening. The daughter's long dark hair streamed down her back. She looked up at me as I passed, her face bunched up in a silent scream.

The little girl-ghost!

My heart rose into my throat and I ran faster to get to Mr. McKensey—and get away from the little girl-ghost and her mother—because I needed to see him.

And then I was there.

Coach Littleton paced back and forth on the sidewalk wringing his hands and muttering. The left rear fender of his turquoise and white Bel Air was bashed in. Steam hissed out of the front of Mr. McKensey's car and water streamed down the street. People stood around watching and talking, but only Skippy and Billy Ray were helping Mr. McKensey.

I pushed through the onlookers. "What can I do?"

"He's trapped behind the steering wheel," Billy Ray said. "We can't get him loose." He'd propped open the driver's side door and ripped his own undershirt off his body. Mr. McKensey's head was resting on the back of his seat. He moaned when Billy Ray blotted the blood off his face with the torn T-shirt.

Skippy was on the passenger side, struggling to push Mr. McKensey's seat back from the steering wheel, which was pressing against the old man's round belly.

Billy Ray looked up. His eyes were wide and his lips quivered. "Help him, EJ. I don't know what else to do."

The sirens were loud now. "They'll be here soon." Some doctor I was going to be.

Across the front seat, Skippy caught my eye.

I took Billy Ray's red-splattered cloth from him and turned to Mr. McKensey. His face was pale. He was bleeding from the nose and mouth and a cut over his left eye. I quickly refolded the torn T-shirt so that the wet parts were inside. My hands shook as I wiped the blood out of his eyes. When he could see, he focused on me for a moment, his lips moving.

"What?"

He repeated whatever he was trying to tell me, but with the noise of the approaching ambulance, I couldn't make out what he was saying.

I lowered my ear to his mouth.

"Don't try *too* hard, son."

I pulled back, horrified at what I thought he might be telling me. Billy Ray ran to the other side of the car to help Skippy. With the two of them pushing, the right side of the bench seat broke free and the pressure on Mr. McKensey's abdomen was relaxed.

I leaned down again. The old man's eyes lost their focus and I knew he was dying. "Good-bye, sir," I said, even though I knew he was already gone.

Part Four

Discovery

1960

18

Billy Ray Parker

April 15, 1960

I SAT IN the tree house daydreaming. Just across the fence and beyond a row of rhododendrons, Mick sat on the front porch of our house, playing his guitar.

Mama stood behind the screen door watching him.

I couldn't make out what she said but he looked up and smiled at her. She said something else and he nodded.

Behind our house across our small back yard, Mr. and Mrs. Vilani were fussing around their carport. It must have been beach night. She was wearing a long muumuu and he had on a matching tropical-themed shirt. They were grilling steaks on a tiny hibachi and drinking Mai Tais.

I picked up Sonny's old binoculars and turned to the other side of my castle.

Mr. Balboa's Soda Fountain was bustling. Young men drove through the parking lot looking for girls or buddies or what passed for trouble in Cold Creek. A couple shared a malted in a '53 Ford and chatted with a carload of boys parked next to them.

We weren't allowed to go there after school like everyone else, because Mama thought the town's teenagers were rowdy and up to no good. Sonny had laughed and said the boys were showing off their modified cars. Mama wanted to know why they thought anyone would want to see such ugly things. Sonny said it was because they worked so hard customizing them and that beauty was in the eye of the beholder. Besides, he'd had fun at Balboa's himself not so long ago. Didn't she have fun when she was a kid? Mama got mad at that and went into her room and slammed the door behind her.

A maroon Mercury pulled up in front of Balboa's.

I ducked below the window and then rose up to peer through the leaves.

Annie Jones and a hefty guy in a black jacket got out of the car and went in. Was that her boyfriend, I wondered. She sat in a booth by the window. I could see her fiddling with something and realized it must be the jukebox mounted on the wall over her table. She leaned back in her seat and snapped her fingers. I wondered what kind of music she'd chosen. "Blue Suede Shoes"? "Tom Dooley"?

A different boy than the one who'd dropped her off at Balboa's appeared at her table. I squinted through the field glasses. It was Billy Ray Parker. They must have argued because Billy Ray stormed out of the soda shop with his fists in the pockets of his jacket. Good.

Annie tapped on the table with her fingertips until the young man who'd brought her came in and sat down beside her. He took off his cap, and I glimpsed his oiled red hair. Butch Murphy. Aside from his hot new car, he was a couple years older than we were and came from a wealthy family. No wonder Annie liked him.

I couldn't watch.

The lot behind the tree house was empty and faced Sugar Maple Drive. Aside from the Vilani's flat-topped ranch and Skippy and Elizabeth's new bungalow, there weren't too many houses back there yet, just neat little squares of land staked out with twine. A lone figure stalked the empty neighborhood. He picked up a chunk of concrete and threw it as far as he could. It was Billy Ray. Annie must have broken his heart back there at Balboa's. Seems Annie was not only my dream girl but Billy Ray's too.

I lay back on the quilt with my hands behind my head. What did it matter? I'd never had the nerve to ask her out anyway. I'd gone to school with her for years and now we were seniors. A breeze rustled the leaves and gently rocked the tree house. I closed my eyes.

* * *

A man held my hand as I climbed the tall concrete steps of a red brick building.

"Where are we going?"

"We are running an errand, Emo."

"I wanted to play with that little girl. I pointed at a group of people back down the road we'd just passed."

"Not today."

"But I want to…" I jerked my hand out of his and jumped off the short stoop. "I want to play with her."

"Emo!"

"No."

BA-BAM!

* * *

The tree shook.

"EJ?" It was a soft whisper.

I sat up.

"EJ, are you up there?"

I stuck my head out of the window. "What?"

"It's Billy Ray. Put down the ladder. "

I gritted my teeth. "Why? "

"Please, help me."

"What's going on?"

"I got mad and shot out the tires of Butch Murphy's car. Butch and his friends are looking for me."

Still miffed that he had the audacity to want my girl, I relented and let down the rope ladder. He scurried into the tree house.

I pulled the ladder up and stowed it under the window. "Why did you mess with Butch?"

"Jealous, I guess. I've been in love with Annie since the sixth grade when we all got the measles. I couldn't stand the idea of him taking her out."

I frowned. "Destroying someone's car could get you put in jail."

"That's better that than facing Butch when he's all riled up."

"You should have thought of that before you shot out his tires."

He leaned back against the tree trunk. "At least he's on foot for a while."

I snickered. "A short while."

"I meant to ask her to the dance but I…well, I didn't get around to it," he said.

"So aren't you afraid she won't ever go out with you now?"

He rose up on one knee to peek through the branches at the chaos at Balboa's. "Yeah, I blew it. " He rubbed his nose with the back of his hand and sat back down. "I probably embarrassed her in front of everyone. She won't forget that for a while."

"Seems to me that you are gonna have more trouble with Butch than with Annie."

"Yeah, she'll get over it. Eventually."

"What makes you think that?"

"Cause she's going to marry me when we turn twenty, and we're going to have three kids and a hound dog named Orson."

I laughed out loud. "How do you know that?"

"Annie told me she dreamed all about it once. She said we'd live over in that new housing development next door to the Vilanis." He jerked a thumb over his shoulder toward the empty lots on Sugar Maple Drive.

I pondered Annie's vision of her future. All my dreams were cloudy or scary, stuff I couldn't forget or completely remember. "Think that will happen?"

"Not if she's gonna spend all her time riding around in the Butch-mobile." He laid his head on his knees. "I always thought she'd be there when I was ready, so I wasn't in any hurry."

The back porch lights came on next door and Mama called, "EJ? Time for supper."

"Coming, Mama!"

"She's gorgeous."

"Annie?"

"She is, too, but I was talking about your mother."

"Aw, man. I don't know. She's my mom and she's strange."

All thoughts about Balboa's and Butch and Annie seemed to have left him. He pushed his glasses up on his nose and stared at my house. "All the guys think she's a real looker, you know?"

Actually I did know it, but it was too weird to think about. "She's okay, I guess."

"What's Vala mean?"

"Don't know exactly. She once said it meant 'singled out,' but when I asked Grandma Arial about it she said she thought it was more like 'chosen.'"

"Whichever. People notice her."

I guessed that was true but she never made friends with anyone besides Zona or went anywhere except Grandma Arial's.

"She's shy, " I said.

Billy Ray shook his head. "Not shy so much as haunted."

"Haunted?"

"Like me."

I cocked my head. In the fading light, he did seem pale and troubled.

"EJ?" Her voice was higher now, annoyed.

"I'll be there in a minute!" I stood up. "You gonna be okay?"

"As long as Butch doesn't catch me."

"Stay here for a while then. He'll get tired of looking and go home eventually. Want me to call your folks and tell them where you are?"

"No. I'll just sit here a bit and think about stuff."

"There's a canteen and a couple of Snickers in that trunk over there. Help yourself."

He nodded and put his head back down on his knees.

I let down the rope ladder. "And don't worry about Annie. She'll come around."

"Will she?"

Hoping that she wouldn't, I climbed down the ladder and hurried through the gate and across the yard to our house.

"What took so long?" Mama stood at the screen with a glass of wine in her hand.

"It wasn't that long."

"Dinner is ready." She led the way to the kitchen where Mick and Sonny were already eating.

"What was all that commotion over at Balboa's?" Sonny handed me a bowl of sauerkraut as soon as I washed my hands and sat down.

"Billy Ray Parker shot Butch Murphy's tires."

"See? I told you it was no good at that place." Mama scooped mashed potatoes onto my plate.

Sonny shrugged. "Probably gave everyone a good scare."

"Why'd he do that?" Mick used a butter knife to spread mustard on black bread.

"He had a crush on Annie but never told her how he felt, and then he got upset when he saw her with Butch."

"How do you know this?" Mama frowned.

"He crawled up into the tree house a little while ago, hiding from Butch."

"Springtime and the young colts start to feel their oats." Sonny sliced the pork roast and doled it out to each of us.

"You are going to feed Billy Ray oats?" Mama sat down and lifted her fork.

"No, he said 'feel,' Mama." Mick put his meat on the bread along with a little sauerkraut.

"What's that mean, Sonny? What's feeling oatmeal?" She wrinkled her nose.

"Not oatmeal, oats. On a farm after baby horses eat, they romp and have a good time. We call that 'feeling their oats.'"

"So young men are like baby horses?"

Sonny winked at Mick. "Yep."

Mick took a big bite of meat and bread. "So where is he now?"

"He's probably still out there moping."

"No, no. No moping." Mama put down her silverware.

"Come on, Vala. For Christ's sake, leave the boy alone," Sonny said with his mouth full.

She was already on her way down the hall to the front porch. The screen door slammed behind her.

The three of us sat staring at each other, trying to swallow food we'd already started. Soon we heard their voices and then their footsteps as they crossed the porch.

"We feed you pork before you call your parents," Mama said as they came into the kitchen. "Sonny, Mick, you remember Emo's friend Billy Ray, ja?"

Billy Ray seemed embarrassed but he nodded to each of us as we stood to greet him.

"Have a seat, young man." Sonny gestured toward a chair next to me. "Vala cooks enough to feed an army."

"But no oats tonight, I'm very sorry." Mama sat down at her place and unfolded her napkin.

Billy Ray glanced at the food on our table. "Oats? What?"

Mick and I laughed until Sonny couldn't hold back any longer and joined us.

Mama patted Billy Ray's hand. "Don't worry, young man. They are laughing at me, not you."

"Mama's got a way with words," Mick said. "I used to think it was because of the difference between English and German, but now I think it's just Mama's way of seeing things."

"Ja," Mama said. "They used to think I was funny by accident." She poured Billy Ray a cup of tea and then topped off her own glass of Blue Nun. "But I was funny in Germany, too."

I was surprised. "What made you laugh back then?"

"Oh, so many things. When I was a girl, I would play tricks on my older sister and her friends."

I swallowed a big bite of sauerkraut and black bread. "Like what?

"I'd steal one of the cards they were collecting and put in one I drew myself. Lana might not find it for days or weeks. She would buy a new card and hurry into her room to add to her box, and when she saw what I did she would chase me, squealing." She hiccuped and took a sip of her wine.

I imagined Mama as a naughty little girl and chuckled. Mick and Sonny smiled, too. We didn't see her this way often.

"What kind of cards were they, Mrs. Logan?"

Mama heaped sauerkraut and pork on Billy Ray's plate. "They were pictures of all our leaders. You know, Hitler, Goering, Heydrich, Himmler. All the important people."

"You mean *Nazis*, Mama?" Mick seemed shocked. "You never told us you knew any of those guys."

"Oh, I didn't, but Lana did. She was popular. I once saw Hoess at a party. He was dancing with his wife. He was born in Mannheim, but they were much older than me. I was just a girl, you know."

Sonny stared at her, his mouth slightly open.

"Who was this guy," Billy Ray asked. "Someone famous?"

"Maybe not here, but in…" She stopped.

Mick and Billy Ray and I leaned forward expectantly. Since she seldom told stories of what she was like as a kid, any tidbit about Mama's life in Germany was enthralling.

"Where?" Mick urged.

Mama's wine seemed to be affecting her more than usual. The whites of her eyes were red.

"Is that who I think?" Sonny's voice was a low rasp.

She emptied her glass and set it gently on the table.

"Vala?"

"I don't think so. No."

"Tell us more. What was Aunt Lana like? Do we look like your family?"

My laughing, tipsy mother faded into the other one, the one who hid from the world and from Mick and me. "They are dead. What does it matter?" She stood up. "Finish your dinner, Billy Ray. Sonny will take you home."

"Can I help with the dishes?"

"Emo will do them, yes?"

I nodded.

"Gut!" She turned toward the hallway. "Mein Bett wartet auf mich."

"Don't go, Mama," Mick said under his breath.

Sonny watched her stumble out of the room before turning back to us. "Finish your pork, boys."

"Who did you think she meant?" Billy Ray asked.

We all looked at each other but no one had an answer. Not even Sonny.

"I'll bring the truck around when we're finished." Sonny took a bite and chewed slowly.

We all bent to our dinner in the sudden silence.

19
Lana's Birthday
April 16, 1960

THE NEXT DAY was a Saturday. Mick and I were in the back yard playing catch with Sonny when Mama came out onto the screened porch.

"What you call this game again?" She sat down at the picnic table. Red wine sloshed over the rim of the goblet in her hand and dribbled on a stack of Sonny's *Hot Rod* magazines.

"Baseball." Sonny caught Mick's grounder, spun around, and tossed it to me.

"Do they play baseball in Germany, Mama?" I missed the pitch, and the ball rolled under the rhododendron at the corner of the house.

"Oooh, be careful Emo. Don't break…den Busch." She dabbed at the wine droplets on the magazine covers with the dishtowel she habitually threw over her shoulder.

"I won't." I panted as I rummaged through the fat leaves, ignoring Mr. Vilani, who was watering his garden and peering over the fence at us.

"Well did they?" Mick threw down his glove and joined Mama on the porch.

"Did what, Milo?"

"Did they play baseball?"

"I don't think so…no…I don't know. But Hitler wanted everyone to be healthy, so we played lots of other games. Lots of running and jumping, you know. He didn't like us smoking, either. He said was bad for the lungs."

"Nothing wrong with being healthy." Sonny stepped up on the porch.

She hiccuped. "Nothing."

From under the rhododendrons, I heard Mama set the glass down on the picnic table.

Sonny said, "How about some coffee, sugar?"

"I don't want to g-g-get up right now."

"That's okay. I can get it," he said. "I'd like some, too."

I sighed and gave up my search for the lost ball. "I'll get it. I want some lemonade anyway. How about you, Mick?"

As I stood up, I saw that Mick had his hand on the stem of Mama's wine glass, slowly easing it out of her grasp.

She stared at it, forehead crinkled, until finally she sighed and relinquished it.

"I love you, Mommy." He handed the glass to me and I hurried into the house and dumped it into the kitchen sink.

I could hear Mama crying and the rumble of Sonny's voice, but they didn't seem to be coming inside yet. I took her bottle of expensive Bordeaux out of the cabinet and emptied it, along with the backup bottle. Then I filled a large mug with black coffee and hurried back outside with it.

"Here he is." Sonny reached for the mug and set it down in front of Mama. "It's hot, sugar, so sip it." He looked up at me. "Maybe some of that Cracker Barrel cheese would help, too."

I nodded and hurried back inside and made another pot of Folgers. While it was percolating, I put a cup and two glasses on a tray along with the pitcher of lemonade, a paring knife, the package of cheese, and some saltines. When the coffee was ready, I unplugged the pot and carried the whole lot out to the picnic table.

Sonny took the pot and refilled Mama's mug. "Try a little more of this. It's fresh."

Mama was too drunk to obey right away but Sonny stood beside her until she lifted the mug to her lips.

While she was drinking the second cup, Mick tore the wrapper off the cheese and cut it up in slices small enough to fit on a saltine square. He popped one into his own mouth and offered another one to Mama.

"I'm n-not a baby," she said but she took the cheese.

I handed Sonny his cup and poured Mick and me some lemonade. "It's a nice morning for a picnic." I sat down across from Mama. She was effectively blocked in now, what with Sonny sitting on one side of her and Mick on the other.

"You are ashamed of m-me."

"Not ashamed, worried," I said. "You're making yourself sick."

"I'm not sick."

"Have some more cheese." Mick handed her a saltine and cheddar sandwich.

She took it but instead of eating it, she laid it on the table in front of her. "I don't think I c-can swallow it just now."

"What is it, Mama? Bad dreams again?" Mick put his arm around her.

"No, no…" The tears finally came. "I'm sorry. I l-love you so much. You should not feel bad because I do."

"Don't push us away, Mama. Please. What makes you so un-happy on a pretty day like today?" I started to refill her coffee mug again, but she shook her head.

"I can't help it, Emo." She rubbed her eyes with the back of her hand and took a breath. Her lips quivered. "Lana's birthday is today."

"Oh?"

Mick and I looked at each other.

"What was Aunt Lana like?" Mick was the first to take advantage of Mama's mood.

"She was smart and interested in politics and science."

Mick perked up. "What kind of science?"

"She studied topics of the day, things like racial hygiene and fr-fren…what is it, Sonny, when you look at the bumps…you know, on the head?"

Sonny shrugged. "I have no idea. What is it?"

"Oh you…" She bit her lower lip in frustration. "You rubbed someone's head and it said whether you were…what's the word… unfit. Yes. The bumps say you are not smart and they…take you away." She stopped.

"Take you away where?" Mick frowned.

"They wanted only healthy people. Beautiful babies. It was sci-ence, you see."

Sonny gathered up the wine-stained magazines and stowed them in the cardboard box he kept by the back door before sitting down to sip his own coffee. I wondered why he put up with all the dra-ma, especially since I knew he had once loved someone capable of loving him back. I was young and frightened when I realized how much Sonny had given up to take us on, scared he would dump us for something easier. I appreciated Sonny now, probably more than other kids who knew their real fathers.

He must have sensed something, because he looked up into my eyes. When I couldn't bear his devoted concern any more, I found the percolator and refreshed his coffee.

"What happened to Lana?" I tried to sound casual.

Mama stared out into the Vilani's garden. "She had a baby, and things didn't go okay."

"You mean she died in childbirth?" asked Sonny.

"No, not that. After the baby, she got very sad. All she do was cry. Every day. She cut herself with the sewing scissors. Here. Mama put her finger under her chin. And then here and here." She pointed to her wrists. "Then one day, Papa found her standing over the crib holding the scissors like this." She held her fists together aiming at her heart. "Papi yelled and grabbed her and she fought him and tried to stab him. Mutti grabbed the baby, and hurried down the stairs screaming for someone to help us."

Mama sobbed into her hands. We stared at her bowed head. Mick's mouth was agape and Sonny lit a quick cigarette, his fingers trembling.

I couldn't stand it. "Did someone help?"

"Papi's men were working in the parlor downstairs. They saw meine Mutti run down the stairs and out the front door with Lana's baby in her arms. They heard Lana screaming and noises like fighting."

Mick put his hand over Mama's. "Where were you?"

"I was in the hall outside Lana's room, watching her try to kill herself and Papi. Then the men ... Papi's men ... they ran upstairs and helped Papi take the scissors away from her. There was blood everywhere, some Lana's and some Papi's."

"How badly were they hurt?"

Mama looked up at me, tears streaming down her cheeks. "Papi had a deep cut on his cheek. It went from here to here." She drew a finger from just below her left eye to the corner of her mouth. And Lana cut herself in the neck. "It was bad but not so bad as it could have been if Papi hadn't stopped her."

"So what happened then?"

"The doctor came and took care of the cuts. He gave Lana a shot that made her sleep for a long time. He told Papi that Lana needed to go to hospital for a while."

"Our grandmother...she saved Lana's baby?" Mick's eyes were as large as saucers.

"Ja, she saved him." Mama smiled at me through her tears and reached out to squeeze my hand. "He was a beautiful baby. Eyes the color of the sky. I didn't see him again for a long time. When I did, I knew those eyes."

"And Lana?" My jaw was so tight that my teeth hurt.

"Papi called his friends. They came and took her to Grafeneck, maybe Hadamar. That's where they took people who were sick in the head. They, you know, they never came back if they were like Lana."

"What?" I kept my voice calm but I screamed inside.

"She wasn't herself, EJ. She bit one of them here." She pointed to her hand. "Maybe they kept her awhile, maybe not. I pretend it's what she wanted for others, so why not for herself? Lana never wanted to be…what's the word? Burden? Ja, burden. I can't imagine how it was for her. She was sick…crazy sick. Every day," she wiped her nose with a napkin, "I still pretend."

"But you didn't see her die?" I asked.

"EJ." Sonny caught my eye and shook his head.

I ignored him. "Tell me, Mama. Did you see her die?"

"I didn't need to see it. I knew they believed that crazy was bad for the Reich. If you went crazy you had to die."

"But maybe she didn't."

"EJ!"

"But Sonny, maybe she didn't die. Maybe we can find her even now. Maybe there's hope. Delores is still looking for her family".

"It's been fifteen years since the end of the war, son. Surely she would have gone back to Mannheim by now. We left our information in case any of your family returned and wanted to find you."

"What happened to her baby?" Mick leaned forward, his palms flat on the table. "If our grandmother is dead, where did she leave Lana's baby?"

"I need wine." Mama tried to stand up but Sonny put his hand on hers and she sighed and sank back down onto the bench.

"He must be alive somewhere," I said. "When was he born? 1940? That would make him three years older than me. What's his name? Maybe we can find him."

"He is lost, Emo. Don't you see? It's hard to find people who are lost in a war." Her eyes were red and swollen, the eyes of a drunk who needed sleep.

"We have a cousin, Mommy. Why can't we know his name?" No one, not even Mama in one of her spells, could resist Mick's sweetness.

"Wolf."

"Wolf?" Mick relaxed. "What was his last name?"

Mama stared at her hands for a long time. "I don't remember."

Mick got up and went into the house. We could hear his footsteps on the stairs and his bedroom door slamming. Then soft chords from his guitar drifted through the house.

I couldn't believe that I had a cousin and this was the first time I was hearing about him. I watched as Sonny helped Mama up and guided her into the house and down the hall to her room. No wonder she was a drunk. She had given up, left all her family back in Mannheim, abandoned every one. Lana and Wolf could be looking for us now. Maybe looking for each other. Maybe we could find them. At least we could try to find our cousin.

20

Sonny's Story
April 16, 1960

A FEW MINUTES later, Sonny came back out onto the porch. "Try not to take it so hard, son." He dumped his overfilled ashtray into the garbage.

I lifted the coffee pot and he nodded. After I refilled his cup, he sat down in one of the wooden patio chairs beside mine. "Whatever torments her has nothing to do with you guys."

"It feels like it has everything to do with us."

"She loves you both."

"We aren't babies anymore, Sonny. We want to know who we are. We need to know. She only tells us a little bit and we're left guessing the rest. Did someone really kill Aunt Lana for being crazy?"

He swallowed the cooling coffee in a single gulp and set the mug down with a thud, as if he was angry. But his eyes were sad when he looked up. "I wish I could help, EJ, but I have no clue about your mom's life before we found her. If she says that's what happened, I'll take her at her word, but it's the first I've heard about it."

"See, that's just it. You never say how you found her or where or, you know, the circumstances."

He gazed out into the yard like he was trying to decide what to do. "Fair enough. Maybe it's time. She ran out in front of our car because she was being chased by some women."

I already knew this part. "Why?"

He took a deep breath. "They thought they saw her at Auschwitz."

The hairs on my arms stood up.

"How much do you know about Auschwitz, EJ?"

I shook my head and then shrugged. "I don't know?"

"What do you mean?"

"I can't decide if I'm remembering something that happened or if I'm remembering dreams."

"Do you want to tell me about it?"

"I can't remember the details during the day but each time it happens—when I first wake up, I know it means something. Then as days and weeks go by, I forget again. When I first read about the camps in American View, the name Auschwitz seemed familiar. I don't know why I knew it. But I knew it had something to do with my dreams."

Sonny lit a new cigarette, inhaled, and held it awhile before letting the smoke come out his nostrils. "The Russians came upon it near the end of the war. Most of the Nazis were gone. Headed back to Germany and into hiding, I guess."

I thought about my dream memories of Gerhardt, and a car ride with Mama and a monster and the bundle in the road. "Ohhhh!" I rubbed my temples. "I remember ghosts—a little girl-ghost waiting in line with her mother...to get in somewhere."

"You were a baby—only two and a half in 1945. Are you sure you remember it?"

I shook my head. "Maybe it's something I made up, but it seems real."

He tossed his Zippo lighter onto the picnic table. "Do you want me to tell you the rest?"

"Yes!"

"I didn't fight in the war, wasn't part of D-Day or any of that. I was too young. In fact, I was still in training on VE Day, the day the war was over in Europe. I got there a few months later as part of the occupation forces. Understand?"

"You didn't fight the Nazis."

"The others, the ones who saw what the Nazis had done or who were part of the invasion, well, feelings were running pretty hot. It had been a long hard slog, and some of them had seen their friends die."

"And you didn't hate us the same way?"

"So much for beating around the bush."

"But you didn't, did you?"

"I won't kid you, son. Some of my buddies did hate Germans based on what they had heard, but not like the fellows who did the actual fighting. Me? When my brother John died in France, it was a private ache and I didn't know quite who to blame. It didn't hurt that our family has German roots. So, going in, I didn't feel anything one way or another. Of course, we didn't know a lot of the stuff Hitler did at that point."

"So what's this got to do with all of it?"

"I'd been there a couple of months when Mags landed their plane in a field near Mannheim. Delores's hands were still pretty bad. She shouldn't have been traveling like that, but I give her a lot of points for nerve and take away a bunch for stubbornness."

"How did you know they were there?"

"I was stationed not too far away. Grandma Arial sent me a telegram so I checked out a car, went to pick them up, and drove them back to town. The city had been bombed pretty bad, and people were trying to clear the rubble and rebuild. It was a confusing time for everyone. The Mannheim Jews had either escaped before the war or died in Auschwitz, but we had no idea about that at the time. Delores still thought she'd find Rosa's parents, at least."

"How did Rosa get out? She would have been a little kid then."

"I don't know the details, but Grandma Arial told me Shirley Maxwell and her dad pulled some strings. The Nazis had rounded up all the Jews in Mannheim in 1940 and shipped them off to a camp in Vichy France. Somehow the Quakers got her out before her family was shipped off to Poland. I understand it was a close call, but that girl is alive today because someone cared and worked hard to find her in time. And even then they say it was luck."

I felt bad about Rosa. She was smart and funny and pretty. And nothing about her life would ever be normal. We had a lot in common that way.

Sonny put out his cigarette. "You done for today?"

"No! Tell me about Mama."

He didn't seem too thrilled about that, but he nodded. "There were a lot of people on the roads those days. Folks who had gone somewhere to avoid the fighting came back to find other families living in their houses and there would be a squabble over who lived where and about furniture and quilts and pictures and stuff. Strangers from all over the world were trying to find lost relatives and came to the DP Camp nearby. The U.S. Army was everywhere you looked. There were a lot of Latvians who had been brought there from one of the concentration camps. They either wanted to get back home or out of Europe entirely."

I picked up the Zippo and clicked it open. "So you and Delores and Mags were driving down the street and ...?"

He sighed. "We were driving into Mannheim where Mags and Delores planned to stay. As we drove down Bismarckstraße, we heard squealing and shouts. A young girl ran across the road in front of us, followed by eight or nine shrieking women. She had a bag of groceries in her arms and she was dressed a little better than the ones who were chasing her. She had on a jacket, at least. As she got to the other side of the street, she tripped over something—a brick or a rock, I think, and fell to her knees. They were on her before I could brake. The car was still rolling when Mags threw open the door and jumped out."

"So maybe they did want her food?"

"What?"

"Mama. Maybe they were trying to get her groceries."

He thought for a moment. "She says that sometimes, but I don't think that was it."

I didn't think it was either, but I was trying to hope. "What then?"

"These women were from Mannheim and they claimed they knew her and Lana before the war."

"Did you talk to any of them?"

He chuckled. "Not me. Before I could get my wits together, Mags waded in, grabbed Vala, and pulled her away from some big gal who had her down on the ground and was punching her in the face. Delores was still in the car beside me, but she's screaming in German for them to get away from that kid. Vala really did look like a child that day."

"I don't understand why her neighbors were after her. Here, okay, I get it. Even though we've lived here twelve years, we're strangers. I don't like when they're mean to Mama, but I get it. We represent the enemy."

"You can't make people get along, EJ. And crazy doesn't go away just because you want it to."

I closed the lighter. "That's what it was? Crazy?"

He thought for a moment. "Sort of a forced crazy. Not liking Jews wasn't new, but the Nazis didn't like all kinds of people—gypsies, those who were mentally or physically deficient in some way, colored people, and ... uh...well, perverts." He squirmed and avoided my eyes.

I flipped the lighter lid open again. "What kind of perverts?"

He grabbed the lighter out of my hand and set it back on the table. "All kinds. Okay?"

I smirked.

"This is serious stuff, EJ. People died. Be respectful."

"I didn't mean any disrespect." My face burned.

"Talk is a powerful thing, son. It can inspire or denigrate. It allows people to share ideas, but sometimes those ideas are dangerous." He stopped. I figured he had something else to say, but he just sat there grinding his teeth so that his jaw moved in and out.

"What kinds of ideas?"

"Well, no one's perfect. It's easy to find some little truth and blow it up into a big lie. When people are going through a crisis, and they're already suspicious of one group of people or another, it's easy to believe a lie and make decisions based on it."

"Huh?"

"I don't know this for sure, but it seemed to me that these women were blaming Vala for something that happened to them."

"Mama? For the war?"

"Your mother's family seemed to be involved in some things that—well, this group of women could have been displaced because of your grandfather's activities, or maybe they really did see Vala at Auschwitz. Hard to figure. She says she was at the camp only once. Or maybe she had something they wanted. All I know is that she ended up with two black eyes and a bloody nose over the whole thing."

"Mags chased them away?"

He grinned. "You should have seen her. She elbowed her way out of that crowd with Vala in tow—Mags was a head taller than any of them—and they backed away. One old biddy finally worked up the nerve to scream something at them as they were getting into the car. She had Vala's bag of groceries and she was handing various items to the women around her. Mags pushed Vala into the back seat and took two steps toward the crowd."

I laughed. "What happened?"

"I guess she figured that Mags meant business. She stopped mid-harangue and walked off. But half a block away she turned around, held up a sorry-looking apple, and took a big bite out of it. Vala screamed something and tried to get out of the car, but Delores grabbed her and pulled her back. The others dispersed on their own once the ringleader walked away. Mags got into the car, and I hit the accelerator before the crowd could come back."

"All that over an apple? I've never even seen Mama eat an apple."

"Bad memories?"

"Maybe." I wasn't convinced. Even if that was it, why did the crowd go after Mama in the first place? If you need food, you just grab it and run. It doesn't take a bunch of people to rip a bag of groceries out of the hands of someone as small as my mother. "So what happened then?"

"Delores turned around to say something, but Vala was wailing because she'd spilled a little can of milk. I didn't understand at the time, didn't speak any German yet, and I was focused on getting us out of that part of town as quick as I could. Delores and Mags both tried to calm her down but she was distraught. Things were tight in Mannheim I guess, but we had plenty of food on the base. And I don't think anyone was actually starving by that point."

"Maybe she was just mad that someone was trying to take her stuff."

"Probably."

"So what happened then?"

"We drove around until we found a restaurant near the train station. Mags treated and we had a nice meal—stew, I think. Mostly, I remember staring across the table as that little thing inhaled her food. When she thought no one was looking, she stole bread off our plates and hid it in her jacket. She wasn't quite sixteen but she didn't look any older than twelve. Mags and Delores and I all agreed that this kid was in trouble, and before we went looking for Delores's family, we needed to see if we could help her."

"And you did?"

"Well, I never was much good at talking to girls. Vala and I had only two words in common at first—nein and sauerkraut." He winked and I laughed. "Soon as she finished her lunch, she started talking a blue streak to Mags and Delores. Delores told me that Vala needed food for her babies, that she wanted to get milk, at least, and hurry back."

"Where were we—the babies, I mean?"

"Vala was dirty and desperate so I figured she was from one of the bombed-out parts of town. Rather than just getting her some food, we decided it was better to get her little family somewhere safe. So we got in the car, and she gave directions. I expected to find the house in ruins but, it was untouched. I pulled up in front and parked. There was a courtyard on the side with a fancy wrought iron fence. It was fall and it was filled with leaves."

"Leaves?"

"You remember it?"

I shook my head. "More of a dream."

"You want me to go on? We've been out here awhile. Do you need a bathroom break?"

"No break. I want to hear it before Mama comes back down and stops us. I glanced up at the window in the kitchen door, half expecting to see Mama watching us even though I knew she was passed out in her room. "I'm okay. There's no one but you and me. I'm older now than Mama was then. Tell me."

Sonny nodded. "Almost done anyway."

"So you got to this house…"

"Mags and Delores got out of the car and headed toward the front porch, but Vala bolted and ran into the courtyard. I followed her while Mags and Delores knocked on the door."

"She won't answer if she knows it's us."

Sonny frowned at me. "What?"

"She won't come to the door. The lady in the big house."

"I'm sorry, EJ?"

"I—it's part of the dream." I felt stupid and depressed.

"Yeah, I know. Been so long, it doesn't feel real to me either."

I leaned back on the wooden chair, put my feet on the picnic table bench, and waited.

"So I followed Vala into the courtyard. She ran to a table in the far corner. When no one came to the front door, Mags and Delores followed us. You and the Mickster were in a box under the table. You got up and ran toward Vala, crying. She scooped you up into her arms and gave you a long hug before staring up at a window on the second floor. We all turned to see what she was looking at."

"Oma was watching?"

"Yes."

"She wouldn't let us in."

"Guess not."

"Grandma Arial would never do anything like that."

"Grandma Arial has your back, son. No matter what."

I took a deep breath and nodded. "Was it cold?"

"I don't think it was cold that day, but it was chilly the night before. You were wearing a blue wool coat that was too small for you. Your arms and legs were bare. The baby…Mick had an old quilt and Vala's coat. Looked like you guys had been camped out in that courtyard for a while."

I trembled. "What happened then?"

"Vala set you down and went to collect Mick. He was asleep when we first saw him, but he was hungry and started crying when she picked him up. She said something to me and Delores translated."

"What did she say?"

"These are my babies—Emo and Milo."

"Little outcasts."

"You always had Vala."

I thought about Mama, two kids before she was sixteen, struggling to take care of us during a war. "She did her best, I guess."

"I never met a more determined person or a more dedicated one. She would die for you guys."

My drunken mother was a hero after all, and my rich grandmother was a villain, like the wicked stepmother in Cinderella or Sleeping Beauty. "So what happened then?"

"You wanted Vala to pick you up again, but she was holding Mick. She tried to take your hand, but you wandered around the patio—sobbing. And then you saw me. We stared at each other for a little bit. You had snot running down your upper lip, but you stopped crying."

"Guess I was a mess."

"I held out my arms. You were scared at first, but then you smiled and came running to me. I picked you up and asked you your name. Of course, you didn't understand me and I didn't understand you, but I knew right then—and you might think I'm crazy saying this—but I knew then that you and baby Mick were the answer for me."

"The answer?"

"It's a long story, EJ, but I was at loose ends along about then. I wasn't as brave as my older brother, your Uncle John, and I wasn't as smart as your Uncle Grant. I was just sort of nothing. I had a girl-friend, but I wasn't good enough for her. She was smarter and better than me in every way there is. I wanted to be worth something—at least in my own eyes. When I saw you and your brother, well, I just knew I was supposed to find you."

"Because we were these pitiful half-orphaned kids?"

"Because you were supposed to be my sons."

I squeezed my eyes shut so he wouldn't see me tearing up. "What about Mama?"

"Well, she was a kid, too…one who was going through hell. I fell in love with you guys first—in one big burst—and then your Mama a little bit every day since."

"Okay." I swallowed a couple of times before I opened my eyes.

"Mags and Delores started gathering your stuff up and putting it in the car," he continued. "We were just about ready to leave when we heard the door to the courtyard slam. While Mags and I looked after you and Mick, Delores and Vala went back to see what was go-ing on. Frau Hess had put three suitcases and a couple of boxes out on the back step—your mother's things. We could hear Vala crying and calling for her mother, but the woman never came back to the door. After Vala calmed down, she and Delores gathered everything and loaded it into the trunk."

"Why was Oma so cold to us?"

"I've wondered that for years. I can't imagine how a woman like that raised a girl as dedicated and loving as Vala. The only thing I can fall back on was the war. It's hard when it comes to your house. Frau Hess had already lost one daughter and her husband. Maybe she was overwhelmed with grief and anger."

I wiped my nose on the back of my hand. "Maybe."

21

The Letters
April 16, 1960

AFTER SONNY LEFT to get cigarettes, I peeked into Mama's room. She lay on her side, snoring. I shuddered and glanced over my shoulder. The house was quiet. I pushed the door open wider. Not even Sonny was allowed in her room, especially when she was sleeping. The old photo album lay on her nightstand. I took a step, holding my breath lest a floorboard creak or my shadow alert her to my presence. I needn't have worried. She was out cold. Maybe she wouldn't even remember she'd been looking at the pictures when she woke up. I tucked it under my arm and hurried out. In the hall, I stole another glance. She hadn't moved.

I closed her door behind me and went upstairs. Mick was lying on his back in his bed, his head and shoulders propped on four pillows and a rolled-up quilt, plunking out a tune on his guitar.

"Is that a new one?" I asked as I tossed the picture album on my bed and flopped down beside it.

"Yep." His fingers flew over the frets and strings. "It's about Aunt Lana's lost baby."

"You've already written the lyrics?"

"In my head."

"How do you do that?"

"Dunno. It's just there."

Where did that boy come from? Mars? I felt like such a dunce around him, but I was proud to be his brother. "It's pretty. Well... sad and pretty."

"Where do you think he is?"

I picked up the picture album and flipped through it. "He's got to be somewhere. Oma probably placed him with some family who raised him as their own." I found a picture of Mama and Lana. Lana glowed with determination and passion. I would have thought her unconquerable, but obviously I would have been wrong. "Think he'd look like her?" I held up the picture.

Mick raised his head. "Hmmm. Dunno. She looks like us. Maybe he does, too."

I examined the picture again and then squinted at Mick. "Just the coloring."

"So look for another blond kid?"

"I guess that narrows it down a little. He would be twenty now. I wonder if he's looking for us?"

"If Oma gave him away, why would he? He might not know he's adopted. Might not know we exist. Might not even know his name is Wolf."

"If his name is Wolf," I said.

Mick strummed his guitar loudly, a final flourish, and set it on the floor between our beds. "If..."

"Just waiting for Mama to get drunk enough to tell us isn't going to cut it with me anymore."

"What other choice do we have, EJ? Besides, maybe Wolf is happy wherever he is. Maybe he wouldn't want to know about all the Hess family craziness. Knowing your grandparents were Nazis is a burden I wouldn't wish on anyone."

It was the first time Mick had ever said how he felt about our German family. "Kids in the neighborhood giving you a hard time?"

"Nothing I can't handle. It's not usually the kids. Their parents can be pushy sometimes. The other day, Billy Ray Parker's mom wanted to know if I kissed the ground when I got off the boat."

"Did you tell her you were two?"

"Naw. I said, 'Sure.' Made her day."

"How do you do that?"

"What?"

"Keep your temper. I can't keep my mouth shut. People ask if Mama keeps Jewish ashes as keepsakes and I want to go after them. Grandma Arial's old lady friends can't let it go sometimes, and I end up being just as rude as they are. And then Grandma is all embarrassed and upset."

Mick stared out the window. "It doesn't usually matter to me, but once in a while, it hurts."

"It makes me want to punch someone."

"Who?"

"That's what's so stupid. Who do I hit? Grandma's biddy friends? I'm not that big of a creep."

Mick laughed. "You punch old lady Spencer and they'll say we have Hitler's ashes in our basement."

"Good trick, since we don't have a basement."

"I think it would be scarier if we kept the old snot in a closet," he sputtered.

"Maybe that's what was in that old suitcase Mama kept in her closet."

"The old brown one?"

"When I had the measles, I tried seven ways to Sunday to get that thing open—even tried a butter knife. When that didn't work, I went through every shelf, drawer, box, and closet looking for a key. I even dumped out her purse. If Hitler's ashes are in our house, I'm betting on that old suitcase."

"No ashes, just papers."

I sat up straighter. "What?"

"Letters and big folders."

"How the heck do you know that?

"I was bored one day and picked the lock."

I grabbed one of my pillows and threw it at him. "You picked a lock and didn't tell me?"

He ducked and the pillow slid off the bed into the space between his bed and the wall. "It wasn't that hard, and I didn't know you wanted to see what was in it."

I smacked myself on the forehead with the heel of my hand. "I nearly stabbed myself to death with a butter knife and you say it wasn't hard?"

"I used one of Mama's bobby pins."

"A bobby pin opened it?"

"I had to mess with it a little, but yeah."

"Is it still in her closet?"

"I don't know."

"Let's go check."

"What if Sonny comes back?"

"We'll just say we were curious and that would be the truth."

"What if Mama wakes up?"

I sighed. "She won't."

We crept out of our room and galloped down the stairs like a couple of elephants. Just to be sure, I peeked at Mama again.

Mick whispered. "Is she still asleep?"

I nodded. My heart beat faster while Mick retrieved the suitcase. I grunted as I hefted it up onto one shoulder.

He closed Mama's door. "So now I need a bobby pin."

"Where are you going to get one?" I hissed as I toted the suitcase up the stairs. "Don't go back and wake her up."

"Shush! I'll get one out of the bathroom in the hall."

"Shush, yourself." I set the suitcase down on the top landing and dragged it behind me, glad that the carpeting muffled the sound. I struggled to get it up on the bed.

Mick stuck his head in the door.

"You found a bobby pin?"

He crossed his eyes and grinned.

"Mick! This is serious stuff." I tried not to start laughing again. "Who knows what's in that thing?"

He stepped inside the room and closed the door. "I told you. Paper."

"Feels like gold doubloons."

"What do you mean?"

"Try lifting it. I about killed myself getting it up on the bed."

Mick struggled with the bag and let it fall back onto the coverlet. "What in the world? There wasn't that much stuff in it before."

"Dig out that bobby pin."

Mick pulled the pin out of his own hair, broke one leg off it, and got to work.

"Just when did you open it?"

"I don't remember, exactly." He focused on the lock. "A few years ago."

"What got you interested?"

"Mama was so upset about that strange fellow at Danny and Teresa's wedding. He was weird, but didn't seem like that bad of a guy."

"You mean Oskar Schreiner?"

Mick looked up at me. "I didn't remember his name, just that he kept knocking on the door, and Mama and I would sit inside the house, pretending not to be home." There was a tiny click. "There ya go." He flipped back the latches and opened the suitcase.

I leaned forward. "Wow."

"Did Mama put all that in there?" Mick reached inside and picked up one of the hundreds of manila envelopes, folders, and bundled letters. "What do you think this is?"

"Breadcrumbs, I hope." I picked up a yellowed piece of newspaper. "Wasn't this in the photo album the last time we looked?"

Mick looked up. "Maybe."

I scanned it. "I couldn't read German that well back then. Wonder why she moved it to this box?"

"Maybe she was organizing things. What's it say, now that you can read it?"

"It's an article from *Völkischer Beobachter*. Looks like it's from August, 1940."

"EJ, what's it say?"

Well-known Doctor Murdered in Munich. Doctor Hermann Freitag's body was found on Schellingstrasse on Tuesday morning. He'd been shot multiple times. Dr. Freitag's work with the state spanned 18 years and his colleagues thought highly of him. He has been a member of the Nazi Party since 1933 and worked with esteemed Dr. Ernst Rüdin in the field of racial hygiene. Police believe that Dr. Freitag's murderer was a Jew.

"Of course, they'd say that," Mick said. "Why would Mama have that particular clipping?"

"No idea."

Mick thumbed through several sheets of typewritten paper in the folder he was holding. "There's so much."

"Are they all in German?"

"At least the ones on top. Where do you think it all came from, EJ?"

I picked up a bundle of letters tied together with ribbon. "They're old. Keepsakes?"

"What are you going to do?"

"Read them."

"All of them?"

I pocketed one bundle and picked up another. "Not all today. We have that thing at the Windshift Inn this evening."

"But some of them?"

"Why do you care?"

"Because I want to read them with you."

I picked out a fat manila envelope and handed it to Mick. "It's a deal."

Untying the ribbon that held the packet together, I picked a single letter to start. I examined the envelope. It was addressed to my aunt Lana. I closed my eyes and took deep breaths. Aunt Lana! Where did this letter come from? I was sure I'd never seen it when I was looking through the boxes and suitcases in the closet before. Why was Mama collecting all this stuff? Was she looking for answers, too?

I glanced at Mick. He'd already opened his envelope. It contained piles of old pictures. He'd dumped them on his bed and was examining them one by one.

I held the envelope in the light streaming from our bedroom window. It was stained with fingerprints and what looked like drops of tea or coffee. Careful not to tear it, I opened the flap and took out a thin sheet of paper. The handwriting was bold with very little slant and the letters had sharp angles. It was short and to the point as if the writer was very sure of himself and very busy.

April 2, 1940

My lovely Lana,

I received your note and I am pleased that you are doing well. That the child is kicking so vigorously tells me it must be a boy. Good. Do as the midwives tell you. Eat well and take long walks. It won't be long before you will deliver a beautiful baby for the Reich.

I am sorry that I cannot visit you. I know that you are upset. I will arrange for some oranges to be sent to you with this letter. Please be patient. I have the weight of the Reich on my shoulders. There are millions of Jews living in our lands. They are reproducing at an alarming rate, working against us, taking bigger and bigger roles in our culture, and despoiling our race. Their goals are nefarious and we must act now. The Führer has a strategy and he has begun the arduous task of implementing it. I am proud to tell you that I personally have a most important role. What I do will ensure a Germany that is respected and feared the world over.

I know that you are concerned about how my wife and family will take my affection for you. I admit it is a problem that we will have to face eventually. I never thought simply doing my part to build a stronger more beautiful Aryan race would lead to this deep passion between us. You are young. That you should love me is a reward for my dedication to the most important tasks of my generation. I know someday we will find more time to be together as proper lovers rather than the short liaisons we have enjoyed up until now. Until then, I hold you in my heart with the same passion I felt when I first kissed you.

R

I refolded the letter and stuffed it back inside its envelope. I felt sick at my stomach. *So this was my cousin Wolf's father?*

Mick looked up. "What did it say?"

"My German isn't as good as I thought," I lied. "And the hand-writing isn't easy to read, but basically it's a letter the father of our Aunt Lana's baby wrote to her explaining why he was too busy to come see her."

"Her husband was a soldier?"

"Everyone who was healthy was a soldier."

"Don't' be so hard on him, EJ. People had to be away from their sweethearts in those days. Soldiers all around the world missed important family events."

"They weren't married."

"Oh." Mick laid down the picture he'd been examining. "There were all kinds of wartime friendships…"

"I think it was something else. It's like they deliberately had a baby for Germany. Like it was patriotic or something."

"You don't think he loved her?"

"Hard to tell. It's a friendly letter, but he was never going to marry her."

"You don't know that. Maybe he would have."

"He was already married."

I couldn't tell if Mick was shocked or just absorbing what it all meant. "So Lana's baby was a bastard?"

It was my turn to be shocked. "I guess so. Technically. But it sounds like everyone thought this was a good thing."

Mick shrugged. "Different countries do it differently maybe."

"Maybe."

"So was she upset, I wonder?"

"I think she had to be, Mick. The way the letter is worded sounds like he was trying to keep her calm until the baby was born. I bet he had no interest in her beyond that."

"Poor Aunt Lana."

"Yeah." I picked up another packet of letters written in different hands. It was embarrassing to read someone else's private thoughts, but I had no intention of putting this treasure trove of information back in the closet.

"What should we do with this stuff? Mama's obviously collecting it all for a reason." Mick held up a faded cartoon showing a muscular Aryan man throwing a Jew off a cliff. It was captioned *Revenge*. "She'll notice if it isn't there eventually."

I evaluated what we had picked out of the suitcase so far. It was a fraction of what Mama had stowed away. "I think we should take as much as we can now and put the rest back."

"We can't keep it in here. She cleans every inch of this house."

I thought for a minute. "The tree house."

"If we are going to put something out there, we better do it before she wakes up and while Sonny's gone," Mick said.

I poked through the suitcase and picked out a couple of manila envelopes and three more letter packets. "Anything I should see in those pictures?" I pointed to Mick's pile of curled and yellowing photos on the bed.

"Mostly strangers. Some are labeled with a name on the back and a location. Looks like most were taken in Mannheim. I think they were taken by a roving photographer because they all have a business name engraved on them."

"Pack them up and I'll take them out to the tree if you can help me get the suitcase back into Mama's closet."

"I can get the suitcase down the stairs by myself," Mick said. "It's almost four o'clock. When Sonny gets here, we'll be stepping all over each other getting ready, so I'll take the bathroom first."

I stripped the case off my pillow and filled it with the materials I'd picked out. Throwing it over my shoulder like a giant hobo's bundle, I slunk down the stairs. At Mama's door, I paused to check on her. She'd rolled over on her side facing away from the door, but she was still snoring.

* * *

As I climbed into the tree house, I felt uncomfortable, like I was being watched. Maybe it was because I'd raided Mama's closet and I felt guilty. Still.

In the tree house, I packed everything into the chest under Grandma Arial's quilt to protect it from the weather. I was putting everything else back on top of the quilt when I heard Sonny's old pickup rattle into the driveway. I inhaled the scent of wood and leaves and fresh air. I wasn't ready to go back to the house to get ready for the party at Myrtle and Jerry Kline's. I wanted a few minutes to unwind, to think about what Mama and Sonny had told us, and to figure out what it all meant.

I peered out the window. Sonny had pulled all the way down the drive and was carrying bags of groceries through the back porch. A movement just beyond him caught my eye. Someone in Mrs. Vilani's garden? A glimpse of dark hair and then a flash as the afternoon sun hit someone's glasses. Billy Ray Parker. What was he up to? Keeping an eye on Mama? She was nice to him one time, and now he was her bodyguard? Crazy kid.

I turned back toward the warehouse and Cold Creek Drive. I could barely see Grandma Arial's duplex across the street. I knew she was getting ready for the walk to the Windshift Inn.

I turned to my left. Balboa's was already hopping. The parking lot was filled with cars. Guys in leather jackets and slicked-back hair were flirting with girls in full skirts and flats. As much as that place intrigued me and I wanted to get to know a girl, I wasn't yet ready to put my heart on the line in front of the whole high school social set. I'd wait until—

Who was that? A brand-new orange Impala was parked on the street facing up the hill toward me. It caught my eye because no one I knew drove a fancy car like that—and because a strange man sat in it, unmoving as a statue.

We knew our neighbors. A stranger was cause for curiosity, if not alarm. Maybe I was overreacting. Maybe it was someone's long lost uncle. I peeked through the slats. The car was gone.

I was relieved but still not ready to go back to the house and get ready for the party. I nudged the trunk with my toe. Maybe one more letter. Just one.

I opened the trunk and unpacked it. Rummaging through the documents, I pulled out the first letter I found. It was from my great-aunt Margit in Stuttgart to my Oma in Mannheim. Since I'd never met either of them and both were dead, I almost tossed the letter back into the trunk. Then I thought about Oma, a cold woman who refused shelter to children. I knew so little about her. Perhaps I would find a clue in this note that would help me understand why.

Oma must have used a letter opener. I visualized her—efficient, bored, distant. The letter itself was on monogrammed stationary dated May 12, 1945.

My dear sister Anna,

I write you with bad news. My darling Siegfried has been killed. My heart is forever broken. He was a guard at Dachau on April 29 when the Americans took over the camp. They were hateful, vindictive, and bloodthirsty. They began killing German guards just because they were at their stations doing what they were supposed to do. A boy who was there told me that Siggie had already laid down his rifle and surrendered. He was sitting in a jeep when an American officer shot him. He was still alive, crying out in pain, and calling for me when another bit of American filth crawled into the vehicle and murdered him.

I hope the men who hurt my baby die in the most painful ways possible. I want their mothers to hurt like I do. I will hate them through all eternity.

I apologize to you, Anna. I had no idea how it was for you when Lana died. When I tried to talk you out of your despair, I didn't understand such unending excruciating pain. I will not live under the boots of the criminals and murderers who have conquered our beloved Germany.

Goodbye forever,

Margit

Great aunt Margit's rage and sorrow was scorching. I'd read articles and seen pictures of Dachau taken by the American soldiers who had liberated it. Those stories focused on the starving and sick inmates—and on the bodies that filled rail cars and ditches and huts. I'd never thought about the fate of the guards—or that I might be related to one. My breathing became faster and more shallow. I felt sick at my stomach and sweaty. And then, I cried. I cried until my head ached and my eyes swelled. I cried for the victims of Dachau and for my cousin Siggie who did what German boys of his age were told to do—and then for my great-aunt who'd been run over by a train the same day she posted the letter to Oma. Finally, no more tears came. Spent, I lay on the floor of the tree house, until my strength returned. And then I got up and went home to get ready for a party.

22

The Park
April 16, 1960

I HURRIED UP the hill, my heart pounding. Mick was ahead of me.

"EJ, why are you rushing?" Grandma Arial panted as she struggled to keep up with us.

"Let them run," Mama said. "All they do is watch television or study. They are like long-legged Apaldoosel ponies. They need exercise."

"Yes, but can't the Apaldoosel ponies exercise slower?"

"Oh, Arial. You are funny!"

I stopped and waited for Mama and Grandma Arial to catch up. My mother's laugh made me laugh too. "Apaloosa, Mama. They are called Apaloosa horses."

"I thought I had it right. Your grandmother said it too."

Grandma Arial winked at me. "I like Apaldoosels better."

"What?" Mama frowned for a moment and then giggled. "Oh. Arial is even funnier than I thought."

"Why are we going to the Windshift Inn today?" I adjusted my pace so Mama and Grandma Arial didn't have to walk so fast.

"Danny and Teresa Kline are visiting, EJ," Grandma Arial said. "They are bringing their new baby. The McDougals will be there too and the Reynoldses."

"I'm excited about little Margaret Kline," Mama said. "I love babies."

"Is Delores bringing her niece, too?" I tried to sound nonchalant but Mama and Grandma Arial exchanged glances. Grandma smiled. Mama didn't.

"She didn't say when she phoned, and I didn't think to ask," Grandma Arial said.

"You like Rosa so much?" Mama's cheeks were red.

"I'm eighteen. I like pretty girls, but I'm scared of them, too."

"Ist fein mit me." Mama's linguistic confusion deepened when she was flustered.

"She's in college now. Pre-med."

"I know this girl is smart."

Her tone irritated me. "I want to be a doctor, too. We have a lot in common."

"I'm going to catch up with Mick." Grandma Arial touched Mama's shoulder before leaving us.

"Let's go through the park." Mama chewed her lower lip. "There's a bench and we can talk."

I shrugged. "Okay." One minute she was joking about Apaldoosels and the next she was upset.

"I don't want to make you unhappy, Emo, but we live in a terrible world." Her jaw was set and her lips were tight. "Maybe another girl would be better for you."

"Why?"

"Because we are German."

"Rosa is German, too. She was born in Mannheim."

"Rosa is Jewish."

I swallowed, visualizing the ugly cartoon Mick and I had found that afternoon. "So is Delores, and you've been friends for years. Is it because of all the stuff that went on during the war? Germans not liking Jews and all?"

"Of course it is!" Mama's voice rose to a loud whisper. "Do you have any idea how it was?"

"You've never told me anything. All I know is what I read."

Tears filled Mama's eyes.

"I'm sorry, Mama. I didn't mean to yell at you, but you say I can't be friends with Rosa and won't tell me why."

"People died. Many people died. For no reason than we didn't want them around. Do you understand, Emo? Rosa's family was killed because they were Jews. People who were married to these people had a very bad time, too. Do you think she doesn't know what we did?"

I opened my mouth, but nothing came out.

"You are good boy, Emo. You should not be punished for what Germany did, but you will be. And Milo, too." She put both hands over her face. "You will be, because of me."

I couldn't imagine what Mama could have done, but I was sure now that something bad had driven her to America and her precious Bordeaux.

"It's different here, Mama. People don't hate Jews here."

She grabbed my arm. "You are young. Differences matter here as much as they did in Mannheim twenty years ago. It is dangerous to ignore the rules."

I winced and tried to pull away from her grip. "Mama, you're hurting me."

"Bad men are everywhere. You have to understand."

"Mama!

"You think I'm crazy and maybe I am. But if you never listen to anything I tell you, you must hear now."

"I'm listening."

She spoke German. "That girl has had more sorrow in her life than anyone deserves, because of us, because of me."

"You can't take the blame for that. You were young like I am now. It was Hitler, not you."

"Yes, it was Hitler." She released my arm and the fury in her eyes burned out. "But Hitler had plenty of help."

I stepped back, rubbing my arm. "Rosa doesn't blame you. Neither does Delores."

"Delores thinks she can fix things. She and Shirley don't understand accepting what is. They don't stop until things are right." She rubbed her eyes with the back of her hand. "No, they don't blame me, but they should. And they will someday."

"Mama ..."

"You must obey me, Emo. Accept that I know better than you for now."

"I don't know what you want exactly. It's not like Rosa is a girlfriend. I like her, of course, but we live in different states. I've only seen her two or three times. She's older than me." I felt sick inside, like I was betraying Rosa even though what I was saying was perfectly true.

Mama frowned.

"What?" I threw up my hands and my voice was louder than I intended. "What do you want?"

"Leave Rosa alone." Her English returned.

I thought this whole upset was silly. "Okay," I grunted.

"You must, Emo."

"Okay!"

"Don't yell at me, Emo. Emo? Emo?"

I stormed off through the park. Her voice got higher and shriller the further away I got.

I bent over, hands on my knees taking deep breaths to calm myself. Even though I could barely hear my mother calling me, her voice irritated me. The whole situation was ridiculous. It wasn't like I was in love with Rosa after all. Of course, Rosa wasn't the issue anyway. Mama wanted to control me, and I wasn't going to put up with it anymore. The stupid war was over, and it had nothing to do with me anyway. If they were so mixed up and hateful back then, so be it. I didn't have to go down that route. I could think for myself.

"Something chasing you, EJ Logan?"

I spun around, searching for the owner of that voice.

"I'm over here. See me?"

"No, who are you?"

"It's Annie, EJ. Annie Jones."

To the left, I glimpsed her sitting on a park bench about twenty yards away. "Hello! What are you doing out here?" I smiled and waved.

She held her arm across her forehead and squinted into the sun. "Thinking. What about you?"

I started to lie and tell her that I was jogging, but the truth popped out instead. "I'm fighting with my mother."

"Aren't we all?" She patted the bench beside her. "Want to tell me about it?"

She had blossomed since the ninth grade. Soft caramel waves replaced her ponytail, and the thin, black sweater she wore tucked into a long, black skirt showed off her new curves. Instead of a necklace, she'd knotted a small black scarf loosely around her throat. All that blackness, with a touch of bright red on her lips, made me think of a fortuneteller—or a vampire.

Trying to keep my appreciation for her new exotic look under control so that I didn't say or do something stupid, I sat on the bench beside her. "Tell you about what?"

"Why are you fighting with your mom?"

"I love her and all, but she makes me mad sometimes."

"My dad thinks she's sexy. Oh, I'm sorry. I didn't mean to embarrass you."

"Lots of people have told me things like that, but it's still weird."

"She's different from your everyday Cold Creek housewife."

I shrugged and sat down beside her.

"She's odd here," Anne said, "but she'd probably fit right in back in Germany."

"I don't know about that. She doesn't fit there either, I think."

"For that matter, I don't know anyone who fits in, really. I don't. You don't...what's the matter with you? Am I mussed or something?"

I had been staring at her mouth. I ducked my chin, embarrassed. "I just...I like your outfit."

"Do you?"

Even though I wanted to blink, I returned her gaze until she looked away. "Are you still dating Butch Murphy?" It slipped out and I wanted to call back the words as soon as I heard them.

She cocked her head. "You've been talking to Billy Ray, haven't you?"

"He was upset."

"Butch is a nice boy."

"I didn't say he wasn't."

"He's older than me and he has a car."

His dad was red-faced and warty and I figured Butch would be just like him one day. "Is that important?"

"That's hardly the point."

"Billy Ray thought you were his girl." It came out sounding like an accusation.

Her eyes were sad. "I'm not anyone's girl."

"Oh?"

"You and Billy Ray jumped to some pretty big conclusions just because I went to Balboa's with Butch."

"I didn't…" I started to lie again, but like before, the truth slipped out instead. "Billy Ray was mad because he wanted to take you to the hop."

"He never asked me."

"He was too nervous."

She sighed. "He's only known me since the first grade."

"So if he asked you now, you'd go with him?"

"Not in a million years. Did you see what he did to Butch's car?"

"No, but I heard."

"It was a mess. Gonna cost a lot of money. Whatever possessed him to do such a thing?"

"I don't know. Guess it made sense to him. He told me that you told him the two of you were going to get married and have kids and a dog named Orson."

"What?" She almost smiled. "I don't remember that. We must have been really little. I do remember Orson though. He was my Uncle Joe's dog when I was four."

"When he saw you on a date with Butch, it tore him up. He really does think you'll marry him when you're twenty."

"I'm not dating Butch. He's my cousin and he's teaching me to drive. *Was* teaching me how to drive. And I'm not going to marry Billy Ray—ever."

Dreams of Annie being my girl came rushing back. "Why not Billy Ray?"

"Oh I love him to pieces and all, but Billy Ray's crazy. Haven't you noticed?"

I supposed shooting up a car was a little crazy. "I never noticed it until the other night."

"He has reason to be, of course, but I don't see him being able to get past it. Don't you remember when we were in second grade and he broke his leg?"

I flashed to Billy Ray coming to school on crutches. "He fell out of a hay loft or something?"

"He *jumped* out of a hay loft at his grandfather's farm. He tied his mother's apron around his neck and his folks told people he thought he could fly like Superman."

"That's right...silly kid." I laughed.

She frowned. "It wasn't true. He was mad because they made him feed the hogs. He was trying to impale himself on a picket fence, which had to be a hundred feet away. He thought the apron would help him glide over to it."

"What?" I was horrified at the thought.

"He fell straight down and broke his leg in several places. I heard it snap, but it seemed like ages before I heard his scream."

"You were there?"

"I was at home, but sometimes I see and hear things when I'm daydreaming."

"Ah."

"Don't look at me that way, EJ Logan."

"What way?"

"Like you think I'm the crazy one."

"I would never think that."

"What do you think, then?"

"That you are the most beautiful girl I ever saw."

Her eyes widened and she flushed. "I wasn't...uh..."

"I'm sorry. I didn't mean to say that...no I meant it, I just..." I turned away to hide my quivering Adam's apple and watery eyes. Of all the stupid things I'd done in my life, this was the worst.

"No, EJ. Don't be upset." She put her hand on mine. "It was a lovely thing to say. No one's ever said anything like that to me. Ever."

"They say it about you all the time," I mumbled.

She squeezed my hand until I looked up at her. "Not to my face."

I was still uncomfortable, but I was beginning to feel like the ground wasn't going to open up underneath me. "I don't seem to be able to talk like a normal human being around you."

"That's because neither of us are normal."

I liked that not being normal was an advantage for a change.

She released my hand. "What were we talking about before we got lost?"

I thought for a moment. "You were saying how you saw things sometimes. Things that you couldn't possibly know. I was going to tell you that I dream things the same way. And I can't tell if I'm remembering something or making it up."

"That sounds scary, too."

"When you see things it scares you?"

"Sometimes. I once saw that everyone in our math class would grow old, but Billy Ray would always be young. I don't even know what that means."

"Were you asleep?"

"No, I was…well, I have a place where I go to be alone and I was sitting there thinking, and that's what came to mind."

"I dream about crying babies and little ghost girls sometimes." I'd never told anyone about my dreams—except Mick and Sonny.

"Do they ever come true?"

There was an edge to her voice that made me shiver. "Do your visions come true?"

"I don't know exactly," she said. "It's a matter of interpretation usually, but close enough to give me the heebie-jeebies."

"My dreams are confusing. I don't think they are about what's happening now or in the future."

She nodded as if she understood. "I once saw a car pass us on the highway, and I thought, 'That guy's gonna lose his bumper.'"

"Did he?"

"Well, it fell off." She laughed. "But he stopped right away and loaded it into the backseat. It wasn't lost."

"That's picky."

"That's how it goes. Things happen that can be interpreted as coming true if you think about it long enough. I sometimes wonder if that counts."

"Was the bumper loose or sagging or something?"

"Not that I noticed. It's just that there was something about the car itself. I know it doesn't make sense. All kinds of things pop into my head that don't make sense though. Remember when we all got the measles in Mrs. Wiggins's class?"

"Miserable day."

"Remember when I thought you put gum in my hair?"

"I'd never put gum in your hair. It's too pretty…I'm sorry."

"Will you stop?" She rolled her eyes. "You aren't insulting me when you say I'm pretty."

"I'm sorry."

We both laughed.

"I'm a dolt."

"I'm trying to tell you something."

"Okay." I suppressed my need to apologize this time.

"That morning when you got sick, I thought you got sick so you could go home, and that there was an important reason you should be home."

"I didn't fake getting sick."

"I know that, silly, but I was absolutely sure that the universe meant for you to be at your house with your mom that day. Isn't that weird?"

I thought about the mysterious strangers in our house and at Grandma Arial's. What would have happened if I hadn't been there? What if John Sarris had hurt Mama? Maybe Annie was on to something.

"Are you okay?"

I avoided her eyes. "I was thinking about some things that happened that day."

"Was I right?"

"In some ways. As you say, it's easy to make it seem true. It's almost like I want it to be, because then there's some order…"

The wind rattled the leaves around us, and it seemed like the park was alive. I wanted to touch her, but I couldn't make myself reach for her hand as naturally as she had for mine. "Today I found out my cousin died in the war." It was almost a whisper at first. My shyness evaporated and I put my arm around her."

She leaned her head against my shoulder. "Did you know him?"

I stroked her hair. "No."

"Lots of bad things happened in that war. In fact, I think the universe is full of awful things waiting to happen. If there is a God, He is either helpless in the face of evil or He lets it happen. That scares me."

That thought scared me, too. "Have you ever told anyone about this theory? Besides me?"

She nodded. "My dad thinks I'm too big for my britches, questioning God and all. He told me he would rather believe and be wrong than take a chance on not believing. My mother doesn't want to talk about it at all."

I imagined that Annie's folks didn't want to deal with their daughter's need to explain what was happening around her—like my mother's refusal to talk about Germany. I was old enough to know it hurt her, but not old enough or smart enough to put the pieces together myself. It was all so ugly. I held Annie in silence until the wind rattled the trees again and we both startled out of our thoughts.

She pulled away from my embrace. "They'll be looking for me."

"Me too." I figured I'd made Mama mad enough and scared enough now. She'd only wait so long before sending Sonny after me.

Annie stood up.

"Thank you. I bent down and grazed her forehead with my lips. I don't expect anyone to understand, but being able to say things out loud helps."

"If you need to talk again, call me."

"I will. I have a place where it's quiet and private."

She patted my shoulder and wandered down the path. In the distance, under the swaying branches of the trees and dressed all in black, she looked like a crow.

Mama was sitting at the bus stop across the street when I came out of the park. The sun was beginning to set, and there was a chill in the air. I waved, but she was absorbed with something in her lap and didn't see me until I was only a few feet away.

"Emo!" She looked up at me and smiled. "Look what found me."

A dirty little dog lay in her lap, enjoying her adoration.

"He's a mutt, Mama, a cute one, but a mutt all the same." I sat down beside her and held out my hand. The scrawny dog sniffed my fingers and then relaxed back onto the sweater Mama had wrapped around him.

"Where did he come from?"

"Back there." She gestured to the creek behind her. It was strewn with tires, rusty springs, and bits of soggy Sears Roebuck catalogs. A wooden bridge needing repair and several coats of paint arced across it.

I rolled my eyes. "The train goes through there twice a day. It's a wonder this little guy survived. He must be street smart."

"Ja, he's a sweet dog." She massaged his back.

I wrinkled my nose. "Old sweety there needs a bath."

"Ja, he needs a bath and sausages and a nice warm bed. Looks like he's been on his own for a while."

"Sonny will tease you."

"Sonny loves lost little things as much as I do."

I laughed. "Yes, that's the both of you. Aren't we invited to dinner at The Windshift Inn? And didn't our little argument make us late? What will you do with this fellow while we eat?"

"I like sweety dog. Maybe I'll call him that. Wait. Not sweets. Maybe Schatzi. That sounds better. It reminds me of the beautiful dogs we used to walk along the Neckar." The scruffy pooch jumped out of her lap and she stood up. "See? Schatzi likes his new name."

I didn't know how she figured that. Schatzi was a tough, homeless terrier who would stay as long as the food was plentiful and to his liking and then take off on new adventures when he got bored. Mama had taken in three pets before him. She still had a cat that came and went as it pleased. Years ago, Mama found a big old hound dog that Mick adored, but it was run over by a car. Not long after that, we had a baby goat sleeping on our back porch until the neighbors forcefully encouraged Mama to give it to the Parkers, who had a farm and other goats. Grandma Arial insisted that Mama's goat was probably an escapee from the farm in the first place, but Mama said her little Gunner was an exceptional specimen and had much finer goat qualities than the common ones the Parkers kept.

"Myrtle won't let him in the inn until he's cleaned up and shows he has house manners."

"My Schatzi is polite baby, aren't you?"

Schatzi, like any number of other creatures, gazed at Mama with utter devotion and at that moment, I swear he was the spitting image of Billy Ray Parker.

I helped Mama on with her sweater. The evening air was cold and Mama didn't seem to mind the stink of stray dog on it.

"Everyone else went on ahead, but you waited for me," I said as we started up the hill.

"Ja." She looked behind her to make sure Schatzi was following us.

"Even though we had a fight."

"You came back to me even though we fight."

We followed the sidewalk to the stop sign and then walked along the berm of the road. The sky was a brilliant pink.

"I love you, Mama."

She put her arm around me. "You are my special boy, Emo."

23
The Party
April 16, 1960

EVERYONE ELSE INVITED to Myrtle's get-together had already arrived. Danny and Teresa sat in the parlor showing off their new daughter. Sonny and Tommy and Delores stood together in the hallway, talking and sipping Jerry Kline's homemade wine. Grandma Arial was busy setting the fancy new table in the dining room. Shirley and Jack Reynolds were in the kitchen chatting with Myrtle as she put the final touches on our dinner. Mick sat at the parlor piano and played *Für Elise* softly while everyone took turns meeting little Margaret Kline. Uncle Grant, as usual, sat by himself and didn't say much.

We had no sooner set foot in the door than Mama rushed into the parlor and made a big fuss over the baby. She'd brought a present wrapped in pink tissue paper, and she proudly presented it to Teresa. "Is for this precious one," she said.

When she opened the package and unfolded an elaborate satin baby dress, Teresa teared up. "Oh Vala, this is beautiful and so delicate."

"Is to remember me and Sonny and the boys."

Teresa hugged Mama and then Sonny. "Thank you, Vala. Danny and I will treasure it."

Mama's smile was radiant. Sonny avoided looking at anyone by staring at his shoes. The whole thing made me uncomfortable. Was Teresa and Sonny's friendship ancient history that everyone but Mama knew about?

Soon I'd had enough of babies and secrets, so I decided to go sit on the front porch. The glider was outside the parlor window. I could enjoy Mick's music, but the voices were muffled enough that I could ignore them. Schatzi lay on the porch. I made kissing sounds and his ears perked up. "C'mon, boy. C'mon!" The little dog turned to look out into the trees. He was already Mama's dog. I closed my eyes and leaned back in the swing. A breeze cooled my face.

Where did Mama get the dress she gave little Margaret? It had probably been white when new, but it had aged to a light watery beige. With embroidery on the sleeves and around the hem, the tiny garment seemed too fancy for an everyday baby outfit. Mama didn't do hand stitching and she hated shopping, so I figured she must have ordered it or had Sonny pick it up at some second-hand store.

Then it struck me. It was from Mama's box of old baby clothes. Was it her christening gown? Or Lana's? Or Wolf's? She had obviously put some thought into this gift, but why not show it to Mick and me first? Didn't she think it would interest us? Why was everything so hush-hush? Okay. So my grandfather was a Nazi and my grandmother was a snobby anti-Semite, and my aunt was murdered because she was depressed, and my cousin Wolf was lost somewhere in Europe. All very bad things. But I managed to learn about them without turning against my mother. What could she possibly be afraid of at this late date?

Something moved in the darkness. Schatzi growled. I sighed.

"Don't think I can't see you out there, Billy Ray."

Billy Ray stepped out from behind the bushes. "How long have you known I was here?"

"I first saw you this afternoon when you were hiding in Mrs. Vilani's garden."

"Why didn't you say anything before?" He came closer.

"Why were you following us?"

"Just wanted to be around your family."

"What about Annie?"

"Annie's mad at me over the Butch thing. Besides, I think your mom needs me more."

Irritated, I fought to keep my voice low. "You think that even with Sonny and Uncle Grant and Grandma Arial and Mick and me, she isn't safe?"

Billy Ray hung his head. "I just want to be around her."

"You can visit us from time to time, but you have your own family. They want you to be with them."

"They don't understand me."

"Does anyone understand anyone else?"

"Don't be mad, EJ. I just don't know what to do with myself. Everyone's talking about graduation and what they plan on doing next. Even Annie says she's going to Ohio State. I can't visualize myself being anywhere but Cold Creek, and I don't see myself studying any more after high school. It's upsetting."

I understood feeling lost, but what that had to do with his sudden obsession with my mother eluded me. "There are all kinds of things you can do here in Cold Creek. Talk with my Uncle Grant. I'm sure he'd give you a job at Logan Foods."

"No offense, but I'm not cut out for industry. I don't like routine. You'll know I've lost all hope if I ever take a job like that."

"What about coaching? You enjoyed football and basketball."

Billy Ray sighed. "Not really. My dad made me participate. He loves that stuff, and he's good friends with Coach Littleton."

I was stuck. "What do you want?"

"I want to be Superman," he said with a straight face. "I want to right wrongs."

"How about being a cop?"

He seemed uncomfortable with that thought, too. "Routine again," he said after a minute.

"Lawyers right wrongs."

"I'm done with school. I have to force myself to go every day. I'd drop out now, but my dad would kill me. I always imagined Sugar Maple Drive and Annie and Orson. I never thought about how to make that happen, or how to support us all if it did. Of course, now that Annie hates me, there's nothing except your mom."

"Mama's fine. What do you think you can do for her?"

"Save her!"

I wanted to scream with frustration, but I could see he was serious. "From what, Billy Ray? From what?"

He shrugged.

Myrtle came to the door. "Dinner's ready, EJ."

"Okay."

"Who's out there with you?"

"It's me, Mrs. Kline. Billy Ray Parker."

"Hello, Billy Ray. Would you like to join us?"

I knew he really did want to, but he shook his head. "Sorry, Mrs. K. My mother's expecting me."

"Maybe next time then."

"Yes, ma'am. Thank you."

I watched Billy Ray walk away, his shoulders slumped, his head down. While I appreciated the world's need for supermen, adventure was in short supply in Cold Creek. What would happen to him when he realized that?

* * *

After dessert, Danny took little Margaret upstairs, and Delores and Tommy began clearing the dishes. Everyone else congregated in the parlor again. Mama swayed against Sonny, dreamily sipping her wine. He stood behind her, his arms around her waist.

Mick grabbed the piano bench and Myrtle joined him. Despite the many decades difference in their ages, music connected them in a special way.

Uncle Grant made noises about leaving, but Jerry insisted he stay a little longer. "Come on, old man. Forgot how to party?"

Everyone laughed and teased Uncle Grant.

"You have the van, Grant," Grandma Arial said. "I'm getting too old to huff down that hill after sundown. You can't leave until I leave, and I'm not leaving just yet."

Everyone laughed, even Uncle Grant. He chose the window seat and I sat down on the floor in front of him.

"Still feels like home," Shirley said as she eased herself onto the couch and propped her crutches against the end table. "I wasn't really a kid when I first came here, but it feels like my life began here."

Jack sat down beside her and took her hand.

I felt rather than heard Uncle Grant's sigh. At first, I didn't understand, and then I remembered that he had a thing for Shirley back when she and Delores were pilots during the war. It had been almost seventeen years since she got polio and broke up with him, yet he still seemed to dote on her. I couldn't understand it. She was adorable, of course, but she clearly loved someone else. And there was no question that Jack loved her.

"It was the war itself that changed things," Delores said. "We never would have had the chance to do what we did, to meet the people we met, if it wasn't for that."

I glanced at Mama. She must have felt awkward. The war and the reasons for it had sent her life into a spiral. She didn't get to do exciting things like Delores and Shirley, and she'd spent the last twelve years being the face of German shame in Cold Creek. I understood her retreat to wine on the one hand, yet these people were her family and friends now. They'd embraced her and no matter how inexplicable that might seem to her, they'd saved us. I was filled with awe and gratitude at that awareness.

Myrtle and Mick literally got their act together, and Mick started playing "Blueberry Hill." By the time he was finished everyone was singing and tapping their toes. Then Mick picked up his ukulele and together with Myrtle on the piano started playing and singing "Tonight You Belong to Me." Soon, we could hear Tommy and Delores singing from the kitchen. Jack jumped up and helped Shirley to her feet and did a little jig around her. Then he lifted her and danced, with her feet dangling inches from the floor, metal braces and all. Her laugh was contagious. Before I knew it Mama and Sonny were dancing.

> *My honey I know*
> *With the dawn*
> *That you will be gone*
> *But tonight*
> *You belong to me*

Uncle Grant got up quietly and went out on the porch. After they finished that song, and Mick and Myrtle started "You Are My Sunshine," I followed him.

"Are you okay?"

He nodded. "Can't hear very well anyway."

"Even with your hearing aids?"

"Music is hard. I feel the rhythm if it's loud, but it's hard to make out words and music at the same time."

"Oh." I tried to imagine what he was experiencing.

He sat down on the glider and lit a cigarette. In the flash of the match, I glimpsed his eyes and quickly looked away. His open sadness made my heart hurt for him.

We sat together, listening to the joyful singing and dancing on the other side of the window.

"It's what I wanted for her," he said. "I wanted to be the one to make her happy, of course. But if not me, I wanted it for her anyway." He coughed into his fist. "It's just this is the first time I've seen her like this."

"She's a wonderful person," I said. "Special."

He pushed the swing back with his feet. "I wish I could be happy without her in my life."

I sat quietly with him until the others were ready to go home.

24
Learning to Drive
April 16, 1960

MAMA AND SONNY decided to walk Schatzi home after the party. Even though I was tired, I chose to walk as well. It had been a long curious day and I thought maybe the night air would lift my mood. Everyone else climbed into Uncle Grant's van and headed down the hill. Mick leaned out the window and waved. Mama blew him kisses until they disappeared on Cold Creek Drive.

Schatzi trotted along in front of us, his pink tongue dangling out of his mouth. He'd made quite a haul. Everyone doted on the little guy and gave him tidbits from their meal. However, he kept close to Mama. Great. One more competitor for her time and affection.

I thought about Annie Jones and wondered if she could really see things no one else could. Then I thought about her breasts. I'd always been drawn to her beautiful hair, but now her breasts captured my imagination. I loved the way they strained against her clothes and I prayed that they would pop her buttons and I'd get to see them, however briefly.

Mama looked back over her shoulder. "You okay back there, Emo?"

I froze. Did she sense I was thinking about Annie's breasts? I hung back hoping the darkness would hide my guilt. "Just thinking about Uncle Grant."

Now Sonny turned around. "What about him?"

They stopped to let me catch up with them.

"Uh ..." I was stuck. "What?"

"Emo, you are funny." Mama hooked her right arm around mine and then took Sonny's with her left. "See we are like scarecrows and lions."

"What?" I knew very well she was talking about *The Wizard of Oz*, but I was stalling—trying to come up with something to distract her from prying into my real thoughts.

"You forget that scaredy-cat lion?"

I'd recovered enough to banter back. "I prefer that guy with the oil can head."

"So we are supposed to skip down the yellow brick road now?" Sonny laughed. "Haven't you done enough dancing for one night?" He gave Mama a quick little side hug.

"I love dancing, Sonny. We should do more." She did a little shuffling jig and lifted both feet off the ground for a quick second, trusting that Sonny and I would hold her up, which of course we did.

She was drunk again, but she was happy for the moment. It was wonderful to see her that way.

Schatzi stiffened and stared into the woods to the right of the road. I heard a crack and some soft rustling in the bushes beside the road.

"What is it, boy?"

Schatzi growled softly.

I knelt beside him trying make out what the little dog saw in the darkness.

"It's probably a possum or raccoon," Sonny said.

"Or that crazy Billy Ray Parker."

"Don't be mean to Billy Ray." Mama wrapped her arms around herself and swayed on her heels. "He's a good boy."

I wanted to go pull Billy Ray out of the brush by his shirt front and send him home with a mock kick in the pants, but I felt sorry for him, too.

"Is that you, Parker?"

More rustling.

"Billy Ray?"

I shrugged. "Whatever it was, it's gone now. Maybe it was a raccoon."

"Come, Schatzi," Mama said. "Let's go see your new house."

With our arms linked, we giggled at our own night fright and walked down the hill to our house, each of us lost in our own thoughts.

* * *

Uncle Grant's Metro van was in Grandma Arial's driveway. Further down the road, Balboa's beckoned with flashing lights and shiny cars and pretty girls and ice cream.

Mick stuck his head out of the van window. "Let's go down to Balboa's and get a bedtime malted. Uncle Grant says he'll drive us and keep an eye on us."

I patted my pockets, checking for the money I'd earned working in the Logan Foods warehouse twice a week after school. "Sounds good to me." I hoped that Annie would be there, although I knew it wasn't likely at this time of night. It didn't matter anyway since at best, my little brother and uncle would be with me and at worst, my grandmother and parents.

"I'm in," Sonny said. "How about you, sweetheart?"

"No sweets for me. My bed calls, but you go. Spend time with boys and brother, Sonny."

I was surprised Mama wasn't going to make a fuss about Balboa's. She must have been drunker than I thought.

Grandma Arial got out of the van. "Me too, Vala. Think I'll take a long bath and relax with a cup of tea. You boys go have fun. Tomorrow is Sunday, and you can sleep in if you need to."

Sonny loved the old cars the young men fixed up and showed off at the drive-in. "You sure, sugar?"

Mama nodded. "Go, go. Eat some boogers."

I groaned and shook my head. "Burgers, Mama. Sheesh."

Sonny gave Mama a kiss on the cheek. "We won't be late."

Grandma Arial climbed the steps to her house and Mama crossed the street and went into ours. The lights went on at about the same time, and both of them waved from the doors to let us know they were in safely.

We stood for a moment listening to crickets in the darkness. Then Uncle Grant gunned the delivery van like it was a hotrod and grinned at me. "Wanna drive, boy?"

"Really? Even though it's nighttime?"

"Gotta start sometime."

"Yes, sir!" I ran to the driver's side door and waited while Uncle Grant scooted across the seat to let me in.

"You are a brave man." Sonny thumped Uncle Grant on the biceps with his fist as he climbed into the back.

"Aw, this boy's almost a man. He can handle a Metro. What's the matter, you afraid?"

Mick leaned forward, the whites of his eyes reflecting in the moonlight. We'd never heard Sonny and Uncle Grant messing with each other this way.

"I'm not afraid of EJ's driving, but you better be scared of what Vala's gonna do to you when she hears about it".

Uncle Grant laughed. "I'm not scared of that little girl."

"Well you oughta be." Sonny sucked his teeth. "She might be a tad under five foot, but she's a sawmill when it comes to these boys here."

Mick and I snickered.

"How do you make it go?" I'd been riding around in it since I was little, but this was my first time behind the wheel. I reached for the key before Sonny or Uncle Grant changed their minds

* * *

We didn't actually get to Balboa's for almost an hour. The sheer joy of driving that big old truck took us through town and two or three times around the school parking lot. Uncle Grant turned out to be a pretty good teacher. He was patient, and he knew how to explain things so that I understood them. I missed a couple of turns and had to back up with Sonny and Mick laughing and teasing me. I loved it.

Inside the restaurant, Uncle Grant bought everyone a milkshake, and we sat around joking about my potential as a truck driver for Logan Foods. Sonny was laughing and mock-punching me in the arm when a siren started.

"What's that?" Mick peered through the window. Sheriff Douglas drove by with his lights flashing, followed by an ambulance and Jimmy Dixon's cruiser.

"Oh my God." Sonny stood up.

I watched him, my last laugh still frozen on my face. "Sonny?"

He was already out the door and running. Mick started after him, but Uncle Grant grabbed his arm. "Hold on, boy."

"Let me go, let me go!" Mick struggled to get away. "He'll need me."

"We'll go together."

A fire truck screamed past.

My ears buzzed. I wanted to swallow, but there was no spit. I couldn't move but my heart was pounding. Then I felt Mick pushing me and heard Uncle Grant's voice.

"Come on, EJ. We need to check on your mother."

That got through to me. "What? What's wrong with Mama?"

"We don't know yet, but that's where the sheriff's going."

Uncle Grant threw coins on the table, and we hurried out to the van.

In the parking lot, Uncle Grant searched one pocket and then the other.

Mick muttered, "Hurry, hurry."

Suddenly it dawned on me that Uncle Grant was looking for the keys to the truck. "Here, I still have them." I tossed them to him and we squeezed into the front seat together.

As we backed into the intersection, we could see a red glow and smoke billowing over the treetops in the direction of our house. Uncle Grant shifted gears and we lurched up the road.

The fire truck was in our driveway and two men were spraying our house with water. Uncle Grant parked a block away and the three of us ran for home. I didn't realize I was crying until I saw Sonny sitting on the front curb holding Mama in his arms. She was curled around him, trembling, and he was stroking her hair and murmuring to her. I caught his eye.

"Is she okay?" I mouthed.

He shook his head.

"Mama?" Mick bent over them. "We're here, Mama."

She turned her head and we gasped. Her nose was twisted and both of her eyes were swollen shut. "Milo." She reached for him with one arm. "Emo?" It was then I realized that she couldn't see us.

"I'm here too, Mama." My voice trembled.

She laid her head back on Sonny's shoulder.

"We need to get her to the hospital, Sonny," the ambulance driver said.

"I'll stay with the boys." Uncle Grant put his hand on my shoulder. "It's been a long night, but these guys are tough."

Grandma Arial came up behind them. She wore her flannel robe and house shoes. "I'm here too, Vala."

Mama reached out to Grandma. Other than our names, she hadn't said a word.

Grandma Arial squeezed her hand. "You are a smart, brave girl."

Mama took a deep shuddering breath.

"I'm proud of you, Vala, so proud. Now let us take care of things here. Rocky will take you and Sonny to the hospital."

"That's right," Rocky said. "It's not that far away. Looks like you'll need a few stitches, and the doctor at the emergency room will want to check for concussion."

Mama let go of Grandma Arial's hand and clung to Sonny.

"I'll be with you, my darling one," Sonny whispered into her ear.

Grandma Arial nodded. Rocky stood on one side of them and Uncle Grant on the other. Together, they hoisted Sonny to his feet so that he never had to let go of Mama. As he turned toward the waiting ambulance, I realized that his shirt was bloody.

We watched as the driver helped Sonny put Mama into his ambulance and climb in beside her. As Rocky closed the back door, we saw Mama reach for Sonny again.

Mick turned to Grandma and wrapped his arms around her. While she was comforting him, I checked out our house, expecting to see it destroyed, along with all of our belongings. The firemen had turned off the water and were retrieving their hoses. Aside from a tall column of smoke coming from the back of the house, everything seemed fine—a bit dirty, but all there. Loud chopping noises told me it was the back porch that had burned and that other firemen were still working on it.

I peered around the corner of the house. Sheriff Douglas and Deputy Dixon were walking toward me with a man. I squinted in the smoky darkness. The figure looked familiar. Was it the man who had broken into our house before? John Sarris? No, not Sarris. I rubbed my eyes. Who was that?

He looked up as they passed. It wasn't some scary Nazi from Mama's past, but our neighbor and friend, Arnold Vilani, the principle of the high school. I spun around and ran across the yard toward them with my fists clenched. How dare he? Someone I knew and saw every day and felt safe with—how could he do this to Mama? To us? I wanted to hit him, stomp on his face until it was as mutilated as Mama's. If I had a knife I would have stabbed him in the eyes. If I had a gun, I would have shot him in the face. I wanted to obliterate him, turn him into a bloody bag of broken bones, rip out his spleen.

I lunged for Mr. Vilani's throat with both hands but Sheriff Douglas stepped in front of me. "We'll take care of him, EJ."

My rage was mindless and wordless. Pushing and punching and kicking, I was hell-bent on destroying the man who'd hurt my mother. The sheriff was a hundred pounds heavier than me. He could have knocked me to the ground with one blow, but he simply blocked me.

Mr. Vilani's glasses were broken and there was a deep scratch on his face. Mama must have fought hard. That thought enraged me further and I tried to get around the sheriff again.

Mr. Vilani's eyes were sympathetic, like they were the time I had the measles and the time I asked to be excused from football. "It wasn't me, EJ." It was almost a whisper.

I screamed and fought to get around Sheriff Douglas and Deputy Dixon.

Uncle Grant grabbed me from behind. "EJ! Son. Calm down."

I blinked. Why were they yelling at me? I wasn't the one who hurt Mama. It was getting harder to breathe. My head hurt—and my chest.

Uncle Grant held me tightly. I struggled, my arms flailing. "EJ? EJ!"

Out of air and overextended, I fell back against him. I thought I might throw up, but before I could, blackness overtook me.

* * *

Ice hung from the trees by the side of the road.

"It's a wolf, Mausi. Run!"

"Mutti?" I stumbled toward my mother's voice in the darkness.

A dark figure came toward me, growling.

I hid behind a bush.

"I have you," someone said into my ear. "It's Opa. You are safe, Emo."

"I can hear you," the wolf said. A hand holding something shiny came through the leaves. I fell back on my butt and something scratched my thigh.

"Mutti!"

The bushes rustled around me and someone grunted.

"Run, Emo." The deep voice behind me cracked. "Run."

* * *

Something cold was on my face and neck. I opened my eyes. "Grandma?"

"I'm right here, sweet boy." She turned the cloth she was holding on my face and it was even cooler.

"That was Mr. Vilani."

"I know."

"Why did he do that to Mama?"

She shook her head, her eyes filled with tears. "I don't know that he did, sweetheart."

I sat up and looked around. Mick was squatting beside me. "You scared us to death," he said.

"I scared myself." I tried to stand up but my arms and legs didn't work the way I expected, and I sat back down in the grass.

"Stay still for a bit." Grandma put her palm against my chest.

"Where's Uncle Grant?"

"He's getting you a glass of water. We can't get into your house until they give the all clear, so he had to go across the street to fetch it."

"What did they do with Mr. Vilani?"

"Took him to jail, I expect."

I shivered. "I wanted to kill him."

"But you didn't." She wiped my face with the cool cloth once again.

"Only because Sheriff Douglas and Deputy Dixon stopped me."

"Feel different now?"

I thought about it. "Hard to say." I was too weak to feel much.

Uncle Grant arrived with a cup and a thermos. "You better, boy?"

"Some."

He opened the thermos and poured me a drink. "Take it easy, now."

"Yes, sir." I accepted the water.

"I talked with Sonny on the phone," he said. "Your Mom's beat up—you saw that—but there's no permanent damage."

"When will she be home?"

"They need to do some work on her, and then she'll be very tired. So she'll spend some time at the hospital where they can watch her for signs of other injuries."

"What happened?" Mick was calmer than me.

"I don't know much," Grandma Arial said. "When I got out of my bath and went into the living room, I smelled smoke and looked out the window. I couldn't see flames but it was clear there was a fire. So I called the fire department and the sheriff, and then I went to find Vala."

Uncle Grant reached down to help Grandma stand up. "Sheriff Douglas said she set the fire?"

"The sheriff told me that whoever did this chased Vala through the house, cornered her on the back porch away from the telephone, and started strangling her. It must have been awful, but she kept her wits and pretended she was unconscious. As soon as he let go and backed off, she grabbed Sonny's lighter off the table back there and set that stack of old magazines on fire, hoping someone would see it and call for help."

"He could've killed her," Mick said almost to himself.

I rubbed my eyes with my fist. "Why? Why would Mr. Vilani do such a thing? We've been neighbors for so long."

Once Grandma Arial had her balance, Uncle Grant reached out to me, too. "Wanna try standing up?"

I nodded. At least I didn't feel like I was going to puke. "She got those scary phone calls whenever Sonny wasn't home. Why didn't we think of a neighbor?"

"Whatever the outcome, this will break Sharon's heart." Grandma Arial seemed unconvinced of Mr. Vilani's guilt.

I rubbed my elbow where it hit a rock when I fell. "Fat lot of good I was in a crisis," I grumbled.

"It's been a long day, EJ. You can't go at this pace and not expect a seizure."

Grandma Arial was right, but that didn't make it any easier.

Mick looked around. "Where's the dog?"

"That poor little thing must have run off. He was used to fending for himself, and like any other creature, he'd be afraid of fire," Grandma Arial said.

"You'd think he would have taken care of Mama." I suddenly hated the mutt.

"Aw, EJ. He couldn't have been ten pounds. Maybe he's hiding somewhere." Mick headed toward the firemen who were pulling the smoldering wooden planks that used to be the porch floor away from the house.

A high wail caused us all to jump. "I knew I shouldn't have gone home!" Billy Ray Parker stood at the edge of our lawn in his pajamas, fists clenched and sobbing. What was it with that kid? He'd always been nuts, but now he was downright annoying.

"It's eleven-thirty," Mick said. "How did you know?"

Billy Ray wiped his nose with the back of his hand. "Everyone knows. The fire alarm wakes the dead."

Billy Ray, whose greatest wish was to guard Mama, had been sleeping—and I'd been learning to drive a grocery van, while Arnold Vilani tried to kill Mama.

25

Facing Facts
April 17, 1960

BA-BAM!

Rubbing my eyes and yawning, I stood up in the seat and looked out the back of the car. There were bright lights and loud voices. Mama and Gerhardt were standing in the road talking to a strange man.

"Mutti!"

"It's okay, baby. I'm coming," Mama called.

I grabbed the door handle and tried to get out. "Mutti?"

"Stay where you are, Emo."

"No." I pushed open the door. The road seemed so far down. I turned around and scooted out on my belly. As soon as my feet hit the ground, I ran toward Mama and Gerhardt.

"Emo. Stop, sweetheart."

Between me and Mama and Gerhardt and the stranger, the monster lay on the ground, groaning.

I froze.

Gerhardt started toward me.

The man on the ground rolled over, holding his side. "Get me that bag, Vala, or I'll cut this kid."

"Who is that, Mutti?"

"It's a wolf, Mausi. Run."

"A wolf?"

"Run as hard and as fast as you can. Now. Before he gets you."

The man lying on the ground coughed and struggled to get up. "You are my ticket, Emo."

As the wolf rose up before me, the light was behind him. I couldn't see his face. The only sound was a wheeze.

I backed away.

"No!" Mama was not far behind Gerhardt. "Don't hurt Emo."

The wolf staggered toward me, arms outstretched.

I turned and ran.

Voices. Footsteps crunching in the snow behind me. Panting and grunting. Someone falling and getting up again.

Gerhardt groaned as if he was hurt.

I turned to see what had happened. The bad man was standing over Gerhardt, kicking him.

I ran off the side of the road and hid behind an icy bush.

"Don't think I can't see you, Emo." It was the monster's voice.

The ice crackled on the trees around me.

"You are a fool if you think money is more important than that particular little boy." The stranger's voice was behind me.

"Then I'm a fool. Give me the bag or I swear I'll kill him."

"The Obergruppenführer will hunt you down. He has eyes and ears around the world."

"Then I should I kill all of you right here."

The bush swayed in the wind and I glimpsed the monster peering into my hiding place.

"I have the gun." Mama's voice quivered.

"Do you think an SS officer would have only one weapon?"

I covered my eyes with both hands.

A loud click.

Someone grabbed me from behind. I screamed and fought.

"Shush, Emo." The stranger whispered in my ear. "It's Opa."

The monster growled. "There you are..."

A flash of light and a loud noise. Opa groaned and let go of me.

Mama screamed. "PAPI!"

The bushes rattled around me as I tried to crawl away.

BA-BAM!

My leg hurt. I touched it and it was wet.

BAM!

The wolf howled.

* * *

I startled awake. I was wrapped in a quilt, lying on Grandma Arial's plastic covered couch. I sat up. My heart pounded and it took a minute for me to realize I'd been sleeping. I pushed back the drapes over the sofa and peered out the window at our house across the street. Steam rose from the roof, black smoke lurking over what used to be the back porch.

"You're awake early." Grandma Arial set a cup of tea on the coffee table for me. "Sure you don't want to rest a little longer?"

"We need to get our things out of there."

"Anything sitting in water is probably a loss, EJ."

I nodded, thinking about the suitcase full of papers. We'd put it back in Mama's closet. Would I find anything besides a smoky paper stew? All that promise of information—destroyed.

Grandma Arial gave me a donut. "Get some food in you. It'll be a big job."

"Has Sonny called yet?"

She sat down on the couch beside me. "He said they've decided to keep Vala in the hospital a couple of days."

"Why?"

"She's not going to die or anything, sugar. She's just beat up and needs attention while she heals."

Grandma Arial was trying to put a nice face on it, but something was up. "Maybe I should go see her before I start on the house."

"They'll be working with her for a while this morning, EJ."

"Maybe she needs some things."

"Her clothes will have to be laundered and pressed before she can wear them. Besides, I'm sure Zona has something in her closet that will work. She'll call when your mama's all fixed up and ready for visitors."

I threw back half the cup of tea. "Okay." I bit into the donut. "What will happen to Mr. Vilani?"

"I don't know."

"Why would he go after Mama like that?"

"Jimmy Dixon said Arnold swears he didn't do it. Maybe he didn't."

"If it wasn't Mr. Vilani, then who did it?" A wave of horror hit me. "I wanted to kill him, Grandma."

"I know, sugar. You thought he hurt the most precious person in the world to you. I understand how angry that must have made you. It made me mad, too, seeing that sweet girl beat up like that."

"Whether he did it or not, I'm ashamed of myself."

Grandma Arial put her arm around me. "That's because you're a good person, EJ Logan." She kissed the top of my head.

I wanted to squirm away, but at that moment, I felt like a stupid, thoughtless kid who, when the chips were down, had been sipping milkshakes instead of watching out for Mama.

* * *

Mick and I had to kick open the front door. The electricity was off and it was dark inside. Using Grandma Arial's flashlight to avoid tripping over things, we went around opening windows and doors.

"So much for Mama's new paint job. " I flashed the light over the wall between the kitchen and what used to be the back porch. "It's all black and blistered."

"She'll be upset." Mick picked up a soggy lampshade. "Looks like this is ruined, too."

Together we gathered up the rest of the lamps and took them out onto the front lawn where we could see them better.

"Even if the silk dries out, the electrical might not work again." Mick set the floor lamp down beside the others. "Maybe we should ask Sonny what he thinks."

"He's got to focus on Mama," I said. "Let's just take them to the dump when Uncle Grant gets here."

"Okay." Mick wiped his hands on the back of his jeans. "What else?"

"You know what else."

He nodded and we went back into the house to fetch the suitcase in Mama's closet. It was pitch black in there. I switched on the flashlight. Everything was standing in two inches of water.

Mick held his nose. "Am I getting used to the smell or is it not so bad in here?"

"You're getting used to it, but we'll need these if we are going to spend any time in here." I handed Mick one of the handkerchiefs Grandma Arial had provided for moments like this.

After we rescued the suitcase, we went out to the hallway and Mick unlocked the little door to the closet under the stairs. He squatted, and waded into the little space. "Anything in particular?"

"Anything that belongs to Mama."

"You aren't interested in saving my old Tinkertoys?"

"Not in the slightest."

He shoved the soggy box full of Mama's memorabilia out the door. When I picked it up to carry outside, water poured out of its seams. "Uh oh," I said.

"Not good."

"Afraid not."

While Mick crawled out of the closet, I toted the box and suitcase out on the front porch. Thankfully, when we'd been rummaging through the suitcase the day before, Mick hadn't relocked it. Even so, the latch was sticky, and it took a moment to pop it loose.

"What a mess," Mick said as he sat down beside me. "Should we just fish out an envelope at a time?"

"The manila envelopes and folders are thicker paper than the letters." I lifted one of the few packets of personal notes that I'd left the day before. "At least they're in one piece. I was afraid the paper would fall apart or the ink had washed away."

Mick took the packet I handed him and examined it. "We ought to peel them apart while they're still wet. If they dry this way, they'll probably stick together."

I didn't ask him how he knew that, but I trusted his judgment. "If you tackle this, I'll carry out the other stuff."

"Deal." I didn't need to make the suggestion. Mick was already absorbed in the problem of rescuing the letters in Mama's suitcase.

"Do what you can, personal letters first, because there must be something about them that mattered to Mama, and then the pictures. I'd like to see the documents too, but if they're damaged, Sonny might be able to get duplicates from the governments involved. I'm sure at least some of them are copies anyway."

Mick cut the ribbon holding the first packet with a penknife and carefully pulled away the top envelope. "I ought to try and get the letters out of the envelopes now, I think."

I went back into the house to retrieve other things from the closet under the stairs. Everything smelled so bad that I couldn't stay inside long before I started coughing.

On my fourth trip to the front yard with my arms full of treasure-turned-crap, I noticed that Mick was making progress with the first packet. He'd rescued eleven envelopes and had taken the letters out. They were lying on the porch in the sun, while he fiddled with the twelfth.

"Looks like you got it figured out."

"Some are harder than others," he said through gritted teeth. "Four of them tore, but maybe we can tape them back together once they dry."

"Notice anything important?"

He pointed to one letter that he'd separated from the others. "That one might choke you up."

I squatted over it. It was the last page of a letter. "Where's the rest of it?"

"That was the only thing in the envelope."

The damp paper made it hard to read. Fact was, it was just plain hard to read.

They knew we didn't want them here. They knew this and yet they stayed. Outsiders say they had lived in Germany for generations, that they were good citizens. I say they invaded my country and bred like rabbits. People say they were patriots, that some of them fought in the war. I say they may have been soldiers, but they were never German. They aren't even human. How

*can a pestilence be human? How can I feel sorry for
them? They caused so much grief and sorrow in the
world. They knew we didn't want them in Germany.
They knew this and yet they stayed. What did they
think would happen?*

Anna Hess

I looked up at Mick. His eyes reflected what I was feeling. A glance into the dark soul of our Oma was harder than I'd
ever expected.

* * *

After Mick left to take Mama's clothes to the laundry, I wandered the marshy yard picking up trash and scorched leaves. As I
rounded the corner of the house, a little brown mutt hurled himself
into my arms.

"Schatzi, where have you been, boy?" I dropped the trash bag
and scratched his ears. "After last night, I figured that life under
the railroad bridge was more peaceful than around here and you
took off."

The dog licked my face like we were long lost pals. He looked
into my eyes and then over his shoulder, back into my eyes and then
over his shoulder.

"What?"

Schatzi jumped down and ran around the yard and then came
back to me.

"You trying to show me something?"

He ran around again and then nosed up against the door to our
shed, snuffling and growling.

"What'd you do? Tree a squirrel?"

His growling grew louder.

My heart bumped in my chest. The door wasn't completely
closed. Had the firemen broken the lock last night?

"Shush, buddy," I said to Schatzi.

The phone in the house was dead. I knew I should go get Sonny,
but what if it was just a chipmunk spooking the little dog? Sonny
needed to stay with Mama at the hospital tonight. Why wake him up
for nothing?

I crept forward and pulled the door open.

As I stepped inside, something crunched under my feet. I tugged on the string over my head. Nothing. "What happened to the light, Schatzi?"

I felt up the string, thinking that the bulb might be loose in its socket. "Ouch!" I shook my hand and used my teeth to pull a sliver of glass from my thumb. Someone had broken the light bulb. The firemen?

I sensed rather than heard someone breathing in the dark corner across from me.

"Stay back or I'll gut you."

I jumped back, tripping over Sonny's open toolbox. Fighting to regain my balance, I recoiled off the wall and fell hard on my butt, scraping my shoulder and bruising my elbow on the door. Schatzi's snuffling turned into a loud squeal.

"Leise!"

The terrier barked.

I stared into the darkness. "Wer bist du?" It was habit, responding to German in German.

"An old friend. Now shut that dog up."

"I don't recognize your voice."

"A really old friend, Emo."

I got up and rubbed my elbow. "I don't remember you."

"Ah, but I remember you."

"What are you doing in here?"

"I need something."

His voice was high and scratchy. I mentally ran through all the male voices that I knew—teachers, relatives, classmates, and neighbors. No one came to mind at first. Then I remembered the dream, a cold night in a car with Mama and the big man in the blue coat. Was the person hiding in our shed the monster of my nightmares? "Seems to me you are hiding. People who need help usually come to the front door and knock."

"Don't mess with me, Emo." The man kicked at Schatzi who howled and danced away.

"I'm not the criminal hiding in a shed."

"Get that beast out of here."

"He lives here." It was only a little lie. Schatzi was definitely going to live here from now on.

There was movement and a soft cough.

"Are you sick?"

"I'll be fine once I get what I came for."

"And that would be?"

"Surely you know, Emo. Your mother couldn't find it—and she was plenty scared and would have produced it if she could. Sonny Logan never knew about our project. That leaves you or the little Pollack Jew. One of you has it."

"Who?"

The man in the shadows sighed through his teeth. "Am I to believe that Vala kept you in the dark all these years? Or are you just scared after what happened to her?"

My hands tightened into fists as I realized that Arnold Vilani was not the man who'd hurt my mother. I took a step forward.

There was a click. "I wouldn't come any closer if I were you." The man leaned forward—and a switchblade caught the dim light from the shed's open door.

I eyed the knife, imagining myself knocking it out of his hand. Then I'd pounce on him and beat him to death with Sonny's crowbar that hung from the pegboard over his workbench. I edged to the right. "What are you looking for, specifically?"

"A suitcase. A cabinet. A drawer. Maybe a sack? Maybe whatever was in that box on the back porch? The one Vala burned."

"Magazines?"

There was a soft gasp. "Vala burned magazines rather than let me see them? What kind?"

Hot Rod. Newsweek. American View.

"What else?"

I shrugged.

"That doesn't make sense." His voice cracked and he coughed.

"I don't know what you want."

"Vala's stash, of course."

The muscle in my thigh twitched. "We aren't wealthy."

"Vala has plenty. Frau Hess would have seen to that."

"You knew Oma?"

He coughed. "Are you an idiot?"

"No." I backed away. "And I'm not afraid of you, so put that knife back in your pocket."

"Bull. You're shaking like a cornered hound."

I swallowed. "I have muscle spasms. It has nothing to do with fear."

"Always an excuse with you. Always a crybaby."

I felt the edge of the workbench and reached for the crowbar. "You knew my grandmother in Mannheim?"

"And a more unpleasant woman I never met."

"How did you know her?"

"She paid me to leave her daughter alone."

I almost dropped the crowbar as it slipped from its hook. "You are my father?"

"You think everything is about you?" His laugh was ugly. "Vala was eleven. I like young women, but she was still playing with dolls in 1940. No, I was in love with Lana, like every other young SS officer in the Reich."

"Lana? What's your name?"

"Oh, you aren't going to get me with that."

"Is it Wolf?"

"I'm asking the questions here."

"Then ask."

"Where is Frau Hess's brown suitcase, the one she gave to Vala when you left Germany?"

I glared into the darkness where his eyes should be, thinking about the mess of sodden paper inside it. "I have no idea what you are talking about."

"The final payment."

"Oma died years ago, and Lana died years before that. There's no one from my family left in Mannheim. That story is over." I switched to English. "We are Americans now."

"And the money Frau Hess gave Vala?"

"I never saw any money. That woman wouldn't let babies in out of the cold. She turned her own daughter and grandsons away. I hardly believe that if she had any money she would send it here."

"You are hard on your Oma."

"She never did a thing for me."

I couldn't make out his features, but he seemed shocked by my attitude toward my German grandmother.

"Frau Hess was a woman of firm beliefs," he said. "True, she was hard, but she wanted what was best for Germany. She was a patriot. That's a good thing, yes?"

When I didn't answer, he closed the switchblade and put it in his pocket.

"So you aren't going to kill me?"

"Not this time." He held out a hand. "Help me up."

"Why should I?" I held the crowbar out of his sight, against my thigh.

"I presume you want me to get out of this shed before your brother comes back."

I put out my forearm and he gripped it with one hand and pushed against the wall with the other one. I pulled and he got slowly to his feet. He leaned his head against the door frame, hacking and gagging.

"Are you hurt?"

"Would it matter if I was?" The sleeve of his jacket was wet with blood. "You aren't going to pass out, are you?"

I shook my head.

He coughed again and spit on the ground. "Why not?"

"It's not me that's bleeding."

"Ha!" He staggered into the yard.

I backed away. When I was sure he couldn't reach me I turned and ran.

"Where are you going?"

"You need a doctor."

"No."

I kept running.

"Emo!"

As I ran across the front yard, Uncle Grant was just arriving in the Metro. I waved my hands. "Uncle Grant! Sonny! Grandma!"

Uncle Grant pulled the truck into Grandma Arial's drive. I knew he hadn't heard me, but he turned toward me as soon as he saw Sonny running down the back stairs and Grandma Arial in the front window of her house with the telephone in her hand.

"What?" Uncle Grant hurried toward me.

"There's a German bleeding in our back yard."

"Stay here," he said as he hurried past.

"No way."

A heartbeat later, Sonny grabbed my shoulders. "What's going on?"

"The man who hurt Mama—the one who cut you—he was in the shed."

Sonny's eyes bore into mine. "Did he...are you okay?"

"I'm fine." I held up the crowbar. "He's sick, I think. Or hurt."

"You stay here and I'll go help Grant."

I turned to follow him.

"EJ!"

"I'm coming."

"Then stay back, in case there's trouble."

I was as tall as Sonny and Uncle Grant. If this fellow gave them any trouble, I wanted to get in a lick or two. I wasn't as crazy as I'd been the night before when I went after Mr. Vilani, but the memory of my mother's swollen and bruised face still infuriated me.

In the back yard, the stranger leaned against our sugar maple tree, talking to Uncle Grant.

"My mother called Sheriff Douglas. He should be here round about now," Sonny said as we approached them. "So don't even think of running."

"I assure you that if I could run, I would have done it by now, Mr. Logan." His English was heavily accented.

"In that case, I'd like to see that knife you tried to stick in my ribs last night."

The stranger took the closed switchblade out of his pocket and handed it to Sonny. "I thought it was all over. Everyone went home. The crazy neighbor was in custody. I figured the last place anyone would look now would be a tool shed." He coughed and spit again. I didn't have anywhere else to go or the energy to get there if I did."

"What's your *name*?" Now that I had my family around me, I was more insistent.

The man turned toward me. "Frank Barnes. That's who I am now."

"And you knew my Opa and Oma and my Aunt Lana?"

He glared at me. "You are a nosey little bastard."

"Keep a civil tone, Barnes." Uncle Grant thumped him on the shoulder. "This young man is being raised to be respectful to his elders—and he expects to be treated with respect himself."

I glanced at Sonny. The corners of his mouth quivered and his eyes twinkled. "Don't mess with Uncle Grant," I mouthed, and Sonny chuckled. I grinned and then turned back to Frank Barnes with a stone face.

"He said he was looking for Oma's brown suitcase. He thinks there's money in it, and he wants it."

"You attacked my wife for money?"

"Some things are more important than a pretty girl, Mr. Logan."

"What makes you think we have suitcases full of cash?"

"It was meant to help certain people get a new start."

"Nazis?"

Barnes's smirk was answer enough.

"And why would Vala have any money for war criminals?" Uncle Grant frowned.

"Can we sit down somewhere? I have never quite gotten over a wound I received in my service to the Reich. And our encounter last night left me needing a stitch or two." Barnes held up his arm for them to see his bloody sleeve.

"I'm afraid we aren't set up for guests at the moment, thanks to you." Sonny pointed to our steaming wet house. "But hold on a minute and Sheriff Douglas will seat you comfortably in his squad car."

Uncle Grant nudged the man, "Where are these Nazis?"

Barnes shook his head and sighed. "Are you serious?"

"Then why should we believe you're anything but a cowardly burglar who beat up a woman half your size?"

Frank Barnes sniffed. "Who cares what you think?"

Sheriff Douglas pulled up in front of our house.

"Back here," I called.

"I think I'm going to move in next door, Sonny," Sheriff Douglas puffed as he joined us. "That way I can finish dinner before arresting the next stranger lurking around your house."

Sonny and I went to meet him. "I think we got the wrong guy last night, George."

The sheriff nodded and turned away from Frank Barnes. "I know." It was almost a whisper. "I had nothing on Arnold except that he was climbing the back fence when we found him. That and he was drunk. After he sobered up, we called Sharon and she picked him up this morning. They're staying with her mother in Medina until I sort through this whole thing."

"What did he say happened?"

"He was sitting out on his carport drinking beer and saw someone on your back porch in the dark. He thought it was one of your boys at first."

I couldn't understand why Sonny and Sheriff Douglas were whispering. Then I realized they didn't want Frank Barnes to know that Mr. Vilani was out of jail already and talking about what he saw.

"So how did Mr. Vilani end up in our backyard?"

The sheriff turned to me. "The fire. He saw the back porch blaze up and Vala fighting with someone. Said he couldn't get the gate open so he climbed the fence. By the time he got here, Sonny was wrestling with this fellow, I'm guessing."

Sonny glanced over his shoulder at the stranger, and then turned back to Sheriff Douglas. "He says he wants Vala's money."

George Douglas laughed. "We'd all be snooping around your house if we thought she had any."

Sonny's laugh was a short smoker's cough. "Heck, I'd get that baby blue Caddy down at Bud Spencer's if Vala had that kind of dough."

"You think that's what those guys who showed up a few years back had in mind," the sheriff asked. "Money?"

"Don't know about the old guy we caught outside, but the scrawny dude who broke in might have."

"Mighty strange, them showing up on the same day, don't you think?"

Sonny glanced at me and shrugged.

"Always seemed to me they were a team," the sheriff said. "They wanted something."

"Probably."

Sheriff Douglas shifted from one foot to the other. "Vala didn't ever tell you what it was?"

"Nope."

"How about you, EJ?"

"Are you kidding? I'm the last to know we're out of milk."

"You didn't remember those guys from when you lived in Germany?"

I shook my head.

"How about this man?"

"I'm not sure. He says he knew me."

"But you don't remember him?"

I squirmed.

"Well?"

"Nightmare," I said under my breath.

"What?"

"I sometimes have nightmares about a monster with eyes like his."

"What kind of eyes is that?"

"Go look for yourself. Almost white. Like an animal's eyes or something".

"Good heavens, boy. You're giving me the heebie-jeebies." Sheriff Douglas snorted and elbowed my ribs.

I rubbed my side, trying not to show my annoyance. "A dream, a scary dream."

"Okay, boy. I'll stop."

"How do we keep jerks like this away from us?"

"Don't really know, Sonny. Running away from something isn't unusual these days. In the case of the white-eyed monster dude over there, it won't be a problem. We got him on assault and burglary and littering and anything else I can think of."

"How about nearly burning my house down?"

"Vala says she did that."

"Only because that lunatic had her by the throat."

"I can probably toss in attempted murder if you want."

A white car with flashing lights pulled up in front of our house and Deputy Dixon got out. "What do you want me to do, Sheriff?"

"Get that fella over there—the one leaning against the tree—take him down to the station."

Deputy Dixon pulled his gun belt a little higher on his hips and straightened his hat. "I got him, boss. Charge?"

"Let's start with breaking and entering. That will keep everyone busy until I can figure out what's going on here."

Jimmy Dixon crossed the yard, fumbling to release his cuffs from his thick black belt. "Don't give me any trouble now."

Barnes held out his wrists. "Don't worry, Deputy, I don't have the energy to resist arrest."

I studied Barnes's face. Other than his eyes, I didn't recognize anything about him. In my dream, the monster was broad shouldered and tall. This man was frail and had poor posture. Still, I was little in the nightmare. Maybe that made everyone else bigger in my mind.

Deputy Dixon took Barnes by the arm. "This way."

As they crossed the yard, I realized that Barnes was limping. I closed my eyes, summoning images that stubbornly refused to materialize in my memory.

"Where will they take him?" I said to Sonny behind my hand.

"Hospital, first, I would think. Then, depending on what they find out about this guy, they'll either arrest or deport him."

"I want to talk to him before they send him away."

"Why?"

"He knew Lana."

Sonny sucked in air through his front teeth. "How?"

"Sounded like he was one of her suitors."

Sonny fished a pack of Camels out of his shirt pocket. "Who knows what these guys are up to? Maybe just trying to avoid arrest for their crimes." He pulled a cigarette out of the package with his lips. "Or maybe they're trying to get the remnants of Hitler's crazy followers together for another go at it. They could just be vengeful murderers out to get back at the world." He patted his pockets looking for his lighter.

"Mama set the porch on fire with it."

He seemed surprised that I knew what he was looking for. "Any idea what happened to it?"

I shook my head.

He stared at the broken bits of charred wood that used to be our back porch. "What would he have done to her if I hadn't left that lighter on the picnic table yesterday?"

I looked around. The tree house was in sight of the yard. But even if I'd been there and not tooling around town in the Metro, would I have been able to get to her fast enough? Mr. Vilani was a lot closer, and he couldn't get there in time.

I turned back to Sonny. "Do you think she's been giving them money?"

He took the cigarette out of his mouth and put it back into the pack in his pocket. "I don't know, EJ. Makes you wonder, doesn't it?"

"Is it wrong if she has been doing it?"

"Those things are hard to decide sometimes." Sonny pushed his glasses up on his head and massaged the bridge of his nose with his thumb and forefinger. "If she did, I'm sure she has her reasons."

"The folks around here wouldn't understand, would they?"

"Afraid not."

"Would Grandma Arial?"

"Probably not."

"Will she hate us? Will we have to go away?"

"Never, EJ. Never. You belong here. We're family."

He never seemed weary of having to reassure me. I hoped he was right. Being German in Cold Creek had never been easy. Even Sonny and Uncle Grant's childhood friends were suspicious. When Mick and I were little, we were oblivious, but as we grew older, we felt the hostility as much as Mama did.

It didn't help that the more I learned about the war, the more uncomfortable I felt. Was I to blame for what my grandparents and parents did? And what did they do, exactly? Should I be as ashamed as I sometimes felt? As much as I wanted to know the truth myself, I avoided conversations about Nazis and concentration camps with my schoolmates or neighbors. "Maybe we should keep this a secret," I blurted out. "They might arrest Mama or something."

"We don't even know if it's true," Sonny said. "Even if Vala had Frau Hess's money at one time, it's gone now."

I thought about it. That's right. Barnes didn't know that when he came nosing around.

We avoided each other's eyes. We both knew this incident wasn't the end.

"I want to talk to Barnes."

"I'd have thought you had enough of his charming personality."

"I should've wanted to kill him. I mean, I went after Mr. Vilani without a second thought."

"I heard."

"Think Mr. Vilani will forgive me? I mean, he was trying to help and all."

"An apology is in order from all of us—and a thank you."

"Sonneeee? EeeeeeeeeJayyyyy?"

Sonny pulled his glasses back down onto his nose. "My mother calls. Let's go eat whatever she's whipped up for lunch."

We started across the yard.

"I mean it, Sonny. I was too scared to ask Barnes all the things I want to know when I first found him."

"I'll see what Sheriff Douglas says. I don't want Barnes in our house or in Grandma Arial's or anywhere near your mother."

I laughed. "I was kind of hoping to talk with him while he's in jail. He wasn't as scary in the light of day as he was in the shed... except for his eyes...but still..."

26

Dolph Jäger
April 23, 1960

"I WANT TO go with you," Mick said as we pulled up in front of the police station. "It's my life, too."

"He specifically said just me. If we break his rules, he might not talk at all."

"Promise you'll tell me everything."

I turned around in my seat. "I promise, Mick."

"The sheriff said forty-five minutes." Uncle Grant tapped his watch. "I'll take Mick to the hospital to stay with Vala and Sonny, and then I'll come back for you."

I opened the passenger side door of the van. "Thank you for this."

"You don't have to stay in there with him," Uncle Grant said. "I don't know what the Israelis think he did, but if they're coming for him, it has to be bad. If he's too hostile or if it's too upsetting, Jimmy Dixon will let you sit in his office until I get back."

"Okay."

I got out and started up the concrete steps of the jail house. As I reached the door, I turned around. The delivery van was still parked at the curb. Mick pressed his face against the window. "Promise," he mouthed.

I nodded and held up my thumb. Uncle Grant put the truck in gear and they drove off.

I took a breath and pushed open the door. Inside, I unfolded the slip of paper the sheriff had sent Sonny. It still said, B14 just like it had every other time I'd read it. I climbed a marble staircase and turned to the left at the first landing. B14 Sheriff's Office was stenciled on the frosted glass door of the first suite of offices. I went inside and stood in front of a wooden desk.

"Can I help you?" A receptionist wearing rhinestone-encrusted glasses and eye-watering perfume peered at me over one of Zona's makeup catalogs.

"I have an appointment with Sheriff Douglas."

She inspected a yellow tablet. "Are you EJ Logan?"

"Yes, ma'am."

She smiled at me and got up. "Would you like some coffee first?"

"No, ma'am."

"Did they tell you that Mr. Jäger will leave here as soon as his escorts arrive?"

"Yes."

"Come with me, then."

We started down a long hall. "First time I ever met an honest-to-God Nazi. They said he worked at that big concentration camp where they killed all those people."

"I heard that, too," I said.

"His soul is as black as a lump of coal."

"Yes, ma'am."

"The Israelis don't fool around with these guys. They'll probably hang him."

"I hadn't thought of that possibility."

"Too good for him, if you ask me," she said.

We went through a door and down another hall.

"I read all about how you captured him after he went after your mother. She must be so proud of you."

"I ... uh ... just found him in our tool shed."

"Would have scared me to death. Those Krauts are a bloodthirsty bunch. Been causing trouble since anyone can remember. After all they did in the war, they're lucky Truman didn't drop a nuclear bomb on them like he did the Japs."

I lowered my eyes, wondering if she realized that Mick and I might be dead now if Truman had done that. "Yes, ma'am."

"Here we are." She opened the door to a small conference room. "EJ Logan is here, Sheriff."

"Thank you, Penny. Hello, EJ."

"You need some more coffee in here?"

"We're fine. We'll talk with Mr. Jäger until the Israelis get here. Check their credentials before you bring them back, though."

"Will do." Penny closed the door behind her and we heard her heel taps retreating down the corridor.

Sheriff Douglas pointed to a chair beside him. "Sit down, EJ."

I took out a piece of folded notebook paper and smoothed it flat on the table before I pulled out the chair.

"What do you have there, son?"

"My questions. You know...so I don't forget?"

The sheriff chuckled. "Good idea. Okay, here's the situation. I'm having Jäger brought up from his cell about forty-five minutes before the Israelis are due here. You and I are going to talk with him easy as you please during that time. We got him on breaking into your house and sending that nice mama of yours to the hospital, but we ain't ever gonna put him away for that. Apparently he's a big fish that the Israelis want for a bunch of bad stuff he did in Poland. We don't even know what all, but this is the biggest thing that ever happened in Cold Creek. Since I don't have to make a case here, you can ask him anything you want. I'm going to be here just in case, though."

"Just in case what?"

"Just in case, EJ."

I sighed. What I wanted to ask Dolph Jäger didn't have anything to do with his war crimes. My questions were personal. I'd expected our talk would be private. What I wanted wasn't going to happen, though, so I decided to make the most of what they were willing to give me. "Okay."

"When he gets in here, the deputy is going to strap him to that chair over there. I want you to stay where you are. Just in case."

"What? Tell me. I'm not a kid."

Sheriff Douglas laughed. "You *are* a kid, EJ, but a smart one. I'm in here to keep an eye on him more than you. These guys, especially ones who were up to their eyeballs in that ugly stuff, when they get caught, they try to take the easy way out. You see?"

My mind spun. Easy way? Did he think Dolph Jäger would try to escape? The courthouse complex was a rabbit warren. It was easy to get turned around once you were inside. They probably brought Jäger in through the underground garage, which made it even more confusing. How would he ever figure his way out?

The sheriff leaned back in his chair. "You don't see, do you?"

I shook my head.

"In the past, when these guys got caught and didn't see a way out, they killed themselves."

"How?"

"They smuggled in cyanide capsules. Hid it in their clothes or shoes, maybe even in little tubes up their butts. When the time came, and they knew they weren't going to escape, they retrieved the capsule and bit down."

"Yuck!" I couldn't imagine doing myself in to spite the executioner. Why not take the extra few hours or days of life? "So you're afraid Dolph Jäger will kill himself if you leave him alone with me?"

"It's a possibility. A disturbing one, I grant you."

I shuddered at the idea of witnessing a suicide. "When will he be here?"

He checked his watch. "On his way now."

I tried to relax before the sheriff noticed my nervousness. It had happened so fast. First Mama found this crazy guy in our house and before I knew it, the town of Cold Creek…the whole world really…was talking about how we caught the notorious Nazi Dolph Jäger. He'd lived for years in Strongsville, Ohio, not an hour from Cold Creek, working in a lab at one of the big research hospitals in Cleveland under the name of Frank Barnes. It scared me that he'd been that close all along.

"You're shaking, son. You can cancel if you want. After what you and your family have gone through the last week, you have a right to take off and go fishing."

"There are things I have to know. Some, I think he wants to tell me because he's evil and likes to hurt people with what he knows.

"Then why let him? There are other ways to find out."

"I don't think so, sir. This may be my only shot."

The sound of rattling chains caught our attention.

"Sheriff?"

"What?"

We both had our eyes fixed on the door.

"What I find out here, if anything…"

"Yes?"

Someone's hand was on the doorknob and it moved slightly.

"Please don't say anything to anyone until I decide."

"Can't promise."

I looked over my shoulder at him. "Just the stuff about my family. Whatever it is, let me tell them first."

"I can do that."

I turned back just as the door opened.

"Es ist ein Fest." Dolph Jäger looked around as Deputy Dixon brought him in and chained him to the chair across the table from me.

"English, Jäger," grumbled Deputy Dixon.

Sheriff Douglas narrowed his eyes. "What did he say, EJ?"

"He said, 'It's a party.'"

Herr Jäger rattled his chains at me and grinned. "Once a Mannheimer, always a Mannheimer."

Sheriff Douglas took a swallow of his coffee and cocked his head toward me. "And what does that mean?"

"Nothing egregious, I assure you, Sheriff." Jäger seemed to enjoy making people feel stupid.

"People from Mannheim have a distinctive way of speaking, I said. He's making fun of my accent."

Jäger turned to Deputy Dixon. "The deal was Emo Johann Hess and me...alone."

"The deputy will be outside the door, Jäger, but I'll be here for the duration." Sheriff Douglas didn't smile.

"That's not what we discussed."

"No, but this is what you have. I'm here or no deal. And you must speak English. Take it or leave it."

I tried to keep from hyperventilating while Dolph Jäger made up his mind.

"He will go?" He gestured with his head toward Deputy Dixon. "Yes."

"No questions about any crimes here?"

"Nary a one."

Jäger nodded his acceptance.

"Stay close, Jimmy."

"I'll be close enough to hear a cockroach fart."

"I expected such crass language from you, deputy." Dolph Jäger took every opportunity to demonstrate his disdain for us.

Deputy Dixon touched the brim of his hat and bowed slightly as he backed out the door. It closed with a click, but we could see his shadow on the other side of the frosted glass.

"A rude man, Sheriff."

"He doesn't like you, Jäger."

"I am a perfectly charming fellow."

"His mother is Jewish."

Jäger snorted. "That is his misfortune, I am sure. It does explain his brutish appearance, though."

"Her family was from Krakow."

Jäger yawned and stretched his arms behind his neck. "They are dead then."

"You're cruel." My tone betrayed my disgust.

"Cruel or not, I speak the truth."

"Truth?"

"Isn't that what you came for, Emo?"

I tapped the paper in front of me with my index finger. "I have questions."

"Go."

"You were in love with my aunt."

He raised one eyebrow. "Love?"

"You know what I mean."

"In 1939, everyone wanted Lana Hess. She was beautiful, and her father was wealthy. And the Hesses were true believers. That made Lana very attractive to the SS."

"Why?"

"If you were ambitious, and most of us were, you needed a wife who was Aryan, from a good family with money, and smart. We were the cream of German society. Our wives had to reflect that if we were to be promoted. Our children had to be beautiful, blond, blue-eyed, tall, broad-shouldered, athletic, and intelligent."

"So did you marry her?"

"No." He winked at Sheriff Douglas. "But I would have proposed if she hadn't...total verrückt geworden."

"Gone mad," I said behind my hand.

"Ja, bad blood. I couldn't have any of that in my family. My line is clean."

"My Oma and Opa turned down your proposal?"

"They were ambitious. They were saving Lana Hess for one of the Reich's top dogs."

"But that didn't happen either. She never got married."

"Not as far as I know. She ended up in the Lebensborn program."

"What was that?"

"Lebensborn?" Jäger cackled. "Breeding."

"What?" I pretended I didn't know what he was talking about.

"Girls with the right physical and mental characteristics were impregnated by the best and the brightest SS officers. They wanted to create a generation of supermen, the future of the Aryan race."

I groaned inside. "So what happened?"

"I have no idea. I saw her one more time in mid-1940. I know that because I was in Mannheim for a meeting. While I was there, I found out I was to be assigned to Auschwitz. I was at the Marktplatz when I saw Lana with Frau Hess and her little sister Vala. They were buying baby clothes. I waved but she pretended she didn't know me. I figured she had found someone who ranked higher than me in Hitler's little world. Maybe an SS Obergruppenführer."

"Major general," I said to Sheriff Douglas, who nodded.

"Did you talk to her that visit?"

"I went to the Hess home one night a couple weeks later. I was... shall we say...curious. Frau Hess peered around the door jamb and told me that Lana was indisposed. I said I'd come back the next day. She suggested that I never come back, gave me twenty Reichmarcks, and closed the door in my face." He clicked his tongue against his teeth. "Poor old thing. If she'd only known who I would become, it would have been different. Perhaps I would have been your uncle, and you would have bragging rights. But then again, perhaps Frau Hess was the source of the sickness that overtook Lana. I heard that whatever it was, she was no longer part of Lebensborn by that time."

I chewed the inside of my lip, wondering if that's what prompted Lana's manic outburst, the one that caused them to send her away to be murdered. I pulled myself together. "The day I found you, you said that you knew me. And obviously, you knew Mama."

"I knew you both."

"Where?" I had almost no wind to push out that one syllable.

The corners of his mouth turned up slowly. "Auschwitz."

"Go on."

"Oh? You want to know that story?" He glanced at Sheriff Douglas. "Aren't you worried what this old battering ram will tell everyone?"

I kept my eyes on Jäger. "I'll take my chances."

He sighed. "If you must know, it was about the bed."

"What bed?"

"Vala's, of course. The gift from your father, I assumed."

"And he was?"

His blue-white eyes glittered. "She hasn't told you?"

Sheriff Douglas slammed his fist on the table. "You have twenty minutes. Quit toying with the boy, Jäger."

"Whatever you say, Sheriff. Auschwitz was like any company town. We were all grateful we weren't at the front. And there were perks for working there. We felt like we were serving the interests of the Führer and the Fatherland by getting rid of the pestilence that had overtaken our country. But we were also young and virile. There were lots of office romances with the Helferinnen, the women who were part of the support staff. We partied together. We gossiped. There was no such thing as a secret. Your parentage was the subject of many conversations."

"Behave yourself, Jäger," Sheriff Douglas growled.

"When that sweet little thing showed up in Krakow, we all wanted a crack at her, of course. Perhaps I should talk about those conversations, Sheriff?"

Sheriff Douglas half rose. "I have time to rearrange that broken leg of yours."

"Such drama. I doubt you want to turn me over to those Jews with fresh marks on me. They want to deliver their own twisted justice on these old bones."

His laugh was defiant, but I also thought I heard a hint of fear. Good. "Please, Sheriff. Let him go on. I can stand it."

Sheriff Douglas slowly sat back in his seat, never taking his eyes off Jäger.

"Why did Mama go to Auschwitz?"

"She didn't, until that last day. She stayed in Krakow. Some people said her Papi had sent her on an errand. Others said she was looking for something or someone. I never asked, she never said."

"She didn't go to meet a lover in the camp?"

"By the time she got there in the fall of 1944, we were very busy processing the trains from Hungary. I didn't have time to keep track of a hometown adolescent wandering the streets of Krakow."

"When did you first meet her in Poland then?"

"That day...the day in January when we finally left."

"Tell me."

"You need to know about Auschwitz. It was war, but not. Those of us assigned there found it pleasant duty indeed. We had access to the finest wines and liquors. Food was plentiful and delicious. We all sent home jewelry, weapons, and money. We weren't supposed to do that, of course, but there was so much, and the Reich never missed it."

"You were stealing from people and murdering them."

He sighed. "It wasn't like that, Emo. Over the years, I've laughed at the accounts in the Jew-owned newspapers around the world. We were under attack by these people. They bought our banks, worked in our hospitals, and weaseled their way into our universities. They cheated us at every turn. They killed the Christ and they polluted our blood. No. I will not listen to this American nonsense about murder. I was protecting my country and my family. I was a servant of the Fatherland."

"Let's get back to *my* father."

"I can only guess who."

I frowned. "How did he meet Mama?"

"I don't know, exactly. We usually met young girls at their bund camps, and they were thrilled to become mothers for the Fatherland. I presume that's how they met. All I know is that in January 1945, the camp commandant ordered me to take Vala and her young son—you—back to Mannheim. Up until that point, I never actually saw Vala in Poland. Seems that Herr Hess sent a telegram to the commandant, insisting that she be escorted home. I assume he used an important name to back up his demand. He wanted to get her out of harm's way, I'm sure. We knew the war was lost and that our dishonorable enemies would punish our bravery and purity of purpose. Russian tanks were coming closer, and the fighting interfered with our mission. I knew it would be bad for those of us who were in leadership positions, so I was happy for the chance to get away."

He was lying. No way would a Sturmbannführer be pulled from his duties to escort us home. "Tell me about the bed."

"It was like this—when the shipments came in, we separated people from their belongings as soon as they got off the train and sent everything over to Canada."

"Canada?"

"That was what the inmates called the section of Birkenau where all the belongings were sorted and cataloged. After each train, there would be thousands of suitcases and bags to process. The guards loved it there. The women prisoners looked like women, unlike those sticks in the rest of the camp."

I remembered the pictures of the skeletons in pajamas in *American View* and shuddered. "If this was such a good post and if there was so much food and drink available, why were the prisoners starving?"

He glared at me. "They were there to work. We were under no obligation to feed them caviar."

I heard a gritty squeaky sound. The sheriff was grinding his teeth.

"Anyway," Jäger continued, "Canada was filled with all kinds of beautiful and expensive things—money, wood, gold, silver, jewels—family heirlooms. What would you bring with you?"

Up until last week, I would've had no idea what I would bring if I was forced out of my home and could only take what I could carry. Maybe I would've guessed money…or family pictures. Now after the fire, I knew that I would see to my family's safety before our possessions. I also knew the sad truth that the simple desire to watch over loved ones was not possible for the people who were my father's victims. They must have known they would be murdered. If not right away, eventually. It was a shattering thought. "So what does 'Canada' have to do with Mama's bed?"

"We used to have some of the Sonderkommandos make things from the stuff in Canada, things we could send to our sweethearts and wives back home."

"Sonderkommandos means special unit," I told the sheriff.

"Yes, very special," Jäger said. "Very special, indeed."

"This special unit, the members were carpenters? Craftsmen?"

"Actually, Emo, they were dead men." He slapped the table with the palm of his hand and cackled when I jumped.

"What else did they do besides make things to send back to Germany?"

Jäger's eyes rested on the sheriff briefly before returning to mine. "They were, shall we say, the cleanup crew. They burned the refuse and took out the trash."

His meaning was clear but this time, I refused to accommodate his nastiness. "They are dead. Is it necessary to continue to talk like that?"

His face changed and he seemed genuinely offended. "You don't know me. You said so yourself. Nothing is as clear as our enemies have made out. They say what they like, because they won the war. For your information, I am a very tender fellow. I love my country even after all these years of exile in Ohio, USA. The decisions were not mine to make. I followed orders like a good and honorable soldier should. I did nothing wrong, and I bitterly resent implications that I did." His face flushed and his voice rose. "In fact, I am proud of my work and of the service Germany did for the world."

"How can you be proud when millions died?"

He leaned forward. "They threatened everything I loved. Surely you can see that. Look at the tragedy that has befallen us. It can all be laid at the feet of the Jews. They caused it all. Our wrath was justified and necessary. They deserved to die."

"Babies, too?"

He sighed as if reasoning with me had worn him out. "A lion's cub is cute and lovable, but one day he will eat you."

"This is what my Oma and Opa believed?"

"And your aunt and your mother and your father. We all worked hard to free the world from the Jewish threat. We were strong and brave in the face of such an enormous task. We should be thanked for the progress we made."

I thought of Delores and her beautiful cousin Rosa who lost their loved ones, and of Oskar Schreiner who lost his sweetheart and his business and his home. I fought back tears. Their suffering could be laid at the feet of my family. No question now. No way to convince myself that it wasn't so.

"Ten minutes, EJ," Sheriff Douglas murmured.

I nodded and checked my list of questions. "The bed."

"Herr Hess sent a car and driver to bring you and Vala back to Mannheim"

"Where was I?"

"You were staying with a family in Krakow. I picked you up there."

My dreams were memories! Vague to be sure, but they reflected something that did happen. My leg trembled under the table. "I remember a lady with silver hair."

"Yes. She had been caring for you for months."

"She cried when you took me." I gasped as I remembered. "You took me away from her!"

"She knew the time would come. She foolishly let herself become attached."

"Where was Mama?"

"She was in Auschwitz, looking at the bed."

"Gerhardt drove us through the camp."

"Yes."

"I saw a little girl."

"I doubt it. Little girls didn't live long at Birkenau."

Surely there was a little girl, the little girl-ghost. I squeezed my temples, struggling to remember. "There was a gate and tall brick buildings."

"Not in Birkenau. Perhaps someone else took you to the main camp."

"Not you?"

"Not me. I picked you up in Krakow and we drove to Auschwitz Birkenau. No side trips. We went to the building where the Sonderkommandos made the beds. They were popular with those of us in the SS."

"What happened?"

"Your mother was there with the commandant talking to an inmate."

"The commandant? Was he my..."

"A little wishful thinking?"

I didn't have time to react to his sarcasm. "What happened next?"

"I saw the bed. It was artistic, and not at all practical. They said all those carvings tell a story," he wrinkled his nose, "but it was too busy and didn't appeal to my cleaner, more modern aesthetic. The funny thing though, at least I think so now, is that no one was talking about the bed once I delivered you to your mother. She focused totally on you, like the two of you hadn't seen each other in a while. Everyone else loaded boxes and suitcases into the car. I never thought a thing about it until after they started closing in on me a few weeks ago, and I knew I'd have to leave Strongsville. One night I was lying in bed, fretting at the injustice of my situation. Then suddenly it came to me. You and your mother were cover."

"You mean you and Gerhardt smuggled something out of Auschwitz?"

"Not knowingly, of course. I remember that there were bags. Your things, I presumed. I had Gerhardt load them in the boot. There was money for me and for Gerhardt. Not a lot, but enough to make it worth my while."

"Who was smuggling what?"

"Could have been your Opa or the commandant. The more I thought of it, the more I realized that someone had been thinking ahead, providing resources for Germany's defeated heroes."

"What do you mean resources?"

He shrugged. "Money? Papers? Tickets? A place to stay?"

"My grandparents helped SS officers accused of war crimes get away?"

"I assume that was the plan...except Herr Hess died somewhere on the road to Poland. And Frau Hess passed away, and Vala ended up here in Cold Creek with the suitcase."

"Five minutes, EJ," Sheriff Douglas intoned.

"So you were the man in the car with us."

"You were a brat. Big for your age. And smart. But I'm surprised you remember as much as you do."

"Did you come with us to Mannheim?"

In the distance, a phone rang. Deputy Dixon left his post to answer it somewhere down the hall.

"You don't remember, Emo?"

I concentrated. "A gun and a sausage?"

Deputy Dixon came back to our door and knocked lightly with his knuckles.

"Yes, Jimmy?" Sheriff Douglas's voice boomed in the small room.

Dolph Jäger sighed in exaggerated exasperation.

Deputy Dixon opened the door and stuck in his head. "They're here. Penny is bringing them back."

"Thank you." The sheriff relaxed back into his seat and nodded at us to continue.

"Listen to me, Emo. Our time is up. Your mother must have something. She may or may not know it, but she has it."

I rolled my eyes. "No way was she helping Nazis get away with their crimes. If so, you wouldn't have needed to beat her."

He frowned. "Don't push me, Emo. Not if you want any more answers from me."

We both knew there was no more time. Now that the conversation was over, my ability to control my emotions eroded. "How do I know any of this is true? My mother was fifteen. She had just given birth to my little brother. I can't believe Opa would risk her life and Mick's and mine on a fool's errand like this. I don't know who our father was, and neither do you, it seems. The only thing I do remember is that you were mean to me, and Mama chased you away with your own gun. You wasted my time and Sheriff Douglas's. You don't know anything."

Jäger's eyes blazed. "Ah, but you see, your Mama never gave birth to any baby in Krakow. It was just you and Vala, until Vala picked up that little 'sausage' off a dead body lying beside the road."

I sat back in my chair, my mouth agape.

Footsteps in the corridor and then Penny's nauseating perfume.

"What do you mean *sausage*?"

"What do you think I mean?"

"Mick?"

Jäger's eyes sparkled with satisfaction. "You should have given me the money and let me leave, Emo."

The door opened.

* * *

I stood on the steps outside the municipal building and looked around for the Logan Foods truck. Not seeing it, I sat on a bench on the courthouse grounds. When I first found Dolph Jäger in our shed, I had no idea who he was or what he had done. However, in the few days since he'd gone after Mama, everyone in Cold Creek had learned about his role in Auschwitz. The very idea of such a creepy villain breaking into our home and attacking Mama made me queasy.

"Are you okay, son? Do you want me to call your folks?" Sheriff Douglas sat down beside me.

"Sonny or Uncle Grant will come soon enough. I need a minute to think before I talk to them."

"What should we do about Mick?"

I shook my head. "He trusts me, Sheriff. He made me promise to tell him whatever this guy said about our family."

"Did you expect this?"

"I knew Mama had a secret, but ..."

"Do you believe him?"

"Do you?"

"I think we have different ideas of truth."

I wiped the sweat off my upper lip. "I wonder if Sonny knows."

"Whether he does or doesn't, he loves you boys like you were his own. Does this change anything for him?"

Did it? Sonny picked up two little boys sleeping in a box on Oma's terrace and gave us a home. Did it matter that one of them wasn't Mama's natural baby? Did it matter to Grandma Arial? No, I knew they loved us no matter what. "No, sir. The only people it would matter to would be Mama and Mick."

"Vala probably didn't say anything in the beginning because she wanted to bring you boys here. That means she lied when she filled out the immigration documents."

"Will she get in trouble?"

"She might."

"That must be why she kept this a secret all these years."

The sheriff nodded.

A black sedan pulled out of the underground garage and headed up Main Street. "Is that Jäger on his way to Israel?" I jerked my thumb toward the sedan.

"Yes."

"Think he really believes what he did was right, like he said?"

"He might, but it doesn't make any difference. You don't need religion to know it's wrong to throw living babies into fires or to bash their heads against the sides of trucks."

"You should feel it in your heart."

The sheriff's shoulders slumped. His face, when he turned it toward me, was weary. "Yes."

I remembered the peaceful expression in Jäger's eyes. "But he doesn't, does he? He knows what he did, but he doesn't think it was wrong."

The sheriff took out his handkerchief and wiped his face. "It's worse than that, EJ." He folded the damp cotton cloth three times and tucked it back into his pocket. "I think he liked it."

"Yeah." It was unfathomable, and yet, I didn't doubt it for a moment.

Sheriff Douglas nodded toward the street. The Logan Foods truck was just passing the black sedan. "Looks like Grant will be here in a minute. What about Mick? Do you think this would upset him?"

"It would me."

"Then why let that weasel cause you to hurt your brother?"

"You'll never tell anyone that part?"

He stuck out his hand. "I promise, son. Mick will never hear it from me."

I stood up and shook his hand. "Thank you, sir."

"You know, I always liked your mother, but this nudges her up a lot higher in my estimation. To take a baby off a dead body like that, the body of a stranger, not just to rescue him but to give him a chance at life when she wasn't but a kid herself, and to carry through with it all these years—well, that's something special, EJ. Don't you forget that about your mom."

"Yes, sir." I marveled at the idea. One baby out of millions! How lucky we were to have Mick. "I can't even imagine life without my brother."

Uncle Grant parked the Metro in front of us. He and Mick got out and came toward us.

The sheriff and I turned toward them.

"Be strong," Sheriff Douglas whispered out of the corner of his mouth.

I squared my shoulders.

27

The Hospital

April 23, 1960

"BUT WHY ARE they keeping her another day?" I said as we pulled into traffic and headed back to the hospital.

"They found a problem." Uncle Grant was nervous. I could tell by the way he gripped the steering wheel.

I twisted in my seat so I could see Mick. "Do you know?"

He frowned. "Just that I couldn't stay with her like we planned. They wouldn't tell me why until we're all together."

I faced forward, my mind whirling. What? What? What? What was worse than being strangled by a Nazi in your own back yard?

"Don't fret. We'll be there in ten minutes and then you'll know." Uncle Grant kept his eyes on the road and there wasn't any further conversation. I didn't know whether to be irritated or more worried.

As we pulled into the hospital parking lot, I unlatched my door so I could jump out the moment the truck stopped.

Uncle Grant bellowed, "EJ!"

"What?"

He braked and put the truck in neutral. "It's not that urgent. Relax. We will go up together."

I pushed back my terror and nodded.

* * *

Sonny was waiting for us outside Mama's room.

He hugged me first and then Mick. "How was the interview?"

"Disgusting. How is Mama?"

Come sit down in the family room. He led the three of us down the hall to a large windowless space. At least there was a door so that the whole world wasn't watching us. Mick and I shared a couch. Uncle Grant took a chair. We waited while Sonny lit a cigarette.

"I know the two of you have been worried about your mom, since the story keeps changing. Every day since she's been here, they told us that she is okay but it would be one more night before she could come home. She needs more tests, she wrenched her back, there's a broken bone in her foot, her throat's so swollen she can't eat, she has an infection from being in the hospital. It's always something."

"Is it more than what Jäger did to her?"

"She's not healing as fast as they think she should, so they've been trying to figure out why. This morning, they decided she's had an emotional breakdown and that's why she isn't responding."

"What's that?"

Sonny glanced at Uncle Grant before focusing on Mick. Your mama is sad—so sad that all she wants to do is sleep or cry."

"Is that why she drinks so much wine?"

"It could be."

"Then it doesn't have anything to do with Dolph Jäger," I said. "Because she's been nervous for a long time."

"I'm sure her encounter with him didn't help. The realization that someone hated her so much that he wanted her dead shook your mama up and added to her other sorrows."

"Do nervous breakdowns run in families?"

They all turned toward me. Mick's eyes were wide. Sonny blew smoke out of his nose.

Uncle Grant was the first to speak. "Don't jump to that conclusion yet, EJ. We'll ask the doctor, but it's too soon to worry about anything like that."

"But it could be," Mick said. "Maybe we'll all be crazy like Lana."

I was sorry that I'd scared my brother, especially since I knew he was safe from any Hess family curse.

Uncle Grant put a hand on Mick's shoulder. "Now, now. Vala has reason to be exhausted. When you think about it, her whole life has been chaotic. That girl has gone through more stress and horror and loss than most of us can imagine. Maybe being attacked in her own home was the last straw."

It was more than I'd ever heard my uncle say at one time. I lowered my eyes. "Yes, sir." I thought about what Dolph Jäger told me. Did Mama really have money or papers to help war criminals escape? We'd been Americans for a long time now. We lived like Americans, thought like Americans. I couldn't imagine her doing anything to jeopardize that.

Sonny put out his cigarette. "Whatever has caused her to be depressed, the doctors think she needs to be sent to a special hospital in Pittsburgh. She needs rest and some time away from wine—and from anything upsetting."

The bottom fell out of my world.

Mick collected himself enough to speak before I could. "Won't being away from us upset her more?"

"Last week, I'd have said yes to that question, but this week, knowing the condition she's in now, both physically and mentally, I think she can't handle everyday life. She's afraid when anyone knocks on the door or when she hears the medical cart being pushed down the hall. This morning she became hysterical when a different nurse than she's used to came to take blood."

Poor Mama. That might seem like paranoia to an ordinary person, but I could understand being afraid, after what Jäger had done to her. "When will you take her to this place?"

"This afternoon, after you and Mick see her."

"So soon?" I needed more time to get used the idea. "How long will she be gone?"

Sonny looked deeply into my eyes. "Until she's better or our money runs out."

I leaned back in my seat. How long would either of those things take? Mama had already been in the hospital three days. I glanced at Mick. He was scared, too. Mama might be having a nervous breakdown, but she still managed to raise us and love us and keep us safe from all the bad stuff she'd had to face. She fought off Dolph Jäger, a long time ago on that frozen winter road and then again last week on our back porch. I was filled with love and admiration for her. "Can we go visit her?"

"When the doctors say it's okay."

"Poor mommy will be so alone," Mick murmured.

"Well...um...not for a while at least. I'm going to go with her. I'll stay with Delores's family in Squirrel Hill."

"What'll happen to us?" Mick cried.

"You'll stay with Grandma Arial at the Windshift Inn. I've already spoken with Myrtle and Jerry. They're getting ready for you to move over there tonight. While we're gone, I need you guys to work with your Uncle Grant to get our house in shape. I want Vala to return to her very own home."

We sat quietly for a moment, each of us pondering our new situation.

"Should I tell her about talking with Dolph Jäger?"

"Maybe not until she comes back from the hospital," Sonny said. "She's not ready for more than a quick chat."

I brought the book we were reading the night before Mama got hurt. I held up a paperback copy of *Old Yeller* that I'd stuffed in my pocket. "Will that be okay?"

Sonny glanced at Uncle Grant. "That might be a good idea, keep her entertained and thinking about someone else's story rather than her own."

"Mick and I can pick a book every week for you to read to her while she's in Pittsburgh."

"That'll be perfect. It'll give her something to look forward to...a new story every week."

"And we'll send her letters and postcards."

A nurse stuck her head in the door. "Mrs. Logan is awake now."

"Thank you." Sonny nodded and the woman left.

I swallowed and then swallowed again. What would Mama look like? Surely the bruises would've faded by now. Was she hurting? What about her arm? Her foot?

Mick was calmer and more practical. "How long do we have with her?"

"About an hour. They're doing the paperwork now," Sonny said. "The Metro would be too uncomfortable so they're arranging for an ambulance to take us."

"What if she gets scared and can't remember how to ask for something in English?"

"I'll be nearby all the time, EJ."

"Can't we visit her in Pittsburgh?" Again, Mick went after information we could use.

"I honestly don't know, boys. I'll call you every day. And as soon as they say it's okay, Grandma Arial and Uncle Grant will bring you to see her."

"Can we talk to her now?" I straightened my collar and smoothed my hair.

Sonny looked at his watch. "Yes, you better get down there. Now that we've made this decision, she feels more at peace. But she's anxious about seeing you guys."

"Anxious?" Mick's voice went from tenor to bass and back to a crackle.

I was shocked at the thought, too.

"Are you guys ready to see your mother?"

Mick and I looked at each other.

"I'm ready." In fact, I was eager. I missed Mama, and I was worried about her. And before that, earlier on the day Jäger attacked her, I'd fought with her. Why was that? Oh, yeah—Rosa. I needed to apologize to Mama.

"Let's do it." Mick's grin was crooked. Neither my mouth nor Mama's did that. Why had I never noticed it before?

"Her room is 223, right down that hall to the right. Grant and I'll get a cup of coffee in the cafeteria while you're with her."

"Okay." I glanced over my shoulder once as we went down the hall. Both Sonny and Uncle Grant were still there watching us. A sudden lump formed in my throat. I loved them so much, and I loved my little brother Mick who was trotting along beside me, trying to keep up with my longer stride.

Grandma Arial sat in a straight-backed chair by the window, knitting and talking to a thinner, paler version of my mother. "Here they are, Vala. I told you they would make it before you leave."

Mama's head rolled across her pillow to look at us. "Meine Kinder."

"Mama." Mick ran to hug her.

"I'm not okay, babies."

The bruises on her face and arms had faded to yellow, and the cut on her lip was healing. However, the whites of her eyes were still red and the bruise on her neck was still dark. Her arm was in a cast and bound tightly against her body. She was hurt in so many places that Mick gave up finding a way to embrace her and simply knelt by the bed and laid his head on her good shoulder. "Oh, Mama," he whispered. "The doctors will help you get better. Sonny will be with you. EJ and I'll help, I promise."

I stood at the end of her bed. Mama had changed since our wonderful evening at the Windshift Inn only a week before. I searched for something nice to say. "Your hair looks pretty, Mama." It was braided around her head. "I never saw you wear it that way."

Grimacing, she patted the back of her head with her good hand. "Arial...she do for me."

"Makes a girl feel good to get a new hairdo," Grandma Arial said. "When you can't comb it yourself and you have to stay in bed awhile, you want to keep it neat."

"Yes, is nice, Arial. Danke."

Mick and I exchanged glances. There was something wrong with Mama beside the obvious. Her eyes were scary beyond the angry red spots in the whites, and her speech was low and slow.

"Sonny says you're going to Pennsylvania," Mick said.

She bobbed her head up and down without lifting it off the pillow. "Ja. Another hospital—Mayview—but they don't say why I can't rest at home."

"They have nice big bathtubs to help you relax, and people you can talk to about how you feel." Grandma Arial was sad and subdued, but I knew she was trying to make Mama feel better about having to leave Cold Creek.

"But why do I need big bathtubs? I don't have time for such luxuries. Meine haus needs fixing." Mama kissed the top of Mick's head. "And you need a haircut, Liebchen, and strudel."

I chuckled. The one thing Mama and Grandma Arial always agreed on was that in times of trouble, strudel was a magic wand that made things better.

"I'll make sure the boys have plenty to eat while you're gone, Vala." Grandma Arial flipped whatever she was knitting over so she could start the next row. "I'm sure you'll like Pittsburgh. Delores will visit you often."

Seeing Mama's beat-up face and bloody eyes, I wondered just how long it would be before she could come home. She had to be sore all over—and scared. She had no idea that her brave fight against that monster of Auschwitz had made her a heroine to the citizens of Cold Creek. Once and for all, she had destroyed their suspicions about her loyalties. And there were at least half a dozen invitations waiting for her at Grandma's to events she would never have been welcome at only a week ago.

* * *

"Vala, while the boys are here, I'm going to check on Grant and Sonny and make sure all the arrangements have been made." Grandma Arial stuffed her knitting into a bag and stood up.

Fear flashed across Mama's face and she stiffened.

Grandma Arial took her uninjured hand. "It'll be okay. We'll all be back shortly."

Mama clung to Grandma Arial. "What if the wolf finds me?"

"Your sons will protect you, darling. You raised two strong young men. You should be proud." Grandma took Mick's hand and placed it in Mama's. "Hold onto Mick. He won't let the wolf anywhere near you. And I won't be gone long. The boys want to talk to you."

"I brought a book, Mama. You want me to read to you?" Mick held up a copy of *Old Yeller*.

"Is that one about the wolf?" Mama's eyes grew suspicious.

Mick glanced at me, horrified. Then he composed his face and turned back to Mama. "*Old Yeller* protects his family. He fights the wolf. Okay?" His voice was smooth and reassuring, like he had everything under control.

"I want my little Schatzi. Dolph didn't hurt Schatzi, did he?" Mama sank deeper into her pillow sobbing.

I couldn't figure out what was bothering her. Everything, I guessed. "Schatzi is fine, Mama. He's staying with us at Grandma's. We gave him a bath and he smells a lot better."

"If they would just let me stay with Schatzi," she wailed.

"We'll bring Schatzi when we come see you in Pittsburgh." Mick handed Mama a tissue and she dabbed at her eyes with it.

Grandma Arial pulled me into the hallway. "Mick is doing fine," she whispered. "But before I leave the two of you alone with your Mama, I need to talk to each of you."

I was surprised at the urgency in her voice. "Okay. What can I do for you?"

"Vala is fragile right now. You can see that."

"Yes." Even though unable to get out of bed, everything about Mama was loud and piteous, like what was going on in her head was bigger and scarier than what was happening in her hospital room.

"Your headache is back?" Grandma Arial put the back of her fingers against my cheek.

"A little."

"No seizures though?"

"Not my regular kind. So much has happened the last week and I'm trying to sort it all out."

"You grew up this week. It's a good thing because we're going to need you. Your mama is going to need you."

I lacked Mick's poise and confidence, so I bluffed. "Whatever it takes."

"I'll take Mick with me in a minute. You spend some time with your mother. Until this past week, she hasn't spent one night away from you and Mick since you came to Cold Creek. She's afraid you boys will feel abandoned and hate her."

"That won't ever happen. I have a brother and Sonny and you, because of her. She's my mother, my link to who I am. I know it was bad for her. Even if I can't understand what's bugging her, I still love her."

We stood there quietly, an unusual tension between us.

Finally, Grandma Arial said, "Do you want to tell me about Dolph Jäger?"

It was the opening I needed. I glanced over my shoulder at Mick and Mama. "Not here," I whispered and pulled her to a couch further down the hall.

We sat for a moment as I struggled to find a way to tell her about the loathsome conversation I'd had with the man who had done this to my mother. Finally, I took a deep breath and blurted out his story about Mick.

Grandma Arial smoothed nonexistent wrinkles out of her skirt. "I hope you can see why we kept Vala's secret all this time," she said without looking at me. "We were glad that you didn't seem to remember that night in Poland and decided to keep quiet about it until you and Mick were old enough not to accidentally talk about it with the neighbors."

I was irked all over again. "I'm eighteen. How long were you going to wait?"

"Until Vala decided that she was comfortable telling you."

Those were two different things, but I decided not to challenge Grandma Arial. I understood that she was limited to Sonny and Mama's decisions. "Besides you and Sonny, who else knows?"

"Mags and Shirley. That's it...until now."

"Not Uncle Grant?"

"No."

I leaned forward, resting my elbows on my thighs.

Grandma stroked my back. "I know you're frustrated and angry, but you need to put all that aside for a while longer. Vala has been carrying some heavy burdens that finally overwhelmed her. That lunatic took away all the security we've been trying to give her. He even took away her right to tell you—at the time and place of her own choosing—about that night in Poland. She needs to heal and rest, and you need to reassure her that you and Mick—"

"And Schatzi." I smiled even though I felt like crying.

"Yes, and Schatzi—will miss her, but that you will be fine while she gets better. And that you both will be eagerly awaiting her return."

"I can do that."

"Good." She kissed my cheek. "Now go in there and send Mick out to talk with me."

"Are you going to tell him?"

"Sonny and I had decided that we would wait until Vala returns and let her do it. If you choose to tell Mick before then, I'm sure everyone, including Vala, will understand. So you have options, EJ. What will you do?"

I shrugged. "Play it by ear?"

The hospital room was on the shady side of the campus. I stood in the doorway for a moment listening to Mick read about a boy racing to rescue his little brother from a bear. Just as the boy realizes he won't make it in time, an old yellow dog—a stray like all of us, it seemed—streaks across the meadow and chases the ferocious beast away. If only it were that simple.

Mama's eyes were closed.

I tapped Mick on the shoulder and gestured toward Grandma Arial in the hall. He handed me the book, and I started reading where he left off. He got up and I took his seat. Mick tapped the top of my head with his knuckles and then joined Grandma in the hall. At first I could hear their soft whispers but then they moved away and the only sound was my own voice.

I glanced at Mama as I turned the page.

"Guten Tag, Emo."

I closed *Old Yeller* and smiled. "How are you feeling?"

"Sore."

The swelling made it hard to look at her face, but I did anyway. As crazy and restless as she'd been a few minutes before, she was lucid now. "Is there anything I can do for you?"

She blew air out through pursed lips. "I hated him, you know."

"Dolph Jäger?"

"He was not friend to my family. Papi didn't like him and Lana was afraid of him."

"Why did you go to Poland, Mama?"

She faded out for a moment, and I was afraid they'd already drugged her for the trip to Pittsburgh. Then she startled and grabbed my sleeve. "Emo, I must tell you this part. I wanted to wait until you were a man, but I might be crazy and I must tell you now."

"I'm here, Mama. Tell me whatever you want." My heart pounded.

"Sturmbannführer Jäger wrote to Papi. He said he found records at the camp about…" Her voice trailed off into a murmur.

"About what, Mama?"

"About Lana's baby's…"

"What did he say about baby Wolf?"

Her eyelids closed and her fingers slipped out of my hand.

"Mama? What did Jäger say? Did baby Wolf die in Auschwitz?"

When she opened her eyes, they had that scary otherworldly look in them again. "I—what did you say?"

"What happened to Wolf?"

"No. No wolf!" She screamed and threw her good hand up as if to protect her face. "Oh, der Wolf kommt für mich."

I tried to hold her but she fought me, screaming. "Mama! It's Emo!"

I fumbled around until I found the call button, then backed away in the face of my mother's rising screams. My leg twitched and I sat down on the edge of her bed, trying to keep my heel from tapping the linoleum.

Teresa Kline appeared at the door. "We'll take care of her, EJ."

I was helpless in the face of Mama's hysteria. "What should I do?"

"Stand outside in the hallway."

As I limped outside, I could hear Mama.

"Der Wolf. I see him. He follows me wherever I go."

"No wolf here, Vala. We are safe from wolves in the hospital. We have a guard. Remember your friend Skippy? He's out front watching for wolves right now."

"Skippy watches?" Mama's voice trembled but she was no longer screaming.

"I promise you."

"What if he doesn't see wolf?"

A nurse and a doctor rushed past me into Mama's room, ready to restrain her if necessary, but Teresa had already gotten Mama past the crisis.

I peeked around the door jamb. Teresa sat by Mama's bed, holding her and rocking back and forth. "It's okay, Vala. You're safe," she crooned.

The doctor checked Mama's eyes and listened to her heart. "Agitated. Heartbeat is up again. How long before the ambulance arrives?"

"ETA is five minutes, Doctor," the nurse said.

"That's close enough. Let's start her medication now. She'll be asleep when the ambulance gets here, and that will lessen the stress of the move."

The nurse left to fetch whatever medication Mama would need to sleep through her long ride in the ambulance.

"Can you go with her to Pittsburgh, Mrs. Kline?"

"Of course, it's already arranged. Vala and I are old friends. No way would I leave her. Danny will come for me in Pittsburgh later tonight."

Sonny, Mick, Grandma Arial, and Uncle Grant hurried down the hall toward me.

"What happened?"

"It's my fault. She got scared about the wolf."

"You stop that, EJ Logan." Grandma Arial put her arms around me. "You didn't cause your mama's problems. Thank goodness you were there to call for help."

Sonny squeezed my arm before entering Mama's room.

I started to follow him but Uncle Grant held me back. "It's getting mighty crowded in there. You can say your goodbyes once they get her ready for the trip. Let's go back down to the family room to wait."

"But I wanted to talk to her more," Mick said as we turned to go.

"I'm sorry. I messed up everything, asking questions."

The nurse hurried past us with a tray, a vial, and a hypodermic.

28

Annie's Magic

April 23, 1960

Rain pounded on the tin roof. I lay on the floor of the tree house, my head propped up on the musty old cushions. Nothing made sense. I wanted to cry but nothing came out—no tears, no sobs, no dry heaves—just a heavy weight on my chest. I took several deep breaths. Relax, EJ. Relax. Don't think. Relax. What was that smell? Rain? Wet leaves. My muscles softened and I drifted off to sleep.

* * *

Tante Magda, I'm thirsty.
Soon, baby. They will give us a drink soon.
Loud noises. BAM. BA-BAM.
I screamed and held up my arms. Hold me!
I can't. You have to walk this time.
I clung to her skirt, sobbing.
She put her hand on the back of my head. Just a little farther.
I'm thirsty, Tante Magda.

* * *

"EJ?"
I opened my eyes.
"EJ Logan."
I stuck my head out of the window. "What?"
Annie Jones shivered at the foot of the tree. "Can I come up?"
"Be careful. The steps are slippery." I hooked one arm around the branch that supported the rope ladder. "Take my hand."
Annie grabbed my arm and scrambled up into the tree house. Once inside, she wrapped her arms around my neck.
"How did you know?" I whispered into her shoulder.
"I felt you needed me, so I went to your house. Your uncle was in one of the upstairs bedrooms. He told me you might be here."
She was soaked but I held her close anyway. "If you had the power to feel that, how come you didn't come before now?" I kissed her passionately before I realized what I was doing.
"EJ…"
I kissed her again.

"EJ, give me a minute. I didn't come for this…" She put both hands on my chest, but she didn't push me away.

I'd have kissed her one more time, but the tears that wouldn't come before my nap arrived suddenly and explosively. I sobbed on her shoulder until no more tears came, and I lay back on the old cushion, depleted.

"I am so sorry about everything that's happened to you this last week." She wiped away my tears with her fingertips.

I pressed the heels of my hands against my eyelids.

"Something wrong?"

Was she kidding? My irritation drained away when I saw the concern on her face. "Crying headaches aren't all that different from ice cream ones."

"I guess not."

"You're cold."

She shrugged. "Didn't expect a downpour when I left for school this morning."

"I thought you knew things."

"Mystical things, not practical ones." Her teeth chattered but her eyes sparkled.

"Smart aleck." I reached around her to Sonny's old trunk and opened it. A threadbare hand towel and a folded quilt covered the books and other things I'd collected over the years the tree house was my sanctuary. "I'm not used to company up here, so I'm not well stocked."

"I came uninvited. I won't stay long."

"Let's get you dry." I handed her the small scrap of terry cloth.

She took off her cardigan, and I draped it over one of the branches that crisscrossed outside the window. Her blouse was damp, too. I tried not to look at her breasts as she wiped her face and neck with the towel. "Thank you for coming to see me. I haven't quite known what to do."

"I heard about that Nazi. That was something, catching a villain like that. It was like a Superman story, only instead of being in a comic book, it was in the *Cold Creek Chronicle*."

"It was great fun having a war criminal try to kill my mother and then having the whole town know about it."

She put a hand on my shoulder. "I didn't mean it that way."

Distracted by her touch, I lost track of what I was doing and froze. Maybe I was too sensitive. Maybe she wasn't making fun of me after all. I unfolded the ragged old quilt and wrapped it around her shoulders. "I know. I'm sorry I snapped."

She touched my cheek. "Just stop it, then."

"Easier said than done when you're a dope." I spread the damp towel on the lid of the trunk. The tree house platform was small and the ceiling was low. To stay out of the rain, we had no choice but to curl up together on the plank floor with our heads on the same cushion.

"This is cozy." I kissed her forehead. A week ago, I was scared to put my arm around her. Now I wanted to hold her until she made me let go.

"How long will your mom be in Pittsburgh?"

I shrugged.

"Where's your brother?"

"He's staying at the Windshift Inn. All of us are, actually. Even Grandma Arial. She wants to keep a close eye on us."

"My cousin went to Mayview." She pulled the quilt up around her ears. "Had twelve shock treatments in three weeks."

"Why?"

"He was a soldier, and I guess he had a bad time of it in Germany. He stopped eating. Just sat around the house, smoking and getting thinner and thinner. Then he stopped talking."

"Nothing at all?"

"Not even to ask for more cigarettes. He'd just throw a tantrum when the carton was empty."

"Is he okay now?"

"He hanged himself."

"No." It was a low exhalation instead of a word. I imagined a young man hanging from an oak tree not unlike the one we were in. The body swung to and fro, until the breeze spun it toward me slowly. The young man's features were contorted, and then I realized it wasn't a man's body. It was Mama's.

"I'm not saying that's what your mama will do!"

Did she read my mind? "Mama is strong. She's been through a lot, you know. She gets sad and drinks too much wine. She's not crazy or anything." The words came out so fast I almost choked on them.

"No one said she was crazy, did they?"

"They said she was exhausted. Anxious."

"She'll be okay."

"Is that a mystic pronouncement?"

"Yeah, but common sense, too. Why would she survive all that she has, only to give up now?"

"Exactly. Why would she fall apart now?" I couldn't imagine a single reason why she would, but my stomach muscles tightened anyway.

"So are we going to talk?"

"We talk all the time." I was beginning to wish she wasn't there after all.

She put a hand on each cheek and looked into my eyes. "You know what I mean."

It felt like she could see into the vault where all my private thoughts lived. I closed my eyes to keep her out. It was my only defense. "I'm not good at that."

"Don't be scared. I won't tell anyone."

All I wanted to do was hold her and kiss her—and maybe touch her breasts. Talking was too hard right then. "What if I tell you something, and then you hate me after I do?"

"People take that risk every day. If they didn't, no one would ever talk to each other."

Did Sonny and Mama talk about anything that mattered? If they did, I never heard them. Mama's English was limited, and Sonny's German was even more so. They kept secrets from each other and from Mick and me—and from Grandma Arial, too. And now, if Dolph Jäger was to be believed at all, I was the keeper of a big secret myself. "Will you tell me things, too?"

"Are you scared that your bad stuff is worse than mine?" She let go of my face and relaxed back into the cushion. "Because if that's the case, you're wrong."

"I'm sorry, Annie. I've always wanted someone to be straight with me, but I guess I never learned how to do it myself."

"What if I go first?"

I was cornered. "Okay."

"You promise never to tell anyone?"

"Sure."

"My mama got pregnant with me when Daddy was away at war."

I rose up on one elbow. "Really? Didn't he mind?"

"I guess not. They're still together and he loves me as much as he loves my brother."

"I guess people don't have to be related to babies to take them in and love them."

"Apparently not."

"How did you find out?"

"Meddling through old boxes of papers. My birth certificate didn't match up with a clipping I found. He was in a tank in the Kasserine Pass when I was being conceived."

"So…who?"

"No idea."

"Your mom never let on?"

"Not a word in my presence."

"And your dad?"

"Nothing."

"Any ideas?"

"I'm the spitting image of my Uncle Harry, but that dog won't hunt either. He was in jail that year."

"No one else?"

"Not that I can figure."

"Your mom never says anything?"

"I never told her I know."

"Why not?"

"Because she's trying to protect me, EJ. So I decided to help her keep her secret."

I sighed. "Yeah."

"It's what people do for each other."

"Is this some mystical lesson?"

"Of course it is."

That hit me wrong. "And living the lie doesn't bother you?"

"Whatever the facts are, EJ, my truth is that they are my parents. They love me and I love them."

"Did you talk with Sheriff Douglas, by any chance?"

"Don't know the man."

"I thought you were related to the Douglases."

She giggled. "He's my second cousin, but he's twenty-five years older than me. I've never had a conversation with him in my life."

Annie didn't come sniffing around the same day Sheriff Douglas and I made our pact because she felt something. I wanted to believe it—but I didn't.

She put her arms around me and whispered in my ear. "Let it go, EJ."

"I don't like life lessons, especially magic ones."

"You're an old grump."

"I am not."

"Okay, a young grump." She giggled and my heart almost melted.

Trying to let go of my frustration, I said, "What's that smell?"

"It's called 'Here's My Heart.' I stole a roll or two from my mother's bottle. You like?:

I wasn't used to strong smells, and my already swollen sinuses burned. "Nice."

She smothered a chuckle with her knuckles. "You are such a liar and you don't even know it."

"I am not."

"Of course you are."

"Okay, my nose is twice as long as Pinocchio's. I tell more big ones than Scarlet O'Hara. I tell three lies before breakfast, and it's a good day for me when I get in seven untruths. Is that what you want to hear?" My rage abated. I lowered my voice. "I'm sorry, Annie. This isn't going well, is it?"

"What's wrong with you, EJ? Don't you know how to goof around? To laugh?"

"I guess not, at least not right now." How could someone I'd dreamed of nightly for years, who'd finally found her way to my tree and into my arms, be so irritating?

We lay there for a long uncomfortable time, listening to the wind rattling the tin roof. She rolled toward me. "I came to comfort you—to distract you, you know? I wanted to make you feel better, not worse."

Everything made me feel worse at that moment, even her apology. "I know."

"Can we try again?"

All I wanted was to be alone to feel sorry for myself.

"Come on, EJ Logan, aren't you tired of feeling sorry for yourself?"

"I'm not—"

"Of course you are—"

"Enough, okay? I guess I'm not in the mood for company right now."

She put her arms around me and pressed her soft body against me. I wanted to respond. I wanted to so much. I wasn't even mad anymore. Just sad.

"EJ, maybe you can't let go right now. Maybe it will be a long time before you can. But when it's time, you must. You'll never understand everything. Okay?"

"I don't know what you're talking about, Annie."

She kissed my cheek. "You will."

* * *

I was asleep, my head on Tante Magda's shoulder.
Somewhere a door rattled open.
Tante Magda's arms tightened around me, "Be quiet, Emo."
A beam of light broke into the room and a gush of air.
"Where is Frau Schreiner?" The voice was insistent but soft.
"Nein," a woman in the far corner answered.
The light moved to the next person cowering in dusty darkness.
"Ver bist du?"
"Angela Sachs. Es gibt kein Baby."
With a hand to the back of my head, Tante Magda pressed my
face tight against her breast.
The light rested on the face of an older woman next to us.
"Und du?"
"Ich nicht."
And then the light was on us.
"Hier!"
Hands reached out of the dark and tore me away from Tante
Magda's arms.
"Emo!"

* * *

I was lying on my back in the tree house when I woke up. Annie was gone. What was wrong with me? I messed up my best chance with her. I pounded my forehead lightly with my fist. I knew—like Annie knew things—that there would never be another one. I'd been a jerk. That sweet, weird girl had only tried to help me, to deliver some kind of heavenly message, and I'd been cranky and suspicious. I'd treated her like dirt. Stupid!

Something was different. I listened. Nothing. The rain had stopped. I got to my knees and put the quilt back over the pile of documents from the smoky house. My mother was in the hospital. The secret that put her there had to be somewhere in those documents. I didn't want to stop going through them, but it was getting dark and I knew Grandma Arial would be looking for me soon. I closed the lid of the trunk and climbed down out of my tree.

29

The Gift

May 17, 1960

OUR HOUSE HAD sat for a month with the doors and windows open when the weather allowed. It still smelled awful. Mick and I spent every day after school wiping down windows, furniture, woodwork, and floors. Uncle Grant decided to repaint all the walls and replace the rugs. Fortunately, Grandma Arial found Mama's original color chips and carpet samples in the shed. They'd just gone into town to buy paint and order the installation of new carpeting.

Mick and I were sitting on the front steps, drinking lemonade that Grandma had left us.

"What do you think about the kitchen wallpaper? Think we ought to peel it off and paint?"

I drained my glass and set it down on the porch. "Depends on how bad the wallboard under it looks. It might be moldy by now and need to be replaced."

A truck with a Jones and Jolly Lumber sign on the doors pulled into the drive.

"Hello?" I stood up and waved. "Are you sure you're at the right address?"

A husky fellow with a clipboard in his hand got out of the truck. "This is 517 Cold Creek Drive? The Logans' property?"

"Yes, sir, but we didn't order any lumber that I know of."

The deliveryman shielded his eyes from the sun with one arm and scanned his clipboard. "It was ordered by a Mr. Arnold Vilani. There's a note here." He unclipped a large manila envelope and handed it to me.

"Mr. Vilani?" Mick got up and peered over my arm as I fished out and read a note. "Wow. That is so nice of him."

"Not just Mr. Vilani. All our neighbors donated something toward materials." I handed the letter to Mick to read for himself, and then pulled out the plans and instructions for a new screened-in porch.

"Where do you want us to unload this stuff?"

I glanced at Mick. "Out back?"

Mick nodded. "It'll be fun." He was practically drooling at the prospect of a new project.

The man turned to the driver of the truck. "Around back, John."

The driver wore a baseball cap with the visor pulled low. He nodded and drove down the driveway into the backyard. As he eased the truck past me, he turned his face away. That's odd, I thought. As he got out of the truck to unload the lumber, something about the way he moved seemed familiar.

"Why do you suppose our neighbors did this for us?" Mick accepted a box of nails and screws from the first man whose name tag identified him as Hank Jolly.

I unlocked the shed and put the plans and a new screen door inside. "They've known our family for years. Sonny and Uncle John and Uncle Grant grew up here. And everyone loves Grandma Arial."

"Maybe, but look at this list. Some of the same families who donated to our porch have suspected us for years. They've never thought of us as real Logans." Mick held up the card.

"Maybe they're getting used to us."

"Maybe they like that you caught a Nazi."

I chuckled. "They always say that. 'Caught,' not 'found cowering in our shed.' I'm gonna stop correcting them. Maybe next time I go Nazi hunting, they'll send us a grill to go on this fancy porch."

"I'd prefer a grand piano if I were the hero of the day."

We both laughed and, with the help of Hank and John, finished unloading our gift in less than fifteen minutes.

"I need you to sign here." Hank held out the clipboard again. "Just says we finished at 4:48 p.m."

I scribbled my name on the form.

"Would either of you like some lemonade? Or some ice water?" Mick turned his attention to Hank and John. "Unfortunately, we don't have any strudel today. Our mother has been ill."

"Thank you. Lemonade would be nice," Hank said. "It's been a long day for us."

We walked around to the front of the house, and Mick poured them each a Dixie cup of lemonade.

"Do you live around here?" I asked John, who had yet to say anything.

He studied his orange work boots and shook his head.

"John's a man of few words." Hank took a pack of Pall Malls out of his chest pocket. "I told him when I hired him that there was more listening than talking on this job."

"Sprechen sie Deutsch?" Something about John irritated me.

John shook his head. He was lying, but what difference did it make?

The men finished their drinks and climbed back into their delivery truck. As John pulled out of the driveway, the sun caught the side of his face. The image of a stranger confronting my mother in our kitchen filled my mind.

John Sarris.

* * *

I arranged planks of wood by length along the side of the shed. "Mr. Vilani made this happen. We owe him so much."

"I always thought he was a strange guy. Never imagined him trying to climb a fence to rescue Mama, though. That was pretty brave." Mick sat cross-legged on the grass, poring over the plans for the new porch.

"And all it got him was a night in jail."

"The cops didn't know any better. Neither did you."

My soul burned with the memory of the way I'd behaved that night. It was embarrassing and scary at the same time. I'd made a big scene instead of helping Mama when she needed me most.

We worked silently, sorting wood screws and springs and rolls of mesh.

"Think we can do this?"

"Piece of cake."

"Will we need any help, or can we do it ourselves?"

Mick put the last of the hardware away in the shed. "We can do it. With Uncle Grant, we'd be faster, but we can do it by ourselves if we want."

I trusted Mick's judgment. I'd never be an artisan, but I could bang nails into wood and screw things together. "Think we have time tonight?"

Mick glanced at the sky. "Couple hours before dark. We could put the frame together."

We set to work, grunting and sweating.

"With Mama needing to go to Mayview and all, we never got around to talking about what Dolph Jäger told you," Mick said as he set two boards in place.

I missed a nail and hit my thumb with the hammer. I screamed and fell backwards into the grass.

Mick dropped the boards. "You big dope. What have you done to yourself this time?"

"It's a bruise. I'll live."

"Trying to get out of this conversation?" Mick helped me up.

I pulled my thumb out of my mouth. "Am I that obvious?"

"I'm not stupid, you know."

"I know." My thumb hurt, but not as much as I let on. This was the fourth time Mick had brought up my conversation with Jäger. I was running out of excuses.

"Let's take a break then." He sat down on the grass. "There's no one else here now. Just tell me."

I sat down beside him. "I've gone over things in my head a hundred times. Sometimes I think what he told me should be a secret forever, that I should die with it inside my head. Because in the end, it changes nothing."

Mick punched me gently on the shoulder. "Then it shouldn't be that hard to say."

"It shouldn't be, but it is."

"You're scaring me, EJ."

"It's actually something that changed the way I look at Mama. It makes me cry."

"That bad?"

"No—yes! I always thought Mama was fragile and naive and maybe a little reckless. This changes all of that."

Mick stretched his legs. "Sonny always said she was tough."

"Did I ever tell you about the dream—the one where Mama and I are on a cold road from somewhere, heading home in a big car with a driver and someone in a dark blue coat?"

He nodded. "And the man hits Mama?"

"Yes, and I call him a monster."

"I always thought that dream must be kind of true."

That boy always surprised me. I took a deep breath and nodded. "I've thought about it a lot since I talked to Jäger and I can't quite figure it out, Mick. He said he was the man in the blue coat. Mama and I were heading back to Germany from Auschwitz, and we had a driver named Gerhardt. It had to be early 1945 since the reason we left was to escape the Russians. But in January 1945, I wasn't even eighteen months old. How can a baby that young remember so much?"

"Maybe you heard it from someone else?"

"Who?"

His eyes turned inward as he absorbed what I was telling him.

"Mama never told us anything about that night, and I didn't remember it. I remember nightmares. But if these dreams are memories, how much can be real?"

"Tell me your dream again. From beginning to end."

I closed my eyes and concentrated. "I want to separate what I dream from what Jäger told me, but that's hard now."

"Just do your best."

I nodded and took a breath. "I hate him. That's the first thing I feel when the dream begins."

"The monster?"

"He's mean to me."

"Is it Jäger?"

I shrugged. "That's the thing. I don't have a reason to doubt him when he says it was him, but I can't remember the monster's face."

"Jäger has those scary eyes."

"The monster had glasses on. It was night and we passed things that were burning, and I see flames reflected in the glasses." I opened my eyes. "That's not the same thing, is it?"

Mick shook his head. "That's a question mark, then. Too bad. They're his only distinguishing feature. He is average in every other way."

"There is his disposition. The monster in my dream is nasty, hitting Mama and me."

"Why?"

Actually I had no idea why. "It was like we were in his way."

"Maybe that's it. He had to ride with you and he didn't want to."

"But why would that be?"

Mick thought for a moment. "You were going home to Mannheim?"

"I can't explain, but I knew Mama and I were going home to Opa and Oma. I didn't remember who they were in my dreams. Just that we were going to see them."

"So you had a driver named Gerhardt."

"Yes, and he stopped when Mama said to." I snapped my fingers. "But he didn't listen to the monster at all."

"So the monster wasn't in charge."

"Maybe he was escaping, and Mama's car was the first he could find that was going west," I said.

"It was dark and there were lots of people walking on the road in the snow..." Mick prompted.

"I remember knowing that it was cold, but something was burning alongside the road."

"And that's when Mama got out of the car," Mick said, "to get food off someone who'd died, right? And the monster didn't want to let her keep it, and she grabbed his gun and told Gerhardt to leave the monster behind on that snowy road."

My mind was racing. Should I? Was it the right thing to do? "Yes, she came running back carrying something—sausage, I thought, in the dream."

"So why did he not want food? I don't understand."

"Maybe my dream was just that. I couldn't possibly remember all of this. I must have imagined it." I was playing for time.

Mick shrugged. "Aside from Jäger saying he was your monster and confirming the general details of your dream, I don't get why you're so reluctant to tell me."

There was no going back now, no delaying. "He...um...he said that *you* were the sausage."

Mick's eyes widened. "What?"

"It wasn't food Mama took off the dead woman beside the road, but a newborn baby. You."

Mick leaned back against the shed, gasping for air. "You mean Mama isn't..."

"Not according to Jäger."

"I don't believe it. He's a bad guy. He's trying to hurt us... and Mama."

"Do you want me to get you another glass of lemonade or call Grandma Arial?"

He shook his head. "Give me a minute."

"Okay." I studied my bruised thumb, waiting for Mick to collect himself.

"I can't imagine how your dream and what Jäger said square up," he said eventually. "How could you mistake a baby for a sausage?"

"I was little."

"I thought Mama had me before the trip back from Poland."

"Mama's never said that, but that's what I always thought, too. Don't know where I got that idea. Maybe that's what she wanted us to think. Maybe it was easier to get us over here if everyone thought you were her natural son."

"Did you talk to Sonny? What did he say?"

"He said the story Mama told him wasn't all that different from my dream. Fire lit the area enough to see people moving around. She glimpsed a woman lying on the side of the road. She asked Gerhardt to stop the car and when he did, she got out and ran back to the woman because she thought she might still be alive. But the woman was still and cold. Sonny said that she'd already ... uh ... birthed you and wrapped you in a piece of her skirt."

Mick shuddered. "That's too horrible to imagine, EJ."

"I guess that's why Mama never told us. Sonny said he and Mama wanted us to be brothers and the four of us to be a family. They put off telling us until they felt we were secure and happy in our new lives. They were also afraid we'd say something to the wrong person when we were little, and they would lose custody of you."

Tears streaked down Mick's cheeks.

I crawled over to him and put my arms around him.

"I'm scared, EJ. Do my papers—do they say I'm Mama's child? If anyone finds out I'm actually some nameless dead woman's baby, will I have to go back?"

"No one is sending you back to Poland. Sheriff Douglas agreed never to tell anyone or to act on this knowledge officially or otherwise. Besides, Mama would tear the heart out of anyone who tried to take you away. And don't even think about what Grandma Arial would do. With Mama in the hospital and the house such a mess, I haven't found all of our documentation, but Sonny said you're as legal as I am…as long as people think you're Mama's natural child."

"Do you think Mama has any idea who my mother was?"

"I was going to ask about everything when we visited her in the hospital before they left for Pittsburgh. But the time wasn't right."

"What do you think?"

"There were lots of people on the road with guards herding inmates from one concentration camp to another. If someone collapsed or stopped walking, they were shot. Sometimes prisoners died from exposure or whatever disease they may have gotten at Auschwitz. Your mother might have been one of them."

Mick pulled away from me. "How do you know all that?"

"Like I told you before, I read the *American View Magazine* that Shirley's father publishes."

"Does this mean I'm Jewish?"

"Maybe, but without identity papers, there's no way to know. The Nazis arrested all kinds of people. You and I are both as fair as Mama. People have commented all our lives how much we resemble each other. It's possible that a Jewish woman at Auschwitz could have concealed her pregnancy, but more likely this was a German or Polish woman, maybe someone who worked at the camp. Or like Mama and me, a visitor who got caught in the wrong place at the worst time."

"I guess I'll never know for sure."

"We can try, but I think you're right. I've had a month to look things up and talk to people who know more than I do. I called

Delores McDougal right after Sonny took Mama to Mayview. She and Mags and Shirley and Sonny and Grandma have been keeping Mama's secret for a long time. But now they're going to help us."

Mick shivered even though it was seventy degrees. "Do you think Mama will ever talk about it?"

"The cat's out of the bag now. Why not?"

"There could always be more secrets. At least now we understand why she was so nervous every time we asked."

I nodded. "Knowing how far Mama went to rescue you, and how much Sonny had to do to get us here makes me appreciate them even more."

We got up and started collecting parts from the porch kit and packing them back up.

"Do you think Mama showing up with a strange baby was the reason Oma wouldn't let us come into her house?"

"Maybe that was part of it," I said, "but Mama would have told her you were her own baby. And remember, Oma wouldn't even let me in."

"You don't remember her at all?"

"Nothing."

"That's odd, don't you think?"

"Everything about our lives is odd, Mick."

The sun was setting. We watched it, each of us lost in our own thoughts.

"Do you think Oma and Opa hated everyone different from them?"

"Yeah, I do."

"Why?"

I took a breath before answering. "Maybe because they were scared."

Mick shook his head. "Or unhappy."

"Maybe."

"I can't imagine happy people chasing others out of their homes and businesses and then murdering them."

"Me neither."

"What were they scared of?"

"Not being in charge, I guess."

After a minute, we put our tools back in the shed.

"It feels weird knowing that Dolph Jäger, the monster of Auschwitz, was hiding in here," Mick said. "It's even weirder that he knew things about us that we didn't even know about ourselves."

"He's nasty through and through. He takes pleasure in destroying people. I'm glad the Israelis are going to take care of him."

"Makes you wonder about all kinds of things, doesn't it? I can understand…"

A soft sound came from the side of the house.

"Who's there?"

A man stood in the shadow of our house. "Hallo."

I stepped in front of Mick. "Who are you?"

"Surely you figured that out by now, Emo. I thought we would be delivering the porch kit to an empty house or I would have found an excuse not to come."

"John Sarris?"

He laughed. "It was silly. I didn't know what to say when your mother caught me in her kitchen. So I acted the bully, anything to cover my true purpose. John Sarris was the name of a man I worked with in the car factory. I was born Gerhardt Schultz and I go by that name now, mostly."

"Except on your uniform." Mick pointed to the patch on his chest.

"Ja, the job, you know. Hank thought maybe it would be a good idea not to scare his customers. If I don't talk, they don't know."

"So why are you here now?"

"I overheard you talking this afternoon about the Nazi. You caught a Nazi?"

"You don't read the papers?"

"Not so much, no. It's hard to read English—takes time, you know."

That explained a lot, but I suspected he couldn't read at all. "Actually, believe it or not, you are the very person I want to talk to."

"Really? The last time, no one wanted to see me. I scared you all, and Vala—Frau Logan—she was angry."

"Gerhardt, we're going to have dinner at the Windshift Inn. Would you like to join us?"

Mick tugged at the back of my shirt. "EJ?"

"That big place on the hill over the little airport?"

"That's it."

"When?"

"We're heading up there now."

"EJ…"

Gerhardt pointed to his work clothes. "I need to clean up. I've been working all day."

"EJ!"

"It'll be okay, Mick. Uncle Grant will be there. And Grandma and the Klines," I whispered over my shoulder. "It's perfect, don't you see? He was on that road that night."

Mick backed away. He'd been through so much in the last few weeks, and unexpected things just kept happening.

I turned to Gerhardt. "Mick and I have to clean up as well. You can use our bathroom at the inn, and I'll loan you some of my clothes."

Gerhardt bowed from the waist. "You want me to tell you things."

"Yes."

* * *

Uncle Grant took a long swig of his Budweiser and suppressed a belch. "You're sure he's not dangerous?"

"Look at him." I pointed my bottle of Orange Soda at Gerhardt. My clothes were too big for him. Sitting in the parlor chatting with Grandma Arial and Jerry Kline, he looked stiff and uncomfortable. "He's a working man. He always has been and probably always will be. I don't think he can even read."

Uncle Grant peered at Gerhardt over his glasses. "That doesn't mean he wasn't part of the craziness that took place in Europe. He broke into your house the same night the other Nazi tried to get into Grandma Arial's."

"Other Nazi?"

Uncle Grant stiffened and avoided my eyes.

"The other guy was a Nazi?"

"He was German, an older man looking for Vala. Sheriff Douglas put him in jail for the night and then gave him a one-way ticket to Florida. It was as far away from you boys and Vala as we could get him with the money we had on hand at the time."

"Grandma says that being German doesn't make you a Nazi."

Uncle Grant flinched as if I'd hit him. For a minute, I thought that I'd hurt his feelings. "I'm sorry…"

"Let's go out on the porch for a minute."

"I didn't mean to upset you."

"You didn't. But let's go out where we can talk in private."

I followed him out the front door. "The swing is more private." I pointed to the wooden seat hanging from chains attached to the porch ceiling. "Sometimes you can hear what people are saying if you sit on the chairs by the window. And sometimes they can hear you."

Uncle Grant laughed. "Why didn't anyone ever tell me that before?"

"I dunno. Maybe because you never said anything embarrassing?"

"Oh I messed up a few times, young man."

We sat on the swing and I told him what Dolph Jäger had said about Mick.

He sighed and shook his head. "So that was it."

"Yes."

"Poor kid."

"Do you hate them now?"

"Who?"

"Germans."

"Here's the situation as I see it, EJ. You and your brother and mother are German. Grandma Arial and Grandpa John's parents moved here from Mannheim in 1892. That means Sonny and I are German, too. That never meant anything bad to me. In fact, I was proud of my heritage. Before this all happened, I'd have defended Germany to anyone who would listen. But the Nazis—what they did in the name of Germany—it's beyond me to explain or forgive."

"Me, too," I muttered.

He took a sip of beer. "Sometimes I wonder if there was something inherently German that created Nazis. Or was it a fluke? Could it have happened in Mexico or Sweden or Nebraska? I feel like everyone else is thinking these things, too. The very thing that I felt so proud of—coming from good, solid, decent people—is lost."

I touched him so he would look at me. "I feel the same way. When I read those magazines, I look around me. Everyone here that I spend any time with is German. My mother—I can't imagine a finer person than my mama. And yet, everything she does or doesn't say, and everything she does or doesn't do—I suspect her. I can't explain it. I trust her, but I know she's not telling me things, and I hate that and I worry. Then I change my mind and think—not her. She's my mama. I know her heart."

Uncle Grant pushed the swing back with his feet and then we glided forward. "When Sonny brought Vala to Cold Creek, I was suspicious, too. I feel bad about it now because she was young and I didn't have any real reason to judge her that way. She worked hard taking care of you and Mick, but the neighbors and our old friends were standoffish. Most of the men had been in the war. Arnold Vilani liberated Dachau. The stories he told about the mess he saw there inflamed Cold Creek folks. So they didn't take too kindly to Sonny bringing a German woman and her kids here. I was mad at Sonny about that for a while. No one ever questioned our loyalty during the war. Both of my brothers served, and I worked hard to do my part. But suddenly, there was talk and I felt helpless and defensive, I guess."

"Uncle Grant…" I wanted to tell him how sorry I was about all of that, but he didn't hear me and just kept right on talking.

"Then with time, you became my family—first you, then Mick, and finally Vala. I'd do anything for you all, just like I would for Grandma Arial and Sonny. You're all I have." He finished off his beer and wiped imaginary foam off his lips with the back of his hand.

I spoke loudly. "Uncle Grant?"

"EJ?"

"I…uh…love you."

He punched my shoulder. "Yeah, me too."

We sat in silence for a few more minutes.

He turned so he could see my face. "What are we going to do about Gerhardt?"

"I want to ask him about Germany, about Mama and Mick, the sausage boy."

"Think Mick's ready?"

"I told him about Poland this afternoon before Gerhardt showed up."

"How did he take it?"

"I don't know really—shocked of course, and he hasn't had time to think about what it all means. He was scared he might be deported."

"Have you thought it through?"

I shrugged. "He's my brother."

"And?"

"And I need to know this stuff. I need to know if my people are good or bad."

"It's not that simple, son."

"I'm scared that if they were bad…"

"That you will be too?"

I was surprised. "How did you know?"

Myrtle came to the screen door. "Dinner in ten."

"Thank you, Myrtle." Uncle Grant lifted his empty beer bottle in acknowledgment. "We'll be in before that."

Myrtle disappeared back into the inn.

"Will you sit with us when we talk to Gerhardt?"

"Sonny left me in charge. You'd have to kick me out. And then I'd break down the door to get in."

"Good because I don't want to be alone when we do this."

"You know you might not like what Gerhardt has to say?"

"He's not like Dolph. I know that somehow."

Uncle Grant got up. "Come on, let's go break bread with the man and then interrogate him."

I laughed at the thought. "Think Myrtle has a bright light we can shine in his eyes?"

"I might have a billy club somewhere."

Joking with Uncle Grant felt good. I felt good, maybe for the first time since Mama got hurt. I thought about Annie and her feelings. Maybe that's what was happening here. I felt like something important was about to happen.

* * *

"Have your talk in here." Myrtle led us to the parlor after dinner. "I'll keep the other guests in the living room."

Gerhardt was stiff—jaw locked, neck rigid, shoulders square, hands behind his back. Maybe he thought his military bearing was respectful, but it seemed odd to me. It clearly put off Uncle Grant and Mick.

"Why don't we sit at the card table? We can have some of Grandma Arial's cookies later."

Gerhardt nodded and stood behind the chair furthest from the window.

I heard the door close and looked around. "Where's Mick?"

"He went upstairs for something," Myrtle said. "He'll be down in a minute."

Uncle Grant sat down at the card table and nodded to Gerhardt, who sat down, too.

"Grant?"

Uncle Grant looked up. I don't know what Myrtle told him in eye talk, but he nodded. She went out and closed the sliding doors behind her.

"Shall we wait for Mick?"

Uncle Grant tapped the end table with his fingernails.

"Uncle Grant?"

"I need to go see about your brother." He stood back up. "This might be too much for him."

I tried to cover my alarm. "Gerhardt and I'll keep each other company while we wait."

"No, go ahead. You can fill us in on what we miss." Uncle Grant also closed the sliding doors behind him.

So much for not leaving me alone with the enemy. My heart pounded. Was Mick upset? Scared? Angry? There wasn't much I could do about it at the moment. I licked my lips and sat down across from Gerhardt.

"The questions?"

"The questions."

"I will answer what I know."

"Who are you really?"

He lifted his chin and stared me in the eye. "I am nobody. A cog. A poor boy from Ludwigshafen."

"How did you end up on that road in Poland?"

"It's a long story and not…aufregend…exciting."

"Tell me anyway?"

"I knew your Grandfather before the war."

"Opa?"

"Ja. He owned die Apotheke…pharmacy."

"I know what Apotheke means."

"Ah yes, so sorry." Gerhardt bowed his head, but I could sense him watching me through his lowered eyelashes.

"So you weren't friends?"

"Friends? No. I was the driver of a delivery van for his suppliers from 1925 until 1935 when he joined the party. Then I saw him at all the functions. I had joined the year before. Right away, the rest of us knew he was a leader, a man who was going places."

"Why did you join the Nazi party?"

"Things were bad in Germany. We were being persecuted for the first war and there was the depression. And the Jews had betrayed us."

"How?"

"What do you mean?"

"How did all of those people betray you? I could see one or two or fifty or a hundred who might have betrayed Germany, but millions?"

"I am a simple man, Emo. Everyone said it was so. That was good enough for me. They lent money, you know?"

Footsteps overhead and a slamming door distracted me. Was that Mick?

"But not every Jew was a banker."

"No."

"And not every banker was a cheat."

"Not everyone."

"Did you know any Jews?"

"I didn't separate people in my head before the party. I didn't recognize the danger. I was a young man trying to make a living.

Times were hard. Enough about Jews. They made enemies in Europe long before the party. Besides, there was more to it."

"And that was?"

"Herr Hitler was interested in making the Aryan race better. No one else in history ever had such noble goals. Think about it, Emo. We were changing what people would look like in the future." He read something in my face and his voice changed. "You do not see this as a noble goal?"

"I want to understand."

Gerhardt shrugged. "The Jews were not as clean as Aryans, certainly not as moral or as motivated. Left to their own devices, they would intermarry with Aryans. Then what would you get? Generations of Germans with diluted blood, until one day our people would be more Jew than Aryan. We would be a nation of Mischlingshunde…mongrels. We changed all of that, although I admit it was controversial." He leaned forward as if to whisper in my ear. "I once drove Eichmann from Krakow to Auschwitz, and he confided in me that if we could delay losing the war for one more year, the Jews would be wiped out. If we could have just held out that long, the world would have thanked us instead of reviling us."

"How do you feel about that now?"

"Feel?"

"Nazis are considered the most evil villains in modern history. How do you feel about that?"

There was a long silence. Gerhardt's expression never changed. "I am a cog, Emo. I worked a machine that broke down many years ago. I found another machine. That is how I feel."

I swallowed back my frustration.

Gerhardt slid his chair back from the table as if he was ready to go. "Now, Emo Hess, was that the real question you wanted to ask me?"

I thought about it for a minute. "Did you know Oma and my aunt Lana and my mother?"

"Not so well in the 30s, but in the 40s, your grandfather became quite successful. He brought in supplies during the war—especially drugs, you know, but other things as well—chocolate, hair oil, cigarettes. Even though the Führer disapproved, many of us smoked behind the potted plants." He avoided my eyes as if I'd think ill of him if he didn't show the proper shame for his disobedience. "And as Herr Hess became more important, he needed a personal driver for party and military business. He asked for me by name." Gerhardt smiled as if that was a pleasant memory.

"So you did know Oma and the girls?"

"You do not remember?"

"I was pretty young."

"Ja. You were young, but I never knew a child like you."

"How so?"

"You were two years old when I came to get you and Fräulein Hess in Krakow, but you were so smart and so big. Your Opa was ecstatic that they had found you, but also worried that there would be trouble on the road as I brought you back."

"I was lost?"

"Oh, yes. Your mama, she cried and cried for you."

"How did that happen?"

"How you got lost? I don't know exactly when it was...it was so long ago, but I remember taking you and Frau Hess to a small apartment on Heinrich-Lanz-Strasse one day. You were an infant then."

"What happened there?"

"Frau Hess took you inside. I didn't go in, but I was nervous. Jews used to live in that building and I was afraid something would happen to her and the baby. But that woman could be difficult. She demanded that I stay in the car. I did not know what to do. If anything happened to Frau Hess, Herr Hess would have executed me with that silver pistol he carried. So I stayed in the car and hoped for the best."

I digested this information. Not only had Oma gotten rid of Lana's baby, she'd given me away, too? Why would she do that? Didn't she like children? Was that why she turned us away from her home in Mannheim after the war? "What was Oma like, Gerhardt?"

He stared at his hands palm down on the table. "Frau Hess was an extraordinary woman. Beautiful. Accomplished. Brave. She was the epitome of what Nazi wives were supposed to be."

"And what was that?"

"Loyal."

Accordion music began upstairs.

Gerhardt startled.

"My brother." I'd been worried about Mick but now I relaxed as I recognized the tune. "He wrote that when he was ten years old."

"It's extraordinary." Gerhardt tapped the table in time to the music. "It has a distinct Germanic flavor, don't you think? Ten, you say?"

I leaned back in my chair and let Mick's music wash over me. "There's no explaining it. Grandma says Mick's a force of nature."

Gerhardt closed his eyes. "It reminds me of home."

"How long since you left Germany, Gerhardt?"

"I left in the last days of the war with—" He closed his mouth abruptly as if to keep the words from spilling out.

I waited, the silence roaring between us, but Gerhardt had decided to hold onto whatever it was he'd nearly said. Maybe if I primed the pump? "I have had a dream ever since I can remember. In it, Mama and you and I and a man in a blue coat are driving on a snowy road on a cold night."

"Ja, Fräulein Hess was fussing over that bed, and that made us late leaving Auschwitz. At the last minute, Sturmbannführer Jäger approached die Fräulein about coming with us. I knew Herr Hess would disapprove, but what could I do?"

"Why would Opa disapprove of Jäger?"

"He pestered Lana."

I nodded, remembering Jäger's version of that story.

"The guards were marching hundreds of people toward Germany, and some of them were too ill to make the trip. They died where they fell or the guards finished them off with a bullet. I had to be careful lest I run over a corpse."

"There are fires in my dream."

"Ja, there were in places."

"And at one of those places, Mama made you stop."

"It was most distressing to Sturmbannführer Jäger. Die Fräulein jumped out of the car and ran back to a woman lying beside the road."

"You got out, too?"

"I couldn't go back without Fräulein Hess. She was my responsibility. When she called for me, I went back to help. The woman was dead. I took die Fräulein's arm to lead her back to the car. Sturmbannführer Jäger was screaming for me to get back on the road again, but Fräulein Hess wouldn't budge. She was convinced she saw something moving next to the corpse. And indeed, my flashlight found a tiny child wrapped in a bloody piece of wool, tucked under the dead woman's thigh. Fräulein Hess picked up the baby and held him close to her. 'He called to me as we drove by, Gerhardt,' I remember her voice was high and childlike. 'He called to me.' Of course, I didn't hear any such thing. I knew Herr Hess would not like his beloved daughter picking up strays that way. I also knew there was no way die Fräulein was going to leave that baby behind, so I hustled her back to the car."

"When Mama came back with the baby, Jäger didn't like it."

Gerhardt's command of English didn't include sarcasm. He rushed to explain the obvious to me. "He was very much a Nazi officer, but he wasn't a good man. He ordered Fräulein Hess to leave the baby behind, right then and there. They got into a fight and before I knew it, he struck her. You started screaming at Sturmbannführer Jäger, and even with a baby in her arms, die Fräulein got hold of his pistol."

It happened. It really happened. "What did you do?"

"He tried to grab you. It was then I realized that he wasn't going to Mannheim on business. He was escaping. If leaders like Sturmbannführer Jäger were running away, the end was near. I was shocked and scared, but I couldn't abandon die Fräulein. I wasn't that big of a coward."

"So what happened next?"

"Your Opa arrived with the Obergruppenführer."

"Who?"

Gerhardt lowered his eyes. "Your grandfather, Emo. They were supposed to meet us on the road hours before, but we were late because of the bed, you see. He had to come farther than he planned, looking for us."

"Opa came for me?"

"And your mother."

"Why were we in Poland in the first place?"

Gerhardt shook his head. "I don't know."

"So what happened?"

"The Obergruppenführer stood up in your Opa's car and shot Sturmbannführer Jäger."

"Who was the Obergruppenführer?"

"A very important man, Emo. Very. He was eager to get where he was going, so he instructed the Standartenführer to watch after you and drove off."

"Wait. I'm confused. Who was the Standartenführer?"

"Your grandfather."

"My grandfather was with an Obergruppenführer that night?" My mind raced. Who was this high ranking officer and why was he concerned about me?

"Ja. And he didn't like Sturmbannführer Jäger very much."

"Okay, and then?"

Gerhardt avoided my eyes. "You ran into the bushes. There was a scuffle, but you came running out. We grabbed you and left Sturmbannführer Jäger lying on the side of the road. I put the car in gear and got out of there as best I could, given the snowy conditions."

"Where did we go?"

"We needed food for the baby. Frau Koblenz had prepareded a basket for us, but there was nothing for a newborn."

"The baby sucked my finger." It was a hazy image.

"Ja, we had no idea how long the poor thing had been there. He was too weak to cry. So die Fräulein gave him water on her finger, and then you wanted to help. She told me to hurry, so I faced forward and drove past the long line of inmates heading west. Once we crossed into Germany, we stopped at a farm off the main road that belonged to a relative of mine. I explained the situation to my uncle who took us in. We hid the Mercedes in a barn where no one would see it. My aunt gave you and Vala a room of your own. My cousin's wife helped with the baby. We stayed there for a while, waiting for the war to end and hoping that the Russians wouldn't find us."

"You never saw Dolph Jäger again?"

"No." He sat erect, not touching the back of the chair.

"Did you ever kill anyone?" It was an obnoxious question. Maybe I wanted to upset him, or maybe I just wanted to know what kind of man he was.

He was aghast. "Oh no. It wasn't in me to kill anyone, not even the foulest Jew."

"Did you try to stop the others from killing people?"

"No. The Jews were our enemies. You don't apologize for ridding your country of those who would bring it down."

"Are you ever sorry?"

The corners of his mouth turned down. "Never."

* * *

The door slid open and Mick peeked in. "Is he gone?"

"Yeah."

"You sad?

"Kinda. And even more confused about Gerhardt Schultz."

"Oh?"

"He's not like Dolph Jäger, but he was in the Nazi Party, too. Turns out he was Opa's driver. That's his only connection. Oh—and I was lost, too. Seems that Oma made it a practice to get rid of her grandbabies."

Mick sat down at Myrtle's new piano and rested his fingers on the keyboard. "Did you ever get to know Mr. McKensey?"

The change in topic was irritating. "No, can't say that I did."

He played a few soft chords. "My earliest memory—the first one that I can relive in my head—was meeting him. I was four, and it was just before we moved into our house. Grandma Arial and I were walking down Cold Creek Drive and Mr. McKensey went roaring past in that smelly car of his and laid on the horn. I screamed and climbed up Grandma like she was a tree and I was a monkey. She had to peel my fingers off her collar. I must have been choking her. She could have scolded me, but she held me tight until I stopped trembling. Mr. McKensey must have seen my reaction in his rearview mirror, because he parked that old monstrosity and came hobbling back to see about me."

"Mr. McKensey?"

"I know, but let me finish. He came back and tried to get my attention, but I was crying and wouldn't look at him." Mick's fingers were agile, the music light and crisp.

"Is that one of yours?" I closed my eyes and kept time with my pinkie.

"Ode to Joy. Beethoven."

"After all of this, you're up for joy already?"

"Shush," he said. "You're wound up like a spring. Relax."

I opened my eyes. His hair seemed blue and pink in the glow of Myrtle's Tiffany lamp.

"Anyway, Mr. McKensey didn't feel bad for his noisy car or for cursing at people or for flipping the bird at anyone who objected. He did feel bad that he'd scared me, though."

"Why?"

"Dunno. Grandma Arial said there was no telling who he'd take a shine to."

"So what happened? Did he stop scaring you with that old car?"

"Oh no. He did that up until the week before his accident. But you know, I got over being afraid of that contraption. Spoiled his fun." He played a few bars loudly.

I startled.

"Fortissimo." He grinned. "Like Mr. McKensey."

It was impossible to listen to Mick play and not feel better. I guess thinking about Mr. McKensey was better than pondering about the Hesses of Mannheim. "He was a strange old coot. I don't think anyone ever figured out what was eating him."

"I'd go visit him from time to time," Mick said. "He loved playing checkers with me, because I let him win."

"You didn't!"

"Wasn't any skin off my nose, and it made an old man happy."

I shook my head. "You liked him."

"Yeah. He told me stories about cowboys and Indians."

"Probably lies."

"Stories."

"Ha!"

"It didn't matter to me whether they really happened or not, EJ. I was a kid. Mr. McKensey didn't know how else to talk with a kid. He liked me, but that didn't change him from being a mean old man. I liked him and treated him with respect anyway."

"Why were you so nice to him? Really?"

"Because Grandma Arial taught me to be that way."

"What if Mannheim Oma had taught us how to behave?"

"Exactly."

I watched his hands on the keys. "I don't understand."

"No one liked Mr. McKensey. He tried to get people annoyed with him to get attention. He chose to be alone, but sometimes he got so lonely that the sadness made him mad."

"And you paid attention to him."

"Yeah, and he paid attention to me back."

"What are you trying to say to me, Mick?"

"We've had lots of surprises lately, and I'm guessing there are more to come. I can be a cranky jerk because my real mother died the night I was born. Or I can choose to be glad that Mama rescued me."

"You choose happy, no matter what."

"Yep." He ended the piece with a flourish. "And you?"

I sighed. "I'll stick with the cranky jerk option for now."

He grinned. "It suits you."

* * *

"This child is Lebensborn."

"I have orders to clean out this rat hole."

"We aren't Jewish."

"Tell that to your Jew mother and Jew father. Get up."

"What about this baby. He's Lebensborn."

A man bent over me. "Circumcised?"

Someone pulled down my pants.

"Look at him! Fair hair and eyes. He is the grandson of Stand-artenführer Hess."

"How did he get here?"

"The boy's nanny was mistaken for a Jew. The SS didn't bother to check the baby's papers."

"Where is she now?"

"They took her."

"Where is this boy's mother?"

"She is coming here, to Krakow. You mustn't take this child now." The woman pushed papers into the soldier's hands. *"Look! Everything is in order."*

The man examined the documents. *"I see. I will take care of the boy. You are all coming with me now."*

"Herr Hess will have your balls if harm comes to that child."

"I will deliver the boy to the commandant. He will see to it Standartenführer Hess gets his grandson back. Now on your feet."

"Please, please! We aren't Jewish."

"Quiet!"

* * *

I sat up in bed.

"Another dream?"

I rubbed my forehead. "Has to be."

"It's about what Gerhardt told you, isn't it?"

"My whole life, I've dreamed all kinds of nonsense. Some of it seemed so real I know it has to be at least symbolically true. That Oma gave me away, too, I never ever suspected."

"That must be why Mama went to Poland. To find you."

I poured myself a glass of water from the ceramic pitcher Myrtle kept on our shared nightstand. "I never thought of that." I drank the whole glass. "Do you think I am crazy, Mick?"

He sat up in his bed and laughed. "Come on, EJ. You aren't nuts, and you aren't going to go nuts. Whatever happened to Aunt Lana and Mama isn't going to happen to you."

I set the empty glass on the nightstand and lay back in my bed. "Maybe it was the war."

"Probably."

"Or maybe they both had some kind of disease as kids."

Mick's sigh was long. "Maybe."

"Maybe you had to be nuts to be a Nazi?"

Mick pulled his thin blanket up under his chin. "Or maybe folks with problems were drawn to the movement."

I thought about that. Billy Ray Parker was a troubled kid. He was always trying to pretend he was something he wasn't. And he was always getting in fights. "Think Billy Ray would have been a Nazi?"

"Billy Ray Parker?"

"Yeah."

"He's so intense that he's hard to be around sometimes," Mick said. "Yeah, he might have joined the party. He needs respect, and if he thought they would help him get that, he would join."

I was wide awake now. "Especially if he got to wear a cool uniform and show off for his friends."

I could feel Mick's breathing slow. He got that way when he was thinking—quiet and calm. "We're never going to figure out why they did it, EJ."

"They couldn't all be monsters," I said.

"No, they couldn't all have done it."

I felt around for the tissues Myrtle kept on the nightstand beside the water pitcher. "But even if they all didn't do it, why didn't someone stop it?"

"Maybe people were too busy living, or scared, or maybe they didn't realize where it all would go."

"I wonder if I'd feel this rotten about things if we grew up there rather than here in Cold Creek, where everyone wonders about us." I blew my nose.

"We aren't German anymore, EJ. We're Americans. Naturally, we feel that Americans are good guys and Germans were bad. Pick up any comic book or magazine. Watch any movie, even TV and radio. Most of the men in town fought over there. It's no wonder they're still hostile. You can't change that. Just be who you really are, a crazy, mixed up, American teenager."

I rolled onto my back and stared at the ceiling. "I feel like I have to make up for it all."

"How the heck are you gonna do that? No way can one kid make it all go away."

"I can try."

He sighed. "That's why I've always admired you. You never, ever, give up."

"But nothing ever gets any better."

"It's better than not trying."

"It's like trying to dig a well with a teaspoon, Mick."

Mick's voice was soft. "What are your plans?"

"Medical school, first. Then try to fix people as best I can."

"That's good."

"Maybe I'll be a surgeon like Danny Kline."

"That's good, too."

I smiled in the darkness with satisfaction, but then the whole doctor thing started to seem so far away. "But what can I do now?"

"Not much you can do now. Not much you can do for Jews, anyway. The world let them down, so they're doing a good job taking care of themselves."

Scared about what he might think, I took a deep trembling breath. "I was thinking more about Negroes."

"What can you do for them?"

"I don't know. Something."

"Mama would have a fit."

"Mama's sick right now."

"We have a lot to do on the house before she comes home. And you have graduation coming up. Maybe we can arrange something after that?"

Was he stalling? "I can see if there's anything the civil rights workers need." I already felt stupid and helpless because I didn't know any civil rights workers. In fact, I didn't even know any Negroes.

"It's late," he said. "Tomorrow is a school day."

"We avoided talking about the dead woman in the road and her baby."

"That's not me anymore, EJ."

"Are you curious about her?"

"Not yet. Vala Logan is my mother, you are my brother, and Sonny is my dad. No matter what happened before I became part of this family, I'm here now. And that's all I can think about until I can talk with Sonny and Mama."

"That's what Uncle Grant said last night?"

Mick got back into bed and pulled the covers up under his chin. "Yep."

"Sounds like something he would say." It also sounded like what Annie told me.

"It was good advice."

"I'm sure."

Part Five

Understanding

1966

30

Home

October 22, 1966

I PULLED INTO the circular drive behind the Logan Foods warehouse and parked. It had been six years since I'd lived in Cold Creek. It felt familiar and strange at the same time. I got out of the Austin-Healy and slammed the door.

A head popped up in one of the warehouse windows. I nodded but I didn't have any idea who worked there anymore.

The man grinned and opened the sliding doors on the loading dock. "Well, look at you, EJ Logan."

The sun was in my eyes but the voice was familiar. "Billy Ray?"

"I didn't think you recognized me."

"That hair confused me.

We both laughed."

"Don't know what got into me." He blushed and ran his fingers through his flat top haircut. "I'm going back to 'high and tight' like yours."

"It's not just the hair."

"I hit a growth spurt right after we graduated. Seven inches and seventy-five pounds." He thumped his hard round belly. "All those years in school, I thought I was Eddie Haskel. And then overnight, I turned into Hoss Cartwright."

I extended my hand. "You look good, Billy Ray. You working the warehouse?"

He pumped my arm. "Supervisor."

"I'm not surprised," I lied. "Married?"

He held up his left palm toward me and stroked his wedding band with his thumb. "Two years now. Remember little Carolyn Spencer? Everyone called her Sissy. She graduated two years behind us."

"The twins' baby sister?"

"That's my girl."

"Congratulations. I'm happy for you, both of you."

He grinned. "Three of us. We got a bun in the oven."

"It's good to see you happy."

"How about you?"

"Engaged."

"Anyone I know?"

I tried not to be annoyed by Billy Ray's curiosity about my private life. After all, I'd asked him about his marital status. "Rosa Singer, Delores McDougal's cousin. She lived in Cold Creek for a while when she was a kid."

"Ah." He had no idea who I meant.

Having run out of things to say, we shuffled our feet and I searched for a way to get away from him.

"Your uncle expanded the business so much he's not around here very often."

I nodded. "He's building three supermarkets in Cleveland. We had lunch in Shaker Heights the other day."

"You're a hotshot doctor in the big city now?"

I laughed. "Not yet. Still in medical school."

"You'll make it."

Another long silence. It had been a long time and we never had much in common except Annie Jones. "You ever hear from Annie?"

"Naw, man. She hightailed it in '62. No one seems to know where she went. Guess she'll surface when she feels like it."

"I never met anyone quite like her."

He sighed. "I nearly killed myself over her. Remember that?"

"You nearly got yourself killed."

"Yeah."

I glanced over my shoulder at our house on the other side of the fence.

Billy Ray must have sensed my impatience. "I was ... I wanted to tell you that I admire what you and Mick did. Riding those buses in Mississippi along with those ... uh ... Negroes."

"I didn't realize folks here knew about that.

"You were on the news."

I felt a flush rising up my neck. "I hope we helped a little."

"You weren't beat up or anything?"

"We were lucky. A week in a hot southern jail with people shouting nasty things at us was as bad as it got."

"I was afraid for you."

I was surprised. "Thanks. Given that Mick is a musician and I was hoping to be a surgeon, it might not have been the smartest thing we've ever done. A real fist fight might have ended both our careers right then and there." I held up my hand and wiggled my fingers. "I'm not sorry, though. It felt right."

I realized Billy Ray had no idea why I'd do such a thing, and he had no interest in asking any more questions about Mississippi.

"You here to see your mom?" That was his real interest. I should have known.

I willed away the tears that burned my eyes. "I never dreamed it would end like this."

"She had four good years, EJ. When she came back from Pittsburgh, she was a ghost, but she got better. I visited her most mornings and we had coffee on the back porch, until she got so bad the last couple weeks."

"She loves that porch. Not just because it's beautiful and useful, but because it was a gift from the town. That meant so much to her, to be accepted."

"Finally."

I was glad he said it so I didn't have to. "Yeah."

"They've all been by to see her since she got the diagnosis. The town biddies took turns bringing green bean casseroles and Swedish meatballs. Zona stays with her every day until time to fix Jimmy's dinner, and the Vilanis check in every couple of hours between the time Zona leaves and Sonny comes home from work, even though your grandmother and that dog never leave her bedside."

"It will be a full house for a few days. Mick and the McDougals are coming tonight. Shirley and Jack will be here tomorrow."

"She's been sick for a while. Why do you think she asked everyone to come this week?"

I knew he wanted an invitation, but that wasn't up to me. "I don't know exactly, but I have hopes for a few things." I glanced over my shoulder again.

"It's still there."

"What?"

"What you came early to see."

I chuckled. "I have some great memories of that old tree house."

"Did you know..." He looked over his shoulder and then down at his feet. "Your mama would go out there sometimes."

"Really?"

"Of course, I don't know when it started." He avoided my eyes. "Maybe not until she came back from Pittsburgh."

That was odd. "Wonder what she was doing up there?" I thought about the *Playboy* magazine I'd hidden under the stack of comic books in the old chest. If she'd ever gone through my things, Mama had never mentioned it.

"Mostly she stared out at your house."

"Probably never felt as safe as it did before Dolph Jäger came calling."

"I never understood what he wanted from her. If it was money like they said, he could have searched the house. He didn't have to hurt her."

"I wondered that myself. He laughed at me when I asked. There had to be more to it, but what?"

"How did you feel when they hanged him?"

"Relieved, mostly."

"One down and thousands to go."

I stared at my feet, searching for something else to say. "Well, Billy Ray. It's been nice talking. I'm sure we'll chat again before I leave."

"Yep. I better get back to work. Inventory, you know."

Before he could engage me in any other uncomfortable conversation, I tramped across the ankle-high grass to the tree house. I touched the trunk, remembering the many nights I'd slept there as I grew up, the hours of cherished privacy, the mental journeys.

I stretched and unhooked the rope ladder. I felt Billy Ray watching from the warehouse, but refused to look back at him. I climbed up into the little room and looked around. The areas I'd patched with the pine planks left over from the new porch were lighter than the rest of the lumber. Grandpa John's father had built the tree house long before the warehouse existed. It was here before our house, too. I thought about Grandpa John who added the ladder and the tin roof for Sonny, the middle son, the sensitive child who needed something to make him feel special.

I sniffed the air. Mr. Vilani was barbecuing on his tiny hibachi. The man was superintendent of schools now. He could afford a fancier house, a nicer car, and a much bigger grill. Why he and his missus stayed on Sugar Maple Lane, no one knew. But we were all glad he did.

I looked out the window toward town. Balboa's bustled, three blocks away. I'd have to get a milkshake with Mick and Sonny and Uncle Grant before I left.

I turned my attention to the inside of the tree house. Its familiarity was soothing. Filled with the odds and ends of my youth—and of Sonny's and of Grandpa John's.

Something was different. I cocked my head. An unfamiliar wooden box sat on top of Sonny's old trunk. I ducked under the branch that supported the roof and reached for it. The top was a carved picture. I dug my handkerchief out of my pocket and rubbed it. The box had been recently oiled and the dark wood glowed in the light streaming through the western window. The carving on the box was a copse of trees and—I squinted—a dog or wolf hiding among the trunks. Like most of Mama's stuff from Mannheim, I recognized the artwork as something she probably got at Schreiner's. She must have loved that place.

I tried to open the box, but the top didn't seem to be a lid. I sighed. Maybe it was just a piece of art. Why did I always try to make something nefarious out everything from Mama's life in Germany? Maybe it was just something she loved and wanted me to have.

Mick's noisy old car pulled into the driveway. I stuck my head out the window and waved at him. "It's about time you got here."

"I don't have a fancy sports car like you."

"That's because you spend your ill-gotten gains on guitars, little brother."

He laughed and gave me a thumbs-up.

I slipped the little box into my jacket pocket and climbed down the tree.

* * *

"Emo!" Mama held out her arms. They were thin and covered with multicolored bruises.

I kissed her cheek. "So what's this all about? Did you get bored and want a party?"

"Ja, you know me well. Is that Milo behind you?"

"Who else, Mama?" Mick bent to kiss her, too.

Grandma Arial got up from her chair beside Mama's bed. "I didn't think you boys would ever get here. I need someone to crank the ice cream for dinner tonight."

"What kind?"

"Peach."

"You're on." I hugged her a long time.

"There, there, EJ. No need to get so excited about ice cream." She patted my back. "I have sauerbraten and nice black bread, too."

"Can't wait, Grandma." I stepped aside so Mick could get and give his hugs.

"Keep it short. It's time for Vala's pain medication. She'll sleep a couple hours at least," Grandma whispered as she edged past me.

I pulled up a chair next to Mama's bed. "You look beautiful. What color is that?" I touched the lace on her peignoir.

"Petal pink. Zona bought it for me. You like?"

"Ja, Du bist wunderschön, Mutti."

She smiled and then turned solemn. "Sonny told you?"

I nodded. "We had such fun when we went to Kennywood last summer. I never guessed you weren't feeling well."

"Emo, what would you do if you knew it was the last roller coaster you would ever ride?"

I squeezed her hand. "I thought it was the first one."

"It was first and last, same ride.

"And?"

Her eyes sparkled. "Es war spannend."

"I'm glad we went. I loved it, too."

"EJ, I can't wait anymore. You know?" Her jaw was rigid. "You are old enough to understand now, anyway."

I didn't like the new hollows under her eyes. I nodded.

"You and Mick. Tonight, when Sonny is here, we will talk."

"We're here for you, Mama. Like always," Mick said.

I stood up. "Rest now. The nurse is here to give you your shot."

"I love you both."

That was something I never doubted.

* * *

We were in the big Mercedes.

I stood on the seat and waved to Onkel Rainer and Tante Renate and Ordella through the back window.

Gerhardt started the car. A box of vegetables sat beside him and a can of milk.

"Where are we going, Mutti?"

"Mannheim. To see Oma."

"I don't want to go."

"It's time, mausi. We have been hiding long enough."

"I want to play with Ordella."

"Your Oma will be so glad to see you." Mama cuddled the baby wrapped in a mended white blanket. "And she will have Strudel for you."

Gerhardt turned around to look at us. "Are you all ready?"

"I want to stay here," I sobbed.

The car started moving.

"I don't want to, I don't want to."

* * *

I was no longer a naughty little boy. I licked my lips and wiggled the fingers of my right hand. I couldn't decide if this particular dream was a memory or a metaphor. It was still light outside. The clock on my nightstand read 3:27. I got up and stretched. Mick and Sonny probably needed a break.

I dressed and went downstairs. Mick was curled up in a chair beside Mama's bed, snoring with his mouth open.

"How can you stand that?"

Sonny put his book aside and smiled up at me. "At least he can sleep."

"I'm going to make some coffee. Would you like some?"

He glanced at Mama, who lay motionless under her blankets. "I need to stretch my legs. I'll come with you. If she wakes, Mick is here."

We shuffled into the kitchen.

"Looks like Grandma Arial's been cleaning again. I rummaged in the cabinet for the coffee pot. Think there's any donuts left?"

"Just the plain. I polished off the maple last night."

"Plain is fine." I spooned Folger's into the aluminum basket, reassembled the pot, and plugged it in.

Sonny set the box of donuts on the table along with a couple of small plates and some napkins. "Feels like old times, doesn't it?"

"Sitting here with you after I got home from a date or when I rolled in from college is one of my favorite memories." I sat down across from him as the coffeemaker made burbling noises. "I didn't mean to stay away this long, Sonny. I didn't realize how time-consuming medical school would be."

"Vala said you were born to be a doctor, and woe betide anyone who dared argue that point with her. I know it's stressful having to live up to everyone's expectations."

"You were good to us."

"You think I brought you here to be mean to you?"

"You know what I mean."

He was quiet for a minute. "You're my family. You and Mick and Vala."

"Mama's been a handful."

Sonny lit a cigarette. "Hell, you've all been a pain in the behind, boy." He inhaled and held it for a moment. "But you've been worth it."

The percolator shuddered and the green light came on. I got up and poured us each a mug. Sonny began his usual ritual of spooning sugar into his coffee.

I took a breath. "Mama says she's ready to tell me." My eyes went to the last spoonful of sugar. Sonny's hand was shaking. "I'm worried she won't be able to tell us everything before it..."

"It's too late?" He laid the spoon on the table beside his mug.

I nodded. "It's still jumbled in my head. What I remember, what I've been told, what I suspect. I'm a grown man now. I need to understand where everything fits."

He coughed into his fist and stole another drag from his cigarette.

Maybe I should start with Cold Creek, a less troublesome start to this conversation than Mannheim. "When we got here, I remember getting off the train and seeing a beautiful woman in a red dress. She knelt down and gave me a kiss. She left a red mark on my forehead and that got Mama going." I blew on my coffee before taking a sip.

Sonny grinned. "That was Teresa. She told Vala she was going to eat you up. I thought I was going to have to use a choke hold to keep mama bear in check."

"Mama spit into her handkerchief and scrubbed my forehead until my skin was raw, but that red mark didn't bother me at all. I thought Teresa was the most beautiful person I'd ever seen." I took a quick gulp and winced as the scalding liquid burned its way down my gullet. "She still is."

Sonny lifted his mug in salute. "Teresa is beautiful deep down in places folks don't usually see."

I touched his cup with mine. "To beautiful women in red, my first confirmable memory."

I waited until he swallowed his coffee. "I need to know the rest, Sonny. She never explained. What if she can't now?"

He stared at the table. "I don't know everything, and I made promises to her."

"Protecting her feelings doesn't matter anymore."

"It wasn't about her feelings so much as helping you and Mick grow up without burdens from the past. That was stuff you had nothing to do with and that she couldn't change."

"Such is my birthright." I balanced my chair on its back legs and put my hands behind my head. "I came out of the bowels of hell apparently."

"She'd bop you upside the head with that towel she kept on her shoulder if she saw you doing that." He slapped his knee in manufactured merriment. "She was always more worried about breaking the chairs than..." He stopped.

"Than what? Stuff that matters?"

For the first time since I'd forced this conversation, he looked at me. I knew I was making him uncomfortable, but as always, his eyes were understanding and kind. "I've been in this box so long, it's easier to stall and see if it'll go away."

I waited but he didn't continue. "I don't have anyone else to ask," I said. "You're the only father I've ever known. Whatever good qualities I have, I learned from you."

"Thank you for that, but did it ever occur to you that I'm not the hero Vala made me out to be? I made mistakes. I was useless and impatient when it came to her problems. When you know everything about your mom, you'll know about my failings, too."

"I'll admit I never thought about that. I respect your privacy. I'm not a snoop." I flushed as I realized that wasn't quite true and that he knew it, too.

"People are complicated, EJ. Especially folks like your mom and me. We come from different cultures. We experienced the war differently. Our dreams were as different as our nightmares. You saw our struggles."

My eyes burned. "I understand those things. I do. I should be and I am grateful to you. Arial is my grandmother as much as that woman in Mannheim was—more so, because Grandma Arial took care of me and loved me. She made me leberknödel and black bread. She came to my school activities. The one in Germany? I can't even remember what she looked like. There are no pictures or stories or memories—well, no memories that make sense. And who was my birth father? I came from someone, didn't I? Even if that someone was a Nazi criminal, surely he had a momma and a poppa and grandparents. Did I come from farmers? Aristocrats? Bakers? Doctors? Mick accepts that he'll never know about his natural family. For him, memory begins in Cold Creek, and maybe that's all that matters for him, but I have these crazy dreams. Maybe all my real relatives were lunatics, and I'll be insane one day, too."

"Take a breather, boy. Some of this is because Vala is so sick..."

"Of course it is," I roared. Sonny's face changed and my rage turned into tears. "Of course it is. I'm losing my mother, and I don't even know her." I fished my handkerchief out of my pocket and wiped the tears from my cheeks. "She's dying and I love her and all, but she's a stranger."

* * *

I met Rosa at the front door. "How strong are you?"

"How strong do I need to be?"

"Strong enough to sit with me when they finally tell me the truth."

"I've already gone through my hell, EJ. I didn't break."

I sank into the sofa and pulled her down beside me. "I might, though."

"You've known where this could lead for a long time." She laid her head on my shoulder. "Our parents came from the same city. Neither family lived more than ten blocks from the Wasserturm."

I held her close and nuzzled her ear. "They might have passed each other on the street."

"They probably spoke the same Mannheimer dialect. But your mother was Aryan, and my parents were Jewish. You know what that meant in the 1930s." Her mood was darker than mine.

I choked back any further merriment. "Do you remember anything?"

"Nothing about Germany. I was a toddler when the Nazis deported us to Gurs. I remember a woman with a giant boil on her hand. I think that was my grandmother, but I'm not sure. Some man cut it with a pocketknife to drain it."

"Do you remember your mom?"

She shook her head. "Nothing."

"What happened to your dad?"

"Delores spent a lot of time and money trying to find out. She thinks the SS separated my parents before they left France, but whether they killed him there or shipped him off to another camp, we don't know. Everyone else went to Auschwitz."

I knew she had lost her family in the war, but the reality of the how and where shocked me. "Why haven't we talked about this before?"

She shrugged. "You never asked."

"I didn't know how, I guess."

"My family talked it to death. Until I was fifteen or so, we couldn't talk about anything else. Then—I don't know why or even when—we just stopped."

"Is someone still trying to find out those details you don't know?"

"Delores. She's persistent."

"And you?"

She patted my chest and withdrew. "I'm trying to live a rational life."

"I understand." I had no idea what she meant.

She stood up and stared out the window at Grandma Arial's house. "What is this all about?"

"Mama is finally ready to talk."

"You came here when?"

"1948."

She turned back to look at me. "In all this time, Vala has told you nothing about her life in Germany or about your family?"

"Dribs and drabs. But I still don't know my father's name—or why she's kept it a secret all these years."

"What makes you think she'll tell you now? Deathbed confessions are rare, you know."

"Maybe I'll get enough information to start figuring out the puzzle."

"What about Mick? Have you asked him what he wants?"

"Mick knows that ghosts ride our backs no matter what we do."

Rosa cocked her head to one side.

"You think I'm being overly dramatic?"

"I think you have a lot to be grateful for. But you only see the mysteries of your mother's past. It could be worse."

"You wanna slap the other cheek now?" It was a weak attempt at humor but it was the only defense she left me.

"As a matter of fact, I do. You can't speak for how Mick feels unless you ask him. Have you?"

Caught in my own exaggeration, I didn't know how to answer her. In truth, I'd described my own feelings. I had no idea what Mick felt.

She pulled me to my feet and whispered in my ear. "Be careful, Emo. This particular path is treacherous." Her irises were almost as dark as her pupils.

I suddenly felt dizzy. My excitement about the pending interrogation of my sick mother turned dark and scary.

"We can't possibly know how our families felt back then or what they thought about the chaos around them. What Vala escaped must hurt every day, and you want to poke her wounds with a stick just to see how deep they are."

"She's my mother. I don't want to hurt her." My eyes filled with tears.

Rosa threw her arms around my neck and I realized she was crying, too.

"Am I a monster? To want to know what these crazy dreams are all about? To learn about the family I never knew?"

"I'm sorry, EJ. Maybe I'm not as tough as I thought," she said. "Something about all this is making alarm bells go off in my head."

"Stay with me, baby."

"No matter where this all goes?"

"Yes."

"My God, you're selfish."

I bowed my head. "I know."

She lifted my face so that our eyes met again. "I don't want any more pain—not in your life and not in mine."

"I can't promise that.

"At least don't seek it out."

I thought about what that meant and about how long I'd waited and about the ticking clock. "I have to." I begged her with my eyes. "I have to know."

She turned away from me. Her hair curled out of its pins and dangled in long tendrils down her back.

I waited. Please, please, please, I prayed silently.

She looked over her shoulder. "What happens if it's not what you expect? If what you learn is unbearable?"

"We deal with it the best we can. Together."

"I wonder if two struggling souls crying themselves to sleep is any better than one."

"At least I won't be alone."

She sighed.

I dug my handkerchief out of my pocket and handed it to her.

She wiped her eyes. "I'll try, EJ. I'll try."

31

Lana's Baby

October 22, 1966

"Емо!"

I opened Mama's door. "I'm here."

Schatzi growled. Then, recognizing me, he retreated back from the foot of Mama's bed to his favorite spot beside her leg, placing his muzzle on her shin.

"Come in and talk." Mama lay on her back, the covers hiding most of her night gown.

"What about the others?"

"Just you now."

"Not even Mick?"

"Not yet."

I went in and closed the door behind me.

"Sit down."

I pulled up a chair. "What is it, Mama?"

She cleared her throat. "I didn't think I'd tell you so soon, but it must be now."

I dreaded what she might say as much as I longed to hear it. "I'm listening, Mama."

"When you were a baby," she started, "...we lost you."

"Oma gave me away?"

"Not exactly." Her voice broke. "When you were little, I took care of you most of the time, but sometimes we took you to das Kindermädchen."

"A babysitter?"

She stiffened and lifted her chin. "I was still in school, you know."

Actually, I didn't know that. I searched for the right tone, soothing and nonjudgmental. "Who was the babysitter?"

"Magda Langer."

"Magda Langer? Why does that name sound familiar?"

"Magda was related to your grandfather's family."

My mind whirled. "Opa?"

Mama took a deep breath and lapsed into German. "No. Your Grandfather John, Sonny's father."

I was stunned. "Grandpa John?"

"Magda married Oskar Schreiner before he escaped to America."

"What happened to Magda?"

"She was deported to Gurs with the rest of the Mannheim Jews in the fall of 1940."

"But she wasn't Jewish."

"She had a little girl—a pretty little thing with dark curly hair—and that child, Schreiner's daughter, was Jewish."

It was interesting but I couldn't figure out what the fate of my sometime babysitter and her daughter had to do with me. "And?"

"You were with them."

"Me?"

"You were tiny. The Gestapo thought you were her baby, too."

"Where were you?"

Mama grimaced and twisted under her covers. Schatzi alerted and whimpered.

"Mama?"

Alarmed and helpless, I watched her ride out the pain. As the intensity eased, she coughed and stretched her legs.

"What? What did you say?" She managed finally.

"Where were you when the Gestapo took me away?"

"I was in hospital."

"You were sick?"

"After Lana—" Her coughing fit went on for a long time. I poured her a glass of water. When the tickle passed, I held it while she took a long sip. She took another breath and collected herself. "After they took Lana and she died, they came back for me."

I sat up straighter. "What?"

"And Mutti agreed with them that it had to be done. For good of the Reich."

"What needed to be done for the Reich?"

"They…steri…what you call it? They made it so I can't have babies, because maybe I might be like Lana and would pass on the crazy to my child. They were right. You remember I was sick in the head for a while after the fire."

Soft taps grew louder and this time, it took both hands to get my leg to relax. Nothing made sense. How could I be deported with my babysitter in 1940? I wasn't born until 1943 when Mama was 14… but they sterilized Mama in 1940. "How old were you when they did that to you, Mama?"

She studied the lace on her coverlet. "Eleven. Almost twelve."

The room was quiet for a long time. Then a buzz began in my ears. Outside the window, the wind rose. Voices in the kitchen and living room seemed especially loud. Down the hall, a toilet flushed. The back door slammed and footsteps went out onto the porch. Every crack and rumble of the old house blended into an unbearable racket inside my head.

And then, the air returned to my lungs and my mind cleared. "Who am I, Mama?"

Her sigh was long and sad. "Lana's baby."

I didn't take another breath for several seconds and when I did, I couldn't tell if I was coughing or crying. I'd never even considered the possibility that I wasn't Mama's child. I thought of the picture of Lana in the photo album under Mama's bed. Then the story Mama had told us the morning before the fire came to mind and with it a sharp pain. "Lana was my mother and she tried to hurt me?"

"Oh no, Emo. No. Something happened. I don't know what. Lana was sad all that week. She didn't get dressed and she didn't eat anything. The doctor visited several times. We worried about her. She and Mutti argued all the time—and then Mutti and Papi yelled at each other."

"What were they arguing about?"

"I don't know, Emo. They didn't tell me."

"Mama?"

"I didn't know what was happening, Emo. I didn't. I was a child."

Tears coursed down her cheeks and I felt guilty for making this so hard for her. I held her hand. "I'm sorry, Mama."

She sniffed. "I'm sorry too, Mausi."

We sat quietly for a moment while Mama collected herself and I tried to rein in my impatience.

"The night before, I heard Lana crying in her room," Mama said finally. Her voice was weakening and I knew we were nearing the end of our conversation. "I went to her room and asked if I could help with the baby. She was holding you when she closed her door in my face."

"Oh, Mama."

"Then, that day, I heard her screaming and ran to see what was wrong. I was in the hallway when Mutti came out of the room with you in her arms. When Mutti ran down the stairs, I peeked into Lana's room. She was crying and screaming. Papi was trying to get the scissors away from her, and they were both covered with blood."

Why would Lana be fighting her parents? What could have been going through her mind? Why would a beautiful young woman try to kill herself? Did her lover—my father—reject her? It didn't make sense.

"Where did Oma take me?"

"Probably Magda." She flinched and fought back the pain that threatened to overwhelm her. "You were back," she panted, "when I came home from school a few days after Lana went to hospital."

"Who is my father?"

"I don't know."

"Mama!"

"They never told me."

I frowned. Surely she had some idea of who he was.

She reached for the tissues on the stand beside her bed, but they were just beyond her fingertips. I handed them to her. "There are no records?"

"Somewhere, maybe." She blew her nose. "I have looked for them since 1948. There were many records from the Lebensborn program, but it was hard to find people after the war. Some of the SS men who participated were married or died during the war or disappeared. Over a long time, I filled a suitcase with what I found, but when I read them, none were about Lana and you. Then, the fire—and they are gone."

I didn't tell her that Mick and I had rescued the suitcase full of letters. It didn't seem important at the moment.

"You will have to start again, Emo."

"Not the monster?"

"What?"

"Dolph Jäger wasn't my father?"

"Oh no, I don't think so. Your father was someone important in the Reich."

"Why do you think that?"

"Because my mother was excited when Lana was pregnant. She said the baby would raise our family status. We would be important to the Reich, and rather than being the wife of an unknown pharmacist and low-ranking member of the party, she would be the grandmother of someone famous."

"Does Sonny know?"

"That you are not my natural child?" She sighed and returned to English. "No. All he knows is that I didn't have your birth certificate."

"Does he know about what they did to you?"

She ducked her head. "Ja. How could he not?"

"And he took us in anyway."

"Sonny is a very kind man. After I brought you and Milo back from Poland, I was afraid that your father—whoever he was—might find us and take you away. Meine Mutter, she was crazy too, of course. She didn't like die Kinder in the house."

"Why not?"

Mama shrugged. "I don't think she realized you were Lana's lost baby. She said that your voice was high and your chatter annoyed her and it hurt her ears when Milo cried for food. She was afraid you would knock over things and break them. Or that Milo would spit up on her furniture and carpets. And she thought that I must have stolen the two of you and that your parents would report us to the Americans. She was scared of everyone by then."

The only fix for that was to keep everyone away from her, I guessed. Especially little kids. Was that supposed to explain why Mick and I slept in a box in a courtyard full of leaves?

Mama's eyelids drooped. "I'm tired, EJ."

"Wait, I have more questions."

"I need a shot." She wadded up her tissue and dropped it into a little wooden pail beside her bed.

"Mama?"

"No, EJ. Tell them to come. I have to sleep..."

"Should we call Doc Wiley?"

"Okay..." Her eyes closed and her voice was so low I could barely hear her.

Gritting my teeth, I held her wrist, searching for her pulse and then relaxing as I felt the light throb. The only thing I'd known for sure, the starting point of my sense of self, was that Vala Hess gave birth to me in Mannheim on September 6, 1943, the night of the bombs. And now even that rock-solid piece of information was wrong.

My mind whirled. Everything changed, as an appreciation of what Mama had just told me sank in. I was two and a half years older than I thought, meaning I was five in January of 1945, not two. Did that mean my dreams of being ripped from the arms of one woman after another were actual memories? Was the little girl-ghost real? I'd always known something was not right, but I'd never expected this, not even after my conversation with Dolph Jäger. How could Mama have kept it from me all these years?

Mama's eyes fluttered and my anger dissolved. I bent over and kissed her forehead. She breathed heavily through her mouth. This woman saved me several times before I was old enough to understand it. I would miss her so much. I should have had years to show her my appreciation. I leaned my head against the carved bed post and cried.

* * *

In the hallway outside Mama's room, I leaned against her door and closed my eyes.

"Can I help?" Zona hadn't left Mama's bedside in days.

"You already are, Zona."

"She was holding on until you and Mick got here." She rose from the kitchen chair she'd been using to guard Mama's door. "She said she had something important to tell you. Did she get it all out?"

I rubbed my temples. "I don't know," I sighed. "Enough, I guess."

"She loves you, EJ."

"I know."

Zona waited while I gathered myself. "Would you like a glass of water?"

I shook my head. "Did she tell you all of this?"

"Probably not. Some.

She needs a shot."

"I'll take care of her, EJ. Do you need to talk to your brother? Or Sonny?"

"Not yet."

"You go find someplace to work things out, sugar. I'll watch over Vala, and I'll cover for you with them." Zona gestured toward the kitchen where Mama's friends had gathered.

"Thanks." I started toward the front door. Halfway down the hall, I stopped, took a deep breath, and came back. "Thanks, Zona." I bent over to hug her. "Thanks for caring about Mama."

She stood on tiptoe and patted my back. "She's the best friend I ever had, EJ. The very best."

I wiped my eyes and hurried out the front door. Outside, I hunched against the wind and headed toward the gate to Logan Foods.

"EJ!"

I ignored the voice and unlocked the gate.

"EJ, wait for me."

I stopped just inside and leaned my forehead against the chain link fence. Rosa was the last person I wanted to see right now, but how do you tell your fiancée to go away?

She hurried through the gate and I closed it behind her. She waited, saying nothing.

"Okay." I held out my hand.

She took it and we crossed the field to the tree house. I pulled on the rope, and the ladder dropped down. She scrambled up and waited for me inside, shivering. I crawled in beside her.

Her eyes were soft with concern. "Are you okay?"

"No."

She caressed my cheek. "You want to talk?"

I shook my head. And then nodded.

"Good," she said. "A man of conviction."

"I don't know how to start."

"Did she tell you what you wanted to know?"

"Some. But it was exhausting and she fell asleep in the middle."

Rosa squeezed my hand but said nothing.

When the silence became to loud to bear, I started. "She...uh... she's not my mother."

"Oh," Rosa whispered.

"I'm her sister Lana's baby."

"Oh."

"Her sister Lana was part of the Lebensborn Project. She was impregnated by some perfect Nazi specimen to create a healthier, bigger..."

"Blonder..." She touched my hair.

I grabbed her hand. "It's degrading! Like breeding cows to produce more milk or chickens to lay bigger eggs. None of it benefits the cow or the chicken. They probably meant to use me in some way, too." The idea made me shudder.

"The flip side of the Holocaust," Rosa said. "Get rid of the undesirables and breed good-looking, muscular, blond boys."

"You sound bitter."

"Do I?"

"Yes." I kissed her forehead. "Save your outrage until you've heard it all."

She raised her eyebrows. "There's more?"

"Oma didn't like kids, so Mama took care of me along with a babysitter when Mama was in school. After Lana's Nazi friends killed her, they took Mama, an eleven-year-old German citizen, one of their own, a whiter-than-white perfect little Aryan girl, and sterilized her." The horror of it hit me and with it came rage. "The bastards." I pounded on the floor planks of the tree house with my fist until my knuckles bled and Rosa grabbed my arm.

"EJ, darling. Oh, EJ!"

"The bastards," I sobbed into her shoulder.

"Shhh...Shhh."

I cried until I couldn't cry anymore. And then I fell asleep in her arms.

* * *

"Hurry, baby. Come to me."

I stretched out my arms and cried, "Don't leave me, Tante Magda."

"If we get separated when the train stops, show this to anyone who talks to you. Show it to the soldiers. Do you understand? The dark-haired woman pinned a piece of paper inside my pocket. Your Opa will find you. Whenever you get scared, remember your Opa will find you."

"Where's Mutti?"

"She will come for you when she can."

A little girl squatted beside me. "Don't cry, little brother. We will be together—like always." A loud metallic screech drowned out her voice and everyone fell against each other.

I panicked, flailing my arms and screaming. People struggled to stand up but it was so crowded they had to use each other to regain their balance. The train rolled a little more and then stopped. We were all thrown down again. A beam of light blinded me as everyone rushed toward the door. Someone tripped and fell on top of me, and it was dark.

* * *

I awoke, cradled in Rosa's arms.

"Do you feel better?"

"Too soon to tell." I opened and closed my stiffening hand.

"It must hurt."

"Yeah. Stupid move, huh?"

"Do you want to go back in the house? Warm up? Soak that hand and let me put something on it?"

"You sound like Grandma Arial."

"She probably has just the thing in her medicine cabinet."

I groaned. "Sadist."

"Now that you mention it, maybe amputation is in order." She leaned down and kissed me. "Good thing I'm a doctor."

We laughed and things felt almost normal for a few minutes. Then the wind made the tree house shiver, and I realized my hideaway might not be Rosa's idea of comfortable. "I'm sorry. You must be freezing."

"Not so much. We have our coats and body warmth. And I found this. She stroked Grandma Arial's ragged old quilt that covered us from chin to toe. In fact, I dozed for a while, too."

"How well do you know Oskar Schreiner?"

"Whew. That came out of nowhere. Why do you ask?"

"He had a wife in Mannheim."

"Oh?"

"Her name was Magda Langer."

Rosa shrugged. "Okay."

I held her tighter. "They had a daughter. And they were deported the same day you were. Because that girl was half Jewish."

She shuddered in my arms. I held her for a while waiting for her to say something. When she didn't, I continued. "Mama was in the hospital that day—being mutilated—and Oma didn't want me around."

"And?"

"And Magda was taking care of me..."

"No. No!"

"I was a baby—like you..."

"Oh, EJ!"

"And the Gestapo didn't care that I was supposed to be the hope of the Aryan race..."

Her fingers bit into my arms.

"And they took Magda and her daughter and me to—"

"The train station in Ludwigshafen," Rosa murmured.

"Do you remember it?" I whispered.

"Of course not. I was a baby, too. But Delores has researched what happened to us. Every step of the way."

"Do you think she knows about me?"

"Maybe not you specifically, but she knows what happened to my mother and grandparents."

"What happened to them?"

"You already know."

"Tell me, Rosa. I need to hear it."

"Auschwitz, ultimately."

"What year?"

"1942."

I shuddered. "That means I must have been taken there in 1942 as well."

"Oh, EJ."

"I read that they killed kids as soon as they arrived. That's what must have happened to the little girl-ghost. And her mother, my babysitter, Magda Langer."

Rosa put her arms around me.

"So how did a sixteen-year-old girl, the pampered daughter of Nazis social climbers, find me—still alive four years after we were all deported—and rescue me from Auschwitz?"

She sighed. "This wasn't what you expected, was it?"

I gazed into her eyes and shook my head slowly.

* * *

Although Mama was no longer well enough to visit with our neighbors, some still sat in the living room sipping tea and waiting for her to wake up and ask for them. When that didn't happen and conversation dried up, they dutifully rinsed their empty cups and put them in the sink. Mick collected their coats while Grandma Arial accepted their kind words about Mama and thanked them for coming. Together they escorted Mama's visitors to the door and waved goodbye.

Knowing that Rosa was watching over Mama while Zona raced home to cook for Jimmy, I hid away with Sonny in his room to avoid having to be nice. He lay on his bed reading old comic books. His eyes were red, and I noticed deep lines forming on his forehead and around his mouth. He had to be exhausted. I certainly was. I turned to stare out the window at our backyard, the old shed, the fence, and the Vilani's house beyond that. The silence was restful.

When the last guest left, Mick came upstairs and tapped on the door. "You guys alive in there?"

"Come on in and grab a seat," Sonny said.

"How's Mama?" It was a stupid question, but it was the best I could manage.

Mick shrugged. "I stuck my head in the door on my way up. Rosa told me Mama was comfortable. Translation—drugged."

"At least when she's drugged she isn't hurting." Sonny was gruffer than usual.

I watched as the Vilanis opened the gate between their property and ours on their way home. "Why do people come visiting when they know you don't feel like socializing?"

"They don't mean any harm," Mick said as he sat down on Sonny's rumpled bed. "They're trying to be helpful."

"More distraction than anything else."

"At least they come bearing food. That helps."

Sonny laid the Captain America comic book on his desk. "What kind of food?"

"Casseroles, mostly."

Remembering neighborhood potlucks past, all three of us made faces at the same time. Not everyone could cook like Grandma Arial.

"At least we can count on Sharon Vilani for fresh vegetables out of her garden." Sonny lit a new cigarette with the butt of his old one.

I watched the Vilanis cross their yard. They were bundled up against the autumn chill. When they got to their back patio, he put his arm around her and said something to her. She stood on tiptoe to kiss his cheek and then his lips. They clung to each other for a moment before hurrying into the house, holding hands.

I closed my eyes, fighting back tears. Sonny had never had that kind of passionate marriage. And of course, neither had Mama. Poor Uncle Grant was in love with a woman he could never have. I dreamed of a life with Rosa. She was affectionate, but…then again, maybe that side of things would explode after we were married. She was smart and fun and strong, everything I admired and wanted to be. And I owed her. After all she'd lost, I owed her.

I pushed the image of the Vilanis' spontaneous embrace out of my mind. "Any idea what this is? I took the little wooden box out of my pocket and tossed it to Sonny."

He turned it in his hands, examining the carvings. "Never saw it before."

"Mama left it in the tree house for me. Another Oskar Schreiner piece of art?"

"Who knows?" Sonny handed it to Mick.

"Does it open?" Mick ran his fingers over the carvings looking for a latch.

"If it does, I haven't found it yet. I was going to ask Mama about it, but she got off on another track and I forgot. And then she was in too much pain to ask."

Mick gave up and handed the box back to me. "It's beautiful."

"I have to talk to Oskar."

Sonny sat up and put his feet on the floor. "Oh?"

"Mama told me something."

I had their attention. "Mama can't have babies."

Sonny sighed and slumped his shoulders.

"What do you mean?" Mick glanced from me to Sonny and back to me.

"She was sterilized when she was eleven years old, in 1940."

Sonny stiffened as the implications of that statement hit him.

"What does that mean, EJ?" Mick's eyes told me he knew very well what I was saying.

"It means I am two and a half years older than we thought all these years. Those dreams I have really can be memories, because memories of a five-year-old child are more real than those of a toddler. It also means that Vala Hess Logan isn't my real mother. Lana was."

"EJ, I never had a clue," Sonny said. "I just knew there'd never be children between your mother and me. Not that we ever actually made love..." He stopped, embarrassed. "That was part of our agreement when we got married."

"That's why she wanted her own room when we moved here?"

He nodded. "Vala was so young and traumatized when we met. I didn't want to push anything on her. I held out hope for years, especially as I began falling in love with her, that we could—you know—grow closer. She never could get past it, whatever it was."

"So what else did she say?" Mick was my brother in so many ways. Who else would know how it feels to find out you aren't your mother's child?

"After Lana died, Mama and a babysitter took care of me. And that babysitter was Grandpa John's cousin's daughter, Magda Langer." I turned to Sonny. "Did you know that?"

He shook his head.

"Do you think Grandma Arial knows?"

He shrugged. "I never heard anyone speak of it. All I know is that Magda was engaged to Oskar and he supposedly left her at the altar when he decided to leave Mannheim."

"Do you know what happened to her?"

"I don't know, exactly. I never met her. She's probably still there I'd guess."

"Mama said Oskar married Magda before he left, and they had a daughter."

"That's news to me."

"She said that because the baby was Oskar's, it was Jewish, so Magda and the baby were deported with the rest of the Jews in 1940...and they ended up in Auschwitz."

Sonny paled. "Have you told Grandma Arial yet?"

"Other than Rosa, you guys are the first to know."

"Why did Mama tell you all this about Grandpa John's relative?" Mick had been quiet until now, absorbing the story. "What's it got to do with you being Lana's baby?"

"That's just it, Mick. I was with Magda and her daughter when the Gestapo came for them. That's the real reason Mama went to

Auschwitz. To find me. To rescue me. There was no boyfriend guard like I suspected all these years. She was trying to *find* me."

"Did Magda and her daughter die there?"

"They must have, Sonny. In my dream, I'm being led through a village, and I see a dark-haired little girl. I know her and want to play with her, but the man holding my hand tells me that she's a ghost. He says—and I think it's Dolph Jäger—that if I don't behave he'll leave me there and tell Vala I got lost."

"How old do you think you were?"

"I don't know. I was conscious of what it meant to be left behind or lost. The Mannheim Jews were taken from Gurs to Auschwitz in late summer 1942, so I must've been two. And that makes me four and a half years old in early 1945 when we left Poland and found you on the road, Mick."

"Where were you between 1942 and 1945?"

"Exactly. Mama or my father or Opa or someone with a great deal of pull must have rescued me from the gas chambers and hidden me somewhere in Poland."

We sat silently absorbing what this meant.

"What is the little girl-ghost doing in your dream?" Mick prompted me.

"She's waiting with her mother to get in…"

"Get in where?"

I closed my eyes, trembling. "Into the building with the big chimneys."

* * *

"Vala?" Sonny's voice was so raspy it sounded like a whisper. "Do you want some tea?" He caressed her ankle under the coverlet.

"I want to go home to Mannheim," Mama murmured without opening her eyes. "I miss it so."

Mick leaned forward and took her hand. "I'll take you there when you feel better."

"I feel better now that I'm packed."

Mick looked me and I shrugged. Who knew what was going on in her head? We waited for her to take another breath.

"He was a demon."

"Who, Mama?"

I was glad that Mick didn't dream about the cold and guns in the distance and thousands of lost souls on a dark road. Good for him.

"Dolph. He is waiting for me."

Sonny's face crumpled and he got up. "He can't hurt you now."

"She's dreaming..." I wanted to comfort him.

He closed his eyes and shook his head before leaning down to kiss her cheek. "He won't be where you are going, my darling one."

She sighed.

We waited.

Schatzi raised his head. His nose quivered and he pawed at Mama's pillow.

Mama didn't move.

Schatzi's first howl was soft. He scratched at the bed-clothes frantically.

"It's okay, boy." Mick reached for the silly little creature.

Schatzi wriggled away from him and sat on his haunches. He threw his head back, and his next howl raised the hair on my arms.

Mick sank back into his chair, and I realized he was crying. So was Sonny.

I looked back at Mama. How like her. No dramatic *good-bye* or tender *I love you*. She just left.

32

What Now?

A WEEK AFTER Mama's funeral, I came downstairs to see Sonny standing in the doorway to Mama's room.

"I don't know what to do now," he said.

I peered past him.

Grandma Arial had stripped the linens off the bed as soon as they took Mama away. The mattress and its plastic cover seemed small inside the big wooden frame.

"About the bed?"

Sonny turned to face me. "No. About me."

"I don't know what you mean."

"Since 1945, I've had a purpose. Now, Vala—well, she doesn't need me anymore. And you and the Mickster are adults."

"I'm sure we'll mess up from time to time." I winked at him.

"I can only hope." His sense of humor was still there at least. "But what do I do in between?"

I squeezed past him and picked up the petal pink peignoir that was draped over the footboard of Mama's bed. I held it to my face expecting to smell Mama's Avon perfume on it, but Grandma Arial had already laundered it. "What 'in between'? I need your help in figuring out the rest of Mama's secrets. Right now."

He followed me into the room and I handed him Mama's negligee. "You already figured out more than I ever knew, EJ. I didn't ask about Vala's past, and she didn't ask about mine."

I ignored his forlorn tone. "Then after we do that, Rosa and I will need you to help us with our wedding." I tapped the center of the headboard with my class ring, something Mama would never have allowed for fear of damaging the enamel mosaic. "Mick will be graduating about then, and he'll need help finding a job in an orchestra or as an engineer. Maybe he'll even have a steady girlfriend by then." I ran my fingers over the carvings.

"What exactly are you looking for?"

"Secret compartments."

"You have several closets of your mother's belongings, and you think she hid more stuff in her bed?"

I tried twisting the finials but they wouldn't budge. "Why else did this ugly old thing mean so much to her? Remember when we were moving in here and the bed arrived from Mannheim? She threw a fit at the thought that you and Uncle Grant might take it apart. Why?"

He caressed the scroll on the footboard. "It reminded her of Germany."

It had to be more than that, but I wasn't going to argue with him. "Mick and I used to sneak in here when Mama was out and try to twist that old bullfrog's head." I pointed.

"She wasn't out very often." Mick stood in the doorway with a mug of coffee in his hand. "What are you trying to do?"

Sonny sat down in Mama's plain American rocking chair and laid her pink nightgown and robe on his lap. "EJ thinks there might be hidden compartments in the bed."

"Could be. I used to fantasize about it when I was little."

I chuckled. "You fantasized about a bed?"

"You bet. The fantasy grew with me, too. When we first set it up in here, I pretended it was an elegant carriage drawn by imaginary horses. And I was a prince out to rescue a fair damsel."

"I can't see it."

"Squint."

Sonny and I obeyed Mick's command. "I don't see a carriage—maybe a sled or something. It would take Clydesdales to pull it, though."

"Then when I was older," Mick went on, "I pretended it was a tank, and I was the driver and was going to smash down walls to rescue people with it."

"If there was that much going on inside your head, no wonder you didn't need playmates."

"The guys my age weren't allowed to play with me until I was in the fourth or fifth grade anyway."

Sonny frowned. "Why not?"

"Because they thought we were Nazis."

Sonny seemed surprised and then angry. "I never heard that."

"It's okay, Sonny. Grandma Arial took care of it. And eventually, the kids came around."

Sonny rocked back and forth in Mama's chair, scowling. "You should have come to me. There was no need for you boys to have one minute of sorrow over something like that. I would've fixed it."

"We survived." Mick sipped his coffee. "Kids pick up things they hear at home and put their own meanings to it. One time, I heard

Mama say that Oma danced with Hitler at a party. I imagined they were dancing to 'Der Führer's Face.'"

That image made me burst out laughing. And for a moment, Sonny's mood broke and he did, too.

"Where in the world did you get that one?" Sonny said when we could talk again.

"It was the only German song I knew at the time."

"Why did you think it was German?"

Mick grinned. "I was six or so, and I still spoke a mixture of German and English—and that song is a mix, too. Seemed normal to me."

"But where did you hear it? Radio?" I remembered Billy Ray Parker's mom humming it whenever she came to pick him up at school and I was anywhere around. She meant for it to make me feel bad. I could tell by the embarrassment in Billy Ray's eyes and the hardness in hers.

"Miss Myrtle was babysitting me for some reason," Mick explained. "She had a stack of Spike Jones records, and that song was on one of them."

"You were that little and Myrtle let you use her prized record player?" Sonny was still out of sorts, even after our belly laugh.

"Not in a million years." Mick's eyes sparkled. "Mr. McKensey and I were rummaging through them and he said, 'You gotta hear this one.' And he played it for me a bunch of times."

"Mr. McKensey had a strange sense of humor." Sonny was less than amused.

"I was oblivious at the time, of course, but I think he loved the idea of me knowing that song. Like it made me really, really American."

"What's wrong with 'God Bless America'?" Sonny growled. "Or 'America the Beautiful'?"

I turned to Mick. "Let me guess. You figured out that song and played it on your accordion."

"It's a catchy tune," he said, keeping a worried eye on Sonny. "But I could never remember the words, so finally, I wrote them down phonetically. I was too little to know which words were German and which were English."

Mick and I both laughed.

"All I can remember is 'We heil right in der Führer's face,'" I said.

"'Star Spangled Banner,' maybe?" Sonny was still grumbling about Mr. McKensey's choice of patriotic music.

Mick put a comforting hand on Sonny's arm. "What is it, Sonny?"

"Just an uncomfortable memory, I guess. We were still in Germany in 1946 when the first war crimes tribunal decision came down. We Americans—the other Allies too, but especially some of the guys I knew—we were full of ourselves. We hadn't fought in a single battle, but we enjoyed lording the Allied victory over everyday Germans. The Nazis had been so high and mighty, pushing people around, and you know, no one likes a bully, not even another bully."

"I can't see you that way," Mick said.

"We were smug and self-important." Sonny's voice rose. "We knew Americans would never do such awful things, and that made us better than the Krauts on two levels. We were better fighters, and we were better human beings. So much for the master race, we'd say to anyone who would listen, which was mostly each other."

I caught Mick's eye and he shrugged. We'd never heard Sonny speak with such self-loathing before. Grief sometimes made people angry. Still this was wise, kind, supportive Sonny talking like Mr. McKensey. It felt weird.

"When the tribunal found the majority of those bastards guilty, especially Goering, it felt like justice. After the prisoners were returned to their cells, a chauffeur waiting in his car outside the Palace of Justice had his radio playing. That song—'Der Führer's Face'—came on, and the driver turned the volume way up."

I visualized the impact the saucy, defiant lyrics might have on Nazi war criminals. "Could the people inside hear it?"

"A friend of mine was a guard. He said the prisoners were quiet at first, contemplating their sentences. The music was loud and silly and everyone, including the prisoners, laughed—even if they didn't understand English."

"Why?"

Sonny patted his chest pocket looking for his cigarettes. "It broke the tension, I guess. They knew it made fun of them, though, and enough of them understood the line, 'When Herr Goering says they'll never bomb this place, We heil heil right in Herr Goering's face.'

"The atmosphere in the prison grew thoughtful by the time the music stopped. There they were, in the bombed-out rubble of Nuremberg, Nazi heaven, and Herr Goering had just been condemned to death. All eyes in the prison went to his cell but he never showed his face."

Mick and I were no longer laughing.

"The ultimate 'up yours,'" I said. "After all the misery they caused, I'm sure most of the world took great satisfaction in taking them down a peg."

"But why does that make you uncomfortable, Sonny?" Mick sat down on the hassock we'd brought in for visitors when Mama was dying.

Sonny found his half-crushed cigarette pack in his back pants pocket. "That was when I realized how small the world is, how connected." He draped Mama's pink peignoir on the arm of the chair, pulled a cigarette out of the pack with his lips, and lit it with his Zippo. "Turned out the girls we knew were related in some way to these prisoners. To them, it was personal and embarrassing. Then I saw Vala's face, and realized how upsetting our behavior toward them had been."

"How do you do that?"

Sonny wiped his eyes with his knuckles. "How do I do what?"

I glanced at Mick and then returned my gaze to Sonny. "Walk that line. The Nazis were villains, the biggest criminals the world has ever known. They killed so many. Destroyed so much. How can you feel sorry for them? How do you still see them as human?"

"Because I'm human, too." He caressed Mama's nightgown as if she were still in it. "I can be just as rotten as the next guy whether I mean to be or not."

"Mama and her family were Christian," I said. "How did they think all the stuff Hitler was preaching fit with that?"

Sonny shook his head. "I've thought about it for years now, and I still don't understand. After the war, we had to live on, knowing that even the most magnificent sounding ideals can be crap. Ours, theirs, anyone's." Sonny blew smoke out of his nostrils as he exhaled.

We sat quietly absorbing that ghastly thought. I knew of so many victims. Oskar and Magda Schreiner and their daughter. Rosa's mother and father. Tante Lana and especially Mama. I didn't know Hitler or Heydrich or Hoess or Mengele, but I did know some of their followers. Gerhardt, Dolph Jäger, Opa, Oma. I swallowed back another load of tears.

Mick changed the subject to something a little less painful. "Remember that lace thing that hung from that?" Mick pointed to the thick wooden frame that arched high over the bed.

I vaguely remembered a time when Mama had some fancy material floating from the canopy frame. I hadn't remembered that it was lace, but now that Mick mentioned it, it made sense. Mama loved frilly things. She had doilies draped all over the place for a while, before she and Zona started buying plastic ones.

Sonny snorted. "I was sure that thing was too high for the ceiling, but it just fit. A half inch higher at the top of the arch and we would have had to raise the ceiling or lower the floor."

"You would have done that for her?"

Sonny sucked his teeth and half-smiled. "By that point, I'd have torn the whole place down if she asked me to."

Mick and I smiled at each other. Mama and Sonny had an unusual relationship, but it certainly had its tender moments.

I turned my attention back to the bed. "Where did she get this monstrosity, do you suppose?"

"No idea," Sonny said. "When we decided to buy Long John's house from his estate, she suddenly started talking about her bed. Her special bed. She had to get it over here, no matter what."

"Where was it?"

"It was stored in the old Schreiner warehouse in Mannheim."

Mick got up and rubbed at the carving on the footboard. "Did the Schreiners make it for her or something?"

"She said it was made just for her, so I assumed it came from your Opa or maybe your natural father, EJ."

I knelt in front of the carving that Mick was studying. "Opa was a pharmacist, not a carpenter, and it seems that my father was a Nazi bigwig. I doubt he ever learned how to carve little animals onto bed frames. He was too busy working out the best way to kill people."

"I imagine one or the other of them commissioned it to be built," Mick said. "It would have two advantages for men like they were. One would be to give Mama something special—"

"This ugly old thing? Ugh!"

"Or two, a way to help a starving artist take care of his family."

Mick could find fine qualities in a rattlesnake with its fangs stuck in a baby's butt. I wanted to be like him, but lately I'd grown cranky and mean. "Probably to show off to his friends that he was such a big shot he could do things like that. I doubt either of them gave two hoots about starving artists."

"There's a signature on it somewhere under the frame." Sonny blew smoke out of his nose.

"Really? Whose?"

He laid his cigarette on the ashtray and got up. "I don't know. I saw it when Grant and I set it up in here. Didn't ring a bell at the time or even seem important. I forgot all about it until just now." He struggled to move the heavy bed. It didn't budge. Mick threw his weight against it, too. Nothing. Then I pushed. Grunting and sweating, we struggled with the giant wooden beast. Together we moved it two inches away from the wall.

"Well, this isn't going to work," I panted. "Do either of you have a plan B?"

"Take it apart is all that I can think of," Sonny said. "Even then, it's going to take more than a couple of us. The individual pieces are heavy and awkward, too."

Mick looked first at me and then at Sonny. "What should we do with it?"

I shrugged, remembering the day it arrived. And Mama's insistence that it not be taken apart. "See what's inside it?"

"What if we tear it apart and it's just a bed, nothing but a piece of furniture?"

"Put it back together and leave it here? Store it somewhere?" I shrugged and we both looked at Sonny.

"It was your mother's favorite thing," he said after a minute. "It should go to you boys, or maybe to your children."

I chuckled at the idea of kids—Mick's or mine—wanting the old atrocity. "I live in an apartment right now, Sonny."

"So do I," Mick said. "There's no way I could get it in the front door."

"It's been sitting here for seventeen years now," Sonny said.

I ran my hand over one of the posts. "Wouldn't you like your parlor back?"

"Naw, this room was Vala's. I've been coming in here to think about her this past week. I doubt I'd want it to be anything else."

"What if you get married again? You think a new wife would want that thing?"

Sonny looked pained. "I can't even think about such a thing, boys."

I stared at it for a long time. "It was probably made at Schreiner's. Who knows when? Maybe long before the war. Maybe it belonged to someone else before it belonged to Mama."

"Why didn't she take to Oskar Schreiner?"

Sonny shook his head. "I don't know, Mick. She just didn't want him around, and I saw to it that he didn't bother her. After all she'd been through, she deserved some peace and privacy."

"Oskar was pushy, and he dressed like an overweight dandy," I remembered. "But he seemed desperate to find out something about his family business. Don't know why he thought Mama might know. He told Grandma Arial and me about when Opa and Tante Lana and Mama visited his business before the war. Opa wanted to buy Schreiner's from Oskar's father. But eventually, as the Nazi laws were instituted, he simply stole it away from the Schreiner family."

Sonny seemed stricken. "She never told me that."

It seemed that Mama and Sonny's pact of living forward had a few flaws. He had been her protector, without knowing what he was protecting. I felt bad for him. "She might never have known that part, Sonny. She was a little girl when it happened."

"So what is the story about the bed, then?" Mick seemed more interested in these things now that he knew he was the bundle in the road that I dreamed about all the time. Knowing he wasn't really a member of the Hess family had probably been both a shock and a relief.

"Maybe before we tear it apart, we should see if the Schreiners ever designed beds with secret compartments," I said. "And if they did, what's the secret password?"

"How do you plan on doing that?" Sonny rubbed the finish on the footboard with his sleeve.

"Where's the Polaroid?"

"In the desk in my room. There's a couple of film packs, too."

"Be right back." I ran out of the room, leaving Mick and Sonny to sigh and remark at my intensity. At the top of the stairs, I opened the door to Sonny's room. It looked like it had always looked, as big a mess after the fire as it was all those years before Dolph Jäger's uninvited visit.

I opened the bottom drawer. The camera was in its box. I grabbed it and a fresh film pack. Beneath them was a leatherette ring binder of Polaroids in cellophane sleeves. On impulse, I grabbed it as well and ran back downstairs.

I tossed the album to Mick when I came into the room and sat down to load a film pack into the camera.

"What are you going to do," Mick said as he opened up the album and paged through the plastic-encased pictures.

"I'm going to take a picture of the bed."

"Why?"

"I'm going to go talk to Oskar. Grandma Arial has his address. He lives in North Royalton and works at the gas company."

"I kicked him out of Mama Arial's house," Sonny said. "And I told him he couldn't come back to Cold Creek. I imagine he's not going to be glad to see you."

"I'll call Rosa and see if she'll go with me. No one can say no to Rosa."

"You can take back the pipe he left at Mama Arial's that time," Sonny said. "It's been in the shed all these years."

"Filled with Hitler's ashes?" Mick elbowed me and we both laughed.

"Old joke," I told Sonny.

"Oh."

Nothing seemed to lift Sonny out of his grief for very long. Maybe we were pushing him too hard. Maybe we should just leave him alone to feel whatever he felt.

"Look." Mick held up the album and pointed to a picture of Mama and Zona hula-hooping in the back yard. "I don't remember this."

Sonny looked at the picture and the corners of his mouth curled despite himself. "We bought them for you and Mick."

"We never had any hula-hoops, Sonny." I squatted and snapped a picture of the bed.

He finally laughed. "No, you didn't. Vala and Zona decided to test them before we gave them to you. Vala spun one of them around her wrist and it ended up hitting her in the head. Zona tried it around her knees. It tripped her and she sprained her thumb when she fell. So Vala decided they were dangerous, and we took them back before you fellas came home from school." He shook his head and handed the picture back to Mick. "Look at their clothes. That must have been around 1958 or 1959. I took that with my old Brownie."

"Figures. They got rid of the cool stuff before you and I ever got to play with it." I said to Mick. I pulled the photo of the bed out of the camera and laid it on the nightstand to develop.

Sonny took the album from Mick and thumbed through the pictures of us as a family. "My God, she was beautiful!"

I took another shot of the bed.

* * *

"Do you want to go with us to visit Oskar Schreiner," I asked Mick after I got off the phone with Rosa.

"When are you going?"

"Saturday afternoon."

"I have a rehearsal with the full orchestra then. How about we meet for dinner afterward, and you and Rosa can tell me all about it."

"We'll meet you at The Arcade at five on Saturday, then."

I got my coat and we went back to Mama's room where Sonny still sat. "We're heading out now."

He nodded but never turned to look at me. The photo album was still in his lap and Schatzi lay on the floor beside his chair.

"See you soon, Sonny." Mick bent down to kiss him on the cheek. Sonny patted Mick's hand absently.

"It's time we left him to deal with what he has to deal with," I said as we climbed into the Austin-Healey. "Maybe our visits are more of a burden than a blessing. We've been down here more in the last month than we have in years."

Mick nodded. "I can't imagine what he's feeling. He gave up his young adulthood to care for us. What does he have now?"

33

North Royalton

November 6, 1966

As Rosa and I pulled into the driveway of a small bungalow on Ridge Road, the drapes covering the window beside the front door twitched.

"Oskar, there's company. Company." The voice was a nasal whine.

"Who do you suppose that is?" Rosa took a compact out of her purse and peered into it, patting her curls into place.

"Perhaps Oskar got married again?" I turned off the engine and took a deep breath. "Now that we're here, I wonder if this is right."

"Oh no, you don't. You've wanted this since Danny and Teresa's wedding. Before even. You crept around your own house, snooping through your mother's life for a definitive answer. We're here now. It might be hard to hear, but it's time we all know."

I gripped the steering wheel, my heart thumping in my ears. The carved box Mama had left in the tree house lay on the seat between us. "Will it make a difference to you?"

She reapplied her lipstick and blotted it with a tissue. "I know you want me to say no—to know for sure that we'll be okay." She put her cosmetic kit back into her purse. "I wish I could be sure, EJ. But how can I be?"

"You could at least have the decency to lie." I wanted to touch her but the distance between us, even in that little car, seemed too much to bridge.

"Whatever Oskar tells us will send us around the spiral one more time. I'm tired of it. Tired of thinking about them and their stupid animosities, wondering how we all ended up a stone's throw from each other, friends. I want a shiny new life now. Uncomplicated playthings in unopened packages. A world free of hatefulness and grief." She looked up into my eyes. "Do you understand?"

I shook my head slowly.

She shaded her face from the sun with her hand. "You do, too."

I put the box in my pocket, got out of the car, and walked around to open her door. "Let's get it over with then," I said.

Rosa's hand was cool when I took it. As we walked up to the front porch of the house, I thought I felt her tremble, but it could have been me.

Oskar opened the door at my first tentative tap. "EJ Logan."

"Yes, it's me."

"I'm sorry about your mother. She was a strong lady."

I remembered the afternoon I watched Mama comfort Zona on the old back porch of our house. I didn't know then what I knew now. Of course Mama understood the sorrow of a childless woman. "Yes, she was very strong. Do you remember Rosa Singer?"

"Sure, I know Rosa. I knew her parents. In Mannheim. You look like your mother, dear. Come in, come in. I knew both of you would come eventually, although I didn't expect you'd come together."

"Rosa and I are engaged," I said as we sat down on his couch.

"You are full of surprises." He put his hand on his cheek, eyes wide. "Your parents would be horrified. Both sets."

"We're American. Those attitudes died with them."

"Oh?" He raised one eyebrow. "Did your time in Mississippi teach you that birds from different flocks can nest together?"

Was he mocking me? Making fun of a serious attempt to stop something that was very much like what had happened in Germany? My cheeks grew hot. How dare he? Oskar Schreiner of all people. How dare he?

Rosa touched my hand and I choked back my outrage. "Herr Schreiner, we didn't come to fight about EJ and me," she said. "We came to talk about your family."

"Oskar, offer our guests some coffee and cake. Cake." The woman was as small as her voice was loud. She was at least thirty years older than Oskar.

"Frieda. Let me introduce you to some fellow Mannheimers. EJ, Rosa, this is my cousin, Frieda Vogel. Her father was my great uncle."

Her gummy smile was gracious. "We have coffee and cake. Coffee and cake."

"That sounds delicious," Rosa said. "Can I help you prepare it?"

"Oh no, dearie. Coffee and cake." She scurried into the kitchen, her soft house shoes slapping against her heels.

Rosa looked at me and then at Oskar and then back at me. Oskar clapped his hands together and said, "Now that Frieda is fulfilled, what can I do for you?"

The tension broke and I blew away its remnants with a sigh. "Mama told me a story before she died. I think maybe it's what you came looking for, that time. Can we share?"

Oskar seemed shocked. "She talked about Schreiner's in Mannheim?"

"She talked about your wife and daughter."

He sat down in an upholstered rocker. It squeaked under his weight. "Magda and Heidi?"

"I didn't know her name was Heidi." Now that I said it, it sounded right, like I did know it somehow.

"What did Vala say?"

"She said that after you left, Magda became a nanny."

"She had no choice. I was here and she was there. I sent money when I had it and long letters but—"

"She was my Aunt Lana's baby's nanny."

His chair squeaked again. "I didn't know that."

I glanced at Rosa and took a breath. "She had the children with her when she was deported with the Mannheim Jews in the fall of 1940."

Oskar stared at his knuckles. "So that was it," he muttered. "I never knew for sure. She just disappeared. I haven't heard from her since the summer of 1940. I thought maybe she simply gave up and remarried. An Aryan, perhaps. It would have solved all her problems. On good nights, I've prayed that she is alive somewhere in Bavaria with a large family, living near a lake with lots of little row boats. I never saw Heidi, not even a picture. Sometimes I forget she even existed."

Rosa leaned forward. "I'm sorry, Oskar."

"I am, too." I coughed behind my fist. Being sorry didn't change a thing. We all knew that, but we had to say something to acknowledge his great loss.

He looked up, dry-eyed. "Did any survive? Do you know?"

"A few. Rosa was rescued by the Quakers."

"At Mr. Maxwell's request." Rosa's voice was soft. "And only because Shirley asked him. She asked because she knew my cousin Delores."

Oskar sighed. "Knowing someone who knew someone who had resources and power could be the difference between life and death. Not knowing anyone...well, I'm here and they are lost."

Frieda came into the tiny living room with a tray. "Sit, sit. I'll serve you. Serve you."

Rosa relaxed back into the couch beside me. "Thank you, Frieda." Glancing at me with amusement, she accepted a cup of the strongest black coffee I've ever smelled.

"Here's yours, Herr...eh...who are you again?"

"EJ Logan. I'm related to Magda's family." The coffee tasted as bad as it smelled.

"Oh, Magda. She was a sweet girl. Sweet girl. Same age as Oskar, wasn't she?"

"She was, Frieda." Oskar passed on the coffee. He didn't feel the need to be polite. "Remember, you used to babysit us when Magda and I were little."

"Magda was a sweet girl."

Oskar took Frieda's forearm. "Yes, Magda was sweet."

Frieda pulled her arm away from his grasp. "Magda was sweet, Magda was sweet, Magda—"

"You know, I need more sugar, Frieda." Rosa's voice was firm, more of a command than a request.

Frieda startled. "Yes. You need more sugar."

"Now, Frieda," Oskar said.

She shuffled her feet in place for a moment before actually moving forward. "I know where it is. I know where it is."

"That was kind of you," Oskar said to Rosa, "and observant."

I looked from Oskar to Rosa and back to Oskar. "What did I miss?"

Rosa set her cup on the metal TV tray beside the couch. "Frieda has a condition that makes her repeat herself, especially when stressed. Sometimes she gets stuck and repeats the same thing until someone introduces a new thought."

I frowned. "Why? What's wrong with her?"

"Any number of things could have caused it," Rosa said. "Frieda's okay. It's not the end of the world."

Frieda reentered the room with a sugar bowl. "You need more sugar."

"Thanks, Frieda." I dipped two spoons full into my coffee.

"You need more sugar, you need more sugar."

"I do." Rosa winked at Frieda as she took the bowl from her. "Why don't you sit down and have coffee and cake too?"

"Join us, Frieda." Oskar guided his cousin to her chair and handed her a cup of coffee and a piece of cinnamon cake. "Frieda is excited. We don't have company very often."

"I'm excited. Excited." She bobbed her head as she stirred her coffee.

I liked Frieda. Weird condition or no, she was hospitable and friendly. I wished Mick had joined us on this trip. He would've thought the old girl was sweet and would've probably written a song about her.

Oskar took another chunk of coffee cake. "Do you remember your parents, Rosa?"

Rosa shook her head.

"Nothing?"

"A woman in a black coat. Rain."

"Your mother's name?"

"I know it, Oskar. I don't remember it." Rosa's glance was questioning and it was my turn to raise a brow. What did Oskar Schreiner want to know really?

"I just thought…you know, maybe Heidi is out there somewhere…and if she is, does she have any memories to help her?"

Rosa set her cup on the coaster Frieda had provided. "Help her do what?"

"Find me."

I opened my mouth and closed it several times before anything came out. "How old was she in 1940?"

He shook his head. "A toddler, not yet two."

"Not yet two. Not yet—" Frieda stopped mid-sentence, her eyes wide. "What?"

Oskar patted her hand. "It's okay, dear. Finish your cake."

Realizing the impossibility of ever finding one little girl pushed everyone into silence.

"Where did they go?" Oskar finally found words.

"At first, Gurs in Vichy France. Then Drancy," Rosa said.

"So, France. There were no death camps in France, were there? They could still be alive." Hope made his eyes sparkle.

"The Jews from Mannheim…from Baden…they went to Auschwitz in the summer of 1942." I watched his face crumple even before I got the word Auschwitz out. I felt like a creep, but he had to know sometime. I was surprised he hadn't found out sooner.

"Excuse me." Oskar Schreiner got up from his rocker and went into the kitchen. A moment later, we heard the back door slam.

"The boy is upset. Upset," Frieda told us.

The three of us got up and went into the kitchen and looked out the window. Oskar stood at the edge of his back yard, staring into a grove of pine trees that stretched away from us for acres.

"He's upset."

I put my hand on Frieda's shoulder. "Let's leave him alone for a minute. Okay?"

"He's upset!" Frieda shrugged my hand away.

"Why did you come to the United States when you did?" Rosa interrupted. "Did you get away before the Aktion?"

Frieda cocked her head like a little dog. "Didn't you know?"

"What?" Rosa followed Frieda back into the tiny living area. "What don't we know?"

I nudged Rosa. "Now you're doing it."

"I was walking on Georgenstraße that day. Georgenstraße."

I lifted my head. "What about Georgenstraße, Frieda?"

She cocked her head. "Vala Hess was there. Little Vala."

"When?" I tried not to seem too eager.

"Kristallnacht." It was Oskar's voice. He came into the kitchen behind us, the screen door banging off his heels. I guess his bad moment had passed.

"Mama had bad dreams about a lady on Georgenstraße," I said as Rosa and I sat down on the couch again. "None of us ever knew what it was all about. She'd be upset for hours sometimes, crying and saying that she was stupid."

"What did she say about it?" Oskar seemed intrigued about Mama's nightmare. And that intrigued me.

I closed my eyes and tried to remember. "In the dream, she's walking down a street—Georgenstraße. There are tall houses on both sides of the road. She's with her mother and sister, I think. She hears a siren and then a truck goes past them and stops a block away."

"Little Vala." Frieda crossed her hands over her heart and crooned. "Vala."

"Did she say more?"

I shook my head. "She sees soldiers. She and Lana and Oma keep walking and just as they get close to the building where the truck is, she'd wake up screaming.

Rosa touched me. "What was she screaming, EJ?"

"Ich bin ein Soldat. Soldaten folgen Aufträge. Soldaten weinen nicht."

Oskar stiffened. "We recited that in school. 'I am a soldier. Soldiers follow orders. Soldiers don't cry.' Funny, I haven't thought of that since I was a boy. I used to think it was noble. That we were a bold, strong people and that our determination was good. A German virtue." He guided Frieda back to her chair. "That's before the Nazis decided that we could no longer consider ourselves German."

"Oh, Vala, little Vala." Frieda wrung her hands.

Oskar patted Frieda's arm. "It's over now, dear."

I frowned. "What?"

Rosa sent me eyebrow messages.

I nodded slightly and lightened my tone. "What's over?"

Frieda looked up at me. "Do you know Vala Hess? Vala Hess?"

I recoiled in surprise. "She was my mother."

"Oh!" Frieda pulled back, her face contorted. "Vala Hess was your mother? Vala Hess?"

"Vala passed away three weeks ago, Frieda. Vala died." Rosa's voice was soft.

Frieda's eyes focused on me. "It was her. On Georgenstraße. Georgenstraße."

"Perhaps this wasn't such a good idea." Rosa placed a restraining hand on my arm. "We've upset Frieda."

"It's thirty years too late to prevent that." Oskar hovered over his cousin. Protecting her from what? Rosa and me?

I ignored them both. "Tell me about it, Frieda. What happened on Georgenstraße?"

"I was walking on the sidewalk, and a block away, Frau Hess and Lana and Vala were coming my way. On the other side of the street. Other side. A truck full of men passed them and stopped at a house a few yards in front of me. The men went inside. Inside." Frieda rocked forward and back in her straight chair. "Frau Hess and Lana and Vala saw them, too. Frau Hess and Lana and Vala."

"And then what?"

"EJ! Your tone."

I avoided Rosa's eyes. "What happened then, Frieda?"

"Crashes. Breaking glass. Screams. Crashes and screams."

"Stop him, Oskar," Rosa cried.

"No. Let him see what's inside the box. He's wanted to know all his life, haven't you, EJ?" Oskar's eyes glinted. Satisfaction? Revenge?

"A woman...an old woman fell out of the third-story window. The window. She fell out of the window." Frieda dabbed at her eyes with the corner of her apron. "The window."

"Then what?" Oskar spoke to Frieda, but he was watching me.

"She crashed on the sidewalk and her head broke like an egg. Like an egg."

Surely that was Mama's nightmare. The death of an old woman in such an awful way. Did a soldier throw her out the window, I wondered. Did she jump rather than live in a world where her privacy was always being invaded? Where people were always taking away her things, her home, her family? Mama must have wondered about that all her life. "Where were the Hesses?"

"Frau Hess and Lana stood where they stopped, staring at the dead woman lying in blood. Lying in blood."

I nodded. "It must have been awful for all of you."

"Vala was a little girl. Little. She saw me. She knew me. She knew me."

That made sense. Mannheim wasn't that big of a city. Of course, people knew each other. "How did she know you, Frieda?"

"My husband and I owned a photography shop. We used to take pictures. Family portraits. Until Herr Hess joined the party, we took pictures of the Hess girls. The Hess girls."

I remembered the FotoAlbum filled with pictures of Mama and Lana. Of course. Before the party, no one realized that Frieda Vogel—born Schreiner—had Jewish blood. People probably did business there all the time.

"Tell EJ what happened after that." Oskar Schreiner's eyes were dark and cold.

"Vala, little Vala. She pointed at me. She pointed at me when the soldiers came out. She pointed." Frieda sobbed into her hands. "She pointed at me and shouted, 'Juden.'"

Not Mama. No.

Rosa gasped. Frieda rocked back and forth, remembering Mama's betrayal, no doubt.

I imagined my mother as a little girl. She would have been nine years old in 1938. Nine years old! She was turning people in to the Nazis when she was nine years old. Lights flashed and I squeezed my eyes closed. "What…what happened then?"

"They beat me. Kicked me. Kicked me. Kicked me. Kicked—"

"Because of Mama?"

Frieda's kind eyes settled on me. "No, EJ. Not because of your mama. Because they were young soldiers out to break things like doors and windows and heads. And heads. Someone called me a Jew in front of little Vala, probably when the Hesses stopped coming to us for their family pictures. So she knew I was a Jew and she pointed me out to the mob. She was a baby, doing what she'd been taught to do. A baby. A baby."

I searched for words. If I'm sorry hadn't seemed right or enough before, it was unusable now. "What happened after they beat you?"

Frieda shuddered, too distressed to answer.

I felt myself shrinking. The furniture, Rosa, Frieda, and Oskar grew huge around me.

"They left her on the sidewalk across the street from where the old woman died," Oskar said. "The two of them lying in their own blood on opposite sides of Georgenstraße. When Frieda woke up, her eyes were swollen shut and most of her teeth were shattered."

I couldn't tell if Oskar was angry with me for pushing, or just angry.

"Her leg was broken and she couldn't get up," he continued. "So she lay there until a baker coming home from work found her and carried her into his home where his wife and daughters tended to her. They had relatives in England and they used those contacts to get Frieda out of Mannheim within days. Her head injury was severe and she was in hospital in London for a while. When she was better, they sent her here before the war started. The timing was fortuitous, as they say."

I was small and Frieda and Oskar and Rosa were big, their voices distorted and loud in my ears. The giant Frieda rocked from side to side, lifting first one foot and then the other as if she was marching.

"And someone here sponsored her." Oskar's voice sounded like thunder. "Good luck all around."

"What about your husband?" Rosa asked Frieda.

"Fritz died in Dachau. Dachau. Dachau. Da—"

"Not because he was Jewish," the giant Oskar interrupted, "but because he had a club foot, or because he was a member of the communist party, or because they didn't like his looks. Take your pick."

"Why did the baker's family take Frieda in as bad off as she was?" The giant Rosa sounded like Boris Karlov.

"They were good people. Good people," Frieda chanted. "Good people."

"Thank God, not all Germans behaved like animals," Rosa said.

No, I thought. Not all Germans were like that. But my family was. Guilt seeped out of my pores and I reeked of shame. This wasn't even the worst that happened. It was just the beginning. There was nothing I could ever do to fix this. It was too late. The perpetrators were either dead or proud of their handiwork, and I was left to face the pain they'd left behind. I felt the seizure start.

"EJ!"

"Get him some water. Water. Get him some—"

"Lie back, my love. Come on. Rally now." I felt Rosa's hands on my leg and realized that it was jerking.

"Take a sip." Oskar's words vibrated like a drumhead. "He's still out. Should we call an ambulance?"

"Not yet." Rosa's fingers pressed into my throat, and then she rubbed my leg again.

Droplets of cold water on my face made me gasp.

"There you are, boy." Oskar held the glass under my bottom lip.

I opened my mouth and when the water brought me around, I tried to sit up.

"Not yet, give it a minute." Rosa pushed me back down on the couch. "Don't want you keeling over again."

The three of them loomed over me, their faces filled with concern and sorrow and something else. I couldn't quite place it at first and then I recognized it. Understanding. They knew what I was feeling. And no one should understand that. No one. I took a deep, ragged breath and as I released it, I coughed.

"Take it easy." Oskar gave me another sip of water.

"What is it? Is it?"

"Something EJ's had all his life, Frieda." Rosa sounded more like herself and less like a giant. "He's okay now. Or will be soon."

"I…uh…" My voice was hoarse. I clung to Oskar's arm. "I didn't hear you. I should have listened better."

"What?"

"When you came to Cold Creek."

"You were a kid. You and Arial Logan listened more than anyone else ever did. Most people don't want to know. The damn Nazis made it easy for ordinary people to justify being horses' asses."

"How can you forgive them? How can you forgive me?"

"I don't. I can't. On my dying bed, I will hate them for what they did. But you aren't them. You had nothing to do with it. Hating you lets the real bastards off the hook."

I pushed the glass of water away. "You should hate me. I benefited from it all. I'm alive and your daughter isn't."

"Your guilt is going to make her live again?"

I coughed once more and then drank the rest of the water in the glass. "I think I remember her, at least I dream of someone that might be her."

Oskar handed the glass to Frieda and sat down in his rocker. "What do you remember?"

"A little girl and I are playing in a dark room. I remember trying to catch her long dark braid as she twirls around in front of me. We are giggling. Suddenly, Tante Magda gathers us up and tells us not to make a sound."

"Is that it?" Oskar stared at his hands.

"For that dream, yes. But I dream about her all the time. I can't remember a time when I didn't dream about her. I call her the little girl-ghost."

"Why do you remember her, I wonder. Strange memories for a German boy." Oskar's anger was white hot again.

It was time to tell Oskar what I knew. "Lana had a baby with someone famous. It was important to my Oma and Opa. It was someone my Oma thought would increase our family's status. And it had to be someone high up in the SS, because it was part of the Lebensborn program."

Oskar frowned. "Lebensborn? A bunch of scientific nonsense, an excuse to replace dark-eyed babies with blue-eyed ones."

It hurt but I couldn't disagree with him. I swallowed back my personal shame and told them about Lana's attempt to kill herself and Opa's fight to stop her. I told them about the hospitals where crazy people were euthanized. And then I told them that I was Lana's child, that I wasn't Vala's baby because she was sterilized when she was eleven.

"Oh poor little Vala. Poor Vala." Frieda was infinitely compassionate, even after her ordeal on Georgenstraße.

"I must say I didn't expect that," Oskar said when I finished.

"Oma must have thought they would hurt me because I was the son of this famous guy and someone who was known to be crazy. So she hid me, I assume, with Magda. She probably didn't know that the two of you were married or that Magda had a mixed-blood baby that put her at risk."

"Maybe she was afraid that this Nazi big shot would try to find you," Oskar said. "Either way, both babies made Magda a target, and I'm sure she had to hide out somewhere."

"Whether Oma was right about me being in danger or not, I don't know. But right after they killed Lana, they came for Mama, so that the Hess family wouldn't have any more defective babies. Mama was in the hospital having the procedure on October 22, 1940, the day of the Wagner-Burckel Aktion. That's when all the Jews in the Baden District were deported. Roughly seven thousand people. I read that the Gestapo had extensive lists drawn up. Wherever Magda was hiding with the two babies, the Gestapo knew where she was."

"That list included me and my mother and father," Rosa said, "as well as my mother's parents and her grandmother. I'm sure my father's family was taken too, but I don't know anyone who survived on that side."

"How did you escape, EJ? You were an infant."

"I didn't. Magda must have protected me and Heidi at Gurs. The French weren't expecting to feed and house thousands of people, and I understand that conditions were bad. Broken windows. Not enough blankets. They separated families, putting the men in one part of the camp and women and children in another part. The winter was exceptionally cold, and disease took those who weren't strong. The only reason we know is that some were able to escape."

"My great-grandmother and my grandfather died that winter," Rosa said softly. "Dysentery, I think. Or pneumonia or some other germ."

"How old were you, Rosa? How old? Old?"

"I was a toddler. Maybe eighteen months, give or take when we got there."

"Do you remember anything? Anything?"

"Mud. Being taken away from my mother and crying. I presume that was when the Quakers rescued me."

Frieda covered her mouth and rocked back and forth in her chair. "Oh, so scary. Scary."

Oskar watched me through half-closed lids. "Do you remember anything about Gurs, EJ?"

"Nothing. I couldn't have been more than a few months old when we got there, but I do have a dream. I am dancing in the mud with the little girl-ghost outside a big wooden building. We were apparently there a year or more before they started moving everyone to Drancy transit camp. So that could be a real memory, I suppose. But maybe not."

"My cousin Delores found out there were six transports from Drancy to Auschwitz in the summer of 1942," Rosa said. "My mother and grandmother were in the second one. She never found my father's name so I'm still hoping, even though I know if he'd survived he would've found me by now."

"Jan was a good man, Rosa. Talented. Younger than you are now when they sent him to Dachau in 1938." Oskar bit his lip, avoiding her eyes and mine.

"Delores is checking to see if she can figure out which transport Magda and Heidi and EJ were on."

"That's kind of her—and you, Rosa. I don't know whether to hope she finds their names or she doesn't," Oskar said. "I'll always regret the calamity I brought to Magda and her family. We were young and in love. We'd known each other all our lives. It was my fault. I still thought of myself as German, not Jewish. I was oblivious to the danger until it was upon us." He squeezed his eyes shut for a long moment. Pushing back tears, I supposed.

34

The Music Box
November 6, 1966

I LOOKED AT my watch. We'd been talking with Oskar and Frieda for two hours. They were exhausted with grief from the memories and the stories we'd brought them. It was clearly time to go, but I had a few more questions to ask. They were actually the reason for our visit.

I started gingerly. "Remember when you told Grandma Arial and me about when Opa and Lana and Mama came to your business?"

"Vaguely."

"You said Lana was standoffish. Was it just that? Or was she depressed?"

"I am not a doctor, EJ."

"Can you tell me about her? What was she like?"

He considered my question. "She was tall and slim. An exquisite girl. Her features were perfectly symmetrical. I was an artist. I noticed things like that."

Rosa leaned forward. "Would she be singled out for that?"

"The Nazis had an image of perfection that few people would fit. They measured kids all the time—how round the skull, the placement of the features, the width of shoulders and hips, the length of arms and feet and fingers and toes. They even looked at the genitals."

"And Lana?"

He shrugged. "All I know is that she was lovely in every sense of the word—physically."

"Just physically?"

He chose his words carefully. "I didn't know her well. She came to Schreiner's several times with Herr Hess and Vala. Vala was a charming little imp, but Lana was quiet. She was there, but not."

"What do you mean?" Rosa asked.

"She was aloof. Ethereal. Wouldn't look at you. I took it that she was too good to speak to the likes of me."

"Did she ever talk?"

I knew what Rosa was thinking and if she was right, it would explain everything.

"If she did say something, it was political. She was a big fan of Uncle Adolf. From the time she was little, they had her out marching and waving flags. Vala too, but Lana was older. She understood and accepted it all. Herr Hess encouraged it, of course, for business as much as philosophy. If the Reich wanted something, that whole family supported it."

"She didn't seem crazy to you?"

"No, EJ. Not at all. Just distant, like what was going on inside her head was more interesting than what was happening at Schreiner's."

I glanced at Rosa. It wasn't enough evidence to diagnose schizophrenia. She could simply have been a shy girl or she could have had a mild form of epilepsy, like me.

"Fritz and I took beautiful pictures of her. Pictures. She was active in sports. High jump. Long jump. Loved the BDM. BDM. She had many friends. Friends. She had friends. She danced with the most famous men in Germany. Famous men."

I was intrigued. "Like who, Frieda?"

"Herr Goering. Herr Heydrich. Herr Kaltenbrunner. Even Herr Hitler, himself. Hitler himself. Herr Jäger was most attentive, but she was interested in bigger fish. Bigger fish. We took pictures at events, until they knew about us. They knew. They knew."

"Where were these parties, Frieda?"

"Around," she giggled like a schoolgirl. "All around. Heidelberg, Munich, a lot. Munich."

I imagined Lana, dedicated Nazi from an early age, lovely, remote, and inaccessible to all but the most prestigious. Supporting the very philosophies that killed her before her twentieth birthday. My real mother. How different she must have been from her warmhearted little sister, Vala.

"I might have a photo. Photo. Photo. Let me look."

"Thank you, Frieda."

She got up and went down the hall.

I turned to Oskar and took the carved snake pipe out of my pocket. "You left this at Grandma Arial's all those years ago."

He took it, smiling. "I'd hoped you would call me about it, or that Vala would. I was looking for any papers about Schreiner's at the time. I was still hoping to get the company back, or at least get paid for it."

"I'm going through all Mama's things and I haven't found anything about Schreiner's except one document from 1945. A shipping invoice. I'll make a copy for you if you want, but I don't think it has anything to do with your father's business."

He held the pipe up to the light. "Did you ever see such exquisite work?"

My tastes were simpler, but I held my tongue. Schreiner's was known for all that fancy carving.

"We sold dozens of these pipes. The snake motif was popular in the 1930s. It was my father's original design, but this particular item was carved by one of our artisans. It was early in his career, but he would have surpassed us all if he'd had a chance. See, that's his signature, right there."

Rosa reached for it. "It's so complex. The snake is beautiful, wrapped around—what is that? A tree?"

"The tree of good and evil." Oskar was bursting with pride.

"Genesis," she said.

"Many religions embrace that story. That's why they sold well."

Rosa turned the pipe this way and that. "Where did you say the artisan's signature was?"

Oskar turned the pipe upside down and pointed.

At first she squinted then she held the pipe to her heart, her eyes wide. "Jan Singer?"

Oskar's smile was broad. "Yes. One of his earliest efforts."

"My father?"

"We've had that for years," I said. "If we'd only known…"

"Would you like to have it, Rosa?"

"Of course, I would." She jumped up and kissed Oskar on the cheek, leaving a faint red mark. "All these years, I've had nothing of his. No idea about his life. Just that we were separated when we got to Gurs and no one ever saw him again."

Rosa's joy made me feel like a jerk. I'd dismissed the pipe as ugly and useless, since no one I knew smoked one. If I'd recognized the symbolism, perhaps I would have understood better what it was. We weren't religious. The only time we went to church was for weddings or funerals. Mama would've recognized it, I'm sure. It was at Grandma Arial's for years, but when she made noises about giving it to Mama, Sonny scooped it up and hid it in the shed. He was concerned that something of Oskar's would send Mama into one of her moods.

"Would you like to hear about your father?" Oskar offered.

"Oh, yes. I didn't realize he worked for you." Rosa sank back onto the couch beside me.

"Jan came to us in 1934 or 1935, I think. He was enthusiastic and talented, and he learned quickly. He specialized in carving little pieces that we could sell for a reasonable price—jewelry boxes, pipes, hair clasps, book covers. He was a storyteller. Every job he tackled told a story, like this one. He was an observant Jew and he loved the main synagogue in Mannheim. He studied the Torah with Rabbi Gruenewald. My family and our employees enjoyed listening to Jan talk about one text or another. We'd been assimilated for five generations, so long that I didn't even realize we were Jews. Jan's enthusiasm for his faith made us smile, especially when it all came down on us and we could no longer fool ourselves as to our status. His stories made us feel part of something bigger, you know? We were pushed out of every business, church, and school that we knew and loved, but Jan made us feel better. Not so lost."

"What...do you remember what he looked like? I have no pictures of him or his family. Just stories from my cousin Gretchen."

"I didn't see him but once before my escape after Kristallnacht." Oskar closed his eyes as if it took effort to think back over the years. "Jan was tall. Dark blue eyes. Light brown hair. A close-cropped beard. He had a scar through his left eyebrow after Dachau. He had delicate hands. Watching him carve was like a dance—light cuts, deep gouges, long slices. I remember he created something for your mother right before their wedding. A jewelry box or something. He told me about Annaliese while he carved his interpretation of the story of Ruth on the lid. He said she was his beshert, that they were destined to be together forever."

I wondered if Oskar was telling Rosa what he thought she wanted to hear. It sounded like bull, as Mr. McKensey would say. I glanced at her. She was eating it up. My heart melted. True or not, it gave her some image of her father. Who was I to challenge Oskar Schreiner's memory of Jan Singer? He had already given me his memories of my mother.

"Here, here, here." Frieda called as she came up the hallway toward us. "Here is the picture. One picture. That is all. That is all."

I stood up.

"See, EJ? There's Lana Hess. Dancing with someone very handsome and tall. Handsome and tall." She held up a photograph of a crowd of people. At first, that's all I could see, a band and mass of people dancing on a wooden platform built in the middle of a town. Was that Mannheim? I turned the picture sideways. Too hard to tell. However, there was a familiar stamp on the back of the print. Vogel Fotografie Studio. I sucked in air faster than I intended.

"See there's Lana. Lana Hess. Lana Hess." Frieda tapped the picture.

A taller more beautiful version of my mother was dancing with a man in an SS uniform. He too was tall, like me, with a high-bridged nose like mine, and blond hair. It was a black and white picture, but the man's eyes were light like mine, too."

"Who is that?" I pointed. He reminded me of some of the pictures in Mama's FotoAlbum.

"Herr Heydrich, of course. He was an important man. Important."

"What was his first name?"

Oskar narrowed his eyes. "Reinhard."

I flashed on the letter Mick and I found in Mama's suitcase so long ago. The letter to Lana from her lover promising her oranges. The letter signed with a single initial, R. "He died, didn't he?"

"Assassinated in 1942," Oskar said.

I couldn't let it go. "What do you know about him?"

"He was a bastard."

"Why?"

"He was responsible for Kristallnacht and the Final Solution."

I was shocked into silence. Surely he couldn't be...no, I couldn't accept that. My father had to be a different high-ranking SS officer. I thought of the stranger who had frightened Mama so much the day John Sarris/Gerhardt Schultz came visiting. The day I was home with the measles. "He reminds me of someone I saw in 1953."

"Heydrich was dead then, EJ."

"But maybe…"

Rosa held the pipe in her lap, embracing Oskar's story about Jan Singer. I was happy that she was happy, but I was also jealous. My life as EJ Logan started the moment Mama and Mick and I set foot in the United States. Despite dreams and vague memories of Germany and Poland, I was an American with no past and no future beyond America. No noble ancestors. Just Mama and Mick and me. And Sonny. Thank God for Sonny and Grandma Arial. I took a deep breath. Maybe I wasn't so jealous after all.

"Thank you, Frieda. I handed the picture back to her."

"No. No. Keep it. Keep it." She handed it back to me. "That's your mama there. Your mama."

I accepted the old photograph. It was a high quality print that had faded little over the years. "Vala Logan was the mother I knew," I said to Frieda. "The one who rescued me and raised me. This is her sister."

Frieda nodded. "Yes, yes, yes."

"But thank you, anyway. I'll cherish this." I could feel Rosa's amusement behind me. I never used the word *cherish*. It was just a word to please Frieda.

I turned to Oskar. "I have a question for you on another matter."

"Of course. What do you want to know?"

I took the Polaroid of Mama's bed out of my pocket. "Do you recognize this?"

He stared at the picture for a moment. "It's familiar in style maybe, but we never made anything like this at Schreiner's."

"Oh? I thought…"

"You look surprised. Why do you ask?"

"This was my mother's bed. I was sure Sonny said it was shipped from Schreiner's warehouse."

"Who knows how the Hesses used the facility after they took it? They were very tight with the Reich, EJ. Herr Hess would do anything to get government business and the good will of the leaders. I have to assume he wanted our business for a reason that had nothing to do with artistry. But to store odd furniture like this? There must be a story, but I don't know what it is." He shook his head as he handed back the Polaroid."

"It's so ugly," I said. "I can't imagine what she saw in it."

"The one thing I learned long ago is that everyone sees art differently. Perhaps Vala's devotion to this piece is personal."

"Makes as much sense as anything else I've considered." I put the picture back in my pocket.

"I wish I could help but I have no idea," he said.

"I have one last thing to ask, Oskar." I pulled the small box from another pocket. "Mama left this for me. I can't figure out how to open it or what it is."

"Oh, my. I haven't seen one of these since 1937." Clearly, the box held more charm for him than Mama's bed. He stretched out his hand and I placed it in his palm. "This is a custom-designed music box. People bought them when babies were born, or a groom had one made for his bride. It plays a tune requested by the purchaser." He twisted the lid several times like it was a jar of pickles. When he let go, the top slowly turned the opposite way and a woman's voice began singing in German, "Leben ohne Liebe kannst du nicht." He closed his eyes and rocked his head from side to side dreamily.

Frieda clasped both hands across her bosom. "Isn't she beautiful?"

Rosa and I looked at each other.

"Who?" I said finally.

"That's Marlene Dietrich."

"You can't live without love…" I translated her words awkward-ly for Rosa.

"It is…special." Rosa sounded tentative. We were used to the Everly Brothers and Roy Orbison. Marlene seemed quaint, lost in someone else's time and place. "You think it was a gift to Vala?"

"Someone loved her dearly. Dearly. Dear Vala."

I smiled at Frieda. "It sure sounds like it." The music box started the song over again. I liked it better the second time around.

"Maybe not Vala." Oskar held up the box so that we could see the sides of it. "Children especially loved these boxes because we filled them with surprises. You could go years, your whole life, be-fore you found them all."

"What kind of surprises?"

"Look at the way the animals are arranged around the sides of the box." He pointed.

It looked just like a bunch of critters running around the four sides under the protecting branches of a tree on the top. A bear or a pig, hard to tell. Maybe a wolf? A bird. And a stag. I shook my head. "Just animals."

Rosa peered over my shoulder. "Oh, look at that!"

"What?"

"See, four letters. Each animal is a letter."

Oskar smiled, so I knew Rosa was on to something.

"Start here, EJ." She pointed at the bird. It was tall and skinny with big feet. The animals are positioned to look like letters. "See? It's an L. And the wolf is an A."

"Oh yeah." I slowly turned the box. "L - A - N - A."

"It was made for Lana." Rosa sounded excited.

"Do you remember it?" I asked Oskar.

"It was a long time ago. I don't remember it specifically, but we were the only woodworkers in the region doing such pieces." Oskar buffed the stained wood with his shirtsleeve. "There were many men in love with women named Lana at the time, I'm sure."

"I still don't get it. This is a music box made especially for Lana?"

Rosa tapped me on the shoulder. "Now, it's something special to you from Vala."

"Why?"

"Perhaps she wanted you to have it in case she died before you got home?"

"She would have had to climb up into the tree house. That's pretty vigorous for someone who thinks death is imminent."

"Maybe it's not as planned as all of that. All of that," Frieda said. "Maybe Vala found it. Found it. Found it."

"That sounds more like it," I said. "I can buy that she found it and decided I might like to have it, but why not just give it to me when I came to visit?" We sat thinking about that question for a minute. When no one had an idea, I changed the subject. "So how does it work?"

Oskar pressed the nose of the bear and a door on the opposite side of the box popped open. He stuck his finger inside. "Doesn't look like this one has anything here." He turned the box sideways, and pressed another hidden button on the squirrel. "Nothing in there. A couple more surprises, maybe." He turned it again and pressed on the wolf. A door sprang open and Oskar fished a small piece of paper out of it and handed it to me.

It was folded several times into tinier and tinier triangles so that it fit into the small compartment. It took several seconds to unfurl it so that I could read it. It was probably the third or fourth carbon copy. A stamp of a large bird holding a medallion with the Swastika covered part of the typing on the bottom left of the page. The typewritten letters were faint, but the heading was still bold: Geburtsurkunde.

"Well?" Rosa was eager.

I felt my face flush as I read my own birth certificate. The real one.

"Are you okay, EJ?"

I folded it and stuffed it into my pocket. "I'm fine."

"Was that a message from your mother?"

"Yes."

"Which one?"

I glared at her. "We need to hurry. Mick will be waiting for us."

Rosa nodded. "Thank you, Frieda. It was wonderful to meet you."

"Was nice to meet little Vala's son. Little Vala." Frieda stretched out her hand. She was such a lovely person, even after all the things she'd been through.

"Thank you for the Kaffeeklatsch." I squeezed her hand. "I hope to meet you again someday."

"Bye, EJ. EJ. EJ."

"Thank you, Oskar," Rosa said. "I will always be grateful."

"I assume that all carvings on bigger pieces work the same way," I asked as I shook Oskar's hand.

He laughed. "Only so many tricks up our sleeves. Push, slide, twist. One will always work."

"Thank you, Oskar. I wish I had better news to give you about Magda and Heidi. I think they probably died as soon as they got to Auschwitz. I know I was with them up until then because I remember…I think I remember, anyway…being on a train with them. I was too little to remember the trip from Ludwigshafen to Gurs, so it must be either from Gurs to Drancy or from Drancy to Auschwitz. Mama found me in Krakow so they must have separated us somewhere in Poland. I've always had these dreams and vague memories. I just never knew that the woman and the little girl were connected to you."

Oskar bowed his head for a moment. "I understand. You were a baby."

"Yes."

He turned to Rosa. "If your aunt finds out any more information, please call me. I am the only Oskar Schreiner in North Royalton, Ohio."

Rosa's smile was sad. "I promise."

I grunted and guided her out the door. Rosa found it a lot easier to tolerate Oskar. I found his barely concealed anger disturbing. He certainly had a right to hate me. It was my family who'd caused most of his sorrows. It disarmed me that he didn't blame me and opened me up to waves of shame. And there was literally nothing I could do about it.

35

Vala's Bed
November 6, 1966

"I SEE." MICK laid down his fork and stared at his linguine.

"I'm sure that seeing a woman fall out of a window and bash her brains out on the sidewalk right in front of you was horrible for a nine-year-old kid," I said. "From everything I've read or heard, Kristallnacht was chaotic. The actions in Mannheim were as bad as they got. People were physically attacked, windows were broken, and the rioters even burned the main synagogue."

Rosa put her fork down too. "Your mother was traumatized, Mick. That she had nightmares about it for the rest of her life tells us that."

Mick's eyes were red, but somehow he kept his tears in check. "One time she was taking a nap. I was six or seven, I think, and I was building something with my Lincoln Logs in the hallway outside her room. She cried out in her sleep, not a scream like when you're startled or scared, but a high keening sound, like a howl. It broke my heart. Still does when I think about it. No one else was home so I ran to her and tried to wake her up. I crawled into bed with her and said, 'Mama?' She startled like she was surprised to see me. After she was really awake, she lay back against the pillow, and I put my head on her shoulder. I think I said something like, 'It's okay, Mama. I'll chase the monster away.' She stroked my hair and said—and I'll never forget this—she said, 'But Milo, what if I am the monster?'"

What a thought. Maybe with my heritage I was a monster too, but wouldn't I know it somewhere inside? Wasn't *good* a standard I could cling to when confronted with tough decisions? Thou shalt not kill—simple and straightforward, the whitest of white and the blackest of black. Unless I was defending myself or my family from attackers. Unless it came to executing murderers. I closed my eyes. Unless it came to flying over big cities and dropping atomic bombs. What about killing for water? Land? Women? What about exterminating hundreds, thousands, millions of people because they might change the course of your national destiny? What about gassing children so that they wouldn't grow up to be an enemy? What about that? My head ached.

"Are you okay, EJ?"

I swallowed. "It's a lot to think about."

"Come on, sweetheart," Rosa said. "Your mother wasn't a bad person. She wasn't anything like Dolph Jäger or Mengele or Hitler. She was a kid who didn't realize what would happen when she pointed Frieda out to the Nazis. She didn't cause Frieda to be hurt on purpose."

I looked up into her eyes. "But Frieda was hurt all the same. Grievously."

Rosa sighed and started to answer. Then she seemed to think better of it and sat quietly, hands in her lap.

Mick picked up his fork again. "So what about the box?"

"A music box with Lana's name on it," Rosa said.

"Music?" Mick brightened. "What kind of music?"

"Marlene Dietrich. Some kind of love song."

I twirled spaghetti around my fork but couldn't bring myself to eat it. Mick and Rosa's attempts to liven up the conversation actually gave me time to think, and their voices blended into the background chatter of the restaurant.

The name on the document in the music box was a weight on my heart that I could never shirk. It was my own fault. Everyone warned me, but I just couldn't let it go until I knew. And now that I did, I realized what a fool I'd been. I stared at my spaghetti and swallowed back the bile. I wished…what did I wish? That the man who'd fathered me was a fishmonger, a simple fellow with simple life and simple beliefs? That he'd never met Herr Hitler or joined the National Socialist Party? That he'd been killed before he unleashed misery on so many millions? I shuddered.

Were the secrets of Mama's bed going to be the same? It had sat in our house from the day we moved in. The way Sonny was talking, it would be there ten years from now—maybe even twenty or thirty. Like the letters in Mama's suitcase, I didn't have to hurry to explore what awful secrets might be hidden inside. I could parse them out over a lifetime.

"EJ!"

"What?"

"We lost you there for a minute."

"Oh. I was thinking."

Rosa got up and collected her purse. "I'm going to powder my nose. When I get back, let's get this over with."

"Get what over with?" I sipped my wine.

She looked at Mick. "You tell him." She headed for the back of the restaurant.

"You're not yourself, EJ," Mick started.

"Ha! I'll drink to that." I drank the whole glass of wine and picked up Rosa's half-empty one.

"I'm on your side. You know that?"

I nodded and polished off Rosa's wine.

"All this stuff we've been learning is awful. No question. That one letter to Oma from the man she hired to find Opa tears me up. And I still think about the one from Lana when she was at camp raving about her dream of one day being awarded Hitler's Mother's Cross. Knowing how it all turned out confuses me. Even though Lana is dead and we'll never know her or have any clue who she would've been as a grown woman, you're here because of her choices. And EJ, I love you and rely on you. Whatever else Lana did, if you are the result, I celebrate her life because I have a brother like you. It's the same with Mama. Whatever else she did, she gave us both life and a life."

Moved, I took a deep breath.

"I know you're sad and depressed about all of it. I am, too. What they felt and did destroyed so many lives, not to mention their own. But we don't have to let it destroy *us*."

I searched for words. "Mama's bed was empty—no lovers, no babies, no future. She was cut off from her family, her country."

"Maybe that was the best thing ever. Sad for Mama, for sure, but she found a new family and a new country with and for us. All that ugliness has to end now, with us. Remember Mississippi? We did something good there, didn't we?"

"We tried." I had my doubts about how much we'd accomplished. I'd watched people beat other people with crowbars for riding a bus through their town. And then those same folks stowed their crowbars in the trunks of their cars and went to church on Sunday with the same moral certainty that Opa had when he stole Schreiner's business. What if, in the long run, I was just as blind? What if my sense of right and wrong was skewed, too?

Mick poured the last of the wine into my glass. "We have to pull together now. I can't have you tearing yourself apart like this. You've got medical school. You've got a charming rascal of a brother who needs you to keep him in line." He wiggled his eyebrows and turned his head to show his handsome profile.

I laughed in spite of myself.

"You've got Rosa, too."

"She's a wonderful woman, Mick, but I don't know how long she'll be able to look at me and not think, 'How much evil did that nut case inherit?'"

"You can't—"

"Are you ready?" Rosa had returned to the table.

My anxieties muted by Merlot, I reached out to her. "Ready for what?"

Mick winked at her. "You didn't take as long as usual."

"I took as long as I needed," Rosa joked back.

"I didn't get to the proposal yet."

I looked from one of them to the other. "What proposal?"

"None of us are hungry," Mick said. "And you're making yourself sick with grief. Not just for Mama, but for things that happened when you were a baby, things you couldn't understand or stop even if you did."

"You don't—"

Rosa picked up her purse. "Will you just be quiet and listen?"

"Let's get this over with fast," Mick said, "like pulling off a Band-Aid. We pack up our delicious and very expensive meals and take them with us. We can take my much bigger and warmer car down to Cold Creek tonight."

"Don't make fun of my vehicle." The banter lifted the momentary cloud from my heart and I embraced lightness, however temporary.

"We'll take Mama's bed apart and see if there's anything in there. Tonight. If there is, we'll deal with whatever it is. If not, we put it all back together and leave it there. Forever. No more worrying about what might be there. We'll know. One way or another."

"What if I can't do that? Leave it there?"

Rosa squeezed my hand. "EJ, darling, don't try so hard. What you do won't make or break the world. It's for your own sake."

Don't try so hard. The last thing Mr. McKensey said to me. *Don't try so hard, son.* I was never sure if he meant don't try too hard to keep him alive or if he meant there were some things I just couldn't change. Was this one of Annie's signs? Maybe Rosa was right. Maybe all my fretting was getting me nothing but more seizures. "I don't know what will be there. I can't promise not to be upset."

"We'll deal with whatever is there. I promise," Mick said.

"Just get it over with?"

Rosa kissed my cheek. "Just get it over with."

* * *

"Might as well," Sonny said as he put our dinners in the refrigerator. "You want to go through the boxes and suitcase too?"

"I hadn't thought of that, but why not? Mick and Rosa want to get it over with." My heart beat faster. "So do I."

"You boys start with the bed. Rosa and I will go through the suitcase."

"I'll get the tool box out of the shed, EJ. Why don't you see what you can find with the push, twist, and slide technique Schreiner told you about?" Mick headed out the back door.

Sonny retrieved the old suitcase and popped it open. I hadn't gone through it since Mama was in Mayview. We'd only given the letters and documents a cursory look then. They were damp at the time, and we spent more time drying them out and repacking them than actually reading them. I was the only one who could read German and it was hard for me anymore. So we'd only digested the simplest ones, the typed documents and the easier to read handwritten notes. The longer pieces and the ones with smears and ornate handwriting, we had put aside. Then life took over and we never got back to them. There were even a few unread pieces still stored in the trunk in the tree house.

I went to the door of Mama's room.

"How do you want to tackle this mess?" Sonny asked Rosa.

"Let's sort by letters and other documents first, and then by date."

I let their voices fade as I focused on the old bed. What purpose was this going to serve? Would it make us love Mama any more or any less? Maybe knowing how she got the old monstrosity would add to our growing understanding of her life and Lana's. Surely I knew the worst already.

"Here we go." Mick hustled past me with the toolbox. "What do you want to do first?"

"Let's start with the engraving on the headboard," I said. "Oskar said it wasn't one of their pieces, but maybe it was just too ugly and he didn't want to claim it."

Mick pointed to an arc of shiny oval or square ornaments creating a mosaic that stood out against the dark wood. Some were pure white, some yellow, and some had flecks of gold paint on them. "I've never figured out what these bumps and ridges could possibly be. I don't see how they enhance the image the artist was trying to create."

"It looks like a gathering of witches around a fire." I touched the flames. "I think this part is just a flat piece of hammered metal pounded into the wood."

"I always liked the wolves hiding in the forest," Mick said. "See, their eyes shine like gold."

Mama had so many images of wolves around her. Her dream about a wolf coming to get her, and supposedly the name of Lana's baby, although my birth certificate, newly retrieved from the music box listed my name as Emo Johann Hess plus another name, my real family name. I closed my eyes and pushed it out of my mind. "Maybe the wolf had special meaning for Mama?"

Mick scratched his head. "Danger, maybe?"

"Wolves live in packs, hunt in packs."

"But in Mama's dream it was one wolf, not a pack."

Mick had a point. I ran my fingers over the bas relief figures. There was only one place where one might press or slide the wood. I pushed against it. Nothing.

"Maybe Mama's dream has nothing to do with the bed," Mick said. "Maybe we're making things up just because we want it to mean something."

"Then let's just take it apart and see."

Mick stood up on the bed frame and examined the canopy. "Where to start? Here?"

"If we get rid of that canopy frame, we'll have more room to work." I examined the joints. "Looks like we have to take the finials off. I've tried that before though, and they wouldn't budge."

"Maybe the wood was swollen." Mick tried to twist the heavy bulbs off the top of the bedposts. "I think they do come off. They're just stuck."

I slipped off my shoes and climbed up onto the bed with Mick. "Let's try together."

Together we twisted the right foot post finial.

"Shouldn't…be…this hard." Mick grunted.

"Keep twisting, I felt something give."

"There it is…"

The big orb slowly turned in our hands. Bits of wood and debris fell out of the inside of the finial as we lifted it off the post. Mick rubbed his thumb and forefinger together. "What the heck is this?"

"What?"

"Dust." He rubbed it between his thumb and forefinger. "Weird. It glitters."

I peered inside the finial. It was hollow but there was nothing inside. A thick layer of oily dust coated the inside surfaces. Disappointed, I examined the thick bedpost itself. "It's hollow, too," I said.

"Anything there?"

"Can't tell. I need a flashlight."

Mick jumped off the bed and rummaged through the toolbox. "Here's a little one. Don't know where Sonny keeps the Eveready now."

"Little one is better anyway. It might fit inside the post." I dangled the flashlight between my thumb and forefinger, focusing the beam into the darkness inside the long hollow tube. "Hard to see but I think there's a package or something down there."

"Can you reach it?"

I stuck my arm down into the hole. "Not even close."

"Maybe a clothes hanger?"

"Let's try it." I withdrew my arm. "What is this?" My sleeve was coated with the same sticky-dry stuff that had been inside the finial. I tried dusting it off but it clung to my clothes.

"Whatever it is, it's disgusting." Mick bent a wire clothes hanger into a long hook.

"It's getting all over the carpet and the furniture."

Mick handed me the wire hook. "I'll get the vacuum."

"No, that would be too loud right now." I inserted the wire into the deep hole inside the bedpost. "I don't think my nerves could stand it."

"We should have started this during the day. There's not really enough light in here to see what I'd be vacuuming anyway."

"What are you guys doing in here?" Rosa held a small sheet of yellowing paper.

"Fishing something out of the bedpost," I grunted as I stuck my arm deeper and deeper into the hole.

"You're gonna get stuck." Rosa reflected my own fear of being in a vulnerable position and having a seizure.

"I hope not." I pulled back slightly and then stopped. "I think I hooked something."

"Here, let me help you." Mick grabbed the wire with both hands and jerked.

Whatever was down there hurtled up the channel and through the top of the bed post. More debris came out with it and a small cloud of dust.

"Oh, for goodness sake!" Rosa coughed into her fist. "What is that?"

I detached what appeared to be a mass of dirty paper hanging from the hook. "Looks like more stuff to go through." I picked off tiny shreds of brown paper that stuck to my fingers.

"My God!" Rosa dropped the sheet of paper she was holding and stood up, looking at her hands. "It's cremains."

I got down off the bed, staring at my own hands. "You mean human remains?"

"Yes. Ashes from a cremation."

"How do you know?"

"I worked in the morgue for almost a year. I know cremains when I see them."

"Mick, call Sheriff Douglas. There are laws."

A moment after Mick left the room, Sonny appeared at the doorway. "Ashes?"

I held up my hands so he could see.

"My God. What did we have in here all these years?"

Rosa got up. "We really shouldn't be breathing this stuff. Let's get some fresh air."

We filed out and I closed Mama's bedroom door behind us.

"I don't know what to think," Sonny said as we went out onto the back porch. "How did she get a bed filled with ashes?"

A cool breeze cleared my lungs and my mind. "And how did the ashes get in it?"

"What did you find besides ashes?" Mick handed us each a towel to wipe our faces and hands.

I realized I was still holding the wad of paper. "This. Looks like whoever made the bed stuffed small bits of paper in here. They're all stuck together."

Sonny poured us each a glass of water, and I realized how thirsty I was. I drank it all down and then accepted Rosa's when she offered it. We sat around the picnic table.

Sonny lit a cigarette with shaking hands. "Do you think the other three bedposts are stuffed with ashes, too?"

I shook my head, too stunned to comprehend the implications of what we'd found. "I don't know."

"How long before Sheriff Douglas gets here?" Mick dipped a dishtowel into his glass and scrubbed his face with it.

"It's not like it's an emergency," Sonny said.

I tried not to show how shocked I was by that statement. There were cremains in Mama's bed! Then I relaxed as I realized that whoever they were, they'd been dead a long time. I looked around at Rosa and Mick. They had understood the situation before I had. Those ashes had to have been in the bed before it left Mannheim in 1948.

"Did Mama know about them?" Mick's face twisted with anguish.

"Of course not," I roared, furious that anyone would think such a thing. "How could she know anyone would put human ashes inside a bed?"

Mick held his head in his hands. "She loved that bed. She always said someone made it especially for her."

I swallowed. "I always thought it was Opa. Her circle of men friends couldn't have been large."

"Maybe it wasn't personal," Rosa said.

"How could it not be personal?"

"Calm down, son. There's no reason to yell at Rosa. Or your brother either."

Sonny was right. I took a breath. "I'm sorry, guys. I seemed to have lost the ability to be polite."

Rosa touched my hand. "It's okay."

It wasn't, but it was the only apology I had in me at that moment.

"While we're waiting, look at this." She handed me the paper she'd been carrying. It's a letter from your grandmother to someone named Margit.

I glanced at the paper. It was the first thing we'd found that was actually in Oma's own hand. "Too dark to make out what it says here," I said.

"Do you want me to help—"

"No! No. I'm sorry, Rosa. I need to do this alone." I went into the kitchen and spread the note out on the counter.

August 19, 1940

My dear Margit,

My note is sad today. Lana's beautiful baby boy has epilepsy, a mild form the doctors say, but still counter to our goals for Lebensborn. They wanted to take him immediately, but Lana has developed a passion for the child that is quite irrational. She says she will never let him go, no matter what any of us say. I'm disappointed in her behavior, I must say. Do we act on our principles or not? To make it worse, Vala adores this baby as well, and treats him like a doll. How did Erich and I raise two such emotional and undisciplined daughters?

They will come for the baby on Thursday next. Our family has been at war with each other since this all began. We have to watch Lana day and night for fear she will run away with the child. Vala can't be trusted to do the right thing, either. We should have listened to the doctor who made the diagnosis and let him take the boy right away. It would have been one bad day, and the girls would have been healing by now.

We are undecided whether to tell the Obergruppenführer about this. I am afraid that this will set our family back, after all the strides we've made with the Reich. Erich and I offered to pay the doctor to say nothing and to alter the records, but he told us we don't have enough money or power to do that. All he could do is delay the filing of the documents for two weeks, to give us time to decide what our legal options are. Once the doctor submits the papers, the boy's father will know, and that will adversely affect us. We are being driven to extreme measures.

Is Wilhelm still looking for work? Perhaps he could help us with our problem. We would pay him six months' wages if he could help us keep the Obergruppenführer from hearing about this flaw in our bloodline. His discretion and yours would be necessary, of course. Please let us know if he is interested before Thursday a week.

I hope that you, Wilhelm, and little Siegfried are doing well.

Your loving sister,

Anna

I recoiled with disgust. Was my grandmother asking her brother-in-law to kill someone? I remembered Mama's newspaper clipping about a dead doctor found in Mannheim in 1940 and shuddered. I'd known about Oma's dedication to the Nazi ideal, but would she really have a man murdered so that my epilepsy wouldn't ruin the family name? If she did, maybe that was the real reason she wouldn't accept us back after the war. My condition ruined things for her.

On the other hand, I was overjoyed that Lana loved and wanted me, epilepsy or not. It was the first time I ever saw any clue that she cared about me. It didn't mean much to the elder Hesses, but it meant everything to me.

"EJ?" Rosa stood outside the kitchen door, peeking through the screen.

"Yeah?"

"You want to talk about it?"

"Not really."

"Sheriff Douglas and Deputy Dixon are here. Doc Riley is on his way."

I refolded the letter and put it in my pocket.

Out on the porch, Sheriff Douglas and Deputy Dixon were solemn.

"EJ." Sheriff Douglas shook my hand first. "I'm sorry to be here like this."

I'd come to like Sheriff Douglas since our interview with Dolph Jäger. More importantly, I trusted him. "I guess the others have told you what we found inside Mama's bed."

He nodded.

Deputy Dixon stood just inside the screen door.

"I'm sorry about this, Jimmy," Sonny said. "I wish you never had to know about it."

"It's part of the job." Deputy Dixon was stoic but I knew that his grandmother had been murdered at Treblinka.

"We found paper scraps in the bedpost," I said to the sheriff. "Looks like notes written in German. They're covered with the stuff too, but I'd like to read them before you take them away."

Sheriff Douglas's gaze went over my head. "Those notes might help us understand what happened, EJ. You know that none of us speak or read German. Would you mind helping us read them after we get them cleaned and sorted?"

I turned to see Deputy Dixon, arms crossed over his chest, nod and smile slightly.

I turned back to the sheriff, "Thank you, sir."

"You need to know. We need to know. Looks like the perfect solution, son."

I relaxed. At least I would know what they said.

36

Inside the Bedpost
November 9, 1966

WE GATHERED AT the police station three days later.

"EJ, you look like crap," Sheriff Douglas told me as I sat down at a long table covered with paper.

"It's been a long haul."

"I can imagine. How come Mick looks like a ray of sunshine?"

"He always looks that way," I grumbled as Mick beamed.

The receptionist set a pot of coffee on a side table. "There's plenty of sugar and cream here. The donuts are fresh from Spencer's. If you need more, just buzz me."

"Thank you, Penny," Sheriff Douglas said. "Have Jimmy Dixon join us as soon as he gets here."

"Yes, sir." Penny's footsteps clicked down the hall.

"Is Rosa coming?"

"I…uh…I haven't told her everything yet."

Sheriff Douglas looked from me to Mick and back to me. "Okay. What about Sonny?"

"He decided to go fishing instead," Mick said.

"Okay then, we're just waiting for Jimmy."

"Guess so."

Mick changed the subject. "How'd you get all that stuff off the paper?"

"Doc Riley and Jimmy worked with little brushes to get them cleaned off so you could read them. And to recover all of the remains for burial."

"Were the other posts filled with that stuff, too?"

"The other bedposts and finials were solid, Mick. Looks like you and your brother picked the only hollow one to open."

I rolled my eyes. "Wonderful."

Someone tapped on the glass window of the door.

"Come on in, Jimmy."

Deputy Dixon carried a bag.

"EJ. Mick." He nodded to each of us. "I brought some gloves for you to use while handling these things."

"Thanks. I appreciate all the work you and Doc Riley did for us the last couple of days."

"First thing," Deputy Dixon said as he laid the folders on the side table and sat down, "these cremains aren't from just one person. There are way too many and they were deposited at different times over the course of weeks or months. Also, the ashes weren't packed into that hole by hand. They floated in from the environment. Meaning that the bedpost was near a crematorium that was discharging ash into the air, also over a period of time."

"Like Auschwitz?"

"Take some breaths, son. Let's not have one of your spells here. We can take it slow."

The sheriff's low and steady tone soothed me, and I forced myself to relax. He was right. No time for epilepsy today. Surveying the table of brown notes, I took the white cotton gloves that Deputy Dixon offered me and slipped them on. "Where should we start?"

Sheriff Douglas pointed to the corner of the table nearest Mick. "They're all dated. We arranged them chronologically starting there."

Mick picked up the first one, holding it gingerly in his gloved hands. "August 3, 1944?"

"That's the earliest one," Sheriff Douglas said.

Mick handed it to me. It was torn and the bottom half was missing. I read it out loud while Sheriff Douglas took notes.

Auschwitz

8.3.1944

> *If you are reading this, you have found the hidden compartment I built into Vala's bed. I suppose that means the war is over and Mannheim has survived somehow, or at least Schreiner's is still standing. I hope you are an American or a Brit. It's not likely you are Jewish for we are being annihilated, and even if the Nazis are defeated, it will be too late for us.*

"This is someone who knew Mama and Oskar Schreiner?" Mick looked like someone had punched him.

Sheriff Douglas scribbled on his notebook without looking up. "Who is Oskar Schreiner?"

"He crashed Teresa and Danny's wedding," I said. "Big guy with a checkered suit?"

"I don't remember them reporting anyone like that."

"I'm not surprised. You know Teresa. She'd welcome the devil himself and offer him a drink."

Sheriff Douglas chuckled. "So what did this Oskar Schreiner want from Teresa?"

"Nothing. He wanted to talk to Mama." I explained about Schreiner's and Frieda and Magda and how they were related to my story.

"And when you showed Mr. Schreiner the Polaroid of the bed, he was sure it wasn't made at Schreiner's?" the sheriff asked.

"Nothing his family created anyway."

Sheriff Douglas nodded and pointed to the next scrap of paper, this one smaller than the first.

8.5.1944

I am a slave now, a Sonderkommando, but I was a healthy young husband only four years ago. My wife was the daughter of a Mannheim jeweler. I had a job and a family. We were newlyweds when the Nazis forced my employer out of business. That was 1938. I was twenty-two.

I looked up. "What do you think?"

"Poor guy." Mick took a sip of his coffee. "I wouldn't want to live like that."

I smoothed the note out and laid it back on the table. "But who is he, Mick? Why would he write letters that no one would get to read for decades…if ever?"

8.13.1944

Train after train. The Hungarians are overwhelming us. Almost six thousand yesterday alone. Surely they are almost gone by now. They've been coming for weeks. We lie to them, lure them to their deaths, and dispose of their remains.

Mick and I looked at each other, stricken.

8.25.1944

> *Planes flew over today. I prayed they would put us out of our misery, but they circled and left.*

"What was that about?"

Sheriff Douglas shrugged. "Dunno, EJ. Reconnaissance, maybe?"

The next note was written with charcoal on a thin piece of wood.

9.6.44

> *I was working in my father-in-law's store when the rioting began. They beat my brother-in-law nearly to death. They broke my eye socket. They burned the synagogue and stamped on the Torah. I couldn't stop them. I coul...*

"That's it for this one," I said. "He must have been interrupted."

"It's a journal!"

I stared at the notes lined up in front of me. Mick was right. This poor soul was just trying to record the last few months of his life.

"How did he do it?" Mick took the last piece of paper from me and examined it closely.

"Hard to tell. They are all different, bigger or smaller, different materials, some ripped from bigger pieces, some neatly folded."

"I bet he stole paper one sheet at a time," Deputy Dixon said. "He lived in a place where paper was so dear he could get his head bashed in trying to get enough to write his biography."

"So he stole so little that no one missed it?"

"That's about the size of it." The sheriff pointed to the tiny sheets. "Not one of them is any bigger than a post card, and most are a lot smaller. He probably tore one sheet into many smaller ones."

Mick handed me the next one. "This one's a scrap and there are big swaths too faded to read."

9.7.44

> *Once th...we returned to Mannheim...Dachau... determi...fight back.*

I looked up. "He wanted to fight back? Against the Reich?"

"More likely just an expression of frustration," Sheriff Douglas said. "I doubt there was very much these folks could do to resist."

9.10.44

Our neighbors called us vermin. My beautiful wife? My mother? Vermin? First Kristallnacht, then Dachau. When I returned to Mannheim after that, I knew what was coming.

9.14.44

The Gypsy children. Eight hundred of them. Even little Bevol, a small boy I shared bread with from time to time, went up the chimneys this afternoon.

9.18.44

I'm hurrying. There's a train from Lodz today. I have little time alone. When I can't get back to the workshop, I roll these notes tight and hide them between my toes. I have survived by making myself useful. They will kill me eventually—or I will die of disease.

9.19.44

I saw guards escorting people to the gas chambers. A woman with a screaming infant stopped me. "This baby is hungry. They told me there would be milk."

They were less than fifty feet from death. I shuffled around them. She grabbed my sleeve. "Have mercy, stranger. We need to care for this little one. Her mother died in the rail car."

Could I rescue one child? Where could I hide her? Before I could decide, a guard forced the woman back into line. I walked a few more steps and looked back. The woman with the tiny baby in her arms was descending the stairway to the gas showers.

Midnight.

I can't stop thinking about the baby who died yesterday. She reminded me of my daughter. Most of the time, I try not to think of my family but my most desperate wish is that some part of me will live on...

9.21.44

Officers come to me with projects. Visiting big shots too. Materials are no problem. They are body robbers and there are lots of bodies. They bring me the Reich's loot. I work with wood, gold, silver, tin, and gems. I've built carved boxes, bas-relief pictures, chests, rocking chairs, and beds.

9.22.44

They separated us in Vichy-France. I remember my daughter's screams as they marched me away. And my wife's eyes. I have to stop thinking about them or I'll go mad, and I have to stay alive until I finish the bed.

9.23.44

Some of the fools who run this place have me make things for their sweethearts. This bed is different though. It's my story, and since the Standartenführer wants it for Vala, I know it will go to Mannheim and one day, she will fetch it from Schreiner's. She is the most willful girl I ever met. I'm counting on that.

9.24.44

An emaciated corpse I slung over my shoulder today was an old acquaintance. Herr Krause was a bully who sold beer to soldiers and local factory workers. I last saw him in 1938. He threw me out of his establishment for being a Jew. When I laid him on the dead cart with the others, I saw that his member was circumcised. It didn't matter who he thought he was. What they thought he was got him killed.

9.26.44

My fellow Sonderkommandos and I can't last much longer. When we are too sick to work, they will kill us, too. My extra efforts in the workshop between shipments will mean nothing.

9.27.44

The teeth I used to decorate the headboard of Vala's bed came from Canada. At first, I pretended they were from some forest varmint. When I could no longer ignore reality, the sheer number of them had me retching behind the sauna. Finally, I saw them as shiny bits of those who were slowly rising up the chimneys. For the longest time, I kept them in my pocket and touched them like one might touch lucky coins. Then to enhance my carving, I polished them and arranged them in an arc, imagining how they would gleam in real sunshine, not this stinking ashen version of daylight. I prayed over each tooth, wondering about its owner—a random soul in a sea of souls.

9.28.44

They brought me a golden necklace today. I laid it on the headboard and stared at it, trying to remember why I once thought that metal was so beautiful. All that's left of me is hatred. I want to join my wife and daughter and all the others drifting on the wind above Poland. Maybe there is peace there.

9.29.44

I cut myself as I carved the wolf on the headboard. My blood dripped onto the wood. On impulse, I rubbed it into the grain so that I too can live on in some far away room where children will be conceived and grow to adulthood free from this unending sorrow.

9.30.44

The headboard is finished.

10.02.44

If you find these notes in Vala's bed, you know about my last testimony, the carved wolf couple and their pups on the headboard. I thought it was appropriate for a child destroyed by her own parents. For a people murdered by their own countrymen.

10.04.44

There is talk of a revolt when they decide to kill us. I can think of nothing more satisfying than to see the crematory I've been feeding these last months utterly destroyed. I will be a part of it.

10.06.44

Tomorrow.

10.7.44

My name is Jan Singer. My wife is Annaliese and my daughter is Rosa. My parents killed themselves rather than leave their home in Mannheim in October 1940. Their names were Jacob and Jutta Singer. Annaliese's parents were Albert and Ilsa Weiss. Her brother was Hans. I think he must be dead, too. Her grandmother Helga was deported with us but died that first winter in Gurs. If you find this note, tell the world that I was a Sonderkommando in crematory IV. Tell them I died fighting.

I leaned back, my mouth open. I couldn't inhale. I tried but no air would enter my lungs.

"I know, I know." Mick put his arms around me. "I know."

"How...How..." The words wouldn't come out.

Deputy Dixon poured me a glass of water. Thinking he wanted me to take a sip, I shook my head.

I tried to get up, but the sheriff pushed me back down into my chair and Deputy Dixon dipped his fingers into the water and splashed cold droplets into my face. I gasped in a lung full of air, before speaking. "Rosa."

"I know," Mick repeated. Then he turned to Sheriff Douglas and Deputy Dixon to explain. "Jan Singer is Rosa's father."

"How do I tell her this? How do I face her?"

Deputy Dixon's face was white. I realized that he was thinking about his grandmother.

"Do you hate me, Deputy?"

He shook his head.

"You should."

"You didn't kill anyone, EJ."

I bowed my head, too ashamed to face him.

The sheriff struggled to keep us on track. "Did you have any memory or idea of this, EJ?"

I shook my head. Who would suspect that some dying Jew made a bed for my mother and decorated it with the remains of those who fell victim to Hitler's lunacy?

"We can ask Gerhardt about the details, then." The sheriff wrote something in his notebook.

"Is he still around?" Mick reached across the table to pat my hand. Last I heard, he wasn't working for the Jollys anymore.

"We'll find him."

"Mama's babysitter," I said under my breath.

Sheriff Douglass cupped his ear with his hand. "What?"

"I think maybe Mama found out where I was and ran away to find me. And Opa sent Gerhardt to find her and bring her home. He and Oma didn't give two hoots if I was gassed and burned."

Mick laid the last note back on the table in its proper place. "So Opa was supposed to meet Mama and Gerhardt?"

I sighed. "In my dream, it's Opa. But what if it was someone who had a stake in my survival?"

"Your real father, if he wasn't dead."

"That's just it, Mick. I don't think he is dead."

All three of them looked at me with surprise.

I'd left out a lot of my suspicions when I briefed the sheriff and Deputy Dixon. "What if my father, the Obergruppenführer, was the one who rescued me from the fires of Auschwitz? What if he paid any number of women to take care of me, and then eliminated them one by one so that my real identity wouldn't ever be known?"

Sheriff Douglas squirmed in his seat. "Whoa, boy. Don't you think that's a bit far-fetched?"

"I don't know, sir. Maybe we've all been counting on a rational answer to all of this. Maybe it's not rational."

"Maybe the Obergruppenführer did love Lana." Mick caught on to my way of thinking faster than the other two. "Maybe when Oma and Opa found out about your epilepsy and decided to let the doctor euthanize you, Lana asked the Obergruppenführer for help to save their baby. All he'd have to do is put Magda Langer's name on the deportation order along with her daughter Heidi and you."

"Would a man like the Obergruppenführer, who organized Hitler's system for murdering millions, rescue a child simply because the baby's mother begged him? It doesn't seem likely." Sheriff

Douglas had dealt with the likes of Dolph Jäger. I guess that taught him to be expect the worst.

"I could understand a man going to great lengths to rescue his own son, EJ," Deputy Dixon said. "Even in a world like the Nazis created, parents loved their children. No matter who you are or what you believe, when the chips are down, your baby matters more than anyone else in the world."

I wanted to say, "Tell that to Lana and Vala Hess." I wanted to say it, but I didn't. Deputy Dixon, a family man without a family, was trying to comfort me.

Even if the Obergruppenführer ived through the war, he would have been tried and executed," the sheriff said. "Unless of course, as you say, he wasn't. I grant you that what you found in that bed is nightmarish. But don't go looking for people that don't exist, son."

I knew Sheriff Douglas was right. Fantasizing that a dead bad guy was really a living good guy who somehow found a way to protect me was foolish. The stuff of comic books and movies. Whether it was my father or my grandfather who shot Jäger that night as I huddled behind the bush was a mystery I'd never figure out. The only people who knew for sure were dead.

I stood up and stripped off the white cotton gloves. "I won't, sir."

"What are you going to do about the bed?" Deputy Dixon sounded as confused as I was.

"What are you and the sheriff going to do with it?"

"Recover the rest of the remains and bury them."

"And then?"

"Return the bed to you."

"I don't know what to do with it, really. It makes me sick now."

"You might not want it now, EJ, but I do," Mick said. "It's something we have to bear together. And however she got it, whatever was hidden in it, it was our mother's."

I nodded. "What's going to happen to the notes?"

Sheriff Douglas looked up from his notebook. "Don't you want them?"

* * *

Rosa's Oldsmobile was in the driveway when Mick and I returned to the house.

We sat in Mick's car for a moment.

"What are you going to do?"

"Give them to her."

"And then?"

"Help her read them if she wants."

"And…"

"Hold her if she wants me to, but she probably won't."

"EJ?"

"And I'll apologize, but we'll both know it won't do any good."

"I'm sorry."

I hugged him. "I admire you, Mick."

"Why?"

"Because you're sunshine, as the sheriff says."

He laughed. "And you're only dark corners? Come on, EJ. Rosa will survive this."

I squared my shoulders. "But what she and I have together won't."

"Don't you love her?"

"With all my heart."

Part Six

Acceptance

Cold Creek, Ohio

1970

McKensey Park

June 5, 1970

UNCLE GRANT DECIDED at the last minute not to drive down to Cold Creek. He said it was because the Logan Foods supermarket in Bay Village was having a problem with a delivery bill. I laughed to myself as I headed south from Cedar Falls. What kind of fool did he take me for? I shopped in that store regularly, and it was a ship-shape property run by an old hand. No way did the manager need the owner of the chain to solve an invoicing problem. Uncle Grant just wasn't ready to tell me about a new development in his life. However, I—and everyone in Ohio for that matter—knew he'd been courting a widow from Rocky River. His "secret" was big news in Cold Creek. Zona saw to that.

As I cruised down Main Street, I beeped and waved at people I knew. Pam Kline was loading grass seed into her old Ford pickup at Jones's Gardens. The Vilanis were at the Esso Station on Spencer Avenue. Deputy Dixon sat in his patrol car outside Zona's Beauty Magic. The little shop was full of women getting gussied up for the evening's concert in the park.

Zona opened her business a year after Mama died, saying she needed something to do. I guess she got pretty lonely. She and Mama had always had something in the works. I chuckled, remembering the winter they'd made an ice skating rink in our backyard. After downing two bottles of wine, they stamped down the snow to make a circle, sprayed it with the hose, and then when it firmed up, piled on more snow and more water. Sonny and Jimmy stood on the sidelines, laughing and taking pictures. By morning, although the ice was a little bumpy, half a dozen kids had strapped blades to their shoes and were twirling, giggling, and falling. They were having so much fun that Mama put on her skates and showed them how to do a spin.

Mama had been gone long enough now that the thought of her made me feel good. I was smiling when I turned onto Cold Creek Drive at St. Mike's. I'd planned on visiting the tree house first, but Grandma Arial was coming out of the newsstand as I pulled up. I flashed my lights and beeped my horn.

"Doctor EJ Logan, you about scared me to death. You didn't tell me you bought a new car."

I rolled down the window. "Would a pretty lady like you want to go for a spin? I hear the rhododendrons are in bloom over in McKensey Park."

"A ride in my grandson's fancy new car or walk four miles... hmm, it's a tough choice."

I got out and opened the passenger door for her. She gave me a peck on the cheek as she got in. I got back into the car and put it in gear. "You look nice. Is everything ready?"

"Almost. The musicians arrived and are setting up. Who knew I would get to meet so many famous people right here in Cold Creek?"

"I never doubted Mick would be famous. He was composing music in Myrtle's parlor when he was seven." I drove out Cold Creek Drive and turned left onto McKensey Park Road. "Of course, I didn't know he'd be so rich, too."

Grandma Arial radiated happiness. "Classical, rock and roll, jazz. That boy has written for everyone from Frank Sinatra to Julie Sullivan. I nearly died when I heard that long-haired folk singer playing one of Mick's songs. I'm so proud of him."

I was, too. How many guys could claim a star like Mick Logan as their baby brother? I slowed as we approached the large gazebo in the park where Mick's orchestra would give their concert.

The parking lot was already filling up. I pulled in as close as possible and helped Grandma Arial out of the car. "Mick told me he had seats reserved for us." I took her hand and headed toward the front row.

A man turned and waved at us.

"Look, EJ. Sonny's already here."

"So he is." I waved back and Sonny got up to meet us.

"I was getting scared you weren't going to make it in time." He gave me a hug.

"I wouldn't miss this for the world. What's the big secret? Does anyone know?"

"No details, but this is the first public performance of Mick's new symphony."

"It must be special, for him to launch it in Cold Creek. I'm sure there are more lucrative venues," I said as I guided Grandma Arial into her seat. She was beginning to show her age, and I worried about her getting knocked down in a crowd as big as this one promised to be.

The front two rows were reserved for Mick's special guests. We never knew who would show up to see and be seen with Mick. Famous entertainers? Scientists he worked with at NASA?

"Hello, handsome." Someone tapped me on the back and I turned to see a beautiful woman wearing a wreath of daisies to contain her long caramel-colored hair.

"Annie? Annie Jones?"

"The very same. Maybe a little worse for wear, but I'm here. I couldn't believe it when I got the invitation from Mick. I assume that was your doing?"

I opened and closed my mouth before deciding that a lie was my best course of action. "I wasn't convinced he could find you, but I'm thrilled you made it." I glanced at Sonny, who tried to hide his amusement. "Where did they seat you?"

She stood on tiptoe and whispered in my ear. "Right behind you."

I took her hand and squeezed it. "Let's catch up after this is over."

She wrapped a big glittering shawl around herself as if she was cold and found her seat. I turned back to Sonny and Grandma Arial.

We'd just sat down when someone else nudged me from behind. "EJ!"

"Skippy, Elizabeth! How are you?"

"Excited to be here. I've never been to a big-name concert before. Never had front row tickets to anything."

Sonny stood up, too. "We've been buds all our lives, Skip. EJ and the Mickster don't remember life without you."

"Can't wait for the show to start. Thank you for including us."

"Don't thank me," said Sonny. "This whole shindig is Mick's doing, start to finish. We all found out about it the same way you did, an invitation in the mail. I tried grilling him about what to expect but that boy can be close-mouthed when he wants to be."

Skippy nodded and started off to find his seat, but Elizabeth refused to follow him. "Can we take pictures? Do you know?" She held up a Kodak Instamatic.

I had no idea, but Grandma Arial said, "Elizabeth, this is our Mick. You take as many pictures as you want."

As they turned to find their seats, I glimpsed an older man standing at the tree line across the street, about fifty yards away. He wore a hat with the brim pulled low over sunglasses. Still, the way he held himself was familiar. I nudged Sonny. "Who is that?"

"Who?"

I gestured with my head and he followed my gaze. "I don't know," he said. But something told me that wasn't quite true.

I wondered if this was the man Sheriff Douglas had kicked out of town back when I had the measles. I started to push Sonny for more information, but decided I was a grown man and could just walk across the road and introduce myself. But by the time that thought crossed my mind and I looked back, the man was gone.

The rows were filling fast. We waved at Jimmy and Zona who were in the aisle seats. She was all dolled up with sparkles in her hair and dramatic eye makeup that made her look Chinese. Jimmy, as usual, hovered over her lovingly as if to protect her from the slightest hint of trouble. It reminded me of the way Sonny used to watch over Mama, and I swallowed back a lump that had formed in my throat.

The last to arrive were Delores and Tommy McDougal and their many children—along with Rosa and her new husband—and Jack and Shirley Reynolds. I hoped against hope that Mags Strickland would magically show up, even though we'd long accepted that she had disappeared somewhere over Southeast Asia.

Grandma Arial leaned toward me. "So much for big shots getting the best seats," she whispered.

Sonny and I looked around. We were surrounded by our special friends, the people who'd rescued us in Mannheim and helped us come to the United States. And there were our neighbors, the folks who brought us casseroles and who rushed to Mama's defense when Dolph Jäger attacked her. These were the families who gave us the kit to replace our back porch and who put aside their suspicions to accept us. I bit my lip, overwhelmed.

A violin broke the rising din of voices. Footsteps crossed the wooden floor of the platform built to house the orchestra inside the giant pavilion. An oboe, high and mellow, soothed me. More footsteps. And then soft blue lights illuminated the stage, and we could see the full orchestra in place, poised.

The audience sitting on the grass around the pavilion saw Mick first and burst into applause. Then as he went up the steps onto the stage, the rest of us stood and cheered.

He looked comfortable in his tuxedo. Tall and lean, his hair glowing under the lights, I could see why young women begged for his autograph on their palms. He came forward and spoke into a microphone positioned at the front of the stage.

"I like it."

Everyone applauded and cheered at his signature welcome.

"Thank you for coming," he said. "Tonight is special for me and my family. Twenty-two years ago today, my father, Sonny Logan, brought my mother, brother, and me to Cold Creek, where he gave us a life filled with love, security, and peace." He paused for a moment and smiled down at us. "And he gave my brother EJ and me a grandmother."

The audience applauded, because whether or not they knew Mick and me personally, everyone knew and loved Grandma Arial. I squeezed her hand and Sonny kissed her cheek as someone came from stage left and down into the area where we were sitting, carrying a giant flower arrangement. He set it down in front of Grandma and stepped around it, to hand her a single rose. Only then could we see it was Uncle Grant.

I rolled my eyes in amusement. So that was why he dumped me. Uncle Grant had Grandma Arial surprise-flowers duty.

"Oh." Grandma Arial flushed and tears rolled down her cheeks.

Uncle Grant bent down and said something to her. She nodded and hugged him and he sat down on the other side of Sonny, leaning forward briefly to grin at me.

"Well, now that we've had our little family drama," Mick said from the stage, "I want to share with you the reason we"—He swept his hand around to acknowledge the orchestra behind him.—"are here. As you know, I muddle around a bit with music."

Everyone laughed as he downplayed the meteoric rise that had made him one of the best-known and most accomplished musicians in history.

"In fact, I've muddled around with the piece we are going to play for you tonight for the better part of the two decades since Sonny brought us here. Other than the people involved in this performance, no one has heard it before. It was my private place where I'd go in my head. It celebrates a complicated young girl who, in a world gone mad, rescued my brother and me and gave us life. We would like to play for you this evening, in honor of my mother, Vala Logan, my third symphony, *Vala's Bed.*"

I fought back the aura that preceded a seizure. This was the moment when all of our paths merged—Mama's, Sonny's, Mick's and mine—and our stories suddenly made sense. I wasn't going to miss a single note of it.

The lights dimmed and someone removed the microphone Mick had been using.

Mick picked up a baton and tapped a bronze music stand holding a thick wad of paper filled with notes. Lightly in the air, he waved the wand three times, establishing the rhythm. Then the oboe once again filled the air for a long moment before the violas and violins began. It was exquisite, and I recognized it as the melody I'd heard

Mick humming from time to time when he didn't realize anyone else was listening.

Grandma Arial wiped her eyes with her handkerchief. Sonny was visibly moved as well.

I took a breath, leaned back into my seat, and closed my eyes. As the performance progressed, I felt them all in Mick's symphony. Mama and Lana and Magda, Oskar and Frieda, and Jan and Annaliese and Rosa. The little girl-ghost and the people on the train and the soldier who tore me from Magda's arms and saved me because of a note pinned to my shirt. The monster who would have killed me except someone rescued me. My Opa who disappeared into the night. My Oma who died alone because no one was good enough for her. And all those who died instead of me.

Mick had captured all of that horror, but his music celebrated healing…kindness over cruelty, acceptance over rejection, and life over murder.

Mama saved the very person in the entire world capable of doing that for me, when she picked up the bundle in the road that night in 1945.

The Stranger

June 5, 1970

I SAT IN the tree house and surveyed the world around me. The Vilanis had returned from the concert and were sitting out on their back porch, sipping their nightcaps and enjoying the stars. Our house was full of people congratulating Sonny for having such an amazing son as Mick. Mick himself was back on his touring bus, headed for his next gig in Columbus.

I turned toward town. Balboa's was looking old. I wondered how long the Balboa family could hold out against the fast-food chains. Still, the lights were bright and teenagers were parked in their cars, eating burgers, drinking root beer floats, and making out.

The air was cool on my skin, and the excitement of the evening left me thoughtful but at peace. I knew that might be temporary. Pain comes and goes. I'd learned to ride out the bad stuff and treasure each moment I felt like laughing rather than crying.

"EJ, it's me."

"Who?"

"Billy Ray Parker."

I stuck my head out the window. "You didn't shoot out any tires did you?"

He snickered. "Naw. Been there, done that."

I dropped the ladder so he could come up. "They have champagne over at the house. All I have up here is warm beer."

"No thanks, buddy. I have a family to see to these days."

We sat quietly. "It's been a long time, Billy Ray."

"Who would have guessed you'd grow up to be a surgeon," he said.

"Actually, I ended up in general medicine. Bad colds and inoculations. I always thought my seizures would go away as I got older, but they didn't. You don't want to be cutting on someone and start shaking or pass out."

"Guess not. Nothing wrong with general medicine though. Maybe you can take over Doc Riley's practice when he retires."

I took a sip of beer. "Yeah, why not?"

"I ... uh...I think it's time I told you something."

"Okay."

"Remember me telling you your mom left that carved box up here?"

"Yeah?"

"That was a lie."

"What?"

"Your Mama never climbed this tree, that I know of, especially after she got sick."

"So how'd she get the box up here? Did you do it?"

Billy Ray ducked his head. "That's the thing, EJ. I did put it up here for you, but it had nothing to do with your mama. She never knew a thing about it."

I was flummoxed. Who else on earth could have had access to my birth certificate? And an ornately carved music box with my birth mother's name? "Then where did it come from?"

"There was this dude who came to town from time to time. I'd see him out here watching your house. After that Jäger fellow got after your mama, I felt bad about not being able to protect her from him. So I—"

"That wasn't your fault, Billy Ray. Dolph Jäger was a psycho, and we were only kids."

"I loved your Mama, EJ. I...you know...understood her."

Like one abused kid recognizes another, I thought.

"I should have been there for her."

I patted him on the shoulder. "You were there for her all the years after she came back from Pittsburgh. Mick and I always appreciated that."

Billy Ray nodded. "So here's the thing. This old guy kept coming back. I watched him, but he never tried to do anything. He didn't break into the house like that Sarris fellow. And he didn't try to hurt your mom, like Dolph did. He didn't even window peep or anything like that."

"What'd he look like?"

"Well, to be honest, kinda like you. He was tall and good-looking. He walked funny, like he was marching or something. He had your nose and forehead. So I figured he was related somehow."

I wondered if this was the same fellow who tried to get into Grandma Arial's house that time. The one that Sheriff Douglas and Deputy Dixon had literally chased out of town. At first, I thought he might have been Opa, but Mama wouldn't have run from her own father that way. She would have been thrilled that he was still alive. I always wondered why she ran instead of coming into the house with us and locking the door. And that guy saw which direction she ran in. It made no sense. I shrugged. "I don't know anyone who looks like that."

"Yeah?"

I shook my head.

"Well, this guy kept hanging around and I kept watching him. And then one day, he confronted me."

"Confronted?" I imagined all kinds of things. "Did he hurt you?"

"No, but he made me think he might hurt your mama. That got my attention even though I knew he was faking it. Don't know how I knew, but I could tell he didn't mean you or your family any harm. He said he wanted you to have that box, but he couldn't give it to Vala and he couldn't give it to you directly. I asked him why not, and he said it was a long story he wasn't willing to share. Anyway, he said he had to go away for a while, and he wanted me to give you the box where no one else would see it. And he…he gave me money."

I could see that bothered him, but I had to give him credit. He could have left that part out altogether, and I'd never have known the difference. "So he gave you the box and you left it up here for me to find."

"That's about the size of it." Billy Ray looked glum. "It didn't look to be dangerous and I thought maybe, since this guy looked so much like you…well, maybe it was an heirloom or something."

"It's okay, Billy Ray. I appreciate you caring about Mama. And the box was important."

"There's one more thing. That man hasn't been around for years, not since before Vala died. Then tonight, on the way to the concert, I thought I saw him."

I closed my eyes. "Did you speak to him?"

"No, he was walking in the opposite direction, and I was driving. Besides—and pardon me if he is your relative—I don't like him."

I chuckled. "Why not?"

"He thinks he's better than everyone else."

* * *

After Billy Ray left, I thought about the man who left me the music box. Could he be the Nazi who sired Lana's baby, my father? That man was assassinated in 1942. That was fact. There were witnesses. And a public funeral, with his family in attendance. Besides, that man didn't have any reason to care about me personally. I was his duty to the Reich. His perfect characteristics blended with Lana's ideal Germanic qualities. That is, ideal until she had a nervous breakdown. Still, the custom music box itself was a romantic gesture to Lana, and someone wanted me to know that.

Was he the one was hanging around the day Gerhardt came to warn Mama? Did she recognize him? She must have thought he was after me. That's why she ran the opposite direction from where we hid inside the house. Her natural instinct was to draw danger away from her children. I rubbed my forehead. But if he really was alive, wouldn't that make her a target? Someone who could report him?

Enough! I'd spent my whole life wondering and feeling guilty. Now I just didn't care. I wanted to be like Mick. Free and joyful. If my birth father was still out there, his existence was a burden and his crimes too monstrous to forgive. I chose to leave him in obscurity, running from one hiding place to another. I wouldn't chase him. My real father was a humble man who gave up everything, including the love of his life, to raise Mick and me. My real father never hurt anyone.

I closed up the tree house, crawled down the ladder, and stowed it.

"Am I too late for our catch-up session?" As always, Annie's appearance was exotic. She looked like she stepped right out of the Coliseum in a thin, almost-see-through Roman toga, wearing sandals with ties up to her knees.

"Where have you been all these years, Annie?"

"Searching for myself."

"Did you find you?"

She swirled around. "For the moment."

"Married?"

"Don't believe in it."

I put my arms around her. "What do you believe in?"

"Love."

I kissed her. "No religion or philosophy?"

"Nope. Well, being happy."

"No politics?"

"Nope."

"You hate anyone?"

"Not a soul."

"Perfect.

Joyce Faulkner

Vala's Bed is Joyce Faulkner's third historical novel after *In the Shadow of Suribachi*, and *Windshift*. While not true sequels, they are related. Faulkner's other books include mystery/thrillers, history, and humor. She was born in Fort Smith, Arkansas, and studied writing at the University of Arkansas in Fayetteville. She also holds degrees in Chemical Engineering and Business.

Faulkner sensed a story when she visited Mannheim, Germany, in 2002. What happened to the Jews of Mannheim? The trail first led to Dachau and then ultimately to Auschwitz. The train station at Oswiecim, Poland, is the end of the line. It was in a nearby hotel, trains screeching in the night, that a tormented young woman first visited the author's dreams. The next morning, Easter Sunday, Faulkner toured the Auschwitz concentration camp and was introduced to hell on earth. Birkenau's gas chambers still vie with the author's belief that goodness and hope can rise from the flames of hatred and cruelty.

Aurora Huston

Huston immigrated to America from the Philippines when she was three years of age. Learning English and adopting another culture led her to depend on art as form of communication. After formal training, the artist began her career in Art Education, teaching for over a decade in Arkansas public and private schools K through 12. Subsequent careers included interior designer, art consultant, public relations director, art director, photography stylist, and painter.

Commenting on inspiration, Huston says, "Life is my medium and my way of depicting the many stages of the human condition. Designing the cover for *Vala's Bed* was a unique challenge. Instead of a beautiful German woman, I found myself completely drawn to the dark sadness of Vala's history. Her haunting memories moved my paint brush quickly and decisively."

www.ingramcontent.com/pod-product-compliance
Lightning Source LLC
Chambersburg PA
CBHW070840260626
47170CB00007B/2445